The Secrets of Drearcliff Grange School

Also by Kim Newman and available from
Titan Books:

Anno Dracula
Anno Dracula: The Bloody Red Baron
Anno Dracula: Dracula Cha Cha Cha
Anno Dracula: Johnny Alucard
Anno Dracula: One Thousand Monsters
(October 2017)

An English Ghost Story
Professor Moriarty: The Hound of the D'Urbervilles
Jago
The Quorum
Life's Lottery
Bad Dreams
The Night Mayor
The Best of the Diogenes Club (December 2017)

The Secrets of Drearcliff Grange School

KIM NEWMAN

TITAN BOOKS

The Secrets of Drearcliff Grange School
Mass-market edition ISBN: 9781785655951
Electronic edition ISBN: 9781781165737

Published by Titan Books
A division of Titan Publishing Group Ltd
144 Southwark Street, London SE1 0UP

First mass-market edition: September 2017
2 4 6 8 10 9 7 5 3 1

Printed and bound in the United States.

For Prano

Contents

First Term

Second Term

The Remove

Drearcliff Grange School Register

First Term

I: A New Bug

A WEEK AFTER MOTHER found her sleeping on the ceiling, Amy Thomsett was delivered to her new school. Like a parcel.

When the down train departed from Exeter St Davids, it was crowded with ruddy-faced farmers, tweedy spinsters and wiry commercial travellers. Nearer the end of the line, Amy had a compartment all to herself.

She first saw Drearcliff Grange through the train's smuts-spotted windows. Shifting from seat to seat, she kept the school in sight as long as possible.

Amy had hoped the name was misleading. It wasn't.

She should have known. Misleading place names like Greenland or the Cape of Good Hope ran the other way, passing off desolate climes as pleasant resorts. Drearcliff was exactly what it sounded like. A rambling, gloomy, ill-repaired estate on top of a cliff. This was wind and rain country. The sky was heavy with dark, roiling clouds.

For a stretch, the railway line ran parallel with the coast.

Waves broke against the cliff, washing through caves, eroding supporting rock. Chunks of North

13

Somerset had sheared away, falling four hundred feet to the shingle. Some time ago, this land-nibbling had reached the Grange. A North Wing had tumbled over the fraying edge. Amid the strew of ruins on the beach, a gothic tower stuck up at an angle, white froth foaming around the base.

Newer wings straggled safely, if dully, inland.

The train terminated at Watchet. A porter walked the platform shouting 'end o' the loine… all orff that's gettin' orff!' The Great Western Railway locomotive discharged excess steam. The clattering hiss was like a rattlesnake with whooping cough.

Amy stepped down from the carriage.

'Ho, Thomsett,' called someone. 'You must be she!'

A tall, ginger-haired girl strode unscalded through the steam.

The hailer stuck out a hand, which Amy shook. Her grip was bone-grinding.

'I'm Walmergrave,' she announced, thumping her chest. 'Lady Serafine Nimue Todd Walmergrave, in full. All and sundry call me Frecks.'

'Crumpets!' exclaimed Amy. 'Why?'

'Freckles. Used to have 'em. Don't now. Too late to chuck the handle.'

Frecks had what Mother called 'a strong personality', which was code for a friend of Amy's she didn't approve of.

'Headmistress has detailed me to slap on the bracelets and ferry you to School. Many new bugs set eyes on the place and flee for the hills. Men with hunting dogs comb the Quantocks for escapees.'

If not for the skirt, Amy might have taken Frecks for a boy. Her brick-red hair was cut short flapper fashion, her lips were the same colour as her face and she had square shoulders.

Frecks wore a more lived-in version of the scratchy uniform Mother had ordered for Amy from the school's recommended London dressmaker, Dosson, Chapell & Co. of Tite Street. Grey skirt with black side-stripe, grey blazer with black piping, grey blouse with black buttons, grey socks with black clocks, grey-*ish* straw boater with black band, bright crimson tie with black-headed pin.

At Amy's old school, girls wore baggy pinafores which made even long-legged Sixths look like children. In a Drearcliff skirt, she felt more like a little adult – on the outside, at least.

On the hankie-pocket badge, a worried-looking woman – Saint Catherine, presumably – hung upside down on a cartwheel above an embroidered motto, *a fronte praecipitium a tergo lupi.* 'A precipice in front and wolves behind.'

If the dreary cliff counted as the precipice, where did the wolves come into it? Those famous hunting dogs?

'This your gear?' Frecks asked. 'All your worldly possessions?'

A porter had hefted her father's old brass-cornered trunk on to the platform.

'Yes.'

Frecks signalled a bent old gaffer, who hefted Amy's luggage on his back and conveyed it to a horse-cart in the station forecourt.

'Joxer's odd-job man and general slavey,' Frecks explained. 'Don't mind him. Shot in the head at Vimy Ridge. Came to Drearcliff with the nag, Dauntless. She was in the War too. Charged enemy guns. Not very bright, if you ask me. Say the name' – Frecks mouthed the syllables *Gen-er-al Haig* – 'and Dauntless bolts. Runs perfectly amok.'

Joxer had the opposite of a beard. His chin was shaven, but thick brownish-white hair sprouted everywhere else on his face except nose and forehead. Cheek-whiskers teased out to nine-inch points. Eyebrows curled like the heterocera of the *dryocampa rubicunda* or North American Rosy Maple Moth.

'Your tumbril awaits, Highness,' said Frecks.

The girl helped Amy climb up into the cart. There were hard benches to sit on.

Joxer let out a sentence consisting of one long unintelligible dialect word and Dauntless began to clip-clop off. One of the conveyance's wheels was a different size to the others. The vehicle listed like a ship holed below the waterline, bravely sailing on to certain doom.

On the narrow road from Watchet to Drearcliff, they acquired a horn-honking retinue of motorists. Frecks smiled and waved at the fuming drivers as if they were all in the Lord Mayor's parade. The growling roadsters could not get by. Ignoring beeps and shouts, Dauntless kept to the middle of the lane. When the slow-rolling cart turned off for the Grange, the cars whizzed past in relief. Amy saw fists shaken and lip-read swear words.

A rutted track led to a tall wall. Broken bottles stuck up from a rind of cement along the top.

'No one knows whether the jagged glass is to keep angry mobs out or hungry girls in,' said Frecks. 'Dr Swan empties all the bottles herself, for personal use. Green for wine. Brown for beer.'

'What about the blue?'

'Poison, my dear.'

They came to a set of spear-tipped gates. Frecks stepped off the cart and opened them, standing aside to let Dauntless through. After fastening the gates, she slipped on to School Grounds by a small, almost-hidden door.

'I trust you're giddy from the privilege, Thomsett,' said Frecks. 'You've just passed through School Gate. You only get to do that again when you leave for good. It's symbolic. From henceforth, you come and go through Side Door. And Girls' Gate, which is further along. Oh, and over the cliff if you can clamber like a monkey or soar like an eagle...'

Considering how Mother had reacted, Amy thought it best not to mention her floating.

'Hop down and we'll walk the rest of the way,' said Frecks. 'It's quicker.'

Amy joined Frecks. They watched as the cart trundled off along a side path, without them but with her trunk.

'Worry not about your gear,' said Frecks. 'Joxer will dump it at the dorms. The Witches will go through it for contraband.'

'The Witches?'

Frecks grinned. 'Whips. Prefects. A superior type of she-imp. If you stashed a precious heirloom in with your scanties, Gruesome Gryce and her Murdering Heathens will have it away. Sidonie Gryce is Head Girl. Wears scalps on her girdle. Did you bring any dollies?'

A dread hand clutched Amy's heart.

'Only Roly Pontoons... I've had him for ages, since I was little.'

Frecks was exasperated. 'I assume you *were* warned...'

Father had brought Roly home from Belgium, on his

17

last leave. After he was killed, she'd liked to think he left the big-headed clown to look after her. Sometimes, she made Roly float in the playroom, flapping his oversize coat like moth-wings.

'Say goodbye to Roly,' said Frecks callously. 'The Murdering Heathens have a burning fiery furnace. Like the one Shadrach, Meschach and the other fellow were bunged in. Prophets prosper in flames. Dollies don't, as a rule.'

The dread hand squeezed. Amy was determined not to cry.

'Gryce will probably dunk you in a horse trough too, or dangle you out of the North Window. Thinks she's a caution. Best to grind your teeth and get it over with. You can shiv one of the minor arcana later, if you've a mind. It'll either get the Witches off your back for a term, or declare a war which can end only in the fall of civilisation.'

Amy didn't know what to make of Frecks. At her old school, there hadn't been any girls remotely like her.

They strolled along a flagstone path between overgrown lawns. On one, a troupe of tall, clumsy girls in wispy Grecian gowns performed energetic leaps and bends under the direction of a large woman who beat time by slapping a riding crop into a gauntlet. On the other, a croquet match descended into a scratching, hair-pulling mêlée as a tiny teacher ineffectually shrilled a whistle. Amy thought she saw blood.

'Unparalleled savagery,' declaimed Frecks. 'That's the Drearcliff spirit. The malleteers are shamming the punch-up, by the way. The Fifth have a pool on who can get Miss Dryden to bust a blood vessel by overtooting.'

The path wound through gardens.

'Our grand tour continues,' said Frecks. 'Sixpence

for the guide would be appreciated. Dorms are in Old House, the one that's falling off the cliff. I'm to get you settled in our cell later. Ames, the birdie who had your perch last, fled to Switzerland for her lungs. Reckon she inhaled ground grit to fake it. Hope you're made of sterner stuff. It's a nuisance having to break in new bugs every twenty minutes.'

Up close, Old House looked no more inviting than from afar. Near the cliff edge, signs warned against straying too close.

They passed through a short, covered walkway into a grassy square surrounded by low-lying buildings. In the centre of the Quad stood a plinth supporting a giant marble foot, broken off at the ankle.

'Professor Clio Chalke McGill, classicist and plunderer, hauled that there tootsie from Ancient Greece and generously donated it to School. Miss Borrodale, who takes Science, says the rest of the colossus must be *hopping mad*. She's mildly droll, though don't get her on Palaeontology or you'll never escape – and watch out for her thwacking habit. This lump is called the Heel. Rumour hath it the whole statue was supposed to be Achilles.'

'Death to King Gustav V of Sweden' was written in red on the white stone.

'Pay no heed to the graffiti,' said Frecks. 'Absalom the Anarchist singles out a different oppressor of the people every week. Almost educational, but a Minor Infraction of School Rules. Clock up six Minors and you have to scrub the Heel with your toothbrush. I've done it twice.'

'School Rules?'

'Yes, nasty little beasts. Set down at the Diet of Worms

in 1066. Memorise 'em, else you'll be constantly in hot water. In some parts of School, it's against rules to wear your boater. In other parts, it's against rules not to. Running from lessons to Refectory is an Infraction. So is *not* running from Refectory to lessons. If a whip slaps you across the chops, you can be Minored for having a red mark on your face. She can keep slapping until you cease Impertinent Display. A Minor is whatever one of the Witches thinks up if she's had a "Dear Jane" from her boyfriend and wants to take it out on someone who can't jilt her for the butcher's lass. I've been Minored for Inappropriate Failure to Whistle.'

'Buttered crumpets!' exclaimed Amy.

'Major Infractions are the serious ones, though. Gross moral turpitude, grand larceny, public indecency, destruction of school property, arson in a naval dockyard. Anything liable to bring the institution into disrepute. Should you be inclined to such criminal endeavours, the good news is that whips can't stick a Major on you without due process. The bad news is that Majors are punishable by fifty lashes with the Cat. Or transportation to the Colonies.'

The north side of the Quad was taken up by a new, three-storey building.

Frecks led Amy to the front steps. Stone eagles perched on low, twisted columns either side of the doorway. They had glass marbles for eyes.

'I go no further, Pilgrim,' said Frecks. 'For me to pass unbidden between the Budgies would constitute a Major. Like School Gate, you only get the honour – if honour it be – of calling in at the Swanage on your first day. Venture within and report to Headmistress, who'll terrify you for a quarter of an hour. Then trot along to Old House and seek out Dorm Three. I'll introduce you to the Desdemona Damsels. With that, I bid you adieu... oh, and don't look Dr Swan in the eye – she's got the fluence.'

II: Headmistress

*S*HE STEPPED INTO a reception room.

One wall was three-fifths covered with framed school photographs, taken annually from 1877. Founding year. Generation after generation of girls. Rising through the years and passing out. Staff growing older and being replaced. Amy estimated Drearcliff Grange would have to start on a new wall in 1961.

A cabinet displayed sporting and artistic trophies. A grinning African fetish of evil aspect was lumped in with silver cups and ballerina statuettes.

There was a strong smell of pure alcohol. A burly woman stood at a table covered with newspaper, using vaporous astringent to clean a disassembled Lee–Enfield rifle. An enormous bunch of keys dangled from her wide leather belt. She looked at Amy through the long thin telescope of the barrel.

'Go up, new girl,' she said, nodding to a stairway. 'Headmistress is waiting.'

Amy tried to put her foot on the first step, but found she couldn't touch it – as if a hard, invisible pillow overlay the carpet. She shot a guilty glance at the custodian. Absorbed in oiling a spring, the woman didn't notice. This wasn't so much floating as standing on air. A slightly sick-making feeling, like pressing bar magnets together when their poles were aligned to repel. Amy was getting more used to it, though the sensation was still disturbing. She couldn't get past the *wrongness*.

Using the banister, she pulled herself hand over hand. Trying not to think about going against nature, Amy glided upwards, toes barely brushing the steps. When she reached the first-storey landing, her usual weight settled back. Her shoes were set down on the carpet. After her floats, she felt heavy, as if Newton himself were paying her back for contravening his Law of Gravity.

A large door bore an engraved brass plate.

Dr Myrna Swan, Headmistress
D. Phil. (Bangalore), D. Eng (Sao Paolo), M. Script.
(Wells Cathedral) & Cetera.

Amy raised a knuckle. A voice came from beyond before she could rap on the door.

'Enter, Thomsett.'

The door opened by itself. Across the book-lined room, a slim, imposing woman of indeterminate age sat behind a lacquer-topped desk.

Amy's hand was still up, where the door wasn't.

'You didn't do that,' said Headmistress. 'I did. I am not in the habit of issuing invitations twice.'

Amy stepped into the room.

Headmistress worked a lever on an apparatus like a typewriter mated with a sewing machine. The door closed behind Amy.

Above the contraption were several copper tubes which ended in eyepieces. Dr Swan had been looking through one. Another tube, with a lens, was out on the landing. It must be an array of mirrors, like a triple-jointed periscope.

Had Headmistress seen her *flying*? Not that it was really flying. Just – *fast floating*.

Dr Swan's jet-black hair was coiffured in a bun on top of her head, with two pearl-tipped needles stuck through it. Her face was white but for red, bee-stung lips and a black beauty mark. Tiny lines showed around her large green-gold eyes. Amy remembered what Frecks said about the fluence. Dr Swan appeared over and over in the pictures downstairs. She had taken office in the founding year. Girls grew up and left, but she stayed the same, always dead centre in the school photograph. Her age must be even more indeterminate than it seemed.

Her tight silk dress was like a long tunic, green with gold griffin designs. A nurse's watch was pinned like a brooch on her breast. Her black academic gown hung loosely. It had sawtooth trailing edges and a flaring demon-king collar.

'Thomsett, Amanda,' said Dr Swan, tapping a folder on her desk. 'Third, Desdemona, Unusual.'

Amy understood half of that.

'Desdemona is your House,' Headmistress explained. 'Drearcliff has five. Ariel, Viola, Tamora, Desdemona and Goneril. Had you arrived at the beginning of year, you would be Ariel. In the circumstance, you fit where you must. Desdemona was down a girl. As for *Unusual*… your mother wrote about "incidents" at home. Footprints on the ceiling. *She* trusts you will grow out of it…'

Amy blushed like a fire engine.

'*I* know you will not,' said Dr Swan. 'Unusuals

have Abilities or Attributes, sometimes both. You are blessed with Abilities. It is our responsibility to help you cultivate them, to find Applications.'

Amy was astonished. This was not what she – or Mother! – expected from her new school. In the months since she first came unstuck from the ground, Amy had been subjected to cold baths, weighted pinafores, long walks, hobbling boots and a buzzing, tickling electric belt. Leeches and exorcism were on the cards. Mother's whole idea in sending Amy to Drearcliff was to clamp down on *floating*.

'We have a tradition of Unusual Girls at Drearcliff. I like to think of them as my cygnets. You've heard of Lucinda Tregellis-d'Aulney...'

The Aviatrix. Britain's flying heroine. The only woman among the Splendid Six, Britain's most unique and remarkable defenders. She didn't just float, she soared. Amy followed her exploits in *Girls' Paper*. Lady Lucinda was currently prominent in the illustrated press for nabbing Jimmy O'Goblins. The coiner-necromancer, whose lightweight sovereigns caused escalating misfortune each time they were spent, was in the Special Prison with a sore head. The Aviatrix was invited to high tea at the Palace with the King and the governor of the Bank of England.

'Tregellis-d'Aulney passed out in '16. She has made a name for herself. So have other Drearcliff Unusuals. Irene Dobson, the medium. Cressida Hervey, the Australian opal millionairess – with dowsing abilities. Monica Bright – 'Shiner' Bright of the Women's Auxiliary Police. Grace Ki, the Ghost Lantern Girl. Urania Strangways, who survived hanging in Montevideo last year. Luna Bartendale, the psychic investigator. I take pride in my cygnets' achievements, whichever direction their enthusiasms take them. You have, I trust, an *enthusiasm*?'

Shyly, Amy admitted 'I like moths. Not collecting them. I don't believe in killing jars and pins. I've sketched three hundred and twelve distinct live specimens. British Isles, of course. I'm nowhere near finished. There are over two thousand British moth species alone.'

'That is *not* what I mean by an *enthusiasm*, Thomsett. Still, it's early days yet. Can you, ah…?'

Dr Swan gestured with her flat palm, lifting it up over her desk.

Amy looked at her toes. She worked so desperately *not* to float, she couldn't unclench whatever it was that held her to the ground.

She strained, eyes shut, making noises inside her head.

'You are trying too hard, Thomsett. Nothing good comes of that. You must *let go*, not *hold tight*.'

Amy nodded and relaxed. She rose an inch or so from the floor, but couldn't stay up. She clumped down again.

Dr Swan raised an eyebrow. 'Promising.'

Amy was exhausted. Had the Aviatrix – who grew temporary wings of ectoplasm – started like this? With tiny floats? Did she ever wake up thumping against her ceiling, blinded by sheets tented around her, in a panic that the world had gone topsy-turvy?

'And the other thing,' Headmistress said. She put a fountain pen on her blotter.

Amy thought about the pen floating, but it only wobbled – and leaked a bit.

She tried to apologise. She could sometimes make things float. More often, she gave herself a nosebleed. Frankly, it was easy enough to pick up a pen with her fingers. Taking hold of things with her mind was a strain.

Dr Swan didn't press her further.

'My eye will be always on you,' said Headmistress, tapping her copper tubes. 'We shall see what can be done with your Abilities. Pick up your Time-Table Book from Keys.'

Amy knew who Headmistress meant.

'*Dismissed*,' said Dr Swan, depressing a lever.

The door opened. Amy backed through it.

III: Dorm Three

OUTSIDE OLD HOUSE, Amy found four Seconds performing an intricate skipping ritual to a never-ending rhyme about drowned black babies in a terrible flood. She asked where she could find Dorm Three. They stopped in mid-chant, staring as if she were a person from Porlock – as it happens, only a few miles away – interrupting Coleridge in full poetical flow. The solemn adjudicator pointed up at the top of Old House, then crossed herself and snapped her fingers to order resumption of skipping and chanting. The terrible flood had to drown many more black babies.

Inside the building, which smelled of rain on rocks, Amy found a tree of signs pointing to destinations as diverse as 'Refectory'; 'Stamp Club', 'Timbuctoo' and 'Nurse'. A broken-necked Mr Punch dangled from the Nurse sign in a hangman's noose, pricking Amy's fears for Roly Pontoons. Higher branches indicated dorms were on the upper floors.

Amy climbed a winding stone staircase. Names, phrases and dates were scratched into the walls. At her old school, boarders slept in something like a hospital ward or a barracks – a big room with beds lined up opposite each other. At Drearcliff, dorms were long, dark corridors with doors off to either side. Amy didn't know where to go from the landing, so she opened the first door. Four beds fit into a room the size of the one Lettie the maid lived in at home. A girl with two sets of extra-thick spectacles – one in her hair like an Alice band – was putting together a tiny guillotine from lolly-sticks and a safety razor-blade.

'You want Frecks' cell,' she said, without looking up from her labours. 'End of the line, new bug. You'll whiff it before you see it. No mistaking Kali's herbal fags. Now, push off will you... this little beast has to be in chopping order tomorrow or I'm for a roasting from Digger Downs.'

Amy ventured on. From behind a closed door, she heard a *quid pro quo* Latin quiz. She caught a peculiar fragrance – heady, a little exhilarating – wafting from an open room at the far end of the corridor.

Sticking her head in, she found Frecks lolled on a cot, perusing a volume with a brown paper cover. She looked up.

'*My Nine Nights in a Harem*,' Frecks explained. 'Fearful rot. Come the deuce in, Thomsett. Meet your fellow dwellers in despair.'

Amy stepped into the cell, ducking to avoid bumping her head on the low lintel. She wouldn't have much room to float here.

'Thomsett, this is Light Fingers...'

A small, blonde girl sat in a rocking chair, deftly embroidering a piece of muslin. She held it up to her face. It was a Columbine mask, with fine stitching around eye- and mouth-holes. Little sequin tears sparkled on one cheek.

'The fuming reprobate is Princess Kali.'

A slender brown girl with a red forehead dot and a gold snail stuck to her nose sat on a mat, legs folded under her. She puffed a slim cigarette in a long holder as if it were a religious obligation. Her eyes were slightly glazed.

'Me, you know,' said Frecks. 'That's your corner.'

Frecks indicated a neatly made, if somewhat forlorn, miniature bed. A dagger was stuck through the pillow.

'Don't mind the pig-sticker,' said Frecks. 'It's not for you. Was sent to the last girl before she took poorly. Never did get to the bottom of that 'un. Many were the questions about dear departed Imogen Ames.'

Light Fingers set aside her needlework.

'She's quick,' said Frecks. 'Her register name is Emma Naisbitt. Her parents are in jail. Which puts her one up on most of us. We tend to be orphans or semi-orphans at Drearcliff. My lot were shot as spies in the War. By the Hun, I hasten to add. All very glamorous and tragic. I was packed off here by my brother. Lord Ralph holds the purse strings till I'm eighteen and past it. Worse luck, since he's a gambling fool and a fathead for the fillies. I fully expect him to run through the dosh and leave me to make a way in the world by wits alone. He's tragic, but *not* very glamorous. Still, I don't have the worst of it in this cell. Kali's Pa had her Ma put to death for displeasing him. He's a bandit rajah in far-off Kafiristan. He's run through dozens of wives.'

Kali rose elegantly, hands pressed together as if in prayer, and stood on one leg like a flamingo. She had masses of very black hair.

'Hya, dollface,' said the Hindu girl, rather musically. 'Whaddaya know, whaddaya say?'

'Kali learned English from American magazines,' Frecks footnoted.

'Ahhh, nertz! I talks good as any other dame in the joint.'

Kali put both feet on the floor and stubbed out her cigarette in a saucer. She had pictures from the rotogravure pinned up over her cot – scowling men in hats: Lon Chaney, Al Capone, Jack Dempsey.

'I forgot to ask,' said Frecks. 'Are you down one parent or two?'

'One,' said Amy. 'My father. The War.'

'Tough break, kiddo,' said Kali.

'Say no more,' said Frecks. 'Mystery lingers, though. Why've you suddenly been sent here? In the middle of autumn term? There's usually no mistake about whether one is or is not Drearcliff material. Born with a caul, font bubbling over at baptism, nannies fleeing with hair gone white overnight, scratches on the nursery wallpaper…'

Amy hesitated. Interest sparked. Frecks and Kali exchanged a Significant Look.

'Light Fingers,' said Frecks. 'You've got competition. We have another Unusual.'

Denial sprung up in Amy's throat, but died. There was no point. It was out before she was properly here. Mother would be livid.

Light Fingers regarded Amy with suspicion, tilting her head to one side and then the other.

'It's not something you can see,' said Frecks. 'Like Gould of the Fourth and her teeth and nails. Or that Goneril guppy with gills. It's something she *does*. Hope you're not a mind reader, Thomsett. They're unpopular, for reasons obvious. Dearly departed Ames was a brain-peeper. Didn't make her happy.'

Amy was tight inside. Close to tears, though she kept them in.

'There there, child,' said Frecks. 'We won't hurt. Tell all.'

'C'mon, doll, cough it up an' ya'll feel better.'

The three girls were close to her now. Amy knew this was important.

'Light Fingers,' said Frecks, 'show her yours.'

The blonde girl reached out and tapped Amy on the chest with her right forefinger, then opened her left hand to show a black-headed tiepin.

Amy, astonished, touched her tie. The pin was missing. 'How…?'

'Prestidigitation, old thing,' said Frecks. 'As practised in the Halls by respected conjurers. And in the stalls by disreputable pickpockets. The hand is quicker than the eye. Naisbitt's hands are quicker than a hummingbird's wings.'

Light Fingers clapped her hands and showed empty palms. Amy found her pin back in place. A bead of blood stood out on the girl's forefinger. Light Fingers licked the tiny wound.

'Gets it from her parents. They had an act at the Tivoli. Doves out of hats. Escapes from water-tanks. Also, a profitable sideline: lifting sparklers from nobs in the audience. Got caught at it. Hence, jail. Captain Rattray nabbed 'em. You know, Blackfist. The big bruiser in the Splendid Six – with the Blue Streak, Lord Piltdown, the Aviatrix and the other two no one remembers. Mrs Naisbitt made a pass for Rattray's magic gem. That was the end of that.'

Amy knew all about Blackfist. Dennis Rattray, a gentleman explorer, had discovered a pre-human cyclopean idol in a cavern temple under the Andes. From its forehead, he plucked the famous Fang of

Night jewel. The story was that when he made a fist around the mystic purple-black gemstone, his body became as impervious to harm as granite and his blows landed with the force of a wrecking-ball. Since then, he had biffed rotters and foiled plots against the Empire. He also concerned himself with less momentous, nevertheless baffling crimes... such as, presumably, the Naisbitts' pilfering spree.

'Mum and Dad could escape any time they want,' said Light Fingers. 'They get out of their prisons and visit each other. All the time. But they go back for the head-counts. Less trouble in the long run. They only stole from horrid people, by the way... quite a lot of rich people are horrid. And Rattray said he'd let them off if Mum went to Brighton with him for a Bank Holiday weekend, so he's fairly horrid himself, no matter what the papers say. After all, he got to be Blackfist by stealing something which was perfectly happy where it was and has the nerve to pinch other folks who are just trying to make a living.'

'Editorial comment over,' said Frecks.

Amy assumed Light Fingers was biased, but what she said sounded likely. It had always seemed to her that Blackfist enjoyed biffing rotters rather more than was entirely healthy. There was once talk of the Aviatrix and Blackfist getting engaged, but that cooled down... and no wonder, if he was the sort to issue improper invitations to married lady thieves.

The three girls looked at Amy, expectant.

'A shy one,' said Frecks. 'Probably taught to hide her light under a bushel. We haven't anything else to show. Kali and I aren't Unusual that way. Just warped. Drearcliff Girls have something extra or something missing. Not just parents. Bits got left out when we were put together. Know what Kali's going to do to dear old Dad when she goes home?'

Kali drew her thumbnail across her throat and made a 'krkkkk' sound.

'Concrete overshoes, wooden waistcoat... curtains, kiddo!'

'Means it, too. She's going to be a bandit queen. She's already coloured in her territory on the map. So, Thomsett, *give*...'

It wasn't that easy. In Headmistress's study, she hadn't been able to perform on cue. Not really. It would be the same here.

'She *is* giving,' said Light Fingers, '*look*...!'

Amy was surprised, then glanced down. She was a full six inches off the floor, feet dangling limp. Her head pressed the plastered ceiling.

Kali and Frecks were wide-eyed. Light Fingers looked a little frightened.

Frecks whistled, long and shrill.

'That was an *appropriate* whistle,' she explained. 'Crivens, you're a pixie!'

Amy went inside herself, and thought heavy thoughts. She came down gently, on toepoints, then settled on her heels.

'I am *not* a pixie,' she said.

'But you can fly!'

She shook her head. 'No, I can't fly. I can *float*. It's not the same.'

The Aviatrix could fly. She could flap her wings, zoom along, bank and roll, ascend and descend, outpace any land craft. Amy could wave her arms all she wanted, but just went up and up like a balloon. So far, she'd only floated deliberately indoors. Once, she had dozed under a tree like Alice and woke up trapped by low branches. Mother said if she didn't stop it, she'd drift away and be lost in the clouds.

'Still, you're an Unusual,' said Frecks. 'Headmistress must love you.'

Kali snarled. 'Stay away from Swan! She's trouble in velvet! A regular cyanide mama!'

'Tell you what, though,' said Frecks. 'Desdemona won't come bottom in netball this term. Not with two Unusuals. Light Fingers can steal the ball and make an invisible pass. Thomsett can float and pop it through the hoop from above. A tough rind for the harpies of Goneril to chew. Must get ten shillings down with Nellie Pugh in the kitchens – she's school bookie, don't you know? – before word gets out.'

For the first time, Amy wondered if Mother was wrong. Maybe floating wasn't entirely wicked.

She was tired of hearing things like 'how are you ever going to get a husband if you can't keep your feet on the ground?'

She wasn't sure about netball though.

A bell sounded, from down below.

'Grub's up,' announced Frecks. 'Form an orderly rabble and proceed to the Refectory. Come on, Thomsett, we'll get you there alive. Then it's down to whether you can survive the worst Cook flings at you. Word to the wise, shun the semolina. I have it on an impeccable authority that it's bat's blood in sick.'

IV: School Supper

THE REFECTORY MADE Amy wonder if Old House had begun as Drearcliff Abbey or Drearcliff Castle. The feeding trough was the sort of place Douglas Fairbanks generally did sword-fighting in, complete with flying buttresses, depressed arches, ribbed vaults and other features of architectural interest.

Stained-glass windows showed men in armour battling she-demons, who were generally getting the best of the fight. Amy wasn't sure the windows were appropriate for younger girls. Several panels showed dismembered knights roasted on spits by happy, red-skinned devil cooks with extra mouths in their bosoms.

Pupils sat on benches at five long House tables, arranged by year. This meant roughly by size, though the odd freakishly tall or stunted specimen broke up any neat arrangement. Thirds had places half-way along the Desdemona table. They could look across at their contemporaries in other Houses. It was not done to pay attention up-table or down-table, where seniors or juniors sat.

Hundreds of girls, talking all at once, clattered to their table-places. The sound of wooden bench-legs scraping on stone set Amy's teeth on edge.

Frecks anatomised the Houses.

'Goneril are Sport House,' Frecks explained. 'Win at absolutely everything, from cross-country runs to tiddlybloodywinks. It's *so* tedious. They used to play boys' schools at football, but an archdeacon's son got crippled – and his side took a ten-two hammering – so that was stopped. Tamora has the terrors. I josh you not. You'd do well to stay away. The most evil Witches are Tamora. Viola are babies. Blub all the time. The Greek dancing on the lawn soppists you saw earlier. Utterly wet and contemptible. Ariel are so stuck up you'd think they were *port over starboard home* through and through. Their people are mostly in trade. We can't stand 'em. Got all that?'

'Sporty, terrifying, babies and posh, yes. What are we?'

'Desdemona? Red-headed stepchildren. Who don't fit anywhere else. Come second in most things. If we're top, it doesn't count because we don't win *properly*. You'll hear that a lot.'

High Table was set on a dais before a triptych of especially ferocious dragons. It had a white tablecloth and the best china. Also, decanters of spirits and wine glasses. Girls made do with tumblers and jugs of brackish water, though Princess Kali surreptitiously dripped something fiery from a bullet-dented hip flask into her tumbler.

Once the girls were settled, they were counted off by Table Captains from each form, with the few absences due to illness listed. Light Fingers was the Third Desdemona Captain. Then, Headmistress made an entrance, cape flapping. Raucous hubbub ceased. After Dr Swan was settled on a throne at the centre of High Table, nine women – and one man! – walked in a processional and took high-backed chairs either side. Teachers wore capes and mortar-boards. Keys, the custodian, had no academic accoutrements, but her jangling keys were a mark of authority. A woman in a white starched wimple and an apron with a red cross on it must be Nurse. The man was very fat, nearly bald and wore a clergyman's collar. Amy guessed he was School chaplain. The Staff faced out at the Refectory, at once on display and commanding an audience.

Servants rolled trolleys bearing cauldrons up and down the aisles, doling something which was either thick soup or thin stew into bowls. Frecks showed Amy how to hold her bowl up with one hand while taking a bread roll from a platter on the trolley with the other. Light Fingers made a show of being slow and clumsy, not wasting her Abilities at supper.

Headmistress made a gesture. The Chaplain got up and mumbled a grace in Latin.

'Bow, you savages,' hissed the Fourth captain up-table, exciting suppressed giggles from acolytes.

Grace concluded, everyone tucked in. Talking resumed and the Refectory filled with din again.

The soup-or-stew was hot and had a distinct, not unpleasant taste. The meat wasn't the best, but the bread was fresh and soaked up the gravy.

Frecks introduced Amy to the rest of the Thirds. The guillotine-making girl, who only wore one pair of spectacles to supper, was Lydia Inchfawn. A bird-boned, pale American girl with long, straight, black hair suffered under the name Ticia Frump and planned to marry as soon as possible to alleviate the burden. The names Houri, Smudge, Peebles and Clodagh belonged to other girls, but Amy couldn't fix which was which. Her head was overstuffed with new names, rules, people and language. Dinner at her old school was supper here, sweet was afters, Scripture was Religious Instruction, prefects were whips.

Martine, the humorous Fourth Captain, took note of a new girl down-table, but her acolytes kept to themselves.

Between courses, a squeaky-voiced, undersized Fifth slipped down-table, with notebook and pencil. She said she was from the *Drearcliff Trumpet* and wanted to interview the new girl.

'Push off, Shrimp,' said Frecks. 'She's not talking.'

The reporter blinked and retreated.

'Can't let her get her hooks in you,' said Frecks. 'Be wary of Shrimp Harper. Girl's a menace.'

'Don't let her sketch you,' said Light Fingers. 'You'll be faint-headed for a week and she'll be bright as a new penny. We tried smearing her cot with garlic, but no joy.'

'Garlic and Shrimp?' said Kali. 'Sounds like a recipe for murder.'

'*Unusual* isn't always good,' said Frecks.

'Mother says it's *never* good.'

'Who's Unusual?' asked Inchfawn. 'The new bug?'

Questions were thrown at Amy by other girls. She wound up talking about moths. No one was perplexed, like grown-ups were, but no one was that interested either.

'You'll fit in,' said a girl with black Indian braids. 'You're ga-ga already. We all go ga-ga at Drearcliff. After a while.'

When afters came, Amy took Frecks' advice and spurned the semolina. She ate an apple, instead.

With the last bowl scraped, the servants returned to collect the crockery. Headmistress stood. Girls sat still and quiet again, as for grace. Amy realised the convention for quiet was not for religious observance but from whenever Dr Swan rose till she gave a nod for din to resume.

'Girls,' she began, 'we must welcome a new sister among us...'

'Oh no, she's not going to...' began Frecks...

'... a new friend, a special gift to Drearcliff, a veritable *ornament*...'

'She bloody is,' said Frecks. 'What a terror!'

'... a shining beacon of potential, an Unusual Talent whose gifts should be nurtured till they reach full bloom...'

Amy didn't hear the rest of the speech. The flagstones had opened and she was pulled under the roiling earth. Everyone in the Refectory looked at her. Her face was flaming red.

'Jammy crumpets!' she exclaimed, *sotto voce*.

'Worse luck,' commiserated Frecks.

'Poison Doll might as well a' stuck a target on ya, kid,' said Kali. 'What happens next won't be pretty. Not ah-*tall* it won't.'

V: The Witches of Drearcliff Grange

A FIRST WENT DOWN on one knee in front of Amy, hands clasped to her chest, ringlets rustling like silenced sleigh bells. The little she-beast declaimed dramatically…

'Welcome, oh sister, oh veritable *ornament*, oh…'

Frecks cuffed the chit about the head. She squeaked like a pig.

'Out of the way, scum, or be mistaken for a carpet and *walked over*…'

The theatrically inclined First was between the Dorm Three girls and the stairs. The little tragedienne's clique had laughed at her turn but now just laughed at her. In the show business, applause was fleeting.

Frecks and Kali picked Bernhardt *fille* up and slung her to one side. She spat 'I'll be revenged on the whole pack of you' and scurried away.

'That exit line was from *Twelfth Night*,' said Amy. 'She's a Viola?'

'You heard the blubbing,' said Frecks. 'Of course she's Viola.'

'It's not Viola's line, though,' said Amy. 'It's Malvolio's.'

Kali gave the departed thespian's audience the evil eye.

'Any a' you mugs got complaints?' she asked.

The down-table girls looked duly intimidated. Kali made neck-breaking gestures. They fled.

'This is gonna get monotonous,' said Kali.

Amy was not reassured.

'It'll blow over when School finds something else to play with,' said Frecks. 'These things pass, like the wind…'

'Wind does damage, sister…'

''Tis true, 'tis true.'

The Dorm Three girls trooped upstairs.

At their landing, Light Fingers made a sign, and they halted.

'Uh oh,' she said. 'We're Belgium?'

'Belgium?' asked Amy, puzzled.

'Invaded and occupied, Thomsett,' said Frecks. 'Likely to be outraged by the Hun. Best get it over with.'

Their cell was already crowded. Amy's trunk took up most of the limited floor-space. It was open, disclosing the rumple of her possessions.

A womanly Sixth sat in Light Fingers' rocking chair, which was much too small for her. She hummed dreamily to herself, as if thinking only modest, chaste, *improving* thoughts. Her complexion was healthy cream, brushed lightly with rose-petal red on her cheeks. She had merry cornflower-blue eyes and rippling golden hair. She looked the sort of angel you'd never sully by placing her up on a Christmas tree. Her grey blazer had gold piping. Above her school badge was picked out, in gothic script, *Head Girl*.

'Gryce,' acknowledged Frecks.

'Shut your hole, Walmergrave,' said a bony, dark girl whose sallow face was half-masked by a wing of black hair. 'This isn't your bailiwick.'

She stood behind the rocking chair, arranged side-on as if to present a thinner target. She had been poking through Amy's Book of Moths with a long-nailed finger.

Frecks held back, along with Kali and Light Fingers. Two other Sixths were in the cell, taking up room: a big-shouldered, tubby girl with a face like one large pimple and rope-braids hanging to her waist; and a fey, huge-eyed sprite with a white streak in her enormous cloud of brown hair. They all had gold piping.

These were the Murdering Heathens.

'Amy, *entrez votre* cell and *asseyez-tu* on *votre* cot,' said Gryce, sweetly. 'I fervently hope we shall be *les amies eternels.*'

Frecks gave Amy a gentle prod between the shoulder blades, and she crossed the threshold. She had to bend and twist to make her way without touching the Sixths or tripping over her trunk. She sat on her cot, knees together, hands in her lap. She tried to ignore the hammering of her heart and the lightness of her spine. This was no time for floating. She *thought* herself heavy. Her cot-springs creaked.

'I am Sidonie Gryce,' she said, looking Amy directly in the eyes. 'I am Head Girl. I embody School Spirit. 'Tis my duty to make *filles nouvelles* welcome. If Discipline is necessary, it is my sacred trust to apply the gentle hand of guidance…'

The dark girl snickered. She had fingernails like painted knives. Her uncovered eye was blue with a dash of red.

'If Encouragement is needed, I shall be at your back, urging you to do your *plus que belle* for School. If Praise is merited, it shall not be withheld. That is the

Code of Drearcliff Grange. *Comprenez-tu*, Amy?'

'I think so,' said Amy.

'*Bonne*,' smiled Gryce, with a flash of steel in her eyes. 'These are *mes amies* and fellow prefects. Beryl Crowninshield...'

One-Eye.

'Dora Paule...'

White Streak.

'... and Henry Buller.'

Pimple Face.

'You will address us properly as Head Girl, Prefect Crowninshield, Prefect Paule and Prefect Buller. *Comprenez-tu*?'

'Yes.'

Gryce reached over, smiling, and slapped her face, then gave a 'go ahead, try again' nod.

'Yes, Head Girl.'

Gryce bent over and butterfly-kissed Amy's stinging cheek, then made a stroke-it-better gesture without actually touching her.

'You see, *mes filles*, a perfect demonstration of the Method Gryce in action. Gentle Discipline. Firm Encouragement. Deserved Praise.'

'Can I Encourage her, S-s-sid?' said Buller, leaning over and putting her blotched face close to Amy's. Her breath was sweet, like violet pastilles.

'Not now, Henry,' drawled Crowninshield. She gave a shoulder-twitch which briefly lifted her hair – revealing her other eye, which was brown – before it fell back in place.

'Prefect Buller's *enthusiasm* is School Spirit,' said Gryce, waving the big girl away. 'Do you have an *enthusiasm*, Amy?'

Amy was not forthcoming.

Crowninshield made a flutter with Amy's book, flapping its covers like wings, flying it around the room like a trapped moth.

'I am a moth,' Crowninshield said, lips shut but throat moving. 'I'm... drawn... irresistibly... *to the flame*!'

Crowninshield fluttered the book into Paule's hair. The Witch who hadn't spoken batted it away with her hands.

'I repeat: do you have an *enthusiasm*, Amy?'

'Yes, Head Girl. It's...'

'Did I ask you what your *enthusiasm* was?'

'No, but...'

The hand went up.

'No, Head Girl,' she corrected herself.

'See, you *can* learn. Now, let us *guess* your *enthusiasm*. Henry?'

Buller made fists, and leaned close again.

'Is it bleeding? Bleeding, while trying not to b-b-blub? Bleeding from something that can n-n-never be fixed?'

'No, Prefect Buller.'

'Beryl?' asked Gryce.

'It's not butterflies, is it?'

'Yes, it's not butterflies, Prefect Crowninshield.'

Crowninshield thought a moment and was pleased. 'Do you hold the position that butterflies are a separate phylum of lepidoptera, as opposed to a sub-species of moth?'

'Yes, Prefect Crowninshield.'

Lepidoptera are not a phylum, but an order of insects, which are a class of the arthropod phylum. Strictly, Amy acknowledged moths were what remained of the lepidoptera once butterflies were excluded. She kept that to herself.

'The taxonomy is not uncontroversial, though, is it not?'

Amy couldn't unpick the contradictions, but intuited her inquisitor couldn't either, and answered 'No, Prefect Crowninshield' with confidence.

'Paule, Paule, wisest of us all?'

'I can't bear moths,' said Prefect Paule in a tiny voice.

'That's not a question,' said Gryce. 'That's a statement.'

'It is all I've to say on the subject. Moths are too Thursday for me.'

Crowninshield tossed Amy the book, which she caught before it hit her in the face. She held it shut in her lap.

Crowninshield tapped her own head. Amy realised what was being asked of her. She balanced the book on her head. At her old school her form mistress was a fiend for deportment, so Amy knew how to keep the book level.

Gryce smiled on her. She began to rock back and forth in Light Fingers' chair, as if daring it to fly into splinters and give her cause to inflict severe Encouragement.

Frecks and the others were out in the corridor, watching. A crowd of Thirds gathered. Had they all been through this? Amy was probably getting an extra helping for being a new bug in the middle of term.

'If the book falls,' said Gryce, rocking faster, 'you'll be marked down as Not School Spirit. *Une vraie salope*! Scrubbing the Heel is a let-off next to the Encouragement visited upon those who are Not School Spirit. Keep a straight spine, moth-girl. Shoulders back. Eyes up, chest up. No, eyes down, showing *la modestie propre...*'

Amy looked down and felt the book tip – but she recovered in an instant.

'There only remains the matter of contraband,' said Gryce, signalling to Buller, who reached down into Amy's trunk and pulled out a blue slip. 'What's this?'

'A gymslip, Sid.'

'Not a Drearcliff slip, though. Excluded.'

Buller tossed it in the air, and Crowninshield caught it.

Mother had not bought new gym clothes from the recommended dressmaker, believing Amy had the proper items – now, it seemed, the *improper* items – already. Her kit bore no emblems associated with her old school, but did not pass.

'Navy is not Drearcliff blue,' Gryce explained. 'Sea-green is Drearcliff blue. *Comprenez-tu?*'

'Yes, Head Girl.'

Yes, you Simpering Witch!

'Don't think of Head Girl like that,' said Paule quietly. 'She won't like it.'

Amy felt stabbed. Paule was an Unusual. Her Abilities included some species of mental telepathy.

Gryce rocked, as Buller raised item after item. Skirts, socks, blouses. The Head Girl didn't even look at them.

'Excluded, Excluded, Excluded, Acceptable, Excluded…'

An old scarf had passed muster, at random.

Amy breathed evenly, trying not to float. She tried to present a bland countenance, tried not to feel anything. This ordeal would soon be over. The Murdering Heathens would not be here all night, could not devote the rest of their year at Drearcliff to this testing of the new bug.

She thought of moths, fixing their distinguishing marks, wing-patterns and antenna shapes in her mind. Moths made sense. *Hepialidae*: *Hepialus humuli* (Ghost Moth), *Hepialus sylvina* (Orange Swift), *Hepialus fusconebulosa* (Map-Winged Swift). Moths were various, but finite. *Cossidae Zeuzerinae*: *Phragmataecia castaneae* (Reed Leopard), *Zeuzera pyrina* (Leopard Moth). Moths flew, purposefully. *Limacodidae*: *Apoda limacodes* (The Festoon), *Heterogenea asella* (The Triangle). Moths were hardy, yet delicate. *Tineidae Tineinae*: *Monopis laevigella* (Skin Moth), *Tinea pallescentella* (Large Pale Clothes Moth), *Monopis weaverella*...

Amy was slapped...

She instinctively raised her hands, to catch the book, but Gryce caught her wrists. Amy cobra-necked and the book didn't fall. She made the book light, almost to the point of floating.

'I said, *what is this contraband?*'

Amy moved her eyes only. Crowninshield held up Roly Pontoons, invading his ballooning clown suit with her hand, waggling his big-nosed, jug-eared head, jingling the bells on his fool's cap.

A tear rolled down Amy's cheek.

She remembered her father making exactly the same gesture. Roly was as much puppet as doll.

'Are you a little child? A little child who *plays with dollies?*'

'No, Head Girl.'

'Then, what is this vile specimen?'

Amy kept quiet. To speak would be a betrayal.

'Not your *poupée*, then, Thomsett,' stated Gryce. 'You wouldn't care if it were hurt, then?'

Crowninshield tore off Roly's left arm, trailing stuffing, and dropped it.

Amy felt a sympathetic pain. The book held firm.

Crowninshield made a scream come out of Roly's open mouth...

'The whip hurt meeeeee, Ameeeeee,' said Crowninshield, in a strange doll-voice. 'You did nothiiiing, you beast. You were supposed to be meee ickle fwend! Meeee not love you any more. Meee hate you, Ameeee.'

'Don't talk like that to a Drearcliff girl,' said Crowninshield, in her own voice, rapping Roly on the nose. 'It's not your place...'

'Nooooooo....'

Crowninshield tore off Roly's right leg and waved the puppet from side to side, screeching from the back of her throat.

Tears dripped off Amy's chin now. But she made no sound. And her book held level.

'Give her the wretched thing, Beryl,' said Gryce.

Crowninshield held out Roly, then snatched him back as Amy reached for it. Then handed him over. Amy couldn't help hugging the mutilated plaything to her breast.

'Now, show School Spirit, Thomsett. Drearcliff Spirit. Can you do that *pour votre amie* Sidonie?'

'Yes... Head Girl.'

Gryce smiled and sat back in the chair.

'*Then tear that horrible thing's head off.*'

Amy froze.

'You heard me, new bug. Tear That Horrible Thing's Head Off.'

'Nooooo, don't, Ameeeeee. Don't kill 'ums. Meeeee soooo saad!'

'Cut that out,' snarled Buller. 'It makes my f-f-flesh creep.'

'There's a lot of it,' said Crowninshield in her own voice. 'Isn't that right, little cripple? Hasn't Auntie Henry got a vast acreage of flesh to creep.'

'Yessums, sheeeeee's as fat as a *cow*!'

Amy hugged Roly Pontoons close. She remembered Father, in his uniform. His Roly Pontoons voice was deeper, jollier than Crowninshield's shrill, cracked whine. 'Hello, Amy, I'm your friend from Belgium. Won't we have jolly fun!'

Moths, she thought, getting a good grip on Roly's neck. *Gracillariidae Gracillariinae: cameraria ohridella* (Horse Chestnut Leaf-Miner). She found stitches weakened by years of night-time hugs and dug her nails in. *Gracillariidae Lithocolletinae: Phyllonorycter coryli* (Nut Leaf Blister Moth), *Phyllonorycter...*

'Off with its head,' insisted Gryce.

'Pleeese, nooooo...'

'Mind that wobbly book, Thomsett,' said Crowninshield, seeming to talk over herself.

Amy thought she was pulling Roly's head, but it stayed stuck. She willed herself to tear, but orders weren't reaching her hands.

From inside her blazer, Gryce produced a pair of man's white dress gloves. She put them on, slowly, flexing her fingers, making and unmaking fists. There were scuffs and stains on the gloves.

Amy looked into Roly's trusting glass eyes.

Jolly jolly fun.

'Noooooo...'

'Okay, that's the limit,' said Kali.

She stepped into the cell and put her hands round the throat of the nearest Murdering Heathen, Dora Paule.

'Read my mind, sister,' she said.

'So angry,' breathed Paule.

'You ain't talkin' horse-feathers. You in the chair, up and out, see. Take a powder. Amscray to Ellhay. Make like a tree and fall down. I ain't just lip-flappin'.'

Buller lunged across the cell.

Without letting go of Paule's neck, Kali angled her body and kicked out – sticking her shoe into the prefect's wobbling tummy. Buller doubled over.

'Any more want a taste of tootsie-to-the-tum? Head Girl?'

Gryce stood, head touching the low ceiling. She was a foot taller than Kali.

'Kali Chattopadhyay,' said Gryce. 'You are not showing School Spirit.'

'Ain't I? Balloon juice.'

'I have no idea what that means.'

Frecks was in the cell, too, now. She stood aggressively close to Crowninshield.

'Prefect Crowninshield, so kind of you to visit. Do call again soon. When you're better.'

Crowninshield gave a half-smile and had to contort to get past Frecks. She was first out of the room. Kali let Paule go, and she helped Buller – whose red face was set in pain – out.

Kali looked up at Gryce. The Head Girl reached out and pinched Kali's nose-snail lightly.

'Three Minor Infractions, for all girls in this cell... for all girls in this House.'

Groans from out in the corridor. Someone muttered 'I've only got the bloody Heel now'.

'And a Major for you, Chattopadhyay. Report to the Whips' Hut first thing after Chapel tomorrow. For Encouragement.'

'I'll be there, Princess. You can be sure of that.'

'Good night, new bug. We'll pick this up when you've settled in. I fear you've made a poor start. *Au revoir*.'

The Witches were gone.

Frecks shut the cell door, barring the rest of the Dorm. Amy stopped shaking and mopped her face. Kali took the book off Amy's head and put it on a shelf above Amy's cot.

'Here,' said Light Fingers.

Amy looked down. Light Fingers had Roly's arm and leg in her cupped, open hands.

'I'll get my sewing things,' said Light Fingers.

VI: Broken In

THREE WEEKS LATER, the whole of Amy's life before
Drearcliff Grange was a fading nursery memory.

Like many a veteran of the Great War, Roly Pontoons
was repaired but not the same. Coffined in a shoebox
under her cot, he was out of harm's way but also set
aside. Her mother's letters, fine copperplate complaints
about Lettie's slackness and the dreadful *nouveau riche*
neighbours, were read once and filed with Roly.

Amy nestled in the heart of a Chinese doll of
institutions, official and otherwise. Frecks' cell, Dorm
Three, Desdemona House and School. At times, she
belonged to forms where Thirds of all Houses mixed
and House Middle School sides where a lumpage of
Thirds and Fourths, along with gargantuan Seconds
and titchy Fifths, was acceptable. She stayed away from
netball, but was recruited for other sports – cricket and
hockey balls were too fast and small to get a mind-
grip on, and the games offered few opportunities for
unnatural leaps and levitations. Her newness was worn
off. Everyone else had forgotten what it was like when
she wasn't at School too.

Every Monday, in Chapel, Headmistress called the

whole register... Abbott, Absalom, Ackland, Acreman, Addey, Aden, Adkins, Ah, Aire... Over three hundred names, called and responded to before breakfast. The first time, Amy was terrified she'd miss herself but piped up a 'present' on cue and the register passed on. She was settled in the Ts... Teller, Thaw, Thicke, Thiele, Thomsett, Thompson, Thorn, Thorne, Thorpe...

A handful of girls were on the register, but not at School. It was customary for their forms to thunder 'absent' *en masse* when they were called. ffolliott-Absent, a fabulously wealthy Ariel Sixth, was famous for her non-presence. She was rumoured to be living high on the Riviera while her guardians assumed she was safe at Drearcliff. She paid off Dr Swan to withhold distressing information from the trustees of the ffolliott estate.

Teachers' names, handles, enthusiasms and tells had been learned. Amy had most to do with Mrs 'Wicked' Wyke, Head of Desdemona Middle, who took Classics, Geography and Gym. Despite her ominous handle, Wicked was a sweet-natured pudding, inclined to fluster and fuss and cluck when liberties were taken – which was, as a consequence, frequently. History, Dance and Deportment were taught by Miss 'Digger' Downs, known for utter lack of humour, malapropisms and spoonerisms and protracted, fiendishly devised revenges against pupils and Staff alike. Wyke lessons were lively, wild-spirited affairs, but Digger insisted girls toil in a silence relieved only by the ticking of the classroom clock or the beat of her riding crop. Her conviction was that Dance was best taught without the frivolous distraction of music. French, Russian and Astronomy were down to Miss Bedale, whose favoured teaching tool was the acronymic mnemonic.

Religious Instruction was the province of the excessively powdered Reverend Mr Pericles Bainter. Some girls fervently believed he was a recruiter for a white slave ring. Several times, Amy was warned in hushed tones that Ponce Bainter made a habit of shipping off Fourths and Fifths to the Orient to become addicted to *bhang*, importuned by Lascars and sold to seraglios. Opinion was divided on whether this was a fate worse than death or an acceptable way of meeting a nice Lascar who would probably turn out, like Tarzan or the Sheik, to be an English Lord raised in foreign parts. English, Poetry and Drama were entrusted to Miss Kaye, 'Acting Mrs Edwards', a sensible flapper – if that wasn't a contradiction in terms – who was on the Staff temporarily while the regular teacher was off having a baby.

Sciences were taken by Miss 'Fossil' Borrodale, a deceptively fair-faced young woman who was the object of Desdemona's most notorious crush, the fanatical devotion which burned in the breast of Lydia Inchfawn. Fossil carried a length of rubber tubing and settled Minor Infractions by calmly offering miscreants a choice between 'the short, sharp shocks' (three thwacks across the open palm) or 'the long, tiresome retribution' (producing a manuscript copy of ten random pages of the *Encyclopaedia Britannica*). Infractors almost always chose the shocks, to the teacher's evident delight. When she administered 'three across the hand', her eyes glittered and she bared her small, pearly teeth. Inchfawn filled up sketchbooks trying to capture Miss Borrodale's expression, and would willingly take the blame for unattributed malfeasance in order to savour short, sharp shocks on her permanently reddened palm. Fossil also commanded the QMWAACC – the Queen Mary's Women's Auxiliary Army Cadet Corps – which spent Thursday afternoons on coast patrol with wooden rifles, looking for spies and smugglers (and ammonites) along the beaches and cliffs. Fossil maintained that Drearcliff was ever ready to defend Somerset from foreign devils, no matter that the most likely invaders of these shores would have to come by coracle from Wales. Smudge Oxenford – Dorm Three's leading Exaggerator – said that on a route march in the rain last term, Fossil had three girls lashed for desertion under fire.

Amy had four Minor Infractions in her Time-Table Book, which girls must carry at all times and surrender to a whip or teacher who wished to mark a Black Notch in the tally-page at the back. Not having the Book about you was good for an additional Minor. After Gryce's welcome-to-school Black Notch, Amy's next Minors came together. Digger Infractioned her for talking in a lesson, to wit: asking Light Fingers for a lend of a pencil sharpener. Amy admitted her Book was back in Dorm, and was ordered to report with it before Prep. Digger dipped her pen in an inkwell and made two thick, practised flick-marks on the tally-page. Carrying the Book at all times wasn't in School Rules, but was an Addendum of Usage – unofficial, but enforced. Her other Minor was malice on the part of Crowninshield. The wall-eyed whip singled her out of a gaggle of Thirds crossing the Quad between lessons and Black Notched her for 'taking the inappropriate diagonal'. A deep voice that seemed to come from the Heel said 'somebody needs a good bottom-kicking.' Amy wasn't sure if Crowninshield's ventriloquism was an Ability… or just a Trick.

Encouraged by her cell-mates, Amy experimented. In Gym, she made herself light as a feather and pulled herself up a rope, arm over arm, legs dangling so she didn't chafe her thighs like others performing this exercise. If she willed a float just as she was taking off for a long-jump, would momentum give her an advantage? She held back from testing the theory. It seemed like cheating, for a start. On manoeuvres with the QMWAACC, she floated herself – Frecks and Kali holding her ankles – to peep over a high wall to see if the Ariel Squad, with whom they were 'at War', were creeping into positions. She hoarsely called out the range for the Desdemona potato-mortars, which bombarded their rivals into calling for an armistice. Fossil sent the Ariels off on a punitive march across the shingle to teach them not to surrender so quickly. So far, few knew the nature of Amy's Abilities. She was keen on keeping it that way. If her floating became common knowledge it would be less of an advantage.

On Saturday afternoons, Wicked worked a projector in the Gym and showed flickers to the whole School. Miss Dryden accompanied on an upright piano with several missing keys and a tendency to go wildly out of tune when she got excited. The films were mostly ancient one- and two-reelers, often parts of long serials screened out of order and never with the opening or closing chapters to explain the story. Girls might hope for Valentino as the Sheik, Charlie Chaplin as the Little Tramp or (in Kali's case) Lon Chaney as a gang boss with no legs (Kali described this film, *The Penalty*, over and over after Lights Out, with elaborations – she proclaimed it as the Greatest Motion Picture Ever Made). However, they made do with 'The Coughing

Horror', one of *The Mysteries of Dr Fu-Manchu*, or 'The Bruce-Partington Plans', one of *The Adventures of Sherlock Holmes*. These were thought to be 'proper stories', held in higher esteem than serials of American origin. In Yank films, soppy heiresses were constantly imperilled by villainous uncles and masked masterminds out to obtain their fortunes. Because they were utterly useless, they often needed to be rescued by handsome fellows. Fossil taught QMWAACC girls how to slip out of even the most elaborate sailors' knots, but such skills were evidently not part of the education of the average American heiress.

The flickers drew venomous hisses from the audience whenever it seemed the hero was on the point of planting a passionate smacker on the heroine's cupid's bow lips but they chickened out at the last moment and rubbed cheeks instead. Scornful of the breed of ringleted and ribboned Paulines, Elaines and Helens, Kali dared express a preference for the honestly naked crookery of the wicked uncles and clutching hands above the hollow charms of the unmanly youths held up as heroes in the chapterplays. Amy's favourites among Mrs Wyke's flickers were not American or British, but French – especially those in which adventuress Irma Vep prowled the rooftops of Paris in a black bodystocking and mask, murdering and robbing at the behest of a secret society called Les Vampires. It occurred to Amy that her Ability might come in handy if she were ever called upon to prowl rooftops. Should she ask Light Fingers how to go about beginning a career in crime?

In three weeks, she had seen and sketched twelve new moths, including the nationally scarce *Discoloxia blomeri* (Blomer's Rivulet), though the Drearcliff grounds were poor moth country. Her *enthusiasm* was noted by Fossil Borrodale, who – when not thwacking Infractors – was a surprisingly good teacher. She didn't baby-talk like Wicked Wyke or insist on rote copying like Digger Downs. Called after lessons to see Fossil, Amy dreaded punishment for some unintentional Infraction – only for the teacher to ask politely if she might look at Amy's Book of Moths. While casting an eye over the sketches, Miss Borrodale admitted she had kept a Book of Fossils when she was Amy's age. Fossil allowed that Amy could examine the Calloway Collection if she liked. The naturalist Damina Calloway – who had taught at Drearcliff around the turn of the century then disappeared in Patagonia – had donated a great number of specimens to the school, including several trays of mounted lepidoptera. Though against killing for science, Amy thrilled at the prospect. The trays had grown dusty and ignored, awaiting someone who shared the *enthusiasm* of the long-gone collector.

Leaving Hypatia Hall – the smelly edifice which contained the Biology and Chemistry Laboratories and the Machinists' Workshop – Amy spied Inchfawn peeping round a corner, boiling with envy. 'It's all right, Inchfawn, I didn't get the thwacks.' That didn't assuage Inchfawn, who darted away, spectacles up in her hair, heels of her hands pressed to her eyes.

Amy now knew her cell-mates intimately. They were together in lessons, at meals, on QMWAACC exercises, between lessons, at the flickers, doing prep, rambling in the grounds, playing sports and games and in the cell, talking in the dark after Lights Out. To everyone else, they were Frecks' cell; among themselves, they were the Forus, a contraction of 'the Four of Us'. If School had a language, the Forus had a dialect – a slang or code comprehensible only by themselves. Frecks was skilled at making up handles and expressions. Each prefect or teacher or girl had a Secret Handle, for use only among the Forus, selected so there was no obvious connection between the handle and the subject's name or enthusiasm or physical appearance. Miss Borrodale was not 'Fossil', but 'Lilac' (her first name was Violet). Miss Kaye was not 'Acting Mrs Edwards' but 'Janet' (J came after K in the alphabet). Dora Paule, known to her relatively few friends as 'Daffy', was simply 'A' (because she was 'A-paule-ing'). Inchfawn was 'Inchworm' to the School, but 'Six' – for Six Eyes, because of her two sets of specs – to the Forus. Only they called whips 'the Witches'; the rest of School called them 'the Sisters'. In Forus lingo, Black Notches were 'Stains' (fully, 'Stains on the Escutcheon'), bosoms were 'beakers' (Light Fingers had the best-developed beakers), prep was 'greens' (as in 'have you eaten your greens?'), serving in QMWAACC was 'being ganged' (derived from press-ganged), custard was 'splodge', and someone with a crush was 'a limpet'.

They all had Secrets. Amy's was the floating. Light Fingers had a stash of stolen objects, picked up while practising hereditary skills. Frecks had a boyfriend in Watchet – a lad named Clovis, who was walking out with her (when they could both escape, which was seldom) though he was supposedly engaged to a little marchioness. Besides her reprobate brother and her spy parents, Frecks' family tree included a glamorous uncle who had flown with Pendragon Squadron during the war. Lieutenant Lance Lake, her mother's brother, had given Frecks some of his kit, including one of the mystic-blessed silvery chainmail balaclavas the Aerial Knights of Avalon believed kept them safe in battle provided their cause was just and true. Kali wore the snail in her nose at least partially to cover a scar given her by her father – who once took it in mind to stick the point of a dagger up her nostril and rip it free.

Amy told the Forus about Mother, and the uncles she had periodically gained and lost since Father died. Light Fingers admitted she'd drawn up, and tested, five plans for escaping from School Grounds, which were set down in cipher in her Time-Table Book. Frecks said she was smuggling vitriol out of the Hypatia Hall a drop at a time, saving enough to throw in the marchioness's face this Easter – using a test tube she'd managed to get her brother to leave his fingerprints on. Kali was thinking hard about her first massacre. You couldn't be taken seriously as a bandit in Kafiristan until you'd supervised at least one massacre.

Originally from Bengal, the Chattopadhyay clan were driven north-east across the entire sub-continent in the 18th Century by the East India Company, who Kali said were worse bandits than anyone in her family. Kafiristan – Land of the Infidels – was properly called Nuristan – Land of the Enlightened – these days, though Kali's family resisted forced conversion to Islam a generation ago and refused to acknowledge what it said on the map. She hoped to be the first of her family to use 'a Chicago pianola' and 'pineapples' rather than kukri knives or strangling scarves.

In books written by grown-ups, there was a lot of guff about school days being either the happiest of your life or a worse ordeal than penal servitude. Headmistress gave speeches about School Spirit and

Wicked Wyke hoped to foment a similar, if more limited Desdemona Spirit which never quite caught on – though Desdemonas bristled at any suggestion other Houses were better in any way, except in games where Goneril won so often no one cared about losing. Amy didn't have the luxury of stepping out of herself and thinking of Drearcliff in terms of Good, Bad or Indifferent. The place was, at times, immeasurably better than her old school (which she could barely recall – she spent twenty minutes nagging at a lost scrap of memory, unable to summon her old school's word for 'greens') and at times far, far worse. She was here, this was (for the time being) her world, and that was that.

She was a Drearcliff Girl.

VII: Kidnapped!

BECAUSE SHE WORE specs, Inchfawn was trusted with the map.

This Thursday afternoon, Desdemona were at War with an unholy alliance of Tamora and Goneril. Ariel were supposed to be on their side, but had capitulated early. Viola were being Belgium, which meant standing in a field and blubbing rather than being bayonetted or importuned by Hunnish hordes.

The berserkers of Tamora wore Art Room blue paint on their faces and brandished hockey sticks decorated with the skulls of shrews. Led by Zenobia Aire, the Fiend of the Fourth, they broke through the Desdemona lines with a great whooping, bashing, screaming attack. It was a rout.

Amy, Kali, Smudge and Inchfawn were cut off from the rest of the House. They had fled to a wooded area outside School Grounds. Inchfawn found an overgrown path she promised was a shortcut back to HQ, but it ran downwards, turning into a small pebble-bed stream, and came out on the beach.

There was a dramatic view of Drearcliff Grange, but no easy way to get up to it.

Floating was an option – but Inchfawn and Smudge weren't in on the secret, and Amy thought it best to keep them in the dark. Smudge, liable to exaggerate, would have Amy zooming about with her tail on fire like Hans von Hellhund, the Demon Ace.

Inchfawn was potentially a Problem.

Since Fossil had taken an interest in Amy's Book of Moths, the teacher's devoted disciple had been at best cold and at worst malicious. Jealousy was a terrible, terrible thing. Inchfawn was rather an unhappy girl and Amy of course felt sorry for her – but she was a drip and a millstone, a burden to the House and a liability to School.

'Some shortcut, sister,' snarled Kali. 'Sure you ain't rattin' for Tamora? If there's one thing I can't stand, it's a dirty squealin' rat. If there's two things I can't stand, it's the wrigglin' portions of a dirty squealin' rat after she's been chopped in half.'

That was a bit strong, but Amy didn't pipe up.

She was cold, bruised and tired. Tuck had run out an hour ago. When they made it back to base, they were sure to be Black-Notched for straying out of bounds. Amy was not looking forward to scrubbing the Heel with her toothbrush. She only had the one, and would have to clean her teeth with what was left of it.

At this rate, they might have to surrender. She hoped they could find a Goneril patrol to be captured by. Then, they'd be marched to neutral territory to sit out the War with the wets of Viola. It would be worse luck to run into a Tamora murder party.

Inchfawn looked at the unrolled map again and shook her head. She offered it to Smudge, who was in her cell, but the other girl wouldn't touch it.

Inchfawn had obviously given up even trying to help.

So far, Amy had stayed away from the beach. Shores were generally not moth country. The most notable landmark was the fallen tower, which was a way off, surrounded by 'Danger – Keep Out' signs. The coast was unevenly eroded, making seaside walks fraught with peril. There was always a risk of being cut off by the tide, which could swiftly transform open beach into a shrinking shingle bay, inaccessible except by boat or climb. Cliff-base caves tempted the adventurous explorer – but they'd been warned against them because, at high tide, the waters washed in and anyone inside would certainly drown.

It was said the caves were used in olden days by smugglers, though Amy supposed smuggling more likely on coasts facing France or Holland than one in sight of South Wales. A few wave-cut overhangs were on their way to becoming caves or catastrophic collapses. Chunks of rock often detached from the cliffs and fell on the beach. School legend had it that two teachers were squashed during a midnight tryst, dying in a compromising embrace.

Smudge pointed out the exact spot where this tragedy had occurred. She spread her arms to indicate the extent of the human pancake found the next morning.

'We believe you,' said Amy, 'thousands wouldn't.'

Smudge stuck out her lower lip. She was very fond of this story. At different times, she had identified six or seven different combinations of teachers in old photographs as the doomed couple. Until 1914, several moustached, jolly-looking masters could be found among the mistresses. Since the War, the only men in the pictures were Ponce Bainter and Joxer.

* * *

Amy knew it was down to her and Kali.

They couldn't go back the way they came. They'd had to move quickly to avoid the Tamora patrol commanded by Crowninshield II, the ventriloquist whip's younger, nastier sister. After taking prisoners, Crowninshield II performed harsh interrogations. Really, what she liked was tying people up. She practised knots on naive Firsts lured to her cell with the promise of lemonade. She might even have got in trouble for it if her sister weren't a whip.

Together, Amy and Kali looked up the cliff.

'There *might* be a path,' said Amy.

'For *you*, maybe…'

'You're a decent climber, Kali.'

They looked at Inchfawn and Smudge.

'If we ditch the baggage, it's a Stain. A whole mess of Stains, doll.'

Amy admitted it. Desdemona didn't abandon its own.

Kali hefted her wooden rifle.

'If this gat were the real deal, we could ventilate 'em a little, put 'em out of our misery.'

Smudge heard that and was alarmed.

'She's just joshing,' said Amy.

Smudge not only spread wild stories, but believed them. It would be all over School tomorrow that Kali had killed several girls and buried them in the herb garden.

Inchfawn sat down and looked at her big clunky wristwatch. It was her prize possession, handed on from a brother who'd been in the trenches. If the hour-hand was pointed at the sun, it worked as a compass – but the day was overcast, if not actually raining, and they already knew which direction they needed to take. It was just that they couldn't go that way easily.

Amy's toe turned something out of the shingle. An old cricket ball, seams expanded but holding together. The School pitch was near enough to the edge of the cliff that balls could be hit for a six into the sea.

Suddenly, they were surrounded.

Kali threw away her useless wooden rifle. She reached under her knee-length khaki skirt to pull a long, straight knife from a holster strapped to her thigh. Not QMWAACC regulation issue. Amy hefted her wooden rifle by the barrel like a hockey stick, hoping to give the enemy a good sloshing.

'Screw off, mugs!' shouted Kali.

Inchfawn had her hands up, in surrender – the weed. Smudge fumbled with her ill-kept rifle, which came to pieces in her hands.

Kali held up her knife and bared her teeth.

A *crack!* sounded. Then, a curtailed ping-*nyeow!*

A shot, and a ricochet.

If Desdemona had knives, trust Tamora to bring real guns.

'I say, you gels are playing rough,' declared Smudge. 'Get things in proportion, why don't you?' – which was rich, coming from her. 'A damsel could get damaged.'

Another shot, and a spray of pebbles kicked up at Smudge's legs.

Amy looked at the enemy and realised there was a mistake. These weren't Crowninshield II's rope-happy Campfire Comanches. Even She-With-No-Mercy Aire wouldn't go this far.

There were eight or nine of them. Slight by grown-up standards, but not all – or not *even* – girls. They wore loose black clothes and matching hoods with eye-holes. Several had revolvers. One held a shotgun.

'Sticky crumpets!' exclaimed Amy.

The one who had shot at them was definitely not a girl. He had a red tuft on the forehead of his hood, a badge of leadership. It looked like a flame. Was it the symbol of a secret society? He took careful aim at Smudge and she shut her mouth.

Had she been wrong about the scarcity of smugglers hereabouts? From their outfits, this mob were up to no good. The hoods suggested *organised* illegality. They reminded her of Les Vampires or the bands of desperate minions employed by wicked uncles to abduct soppy heiresses.

Kali gave a battle yell and charged.

Amy's heart clutched and she was sure her friend would be shot. She swung her rifle, which left her hands and cartwheeled through the air until it smacked against a hooded head. A torrent of frightful masculine swearing poured forth.

Kali went for the leader, who sidestepped her charge and cold-cocked her with his pistol butt. She dropped her knife.

Two others caught the stunned girl and bound her with ropes. They were as practised as Crowninshield II.

With his gun, the leader indicated that Amy and the others should not interfere.

The prisoner was dragged, a deadweight, along the beach. The fellow Amy had beaned was still angry, but his leader indicated they shouldn't stick around. They had what they'd come for.

Kali.

'You can't do that, you bounders,' Amy shouted.

They didn't reply and kept on doing it.

'You won't get away with this,' she added.

She didn't sound convincing to herself.

The hooded men moved quickly. They were nearly out of sight beyond a cliff outcrop. Amy picked up the old, wet cricket ball and bowled it at the leader's head. She made the ball light as it left her hand, then let it recover its weight as it flew long and straight. She had tried this before.

The hooded leader turned to look back and was struck between the eyes.

'*Thrown*, Amy,' applauded Smudge.

The hood must have protected the leader, for he didn't fall down dead. He shook a fist back at the girls. Amy picked up stones. The leader made a sign to a minion, and the shotgun was discharged in their general direction. Pellets pattered on the beach. Then, the gunman took careful aim with the other barrel. Reluctantly, Amy dropped the rocks.

The abductors hustled away.

As soon as they were round the curve, Amy would follow, keeping close to the cliff, hiding, floating if need be. She could not let smugglers take her friend.

Smudge grabbed her arm, holding her back.

'They'll shoot you,' she said.

'I don't care,' said Amy.

'They might shoot Kali,' Smudge argued.

'If they went to the trouble of tying her up and carting her off, I should say not,' Amy reasoned. 'Her father has enemies. The kidnappers probably intend to ransom her.'

'It could be Ponce's white slavers,' put in Smudge. 'Not that Kali's white, but, you know, for her I expect they'd make an exception... She's jolly saleable, I should say.'

'I don't care what colour she is,' said Amy. 'She's a Desdemona of Drearcliff. We can't let her be snatched without a fight.'

Amy broke free of Smudge.

'I wish Miss Borrodale were here,' said Inchfawn.

Then, suddenly, she was.

'You girls,' said Fossil, 'War's over. You're casualties.'

VIII: Treachery

SMUDGE TOLD THE story first, which was a disaster. After confirming that Kali hadn't turned up back at School, Miss Borrodale took Amy, Smudge and Inchfawn to Headmistress's study. Dr Swan asked Keys to sit in on the interview. Small chairs were brought in for the girls.

'Chattopadhyay is missing,' stated Dr Swan. 'Tell me what you know.'

In a gush, Smudge got out her version of what happened on the beach. She had most of it straight, but embellished details. Instead of a sewn-on red patch in the shape of a flame, Smudge said the leader's hood was actually on fire. She claimed the abductors had popped out of foxholes on the beach – which might have been true, but sounded silly.

The tide was in now, so any evidence – spent shotgun pellets, for instance – was underwater.

Smudge wasn't believed.

Amy calmly confirmed most of the story and insisted the police be called at once. The country must be searched, trains stopped, roads blocked, airfields shut down. It was vital action be taken now.

Dr Swan and Fossil exchanged *looks*. Amy was still a new girl to them. They now thought she was following the errant path of Smudge Oxenford into realms of faerie, flight and fancy.

The spotlight fell on Inchfawn.

Surely, the grown-ups would have to believe three girls telling the same story!

Inchfawn took off her glasses and cleaned them with a hankie.

'Kali ran off,' said Inchfawn. 'She talked about it, then she did it. She said she could get back to School without us. She said we were *baggage*.'

Headmistress's eyes nearly closed.

Any girl who knew Kali could tell this was rot, but Amy understood that – to the tiny mind of a grown-up – Inchfawn's version sounded more believable than a wild romance of hooded villains. Especially if the primary source was the School's most famous Exaggerator. Smudge invoked smugglers, white slavers, anarchists, spies and members of secret orders of demon-worshipping monks so often that patience with her had run dry.

Amy had a spurt of pity for the Exaggerator. At last she had a true story of crime and terror to recount, but her previous yarns rendered it worthless. Amy felt only cold contempt for Inchfawn. She wanted to slap her, but knew it would make the drip seem even more like the put-upon truth-teller in a nest of verminous fibbers.

Headmistress asked Fossil to escort Inchfawn to Old House, where she was to clean herself up for supper. A-tremble at being entrusted to her idol, Inchfawn ignored Amy's thumb-through-the-fist sign. The traitor couldn't cling to Miss Borrodale's skirt forever. Eventually, she must answer for her crimes.

Amy and Smudge remained with Headmistress.

'It is a serious matter to voice untruths in this study,' said Dr Swan. 'Even in the cause of protecting a House Sister.'

Now it looked even worse. Kali had run off like a sneak and her friends were lying to cover up.

'Do you have anything to add to your account of this afternoon's incident?'

Amy and Smudge did not.

'Very well,' said Headmistress. 'This matter will be resumed.'

'Aren't you going to call Scotland Yard?' asked Smudge.

'We make our own laws at Drearcliff,' said Dr Swan softly. 'Keys will find Chattopadhyay.'

Keys nodded. She had a waterproof cape to hand and was set to go out in search of the missing girl. At least something was being done, though it was scant comfort.

Dr Swan considered the girls, drummed her lacquered nails on her desk, and said, 'You are dismissed.'

IX: The Moth Club

'KEYS WON'T FIND Kali,' declared Frecks. 'The old trout knows School better than anyone, but hasn't been off grounds this century. When she was a Sixth, she was engaged to a young officer. He only went off and got beheaded at Khartoum with General Gordon. Keys took a vow not to leave Drearcliff Grange. Graduated from Girl to Staff and stayed put. Wants to be buried in the cricket pitch. Under the crease.'

'Could hardly make it any lumpier,' Amy commented.

Frecks and Light Fingers tittered at the drollery, then remembered how grave things were.

They were in their cell. Amy had told her friends all.

'Keys has been scouring the school for sign of ffolliott-Absent for two years and is no closer to laying a hand on her.'

'Surely, ffolliott absented herself?' Amy said. 'Isn't she on the Riviera?'

'Did you hear that from Smudge?' asked Frecks.

'Well, yes.'

'... *quod erat demonstr.*, eh? Smudge told *me* that ffolliott-Absent went in a burnoose to trail after Lawrence in the desert, having been fired up with Mohammedanism by anonymous postcards from a sheik. Yes, Smudge said the postcards were both anonymous *and* from a sheik. She meant an anonymous sheik, I suppose. Wherever Enid ffolliott is, I doubt she's in this. It's not like sardines, where each disappearee crams in with the last until there are more of them than the stay-behinds. Whatever has become of ffolliott-Absent is of a different order of strangeness to Kali's abduction.'

'The kidnappers will have Kali in an aeroplane by now,' ventured Light Fingers. 'Or a sealed train carriage. She'll be bundled up like an invalid. Bound to have been drugged too.'

Amy wasn't sure about the theory.

'I don't know why,' she said, 'but I believe Kali hasn't been taken far away, *yet*. The hooded men were only after *her*. If they were white slavers, wouldn't they have taken all of us?'

'I doubt even the most depraved oriental potentate would offer cushion-space to Inchfawn,' said Frecks. 'She'd have to be a Special Bonus Offer, thrown in with better quality merchandise.'

'She wasn't much use in the pinch,' admitted Amy. 'Poor girl.'

'I wouldn't "poor girl" Inchfawn,' said Frecks. 'That one has a sly, cunning streak. And a mercenary nature. Brain-peeping Ames always shied clear of her. Just like Six to turn yellow in a pickle.'

'Funny thing, though,' mused Light Fingers. 'I was in Inchfawn's tent when we went hiking last year. We got early tea every day because we were first to pitch camp. Inchfawn was a whizz at map-reading. I'm puzzled she should have lost the knack. Her brother's watch works like a compass.'

Amy snapped her fingers. 'Crumpets!' she exclaimed. '*Her brother's watch!*'

'Do tell,' urged Frecks.

'She snuck a look at the watch just before the hooded men appeared out of nowhere. As if she were waiting for them! We wouldn't have been on the beach at all if it weren't for her mucking up with the map... So how did they know where to find us?'

The three girls goggled at each other. Inchfawn was in with the abductors!

'It's a Hooded Conspiracy!' declared Frecks. 'I knew it in my bones!'

Amy found such malignancy difficult to credit, but it solved the riddle of why Inchfawn had fibbed to Headmistress.

'What a cow-bag!' said Light Fingers.

Frecks knotted a dressing-gown cord.

'Kali showed me how to do this,' she said. 'Put a florin in the knot, to give weight. Hey presto – Thuggee strangling tool! Justice will be swift. Show no mercy.'

Frecks snapped the cord, which twanged like a bowstring.

'*Whoah, Nellie,*' said Amy. 'Let's not go off half-cocked. Yes, Inchfawn's in on a terrible, terrible crime. But knowing she's in it opens the door a crack. We were at a loss. Now we have a *clue*. If we play this cleverly, we've a chance at doing what we know Keys can't. Find Kali and get her back...'

'...and see off those dastards in the hoods and all their drippy minions.'

'*Minions?*' Light Fingers asked Frecks.

'It won't be just Six. If they've signed her up to the Hooded Conspiracy, who knows how many other girls – teachers, even – are in it? Could go all the way up to High Table. Might even be a pinch of truth in what Smudge says about Ponce Bainter. On principle, we can't trust anyone outside this cell until they prove themselves. Smudge is probably sound, from what you say, Amy. Can't see what earthly use she might be, though. It's down to we three. We must apply ourselves – use our Abilities. Without Kali, we're the Forus no longer. To go up against the Hooded Conspiracy, we must form a conspiracy – a secret society – of our own. Now, what should we call it? The League of Avenging Justice? The Three Good Girls?'

'The Scarlet Slippers?' suggested Light Fingers.

Amy had it. 'The Moth Club.'

The others looked at her, puzzled and a little disappointed.

'The Moth Club?' exclaimed Frecks, in disbelief.

'All those other names *sound* like secret societies,' Amy explained. 'The Moth Club doesn't…'

'It sounds *boring*,' said Light Fingers.

'Moths are *not* boring,' said Amy, a little stung. 'But, I admit, my enthusiasm isn't generally shared. If we talk about Moth Club doings, people will yawn and not think any more of it. Only we'll know it's important. That's a super way to keep a society secret.'

Frecks saw sense. 'The Moth Club it is!'

'I liked The Scarlet Slippers,' said Light Fingers, weakly.

'We'll have another society called that,' said Frecks kindly. 'A pretend secret to cover up the real one. A good name should not go to waste.'

Amy felt a sense of purpose. After the worrying, dizzying helplessness of the afternoon, it was a relief, almost an intoxicant.

Something was being done.

Now they had a name, the Moth Club needed a charter. Amy turned her Book of Moths upside down, and opened the blank last page. She fetched out pen and ink and wrote 'the purpose of the Moth Club is to study moths in their habitats, to list and sketch any species found on the grounds of Drearcliff Grange School, to defend the honour of moths against the calumnies of the supporters of trivial butterflies and to take steps to prevent the wanton murder of moths by certain boys who stalk them with poison and kill them in jars for the empty achievement of building a collection of dead things.'

'Phew,' said Light Fingers.

Amy pressed pink blotting paper to the page. She held it up and saw the charter in mirror-writing.

'That's the *official* story,' said Amy. 'Now, pass me that pencil.'

Pressing firmly, writing between the lines of the previous passage, she wrote 'the true purpose of the Moth Club is to oppose the Hooded Conspiracy, no matter who their agents or masters might be, to rescue Princess Kali Chattopadhyay from their vile clutches and return her to safety. We vow not to rest until this purpose has been achieved, and that none of the undersigned shall betray her cell-sisters on pain of death by strangulation. We shall triumph.'

She showed this to Frecks and Light Fingers, who approved.

Then, using an India rubber, Amy wiped away the pencil – rendering invisible the secret charter of the Moth Club. Its imprint remained on the paper and would emerge if anyone were to rub a pencil-nib over the seemingly blank spaces between the lines.

Amy signed her name in ink under the official and shadow charter, and passed the book to Frecks, who signed with a flourish, and Light Fingers, who had to think hard to make her signature.

'We should take code names,' said Frecks. 'Secret *secret* handles. Moth names. Thomsett, you're the expert. You pick.'

'Where are your people from?'

'Lincolnshire,' said Frecks.

'Willow Ermine,' she said, printing it in small letters under Frecks' swish of a signature. 'Its wings look like little Lords' robes, white with tiny black spots. Light Fingers?'

'I'm not from anywhere. Mum and Dad were theatricals, on tour all the time.'

'Where were you born?'

'The Theatre Royal, King's Lynn. Between houses.'

'Large Dark Prominent.'

'Pardon?'

'It's a moth. Very rare. The only specimen known in the British Isles was bred in Norfolk, near King's Lynn.'

She wrote down the name.

'What about you?' asked Frecks.

'Kentish Glory,' said Amy, lettering it under her signature.

'But you're from Worcestershire,' complained Light Fingers.

'So is the Kentish Glory,' she said. '*Endromidae: Endromis versicolora*. Catalogued by Linnaeus in 1758.'

She flipped back the pages to show the sketch – mostly in brown pencil – she had made. The Kentish Glory was the rarest moth she had catalogued to date. It had visited her grandmama's garden two summers ago, and had held still on a leaf as if posing for Amy's pencils, fluttering off as soon as the sketch was finished.

Light Fingers produced a needle from her sewing box. They all pricked their forefingers, stuck little full stops of blood after their names to seal the pact, and sat on their cots, sucking their fingers.

The Moth Club was founded.

X: Midnight Retribution

THE NEXT NIGHT, well after Lights Out, the Moth Club crept along the corridor. They presented strange figures.

They reasoned that if their foes were *hooded*, they must be *masked*.

Born and raised in theatres and naturally quick with a needle, Light Fingers was an Old Reliable for the Drearcliff Ballet Club, the Viola Dramatic Society, the Arthur Wing Pinero Players (who existed thanks to a bequest from an Old Girl which maintained the Drearcliff Playhouse in a state of acceptable plushness – on the condition that the school mount annual productions of a work by the author of *The Gay Lord Quex* and *The Second Mrs Tanqueray*), the Ragged Revue and the Christmas Mummers. For every play, recital or presentation, Light Fingers made or altered costumes to order. Therefore, she had knowledge of and free access to the catacombs under the Playhouse. Here, props, scenery and costumes – some dating to the last century – were stored. Smudge said the storage cellars were haunted by a Viola Fifth who foolishly drowned herself while taking the role of Ophelia too seriously in the '08 Senior Production of

Bowdler's *Hamlet*. The theatrical spectre purportedly dripped on the floor and wailed her mad scene among hanging doublets and hose. Light Fingers was not afraid of such silly-goose ghosts.

There were no lessons on Saturday afternoons. Girls were expected to pursue their *enthusiasms*. Having raided the catacombs for raw materials, Light Fingers worked in their cell – prickling somewhat at the many and contradictory suggestions from her 'customers' – to run up ensembles suitable for the Moth Club's secret missions.

Now, Amy, Frecks and Light Fingers wore wood-nymph body stockings from some forgotten sylvan ballet, tight-fitting balaclava helmets from an unsuccessful dramatic recital of *The Charge of the Light Brigade*, sturdy dance pumps, and light-weight cloaks passed down through generations of 'courtiers, attendants, guards, clowns, & co.'. The costumes were set off by moth-shaped domino masks, with feathery pipe-cleaner antennae and trailing wings which covered their lower faces. The cloaks, masks and body stockings were appropriate for their code-name species: Kentish Glory was a brownish rust, Willow Ermine white with small black dots and Large Dark Prominent speckled grey-brown.

Light Fingers silently opened the door and the Moth Club slipped into Inchfawn's cell.

As they entered, someone stirred. It was Smudge. She caught sight of the masked intruders in the moonlight and shoved the edge of her sheet to her mouth.

For a moment, Amy – Kentish Glory – fought panic. She didn't know which of the three sleeping Thirds was their quarry. Then she saw two pairs of spectacles neatly folded on a small table by one of the cots.

The Moth Club laid hands on Inchfawn.

Amy pressed a face flannel into the girl's mouth. Inchfawn was awake, but too terrified to struggle.

Smudge mumbled a quarter-hearted protest. Frecks raised a finger to her mask-covered mouth. Smudge buried herself under the bedclothes.

Between them, the Moth Club got Inchfawn cocooned in a sheet and carried out of the cell. The other Thirds didn't even wake up. Smudge could tell them what had happened. She'd exaggerate, of course – and spread lurid tales of deaths-head monsters spiriting Inchfawn away to glut vampirish thirsts. Frightening rumours about the Moth Club might serve a purpose. Wrong-doers *should* be afraid of them.

They carried their muffled burden up the backstairs. Having hold of Inchfawn's head-and-shoulders end, Frecks bumped the bundled-up bonce against walls and doors a little more than was strictly necessary. A door which should have been locked wasn't. Through this, they reached the flat roof. The cloud had cleared off for once. A full moon bathed Old House in pale light. Perfect for nocturnal lepidoptera. Chimney stacks threw stark, deep shadows.

The scene had been prepared. Light Fingers' rocking chair was tipped against the low guardrail, with ropes prepared for the accused's neck and ankles. Inchfawn was unrolled from her sheet and tied to the chair. Her hands were bound behind the chair, and the gag taken from her mouth.

A kick set her rocking.

'You will not scream, *wretch*,' said Frecks, putting on a deeper, more ominous voice in her guise as Willow

Ermine. With wind whining in the chimneys and waves crashing hundreds of feet below, it was deuced eerie. Amy's hackles rose.

Inchfawn opened her mouth, but swallowed a cry. Without any of her glasses, she looked like a different girl.

'Lydia Inchfawn, Dorm Three Desdemona, you are accused of treason against your House Sisters,' declared Amy, finding her own hollow voice for Kentish Glory. 'It is proven that you did collaborate with the Hooded Conspirators who abducted your House Sister, Princess Kali Chattopadhyay. Furthermore, you did perjure yourself before Headmistress...'

'Who is that?' asked Inchfawn.

'Silence, *weasel*,' boomed Frecks. 'You will hear the charges.'

'...you did perjure yourself before Headmistress, to hinder attempts to pursue the Conspiracy and rescue Princess Kali. These things are known. Now, sentence must be passed... and *executed*.'

This was the trickiest part of the plan. And it depended on Amy. Even if Inchfawn guessed who was behind the mask of Kentish Glory, there was a thing she did not know about Amy Thomsett.

She could float and she could reach out with her mind and make others float.

Since making a poor start with Headmistress's pen, she had been practising and was more confident.

'Ha ha, very amusing,' said Inchfawn unconvincingly. 'Now, if you'll untie me, we can all get back to bed... and nothing more will be said, all right? No need to trouble Headmistress – or the whips! – with this raggishness.'

Frecks and Light Fingers hefted up the chair, and set it on the guardrail, holding it steady.

Inchfawn squeaked.

The accused was tilted backwards, over the edge.

A grassy strip separated the outer wall of Old House and the cliff edge. Depending on the wind, a person falling from the roof might bounce on that ledge or miss it entirely. Whichever, they would plunge to the shingles. It was remotely possible they'd be impaled on the flagpole which still stuck up from the broken-off tower.

Frecks and Light Fingers struggled with the weight. Light Fingers had only lent her chair to the Moth Club on the condition it be returned safely. It was a prized possession, one of the few things she had brought with her to School. It had accompanied her to the dressing rooms of all the great theatres of the kingdom. Amy felt a responsibility for the furniture.

She reached out with her mind, feeling the shape and weight of the chair and its prisoner, then took a firm hold on the lump they made together. The chair juddered a little, as if trying to free itself from the other girls' grips. Now Amy made it *lighter* and herself *heavier*. Anchored to the roof by her increased weight, soles sinking a little into soft tar, she held the chair as if invisible strings ran from her eyes to its points of balance.

Amy raised her arms – her wing-like cloak spread out – and took all the weight on herself.

Frecks and Light Fingers let go of Inchfawn.

The chair wobbled, but did not topple.

Amy let out the invisible strings and the chair tipped backwards.

'No,' screeched Inchfawn, fat tears streaming down her cheeks. 'It wasn't my fault, you beasts! They said no one would be hurt! I was made to do it! It was... a whip, I tell you. A whip!'

Just as Frecks had theorised, the Hooded Conspiracy ran through School.

The chair was floating now, like a large balloon. Amy didn't think Inchfawn even noticed. If she looked down, she would see dark sea and the white froth of breaking waves. That would be enough to stop most people's hearts.

Amy began to reel the blubbing culprit in.

'What have we here?' drawled a voice from behind them. 'Such a shocking spectacle,' it continued, from another direction. 'I should say this was unmistakably a Major,' from one of the chimneys. 'What do you think, Head Girl?'

It was Crowninshield, throwing her voice about. All the Murdering Heathens were here, in grey nighties and dressing gowns. They carried hockey sticks or cricket bats. Henry Buller had one of each, hefted on her shoulders like the crossed swords of a barbarian gladiator. Crowninshield II was with them, a cadet Witch, drooling at the sight of a trussed Third.

'I fear very much so, Prefect Crowninshield,' said Gryce. '*C'est tres mechant… tres mechant* indeed.'

The surprise jarred Amy's concentration. Suddenly, she wasn't *heavy*. The chair was let go, over the edge.

Inchfawn wasn't the only one who screamed.

XI: In the Ruck

BEFORE SNATCHING INCHFAWN from her cot, the Moth Club had prepared the roof. In case of eventualities like this, a stout cord was tied between guardrail and chair-back. The prisoner dropped barely five feet before the rope cracked taut like a hangman's neck-breaking noose. Knots tied to QMWAACC standards held. The chair stayed as securely tethered to the rail as Inchfawn was to it. She might not be exactly comfortable but was in no real danger.

Still, her nasty tumble was a useful distraction.

Amy reached out with her mind and tried to float Henry Buller. The Sixth was hefty. Her flat feet were planted firmly.

'I say, g-g-g-girls,' stuttered Buller. 'I've come over queerly…'

Buller's waist-length braids rose as if on stiff wires and bobbed like charmed snakes. Her crossed bats lifted from her shoulders, seemingly of their own accord. Her eyes almost popped – which wasn't Amy's doing, just a natural reaction.

Dora Paule hissed. An Unusual herself, she recognised another.

'I d-d-don't like this,' said Buller, her croak close to cracking. 'S-s-s-Sid, m-m-make it s-s-s-stop!'

The bats were tugged out of Buller's hands. Amy made them dance in the air like dangerous puppets. She let go and the bats clattered, thumping Buller's shoulders as they fell.

Inchfawn, out of sight, was still making a fuss.

'Cut out the yelpage, stoat,' said Frecks. 'Dangle with some dignity. For the House's sake, if not your own.'

Seemingly unperturbed, Gryce signalled her Murdering Heathens to spread out, cutting off the Moth Club's avenues of escape. Buller was *hors de combat*, but the Head Girl had other minions. The Crowninshield sisters took flank positions, chins down as if expecting a charge, evil mismatched eyes peeping up through long fringes. Their identical smiles of unhealthy excitement were all the scarier in moonlight. Paule seemed, as usual, distracted – but was stationed between the Moth Club and the access door to the backstairs.

'How gaudy you look,' commented Gryce. 'I note a dozen Minor Infractions of the dress code. Or has there been some *minuit masquerade* to which, by an oversight, we were not invited? In any case, *mes enfants*, the party is *fini*.'

This was worse than facing the Hooded Conspiracy proper. Grown men might shoot at you, but couldn't dish out extra punishments for having the temerity to fight back. If the Moth Club survived and were unmasked, they would be cleaning the Heel with their tongues and have burning bamboo shoved under their fingernails in the Whips' Hut for the rest of their lives at Drearcliff.

'*Mes filles*,' said Gryce, 'let us see which spotty faces

cower behind those ridiculous bug disguises...'

The Crowninshield sisters stepped forward. They had rounders bats. Frecks had taught Amy 'only bounders play rounders', a game for twits who had not the patience and poetic soul for cricket. Buller was now superstitiously afraid of her own weapons, but her ham-sized fists were clenched.

It was going to be a ruck.

'Let the Witches have it,' cried Frecks. 'Tally-hoooo!'

Light Fingers, faster than a nocturnal hummingbird, zig-zagged towards Crowninshield, but stepped into a shadow at the last moment, leaving the whip blinking. Then, swiftly, she came out of the lea of a chimney and tweaked Crowninshield's nose. She could keep this up all night. Frecks stepped under a bat-slosh from Crowninshield II and punched her square on the nose, staggering her back. She ripped her opponent's weapon from her hands and sailed it off over the edge of the roof.

Amy realised she was *floating*. The thrill of the moment had made her lighter. Her feet hung limply, about nine inches from the rooftop. Using her moth-wing cloak, she tried to swim through the air towards an astonished Buller, but found herself flapping in place. The gentle-seeming wind filled her cloak as if it were a sail. She had to resist being borne backwards over the parapet.

She made herself heavy and landed hard. Her ankles hurt.

Buller charged her, snorting like a heifer. Amy wished she had persuaded Kali to teach her Kafiristani foot-boxing.

She held out a hand and floated Buller's dropped cricket bat, tripping the girl up.

Then, she took the fight to the Queen Heathen.

Pushing Buller aside, giving the Sixth enough extra weight to keep her sprawled on the roof, Amy ran at Gryce. The Head Girl was used to delegating the thumping and scratching to her Murdering Heathens. Amy had an idea she was, like all bullies, a coward at heart.

Amy screeched. This was her moth-cry. She had practised. She knew it set teeth on edge.

'*Filles*,' shouted Gryce, calling for help. '*Beryl...*'

The trailing mask-wings tickled Amy's mouth as she kept up her cry. She saw fear in the Head Girl's eyes. It was welcome.

In this disguise, the Kentish Glory costume, Amy was not a feeble Third, a new bug who could be shoved around. She was a mystery, a creature, a terror to the wicked, an angel to the well-intentioned. Free of the weaknesses of her person and position. Free to strike!

She pushed Gryce up against a chimney stack and drummed fists against the girl's chest and face. She grabbed handfuls of the Head Girl's unbound hair and tugged. She screeched in the Witch's face.

Gryce was helpless.

Amy kept up the attack.

Crowninshield did not come to help the Head Girl. She was dancing around the roof with Light Fingers, tossing her voice to throw off her opponent but too slow to avoid swift slaps and cuffs. Having put Crowninshield II down with a bloody nose, Frecks laid into Buller with the prefect's own hockey stick.

The Moth Club were giving a good account of themselves.

Why had Amy been intimidated by the Murdering Heathens? Gryce was blubbing as badly as any Viola First now.

A hand clasped her shoulder, and a mouth pressed to her ear.

'*Amy Thomsett*,' whispered Paule, 'stop this. *Now!*'

There was a light, and a smell, and the sky changed...

XII: The Real *Head* Girl

THE ROOF WAS bathed in the harsh purple light of three big, shining moons. All was still. Amy's cloak collar itched. Her new costume felt heavy, the domino tacky against her cheeks.

She could no longer hear the sea. Far off, something wailed musically. Soft and mournful, but bone-scrapingly *wrong*.

To Amy's surprise, *everyone else* was floating. They weren't drifting ever upwards to be lost in the stratosphere – which Amy was always afraid would happen to her. Frecks, Light Fingers and the Murdering Heathens bobbed gently a few inches above the roof, as if suspended in invisible liquid. To Amy, they looked like waxworks – frozen in mid-air, mouths open, clothes stiff, hair starched. She let go of Gryce and the Head Girl drifted away. Her face was a contorted mask, eyes open but unseeing. Her hands were raised in defensive claws. She looked silly, but Amy wasn't inclined to laugh.

She turned, *knowing* this was Prefect Paule's doing.

Amy had thought Dora Paule wasn't quite there. Now, she knew that was the honest truth.

Paule wasn't a floating waxwork, but wasn't herself

either. At least, not the self she usually showed.

She was like a balloon person who'd been blown up irregularly. The head was five or six times normal size, swollen cranium distinct beneath a vast dandelion clock of hair. The rest of her was undeveloped, with feeble, withered limbs. Her feet trailed on the roof, but her head must be floating. Her spindly body couldn't otherwise support its weight.

The face, though expanded, was unmistakably Paule.

'Good evening, Amy,' she said, mildly. 'This must be a shock. Did you think you were the only Unusual? When I first came to School, I did. It's natural. You read about Blackfist, Dr Shade or the Slink in the story papers, but never think "*they're like me*".'

In this purple light, Paule sounded less mad. That was not comforting.

'Where are we?'

'A step outside,' said Paule. 'I call it the Purple. I'm always half-here, which is why I'm half-gone Back Home.'

'Do you really look like that?'

'In the Purple, yes. Don't take it seriously. Consider yourself. You have wings here.'

It was true. The itching tug Amy had felt was not the cloak Light Fingers had scavenged, but a set of moth wings anchored to her shoulder blades. She shrugged and they spread in display – but she didn't know how to flutter. It must be a knack you had to learn, like wiggling your ears. Her forehead tingled where her antennae were rooted. She had smells in her mouth, tastes in her eyes, colours in her ears.

'Why've you brought us here?' Amy asked.

'Not to save Gryce,' said Paule. 'She can take her lumps. Though she's not who you should worry about.

She's no real idea what's going on. No one does, except me. Looking at Back Home from the Purple is like watching a play with the script in your hand – you can flip back and forth, read the stage directions even, know what's coming. But you can't change the story. For that, you have to be Back Home.'

Amy, fascinated, touched Gryce's frozen face. Her skin was warm, but not pliant.

'So you're claiming Gryce isn't in the Hooded Conspiracy? That Inchfawn was fibbing?'

'Yes and no.'

Amy's antennae prickled with irritation.

'No,' said Paule, picking up her reaction, 'I'm not being wishy-washy, I'm answering both your questions in order. Yes, Gryce is not party to the kidnap plot. No, Inchfawn was telling the truth when she said a whip made her dupe you on to the beach. It was Crowninshield. She's clever. She works at it, like she does her ventriloquism. She's not a natural Unusual, but thinks she can gain Abilities. It's all about money. She hires out. The people you call the Hooded Conspiracy gave Beryl ten pounds to make sure Princess Kali was on the beach yesterday. That's not important. *We're* important. So's Emma Naisbitt, if only she'd look beyond the ends of her fingers. We are the School Spirit. You know what it means to be a Drearcliff girl...'

Tendrils of thicker purple, like the ghosts of eels, wound at ankle height. The quality of the light was unpleasant in this place. Though there was no heat, the moons' shine was as oppressive as a blazing summer's day. The wailing was closer and raised Amy's hackles like the brush of razors. Her antennae stung. She felt sparks behind her eyes.

Paule leant towards her. Her forehead seemed to be expanding further. Her eyes were the size of apples.

'Why do you think they send girls to school, anyway?'

Amy was taken aback by the question.

'Your mother said it,' began Paule, '"Boys grow up and go out to conquer the world, make fortunes, fight battles, invent aeroplanes and miracle cures and the wireless. Girls get married and have children. Why fill their heads with anything not relevant to that?"'

Once, when she didn't think Amy could overhear, Mother said that to her own mother. Grandmama – a lifelong suffragette – had marched, broken windows and chained herself to railings to get the vote. Since female enfranchisement, Mother had pointedly never voted. They had *differences* over Amy.

'"School prepares a girl for life,"' said Amy, quoting Grandmama.

'Yes, exactly,' said Paule. 'Ordinary schools prepare ordinary girls for ordinary lives. Babies and cakes and wallpaper. Drearcliff is not an ordinary school. We are not ordinary girls. We will not have ordinary lives. Certainly you won't, Kentish Glory.'

Amy's wings stiffened involuntarily – with something like pride, but also apprehension. She didn't want to know what happened in the last act before the overture was finished.

'Back Home, there's a demand for *educated* girls,' said Paule. 'Not too educated, but enough. It's like white slavery. Girls are put on the market and bought with a wedding ring or a villa in Nice or an endless supply of dear little hats. Drearcliff girls don't marry masters of foxhounds and raise gallant captains for the next war. The men we end up with are different. Unusuals. There are more around now than before the War, have you noticed? Men with great and secret purposes. Freakish geniuses and bold explorers in nether regions. Men with Abilities and Attributes. Unusual men need Unusual women. Swan realised that when she started. She saw what was coming, saw the need for *Drearcliff* girls. An ordinary fellow wants a wife who serves tea prettily and puts up with mess in the bedroom in order to pop out healthy children. Other men want a woman who can walk through the walls of the Tower of London with a crown jewel in her mouth, or keep an entire tribe of pygmies on mind-strings under the impression that she's a volcano goddess. Some men want women who actually *are* volcano goddesses or winged creatures or night-gaunts. Those are the lives Drearcliff prepares you for. Who do you want to marry when you grow up, Amy? A curate, or a masked mystery man?'

Amy wasn't sure she wanted to marry anyone.

'You can forget the curate,' Paule continued. 'It's too late for him. Look how you're dressed. Think what you can do. No matter what your mother wants, you can't cut out the part of you that *floats*. That means you've got no choice but to live in a night world.'

Amy looked at the other girls, the frozen ones. Light Fingers was an Unusual, in the sense Paule meant. The rest – Frecks, Inchfawn, the Murdering Heathens – were... well, not Ordinary, not exactly. There was even something odd about Henry Buller, with her mannish arms and stutter, or Crowninshield II, with her knot-making fingers and cruel twist. Unusuals? Not entirely. But they were unmistakably Drearcliff Girls.

'Do you know who sends their daughters to Drearcliff?' asked Paule. 'Criminal masterminds, outlaw scientists, master magicians, clubland heroes. Sally Nikola of the Fourth is the daughter of the Fifth Most Dangerous Man in the World. Did Swan mention the Drearcliff girls who have been hanged? Two for murder, one for treason. We have three or four girls at present who aren't strictly human. Janice Marsh, the girl with gills, for a start – but she's only an obvious one. Polly Palgraive, the Second who smiles all the time and never closes her eyes, has been asleep for six months. A parasitic maggot crawled up her nose into her brain and works her like a puppet. If you try to have a conversation with her, you're actually talking to the maggot. I'm not sure myself if I'm human. I've been kept back while I develop. I came to Drearcliff when Victoria was Queen. Back Home, I've stopped growing, but in the Purple I still have a way to go.'

Paule flapped her flaccid hands apologetically.

Amy was worried about what the prefect had said.

'Oh, you're human, all right,' Paule reassured Amy. 'You only have wings and antennae because I've brought you into the Purple. Back Home, you'll be you again. But you'll still have the knack of *floating*.'

The tendrils were thicker now. One brushed past Amy's legs like sandpapery seaweed.

'You'll have to leave soon. Apart from me, girls generally can't stay in the Purple long. Others attract undue attention. That's not pleasant. I learned my lesson after I lost some visitors. Misplaced, rather. I'm sure they're here somewhere. I'm glad we've had this little chat, though. We should be friends, if you can be friends with the half of me in the Back Home. We are both *in the know*.'

There was something desperate, something *yearning*,

in Paule. If she had to keep repeating the Sixth Form – while other girls left School to get on with the lives for which they had been prepared – she must be lonely.

Amy understood that. She had been lonely too. Keeping her secret.

…but she wasn't lonely now. She had Frecks and Light Fingers and Smudge and… and Kali. She had her cell, her House, her School.

She realised something about the Purple. It was a deadly distraction. Here, you thought about what Paule wanted you to. You paid attention to her. This place had three moons, but Dora Paule was its star, its sun.

Back Home, other things were important. Amy concentrated, her antennae taut and curved. She remembered the secret charter of the Moth Club.

'…to oppose the Hooded Conspiracy, no matter who their agents or masters might be, to rescue Princess Kali Chattopadhyay from their vile clutches and return her to safety. We vow not to rest until this purpose has been achieved.'

Paule's head was so large now that her body was like the basket hanging under an air balloon.

'Paule,' said Amy urgently, 'where's Kali?'

'Oh, she's Rapunzel, waiting,' Paule said, off-handedly. 'She won't be got rid of till the third dawn.'

The purple light shut off.

Gryce was screaming again. A full three feet off the ground, Amy grabbed Gryce's lapels. She tugged the Head Girl upwards and plopped her bottom in a chimney. Gryce stuck fast, arms and legs waving, yelling like a dervish.

Amy landed on the roof, better this time, bending at the knees.

Dora Paule, regularly proportioned, stood aside.

'What did you mean?' Amy asked her. 'Rapunzel? Got rid of?'

'Mean? I'm not mean. I don't mean. I... oh, good night...'

Frecks, breathing heavy, wings torn, tugged at Amy's cloak and made for the open door, dragging Amy away from Paule, who fluttered her fingers in a distracted farewell. Light Fingers was already on the backstairs.

The Murdering Heathens clustered around the Head Girl, wondering how to get her out of the chimney without being hurt by her kicking feet or flailing fists.

The Moth Club rattled back to their cell, divesting themselves of their costumes en route.

A thin voice sounded from outside the window. Inchfawn dangled still.

'That reminds me,' said Frecks. 'Light Fingers, go rouse Wicked Wyke. She'll be up early, since it's Sunday Chapel at seven, Lord help us! Report that some larcenous harlot has stolen your rocking chair! Best shift any oncoming blame on to persons unknown, eh? Say it was probably one of Ariel's well-known not-funny japes.'

Light Fingers got into her dressing gown and hurried off.

Frecks was abuzz, exhilarated at the Moth Club's first outing. While Amy had been in the Purple, no time at all passed for the others.

Amy didn't know what to tell Frecks.

Rapunzel? *Got rid of*!

'Crumpets,' she exclaimed. 'Calamity and crumpets!'

XIII: Chapel

SUNDAY CHAPEL AT Drearcliff was more about mystery than enlightenment. All School – no excuses accepted, including deathly illness – filed in and took their pews. Miss Dryden, of the futile whistle, improvised at a wheezy organ, pumping stately, presumably devotional music with an occasional shrill screech or dramatic detour. Frecks claimed Dryden sometimes played 'Yes, We Have No Bananas!' very slowly as if it were solemn and religious.

Most of the Staff – and not a few of the Fifths and Sixths – looked as if they'd spent the night at a cockfight in an opium den followed by an orgy in a gin-house, then come straight to the Chapel without going to bed. The unscratchable Gryce might have looked fresh from eight hours of innocent sleep, but Crowninshield and Buller showed a satisfying collection of cuts and bruises. Paule was distracted, as usual. Did she even properly notice what happened outside the Purple, or even remember what she'd said last night?

'*She won't be got rid of till the third dawn.*'

If Paule meant the third dawn after Kali's abduction, that would be first thing Monday. Tomorrow morning!

In a terror spasm, Amy envisioned a scimitar held up to catch the sun's first rays and Kali's lovely neck stretched on a chopping block.

Miss Dryden's straining organ rose in a crescendo, giving the Reverend Mr Bainter his cue. The chaplain had to hide behind a curtain while Staff and Girls took their pews. He emerged, wearing a peculiar tricorn mitre with candle-tassles which burned like slow fuses and smelled like Kali's joss cigarettes.

With his hair-slickum, cheek-powder and a lotion which whiffed powerfully of aniseed, Ponce Bainter took to the pulpit like an ageing prima donna to the stage. Amy had thought all clergymen orthodox, respectable and slightly dull. Bainter was more than slightly dull, given to prefacing and concluding sermons with droning Tibetan chants, but was far from orthodox and, as all the girls were certain, quite the reverse of respectable. He seldom mentioned Our Lord Jesus Christ, an important figure in the sermons Amy had heard elsewhere. His vestments and altar cloths were embroidered with symbols not found in other churches – mediaeval scientific implements, monocular starfish, bipedal goats, wavy lines, the constellation of the Plough and snarly faced moons. The upside-down woman on the wheel, as represented on the school badge, featured heavily.

The text for today's sermon was the school motto, *A fronte praecipitium a tergo lupi*. Amy, incapable of concentrating on Bainter's windy talk, still didn't find out where the wolves came into it.

Mentally, she wrestled with a different text, '*Oh, she's Rapunzel, waiting.*'

Amy was stumped as to what Paule could have

meant. Kali didn't have particularly long hair or (so far as Amy knew) a devoted swain intent on spiriting her off. Some wet girls whispered she'd eloped with Ivor Novello, but that was tommyrot. Kali detested matinee idols, and preferred a mug with a snub-nosed 'gat' in his fist to a gent with a high-pitched serenade. Now, if Lon Chaney were walking around North Somerset on his knees, snarling insults, then Kali might have been tempted... Kali *was* a princess, but Rapunzel was practically the only fairy-tale heroine Amy could think of who wasn't. Technically, Rapunzel probably became a princess after the story was over – provided the prince who climbed up her hair did the decent thing and married her. Wondering why Miss Kaye obviously skipped passages in reading aloud to the form, Amy had looked up the original Brothers Grimm; in that, the prince caddishly got Rapunzel preggers and was blinded for it. Rapunzel was famously a prisoner in a tower, so maybe Paule meant Kali was being held captive. Rapunzel's gaoler was her stepmother, but Kali's father went through wives so rapidly no stepmother stuck around long enough to plot against her.

'You, Amy Thomsett, Desdemona Third,' shouted Bainter, raising his voice, pointing a finger. Girls edged away, putting clear space between them and Amy.

Had Ponce known she wasn't paying attention? If so, why single her out? If anyone in Chapel *wasn't* thinking of something other than the sermon, it would have been a miracle.

'Answer the Question!'

Amy ummed. She had no idea what the Question was.

'"With a precipice in front and wolves behind,

what would you do?"' rasped Frecks out of the side of her mouth.

Amy said the first thing that came into her mind.

All School tittered, except Ponce – whose eyes bulged with fury.

Amy caught herself. She had said 'I'd *float* over the precipice…'

Dr Swan, eyes firmly shut throughout Bainter's sermon, blinked alert and clapped once, silencing laughter.

'…the wolves would rush over the edge,' continued Amy, hoping she could claim she was trying to be funny, 'and be dashed to death on the jagged rocks below.'

'And *you*, Thomsett, where would *you* be?'

'Ah, away with the fairies?'

Thunderous laughter. A note was passed along the pew and pressed into Amy's hand.

She looked. It read MAJOR INFRACTION, R. Wyke (Mrs).

XIV: At the Heel

CLEANING THE HEEL wasn't quite as frightful as advertised. It *was* done with toothbrushes, but Infractors didn't have to use their own. Stout-bristled specimens were provided. Buckets of water and carbolic soap were also involved. Amy had imagined toiling alone, perhaps with hobbling weights, but reported to the Quad after Chapel to find herself in with a shower from all Forms and Houses. These miscreants had either clocked up enough Minor Infractions to qualify for the punishment or – like Amy, convicted of Impertinence in Chapel – gone for the High Jump and got caught in a Major.

School Rules decreed that a Major Infraction automatically got you the Heel, but – in a rare, merciful touch – obliterated outstanding Stains like the four Minors Amy had in her book, so you started fresh next week. Anyone with five Black Notches who wanted to do something appalling might find it almost worth the throw. Unity Crawford of Viola, known to all as 'Vanity', was here for pouring red ink on the dress shirt of a girl who had beaten her to the role of Lucas Cleeve, male lead in the Arthur Wing Pinero Players' production of *The Notorious Mrs Ebbsmith*. Polly 'Perky' Palgraive was here because her constant smile irritated the Witches so much they piled Minors on her in the hope of wiping it away. She was cheerful, if glassy-eyed. Amy remembered what Paule had said about the maggot in her brain and decided to start cleaning at the opposite end. The anarchist Hannah Absalom – who mortified a different monarch, plutocrat, churchman or politician every Monday – was up on her regular Major. She set grimly to scraping 'Death to President Zog of Albania!' off the Heel, cleaning the canvas for next week's message of terror.

This week, the Heel was supervised by Miss Kaye. She brought a lawn-chair and a book, and let the girls get to it. She had a hamper and promised lemonade at the end of the job. Amy gathered they were lucky. When Fossil was in charge, she stood over Infractors with her Bunsen burner tube and added extra *encouragement* if the pace slackened.

Still, this was a pestiferous bother.

Every moment she was here, scraping grime out from under Achilles's marble toenails, she wasn't looking for Kali. If Paule were right, the Moth Club had to find – and *rescue* – their cell-mate before sun-up tomorrow.

It was done inside an hour. Miss Kaye inspected the Heel, deemed it suitably spotless, and gave the girls – Infractors no longer, their records clean as the marble – lemonade. Absalom refused hers on political grounds.

Miss Kaye – Acting Mrs Edwards – wasn't like other teachers. She wasn't here for life, so lacked the cowed, cringing attitude even termagants like Fossil had around Dr Swan. She had read out 'Rapunzel', albeit in edited form – so she might have an idea.

Amy asked, 'Why would anyone say Kali Chattopadhyay was "like Rapunzel, waiting"?'

Miss Kaye was surprised.

'Chattopadhyay's hair isn't long,' she said, touching her own trimmed bob. 'And she didn't wait. She took off. If found, she'll be scrubbing the Heel all term. Headmistress takes a dim view of absconders. Though she's been in less of a bate about Chattopadhyay than Ferrers III last term. Funny, that. When Ferrers III went over the wall, the Chief Constable was summoned, notices put in the papers, the countryside combed by search parties and the truant tracked by private detectives to a boarding house in Torquay. I'd have thought a Kafiristani princess an even greater loss. But there's been little fuss.'

Was Dr Swan trying to avoid bad publicity?

'Kali's father happens to be in Birmingham on business,' continued Miss Kaye. 'Buying rifles from Webley and Scott, I believe. He is due to pay a call on School tomorrow. That will, I imagine, be an uncomfortable occasion. Parents don't generally take it kindly when their daughters go missing.'

Vanity snorted. She had the full set of parents, but still played the orphan. She acted up fearfully in the forlorn hope of getting attention. Amy suspected Vanity regretted not thinking of running away, preferably in disguise, to become the centre of a whirlwind of speculation. If she scarpered now, she'd be accused of imitating Kali – a severe blow to her reputation as an 'original'. Of course, it wouldn't be plagiarism. Kali had not, despite what Inchfawn swore, gone off on her own accord. She'd been snatched!

'But why "Rapunzel, waiting"?'

Miss Kaye shrugged, not casually. Her eyes showed lively interest. There were some – well, Smudge, inevitably – who said she was a spy. Frecks, who knew about the espionage game, said Oxenford wasn't as far off as usual about Miss Kaye. There were 'tells', apparently. After last night, Amy wondered if Smudge wasn't imaginative *enough* – her fictions paled beside the unexaggerated truth of Dora Paule and the Purple. From now on, she might believe the girl on principle. The verdict was that Miss Kaye was at Drearcliff for some purpose beyond filling in for Mrs Edwards. Amy felt she could trust the temporary teacher in a way she couldn't trust Headmistress or Ponce Bainter or Miss Borrodale.

'Rapunzel sat in her tower, waiting for her prince to call "Rapunzel, Rapunzel, let down your hair",' said Miss Kaye. 'The story seems to have gone beyond that in Chattopadhyay's case. Her prince has already come and spirited her off.'

'But, Miss, it wasn't like that. I saw hooded men take her away. Against her will.'

Miss Kaye's eyes narrowed. Amy could tell Miss Kaye had no reason not to believe her and maybe more than reason to doubt Inchfawn's story.

'When Rapunzel was waiting, she was in a tower,' said Miss Kaye. 'With no way in but an upper window.'

Amy had to concentrate hard to keep on the ground.

That was it! The tower! Kali was being held in the tower. The broken tower on the beach, surrounded by 'Danger' and 'Keep Out' signs. What better place to keep a prisoner?

She must tell the Moth Club.

XV: A Meeting of the Moth Club

WHILE AMY WAS taking her punishment in the Quad, the rest of the Moth Club had not been idle. Returning to their cell, she found Light Fingers picking twigs out of her Sunday pinafore and Frecks in a state of high excitement.

'After Chapel, we spotted Crowninshield and her homunculus of a sister sneaking off grounds,' Frecks explained. 'Light Fingers tailed them. She can dog a person's tracks without being seen. Useful knack if you can come by it. There's a secret way through the wall, hidden by ivy. Which is nice to know. No more braving the glass spikes.'

Light Fingers had worn her Large Dark Prominent domino, but not the full Moth Club get-up.

'They took a hamper down to the beach,' said Light Fingers. 'Contraband from the kitchens.'

'You'll never guess where they were headed!' declared Frecks.

'I bet I can,' said Amy. 'The tower!'

Frecks and Light Fingers presented studies in bugging eyes and open mouths.

'Good gravy, Thomsett,' said Frecks, 'how the diddle did you tumble?'

Amy hadn't told her chums about the Purple, not to keep a secret but because she didn't think she could explain without seeming potty. Floating and gills and hummingbird hands fell within the accepted realms of Drearcliff strangeness, but Paule's peculiarity was excessive even by School standards.

'Someone mentioned Rapunzel,' Amy said weakly.

'Ah-hah,' said Frecks. 'She of the upstairs dungeon. The mists clear!'

'When the weird sisters got to the tower, a rope ladder was let down from an upper window,' said Light Fingers. 'There's no other way in. The hamper was hooked to the ladder and pulled up. I didn't see who was doing the pulling...'

'It *must* have been the Hooded Conspirators,' enthused Frecks. 'If they've got Kali, she's in the tower!'

'Crumpets,' exclaimed Amy.

'I don't see why they *haven't* spirited her away or done her in,' said Frecks. 'They're running a fearful risk sticking close to School. Perhaps Kali's being held for ransom and Swan's keeping mum?'

'Miss Kaye said Mr Chattopadhyay is coming down tomorrow. Perhaps he's bringing a princess's price with him. Kali's weight in gold coins or blood rubies.'

'*I* wouldn't cross Kali's dad,' said Frecks. 'He's not the sort to take Hooded Conspiracies with a song and a philosophical laugh. He's the sort who hunts down enemies and garrottes them, their children, their parents, their friends and their pets. Come tomorrow, I shouldn't care to be a white mouse owned by the sweetheart of a cousin of a Hooded Conspirator!'

'We can't wait for tomorrow,' said Amy. 'Mr Chattopadhyay will be too late. Even if he takes the earliest train from Birmingham, Joxer won't get him to School till well after dawn. And that's when Kali will be got rid of. The third dawn!'

'How do you know this?' asked Light Fingers.

'I feel it in my moth antennae,' Amy explained. 'Really, I do. You'll have to take it on trust.'

That hung there in the cell for the briefest flicker.

'Good enough for me,' said Frecks. 'The word of a Moth Club girl is not to be doubted!'

Frecks stuck out her paw, which Amy gripped. Light Fingers grasped their enlocked hands.

It was already getting dark. Girls were drifting towards the Refectory.

'We can't hare off now,' said Frecks. 'If we're marked absent at Supper they'll raise the whole School after us. It'll be torture sitting and eating as if nothing were amiss, but we've got to be valiant. After nosh, we fly!'

XVI: An Upstairs Dungeon

THE MOON WAS just past full, the night sky clear. Wet shingles shimmered and tidal pools reflected constellations as the Moth Club – in full costume – crept towards the tower.

Being off School Grounds at any time was a Major Infraction. At this hour it was probably cause for expulsion and disgrace. Their cots were stuffed with pillows, in case Wicked Wyke sprang one of her occasional inspections.

'Should we call "Rapunzel, Rapunzel, let down your hair"?' ventured Frecks. 'Might give Kali heart to know rescue is at hand.'

Amy – Kentish Glory – shook her head. Stealth was the order of the evening.

The three girls blithely passed Danger! and Keep Out! signs, and climbed the rocks and rubble piled around the base of the broken tower. The footing was unsure. Rubbery, slippery seaweed-coated broken, tilted surfaces. Deceptive pools were populated by scuttling crustaceans with angry eyes on stalks. Up close, there was more of the tower than Amy had thought. What had sheared away with the crumbling cliff was the top of a fortified lookout post, built when Somerset expected invading Welsh warriors any minute. They would have had names like Dai the Dreadful, Evans the Eviscerator and Bloodthirsty Blodwyn.

Like Rapunzel's upstairs dungeon, the tower had no ground-level entrance – and no windows for the first thirty feet or so. Leaning inland at a greater angle than the Tower of Pisa, it was a wonder the remnant hadn't completely collapsed. Smudge claimed it had been shored up in olden days and used as a lookout post by Cap'n Belzybub, the masked raider who once reddened these waters with the blood of innocent sailors.

Light Fingers indicated the window from which the rope ladder had been lowered. It was near the top.

It was down to Kentish Glory to swarm the tower.

Looking at the window, she made herself light. She floated up two or three feet in a spurt and bumped against the inclining stone wall. Her friends winced in sympathy, but she held her tongue.

The wall was rough enough to afford handholds every few feet. The way was too crumbly and irregular for mountaineering, but she was a floater not a climber. She pulled herself up, careful not to get too far from the wall. She angled her body to avoid scraping her legs. It was like swimming through air. The cloak-wings helped her manoeuvre. Could she ever use them to fly properly? A strong wind blew. She had to be wary of being caught by a gust and borne off into open air.

She had a moment to realise she'd never floated this far off the ground before. Then, near the window, the urgency of her mission overcame other concerns.

She heard voices inside the tower. The shock made her suddenly heavier. Gravity tugged and she slithered down a few yards, then flattened against the wall, sticking like a moth, cloak spread around her. It took all her concentration to stay light and hold her position.

The talk was in a language she didn't know. Eastern gabble, she thought. Mr Chattopadhyay had many enemies in his home country, especially former in-laws. Could this be a revenge plan? Using the bandit rajah's daughter to lure him to a spot where he could be assassinated. If someone else killed her father, Kali would be furious.

Amy inched up towards the window. Rather than pop her head over the sill, she climbed beside the opening and listened. The conversation stalled. She detected dim light from inside the tower.

Then, she surged up the final few feet and reached the broken battlements. She hopped over, and made herself heavy enough to put her feet on what turned out to be the rotted timbers of a platform-like roof. Creaking wood began to give way under her. She had to float again, taking her weight off the unsafe roof, and gripped the secure stone. She sat in a gap in the battlements and listened. Her racket had not alerted the Hooded Conspirators.

She looked down and waved. Frecks and Light Fingers – Willow Ermine and Large Dark Prominent – waved back...

...when Kali was in the Moth Club, what name would she take? Amy hadn't looked up the moths of Kafiristan, but suspected they were exotic species.

She hooked her feet around stone and let herself float face down. At full stretch, she reached the window – and peeped in from the top.

The window let into a small room. No one stood

guard here. Amy made out a coiled rope ladder, attached to pitons newly hammered into cracks between the flagstones. She also saw the famous hamper, open and empty. It wasn't large enough for a feast, so she assumed only two or three Hooded Conspirators guarded Kali. Did the villains bother to give their captive anything to eat or drink? It would be just like them not to.

Crawling insect-like, Amy entered the room.

Letting go of the window-rim, she bobbed up against the low ceiling. She gradually thought herself heavier and settled her ballet pumps on the floor.

There was a doorway, which had stout, rusted iron hinges – but no door. That must have rotted ages ago. Beyond the opening was a light. Poking her head out, she saw a winding staircase. She went back to the window and quietly let down the rope ladder, which Frecks and Light Fingers caught before it flapped away in the wind.

Soon, all three girls were inside the tower.

This time, Frecks had brought a hockey stick for use as a cudgel.

Amy remembered that the Hooded Conspirators had firearms. Was their leader here? The fellow she'd beaned with a cricket ball. She hoped his head was still splitting. He must have a good-sized bruise under his hood.

The Moth Club silently made their way down the spiral stairs.

Then, they heard voices – and froze, a tableau of cloaked, masked figures. On the next landing was a room. Lantern-light spilled out.

'... there, the princess won't slip from that so easily,' drawled an all-too-familiar voice – Crowninshield. 'My sis is an expert in these things. Houdini himself couldn't get out of one of her corned-beef constrictor knots. Much less Nut-Brown Nancy here.'

Frecks quietly slapped her hockey stick into her hand.

Kali was here! And the worst of the Witches!

'Wriggle all you like,' Crowninshield crowed. 'The rope only gets tighter. Minnie had more badges for knots than anyone in the Brownies, before they court-martialled her for demonstrating grief strangle knots on Brown Owl's Pekingese.'

'She does look funny, Beryl,' said Crowninshield II. 'I didn't think girls her colour could go red in the face.'

An mmpphing noise suggested Kali was gagged. The tone of her muted protest indicated dire promises.

'Now, give us some of that bottled beer, like you promised,' Crowninshield demanded of her unknown confederates. 'You chappies may be the most desperate Thuggees in far-off Whateveristan, but you're no match for a Drearcliff whip! It's a wonder Red Flame lets you hang around.'

Red Flame – the Leader of the Hooded Conspiracy!

Of course, who else would be the arch-enemy of the Moth Club but a flame?

Frecks was all for charging in, but Amy held her back. They were too close to blow the game by indiscriminate action.

A hooded man came on to the landing. The Moth Club stuck still, hiding in the dark. The wretched sisters trotted after him. Crowninshield was smoking a black cigarette and wearing make-up. Crowninshield II was fiddling with a cat's cradle.

'Beer's down below, eh?' said Crowninshield. 'Makes sense. Keep it cool in the depths.'

'Drink meeeee-eeeee,' came a tiny, shrill, liquid voice from the lower floor.

The Hooded Conspirator, unused to Crowninshield's vent act, clutched his throat in terror. She laughed nastily.

'Give all your beeeeeer to Beryl,' said a voice from nowhere. 'Or face the wrath of the Great God Jumbo-Omooo!'

Crowninshield II tittered nastily.

The Hooded Conspirator produced a curved knife from his loose black blouse, but Crowninshield brushed it aside.

'I say, for desperate characters, you mob are utter clots, aren't you? There are Firsts who wouldn't fall for that. Come on, bucko, let's get that beer!'

Crowninshield prodded the knife-man with rather more confidence than Amy would have shown around such desperate fellows. With abduction and assassination to their credit, they'd scarcely stop at tossing a couple of extra heads on to the pile.

The sisters were led downstairs, away from the landing.

In the room, Kali mmmppphhed some more. Amy judged that at least one Hooded Conspirator was left to guard her – but probably no more. These were the best odds they would get.

She gave a low whistle, and the Moth Club sprang into action.

XVII: Desperate Rescue

KALI WAS TIED up. Seemingly every part of her was individually tied to a particular part of a stout chair. A white scarf wound round the bottom half of her face, lipstick smile painted mockingly over her mouth. Her exposed eyes were darkly furious.

There was indeed but one Conspirator in the room, not even Hooded. He had taken off his mask to drink a mug of tea, and looked stricken to be caught with a naked face when the Moth Club burst in. He was an Englishman, to judge by his colour – but unthreateningly middle-aged. Hood-wearing had scraped his hair into a funny shape.

Frecks conked the Hoodless Conspirator squarely on the noggin. He went down like a slaughtered bull. His eyes rolled up and blood came out of his nose, but Amy didn't waste sympathy on him.

Light Fingers patted the prone guard down, and came up with a knife which seemed cousin – if not twin – to the dagger waved by his mate when Crowninshield was showing off her voice-throwing.

Amy got the gag off Kali's mouth.

'Mother of pearl, that's a relief,' said Kali. 'Who the heckle are you gals?'

Amy flash-lifted her domino.

'I mighta knowed. Get these strings offa me.'

Light Fingers sawed rapidly, severing knots which couldn't be untied.

Kali recognised the swiftness of movement.

'Light Fingers? And the frail with the blunt instrument has gotta be Frecks. I'm mightily impressed. I was workin' on a coupla ways out, but this saves time an' motion.'

Kali was free. She stood up, but wasn't steady. Amy supported her.

'I've got pins and needles all over,' said Kali.

Amy helped Kali out of the room. The Hoodless Conspirator groaned and Frecks gave him an extra love tap.

On the landing, they found Crowninshield II. She had a bottle of ginger beer.

'Ber-ylll,' she yelled, 'it's the Moth Girls, again!'

Kali, arm around Amy, lifted up her leg and planted her foot squarely on Crowninshield II's chest – then gave her a shove which tumbled her backwards down the stairs...

'Oh, ow, oh, ow-www, watch out...'

The Fourth rolled out of sight and collided with bodies rushing upstairs, summoned by her cries. Crowninshield swore loudly, unintentionally throwing her voice so that oaths bounced back from the walls.

'Exite, rapido,' said Amy.

The Moth Club got Kali up to the window-room and helped her on to the ladder. There was a tense moment as it seemed the ex-prisoner's hands couldn't get a grip on the rungs, but her circulation started flowing again and she scrambled down like a monkey.

Frecks and Light Fingers followed.

Amy watched the doorway.

The Hooded Conspirator charged in. Amy threw herself through the window – hoping she'd float not fall. She soared away from the tower and thumped against the cliff. Kali was about half-way down, legs caught in the rungs. Frecks and Light Fingers were stuck above her.

'Give me that shiv,' said Crowninshield.

Leaning out of the window, the Witch started cutting rope. The three girls lurched dangerously. Kali got free and started moving down again.

'You're going to faa-aalll,' mocked a voice from the winds. 'You'll be squashed flat as a pan-caaake!'

One of the main ropes was severed and the other went tight. Crowninshield got her blade to it.

Amy pushed against the cliff face and launched herself at the tower, aiming for Crowninshield. Her cloak filled with wind, and she rode the air like a glider.

She held her arms out in front, hands knotted into fists. Like a battering ram, she thumped into Crowninshield's face. The whip raised her knife, but Amy back-pedalled in the air and floated out of slashing range.

Bleeding and hurt, Crowninshield took a moment to be astonished by the flying girl.

Kali was on the shingles, the others not far off.

The rope parted, but too late. Frecks and Light Fingers were on the ground.

The ladder fell in a coil at the foot of the tower.

'Beryl, how are *you* going to get down?' asked Amy sweetly.

Crowninshield hissed, snarled and flung the knife –

inaccurately – in Amy's direction. It thumped against the cliff.

Amy let herself descend slowly – she was becoming more expert – and landed on the beach. The others were well ahead, and running.

She looked up and saw the trapped Witch shaking her fist.

They would soon be back in their cell. All four of them.

XVIII: A Parental Visit

NEXT MORNING, KALI reported herself present to Wicked Wyke. She said she had been abducted, held prisoner and rescued, but claimed truthfully that her saviours had been masked. She did not mention that she knew who they were. Though the outcome had been for the good, Drearcliff was not one to forgive Thirds who were off grounds without permission after Lights Out.

Should anyone be inclined to doubt Kali's narrative, they were welcome to visit the scene of the crime, to wit: the tower. Since Crowninshield had cut off their only means of egress from the secret hiding-place, the rump of the Hooded Conspiracy were still in residence, stewing mightily. Wicked sent a Second with a note to Headmistress, who detailed Keys to lead a deputation to the scene of the crime. The party consisted of Keys, Mrs Wyke, Kali the Accuser and, in the event that a) there were villains and b) they were inclined to put up a fight, the reassuringly male Joxer. Amy suspected that, of the four-strong expedition, Joxer was least able to take care of himself in a mêlée.

Amy, Frecks and Light Fingers had to endure

Monday morning lessons as per usual and missed out on the excitement while listening to Digger getting her Tudors and Stuarts mixed up. It was a wonder a period of history so full of people having their heads chopped off could be made to seem so blindingly dull.

Mid-morning, the Moth Club met up in the Quad, between lessons. The Heel, clean yesterday, already bore Absalom's message of the week, 'Death to President Juan Vicente Gómez of Venezuela'.

Kali gave them 'the low-down'.

'Swan's called in the cops – you know, that broken-down sergeant from Watchet. The Sadista Sisters are tryin' to make out they was snatched too, the doity bums. They're sellin', but Swan's not buyin' – though she'll let 'em off, since she doesn't want to dish out another multiple expulsion this term. If I were the Crowninshields, I'd take a spell in the slammer rather than stick around School. Beryl the Vent has had her whip's licence yanked. They've stripped her gold piping off, which makes her meat for anyone with a grudge – and you'll find me at the head of the line. The Hooded Creeps ain't squawkin' – they don't know enough to be more afraid of Headmistress than their bosses. They were hired goons anyway. I got that much out of 'em.'

'You've no idea what it was all about?' ventured Amy.

'Were you up for ransom?' asked Frecks.

Kali shrugged. 'They was tightmouth. Something was gonna happen this morning, though. Something permanent, I figure. I lost my hat in the tussle, and one of the jaspers said I wouldn't be needing one after Monday sunrise. He said a tourniquet might suit me better.'

Kali drew a thumb across her neck.

'You know your father's coming,' said Amy.

Kali looked down. 'Yeah. How about that?'

'I doubt we'll ever get to the bottom of this,' said Frecks. 'Still, no real harm done. Jolly jape, as it happens. Kali rescued. Witches routed. Up the Moth Club, down the Murdering Heathens. Hurrah for School!'

Kali knew all about the Moth Club now.

'It'll be a shame to hang up the costumes for good,' said Light Fingers. 'I've ideas on how to improve them. But Kali's safe, so our charter purpose is fulfilled.'

Amy thought about it.

'Don't put the costumes where we can't get at them,' she said. 'I've a notion we might need them again. Paule said as much and she's supposed to be able to see the future.'

Amy couldn't help wondering who was behind the Hooded Conspiracy. Had Drearcliff heard the last of them? Red Flame remained at large and unknown.

'Uh oh, here comes the Old Man,' said Kali.

Dr Swan was coming across the Quad with a tall, dark, dramatically bearded man who wore a white western suit and a cherry-red turban. He had electric eyes, like his daughter's. They flashed as he saw the girls in a gaggle by the Heel.

'Don't get hitched to him, that's my advice...'

'No fear,' said Frecks. 'He's *ancient*!'

'My last stepmother was a year younger than me.'

'Crumpets,' gasped Amy.

'Don't worry, doll,' said Kali kindly. 'Pop likes 'em fleshier than you.'

It wasn't the prospect of matrimony which had startled Amy. It was the large pink sticking plaster on Mr Chattopadhyay's forehead. The patch barely covered a bruise which looked for all the world as if an accurately chucked cricket ball had struck him between the eyes.

'Double crumpets,' exclaimed Amy again.

Second Term

1: The First Drop of Rayne

EARLY IN THE new year, Amy returned to find Drearcliff Grange School transformed into a fairy-tale castle. House and grounds were blanketed with thick, white snow. Translucent stalactites hung from sills, gutters and eaves. Frost shapes sparkled on windowpanes. There was delight, especially among Firsts who had yet to experience a Drearcliff winter. Amy had an inkling that living in an icebound palace would have drawbacks, but was still struck by its prettiness.

Headmistress, swathed in white furs like a lady Cossack, greeted the back-from-the-hols rush of girls with cautions not to run on slippery flagstones. Nevertheless, there were outbursts of snowball-chucking, snowman-making and tea-tray tobogganing. Nurse had laid in a supply of ointment, bandages and sticking plasters. Casualties were inevitable.

Night fell in mid-afternoon. Joy sputtered.

Everyone realised how cold it was. Deucedly, devilishly, perniciously, pestilentially cold. Drearcliff wasn't Fairyland, but Hell Frozen Over. No matter how much fuel Joxer fed into the furnace, scant warmth seeped from the basement to the rest of School. Piping-hot soup was icy by the time it got to table. The water closets were frozen solid until Keys went round with a hammer.

Rumour had it that the wolves of the motto loped from their caves when the weather turned. Smudge – who had *not* learned her lesson from the Affair of the Hooded Conspiracy – recounted stories of growling in dorm corridors at night and scratches found on cell doors in the morning.

This was not happy weather for moths.

The next day, Hale of the Fifth, the Goneril cross-country champion, refused the option to take part in indoor games for the duration and set out on her habitual run through the woods. In her usual kit of shorts and singlet, she waded through thigh-high drifts to her starting post, cheerfully proclaiming she'd warm up when she hit her stride. Hale and Hearty Hale, a heroine to her House, was cheered at the off, though even her most staunch partisans nipped back inside sharpish as soon as she was out of sight. Three hours later, a search party found her, barely a hundred yards along her route, blue-limbed and frostbitten. Hale mumbled about golden eyes glittering in dark places between the trees before swooning. When she came round, her new handle was Swot of the Antarctic.

The cold became the only topic of conversation. A thousand schemes were hatched to mitigate its numbing, creeping, deadly effect.

In their cell, the Moth Club piled every blanket and garment they possessed on to their beds, then burrowed into the cocoons. Even at the bottom of the pile, Amy had to set her jaw to keep her teeth from chattering. Sleep was troubled by the shivering and moaning of her comrades in distress. She wore mittens over gloves and three pairs of socks to bed, but her hands and feet still froze. If wolves dared trespass in Dorm Three, they'd most likely be skinned by desperate girls, so their hides could be quilted into fur coverlets.

Frecks opined that Napoleon's retreat from Moscow was a charabanc outing to Eastbourne next to winter at Drearcliff. Kali said the eerie high mountain peaks of the Hindu Kush, haunt of the fabled *yeti* or *mi-go*, weren't as dreadful as North Somerset in January. Howling blizzards came regularly, rattling the windows. Kali said if you listened hard, you could hear *yeti* calling each other in the wind. Each fresh snowfall obliterated pathways and further burdened straining roofs.

The Heel was buried under a white mound until the first week's Infractors – mostly Seconds who disobeyed Headmistress's decree about running on flagstones but could still walk afterwards – had to excavate and uncover the relic. Allowed small shovels in addition to the traditional toothbrushes, the punishment party discovered 'Death to King Herod of Judea... and a Merry Christmas to All Our Readers' painted on the marble in extremely large red letters. This earned Absalom another term's worth of Sunday detentions. 'I'm a second Dreyfus Case,' she complained, but Amy suspected she welcomed political martyrdom.

Curious, Amy asked Absalom how anarchists celebrated the holidays. The girl explained her family exchanged radical pamphlets and gelignite recipes while dining on a roast swan her father had specifically poached from a royal estate. Instead of carols around a tree, they sang revolutionary songs in front of a fire into which they threw straw dollies made in the image of kings, presidents, colossi of finance and secret police chiefs. Absalom and her sisters nibbled biscuits decorated with red sugar stars and slogans of the struggle.

An anarchist Christmas sounded more fun than Amy's hols. Arriving home after her first term away, she found Mother bright-eyed with expectations of a change in circumstances. Mother felt that, warmed by grog and mince pies, Amy's latest uncle could be inveigled into addressing a Certain Pressing Matter. She ordered Lettie to decorate and sent Cook out to fetch a goose... but an 'incident' at a cocktail party in Altrincham prompted the revocation of Uncle Horace's dinner invitation.

By Christmas, the house was left half-decorated and presents were returned unopened. On the day itself, Mother took to her bed with a headache. Lettie and Cook were with their own families and the goose was forgotten in the pantry. Amy worked on her Book of Moths. In the evening, she put a Chopin *Étude* on the gramophone and defiantly floated around the drawing room in her nightie, pushing herself off the walls and ceiling to drift gently like a balloon. She rolled herself up into a ball, tucking in her knees, and bobbed about the chandelier, then concentrated hard on becoming steadily heavier and setting down on the carpet. She wished she had thought to bring her Kentish Glory costume. She floated better with the leotard and mask.

On Boxing Day, Uncle Horace came round to apologise and left with a black eye and tea all down his shirt. He had not been one of Amy's more inspiring uncles... indeed, he scored near the bottom of a bad bunch. Only after four or five of the beasts did Amy notice what they had in common. They were all fellows who had found some excuse not to be in the War. Uncle

Horace, an alderman, said he would have happily served at the Front, except that someone sensible had to stay behind and keep the women-folk in line. He was proprietor of a munitions factory where girls who protested about the ratio of sawdust to gunpowder in the shells were dismissed out of hand. Army protests about Uncle Horace's habit of sending them misfiring duds failed to effect a change of purchasing policy, thanks to his expert toadying, lobbying and backhanding. But getting round the War Production Board was easier than appeasing Mother.

Amy wouldn't be surprised if Uncle Horace were mysteriously shot.

Worcestershire would scarcely be bereft were someone to collect the full set by potting Uncle Simon, Uncle Ernst, Uncle Clive, Uncle Peasegood and Uncle Stanislas like china ducks in a fairground shy.

Two weeks into term, snowmen made in fun on the first day were no longer jovial, friendly presences but visible minions of an invisible enemy. The unmelted monsters mocked the warm-blooded fools who had created them. Coal eyes took on a malicious cast, carrot noses sneered at shivering mortals and jaunty brooms were shouldered like rifles.

Girls began pitching cricket balls at the snowmen, knocking off hats or punching holes through heads. At first, superstitious Firsts and Seconds effected repairs, trying to placate idols who'd been given appealing names like Captain Freezing or Mr Cold. Offerings were laid on altar trays placed before their squat, primal forms. As conditions persisted, the worshippers fell away. Apostates took to bitterly denouncing their former beliefs.

Smudge, of course, said the snowmen came to life

at night – in league with the prowling wolves. Even those who should know better started listening to her. With long, long nights and not much else to do for entertainment, there was an epidemic of ghost-storytelling. Not just from Smudge. Peebles Arbuthnot – hitherto taken for a sensible lass – came back to the dorm in a tizzy one evening, gabbling about a brush with a glowing violet apparition in the covered walkway leading from the Quad. She described a partially transparent girl, posed in an attitude of terror. One moment, she was there; the next, she was gone, leaving behind a whiff of chem lab stinks. Peebles' House Sisters assumed someone was ragging her. Frecks suggested this was one of Ariel's unamusing practical jokes. Peebles wasn't especially high-strung or imaginative. Amy saw she was genuinely spooked.

'I jumped,' Peebles said, 'but *she* was the frightened one… and not by me. I could see her, but she was looking at something else, something *terrifying* I couldn't see. The expression on her face was awful. I'll be walking the long way round from now on. I shouldn't care to encounter that ghost girl again if I were let off R.I. for a whole term.'

It transpired there had been other sightings of this purple spectre – some highly dubious, a few unnervingly credible. She already had a name, Mauve Mary. Bowman of Tamora and Laverick of Ariel had seen her in the same spot. It took a while for the story to get beyond their dorms. Mauve Mary always appeared to a girl walking alone, late in the afternoon but after dark.

The apparition's purple hue made Amy think of Dora Paule.

Was this a case for the Moth Club? With the Hooded Conspiracy in abeyance, they could do with a fresh mystery. They resolved at least to investigate. Pretending to be from the *Drearcliff Trumpet*, Amy and Light Fingers interviewed Laverick and Bowman. Laverick sent them to Trechman, an Ariel Third who'd been teased last term after reporting what now seemed to be the first Mary sighting. A chem whizz, Trechman was trying to concoct a brew to match the spook's stink. She compounded something truly disgusting, but admitted it wasn't quite the right order of pong. Trechman didn't believe in ghosts. She insisted Mauve Mary was simply a phenomenon which would be dispelled by scientific explanation... as soon as she could come up with one.

Everyone who saw Mauve Mary agreed she wasn't a girl they recognised, though she wore Drearcliff uniform. Amy told Peebles to find an excuse to visit Keys' office and look at the old photographs to see if she could find the ghost among the classes of yesteryear, but Peebles was more afraid of the custodian than any mere supernatural presence.

The Moth Club investigation stalled. Since Mauve Mary wasn't *doing* anything except popping up and popping off again, it was hard to determine whether she should be banished by exorcism or helped against whatever it was that terrified her so. From what they gathered, Mary was in distress – but Kali warned Amy that ghosts were slippery customers, who'd pull a pitiful act in order to get close enough to tear your ears off. None of the Moth Club had seen Mary themselves. Once the story got about, knots of ghost-finders were always poking around the walkway in the hope of scaring up the spook. That seemed to frighten her off far more than bell, book and candle.

A vaguely worded rule against dawdling was invoked

to crack down on loitering in Mauve Mary's walkway. A little shrine appeared at the spot where the spectre was habitually seen. A cult of Ariel Seconds adopted the phantom as a House Sister. They left paper flowers and cut-out dolls for her. Amy was surprised the whips didn't order the mess cleared away, but Ariel always had more licence than other Houses. Smudge said any who tampered with the shrine would wake in the night to find a huge violet face pressing down on theirs then die of stark terror.

One Break Amy ventured into hostile territory – the Whips' Hut – to seek out Dora Paule. The prefects' lair was more of a bungalow than a hut, and usually shunned by girls who didn't wear gold braid. Having drifted away from the Murdering Heathens last term, Paule was no longer in any particular clique. Amy couldn't tell whether the other whips were wary of her or protective. Daisy 'Even' Keele, who let her into the Hut, warned her that Paule was 'having one of her confused spells today'. Keele, a Desdemona set upon becoming a woman doctor, showed Amy through to a snug little room where Paule had a favourite wonky chair.

When Amy tried to ask if Mauve Mary had anything to do with the Purple, Paule went off on a verbal tear about goblins and giblets and golems and guillemots. It might be a nonsense rhyme or a witches' spell. Too much of Daffy Dora's mind was elsewhere.

Keele shrugged, not unsympathetically.

'My great grandmama was like this,' said the whip. 'Couldn't remember who we were fighting, but knew there was a war on. Kept a cutlass under the bed in case Boney came to Sevenoaks. Ninety-three when she pegged it. I reckon she kept Boney off for a good long while.'

'There'll be wars here soon,' said Paule. 'Wars between colours.'

That made no sense to Keele, but Amy saw a glimmer of meaning.

She was tempted to ask Paule to take her to the Purple again. Right now, conditions at Drearcliff were so grim the twilit realm almost seemed an ideal holiday destination. Amy would also have liked to have the complete Paule to talk to. The sliver of the girl left 'Back Home' was poor company.

Sadly, Amy stood up to leave.

'Call again any time,' Keele said satirically. 'We're open all hours.'

'Amy,' said Paule, just as she was nearly out of the room. 'You'll think it's about Black and Grey, but it's not… it's about Purple. It's always about Purple.'

'What's *that* about when it's at home?' asked Keele when they were out of the room. 'How do you even know Daffy Dora? You're a Third, aren't you? Desdemona.'

'We're interested in some of the same things,' Amy said.

'Really? What manner of things?'

'Moths,' said Amy.

'Ugh. Can't stand the smell of those balls.'

'Me too. I'd rather have a dress with a few tiny holes no one can see than one whiffing of poison.'

Keele was suspicious now. Whips were trained to ferret out hidden Infractions. Girls who fraternised across the lines were usually up to something rum. If in different Houses or Forms, sisters or cousins brought up together went through School without acknowledging each other's existence.

'Are you one of *them*? An Unusual?'

Amy didn't like to say. Keele was decent as whips went, but people were funny about Unusuals. Light Fingers was always pointing out the little ways they were treated differently from the Ordinaries – not even with malice, but tiny stings all the same.

'If you've any idea what can be done for Dora, speak up. Great Grandmama was a dear old stick, no matter how much Clan Keele wanted her shut away. We *should* all be ready to fight Boney. She didn't just mean Napoleon. Boney was around before Mr Hat-on-Sideways and didn't die on St Helena. Even Napoleon had to fight Boney at the end. Daffy sometimes talks about Boney too, but only to me. She knows what Boney is for everyone. Davey Jones for Hern and the Cold Knights for de Vere. Is it the Purple for you? This Mauve Mary story that's going around?'

'I don't know yet. I'm a Third. For me, Sidonie Gryce is Boney.'

Keele was shocked. Amy feared she'd presumed too much. She sensed that she might get slapped with a Major for Impertinence. Stabbing a Second was a Minor, but cheeking a Sixth was punishable by burning at the stake... or at least a term of scrubbing the Heel with Absalom, Palgrave and the recidivists.

Then Keele melted and she laughed. Not every Sixth liked the way Gryce did business, but rifts in the united front were rare. In the Whips' Hut, there were possibly concealed phonograph recorders and certainly ears out for potential treason.

'There's no harm in Daffy,' said Keele. 'And she's not as doolally as some folk think. Sometimes I think she's what School is all about.'

'She's the real Head Girl,' said Amy.

Keele laughed again, but was then thoughtful.

'You're very sharp, Thomsett. My eye is upon you.'

Break was over. Amy hurried on to French with Miss Bedale. It was even harder than usual to concentrate on irregular verbs.

Her mind was infused with Purple thoughts.

Since her brief transportation last term, Amy dreamed often of the sky with three moons and the trailing tendrils... and other things, which she hadn't seen for herself but still knew were of the Purple. A twisted, leafless, ancient tree with eyes in the knots of its bark. A sea of ankle-deep sludge, boiling with reptile spawn. A circle of chanting priests or devotees in pointed hoods – some misshapen by swollen heads or antlers – holding up their arms and waving in unison. A burning sensation in her back, as if her shoulder blades were straining to break free of her skeleton.

Sometimes, Amy dreamed she stood in the middle of a flat desert where an intricate diagram was scored in the sand. Slowly, she would rise above it on moth wings and the design became apparent. It had to be looked down at from on high to be seen in full. Entwined spirals drew the eye towards a centre that was painful to look at directly. At points where the spirals crossed over each other were placed large white eggs, which shook and cracked as they hatched. If she was far enough above the sands to make out the whole pattern, she was too high to make out what manner of creatures were emerging from their shells.

When she dreamed of the Purple, she was difficult to wake. Light Fingers told her she floated in her sleep and only a great deal of shaking brought her out of it. Amy still hadn't told the Moth Club about the Purple.

Hooded Conspirators and Mauve Mary were everyday topics of conversation, but the Purple was too weird to mention without seeming potty. The example of Dora Paule was there to prove that.

Being an Unusual didn't bestow special advantage in winter.

Amy tried floating over the muddy frozen slush the snows turned into after a few days, but the cold numbed her Abilities as well as her toes... so she had to trudge with all the rest. Light Fingers kept her hands in constant motion, rubbing her arms and legs. She reported that it made little difference. Gould of the Fourth, who was supposed to have wolf blood, shivered and went blue-limbed on the hockey field like everyone else.

Joxer's seaweed – Drearcliff's prime meteorological resource – was frozen stiff, suggesting spring was a good long way off. At this rate, not everyone would make it through winter.

On the third Saturday afternoon of term, Marigold de Vere – least hated of the whips – pitched up at Hypatia Hall. Amy had taken the extreme measure of asking Miss Borrodale for extra prep involving Bunsen burners in the hope of warming her perpetually chilly hands. De Vere put out a call for volunteers.

This was unheard-of. Whips, as a rule, press-ganged, enslaved and commandeered.

'It's been decided that the snowmen must go,' announced de Vere.

Slightly warmed hands – including Amy's – shot up.

De Vere smiled broadly. She was a humorous Desdemona Sixth, with dimples, wavy blonde hair and a brother who drove racing cars. If Gryce ever fell from power, it was thought de Vere would replace her as Head Girl. Some invested hopes in a de Vere ascendancy the way pre-unification Italians believed in Garibaldi, but the hour of liberation was certainly not at hand. Gryce might have lost a few lieutenants – the Crowninshield Sisters skulked about together, avoiding the vengeance of those emboldened now the older witch was no longer a whip – but Head Girl was secure in her position. De Vere was too mild, easy-going and straightforward to undermine a rival, though many of her supporters weren't above chicanery.

Amy remembered what Keele, a chum of de Vere's, had said. Her Boney – the phantoms that troubled her dreams the way those hatching eggs disturbed Amy – were creatures called the Cold Knights. How did Amy know it was spelled that way? She just did – it was an unsettling insight. That came with being Unusual.

The murder party consisted of Amy, Light Fingers, FitzPatrick and a random Ariel Second called Mrozková. De Vere marched them to Joxer's shed, wrenched open the door and issued weapons – a rake, a hoe, a cricket bat and a long-handled axe. The whip herself took a paraffin blowlamp and lit it with a long match. She puffed an experimental burst of flame in the air. FitzPatrick jumped out of the way to avoid losing her eyebrows.

'Leave no snow blighter standing,' de Vere ordered.

Captain Freezing, first and foremost of the snowmen, commanded the front lawns, in sight of all School. The eight-foot creature wore a plumed shako from a bygone Austro-Hungarian pageant. Leftover Christmas holly and ivy garlanded his broad shoulders. The very model of a Cold Knight. Ice-hearted to the core, the Captain

139

had to go. De Vere strode across the snows, lamp thrust forward and upwards, and squirted fire into Captain Freezing's face. His rope moustaches caught light. His head hollowed out. Hot meltwater gushed over his chest, eating like acid.

De Vere stood back and signalled a general attack. Amy swung the axe, which sliced through Captain Freezing's snow torso without doing much damage. FitzPatrick's cricket bat was much more effective in smashing the snowman's insides out. With savage glee, the party brought down the Captain and kicked his remains across the lawn. Mrozková raked over the spot where the Cold Knight had stood until only the flattened shako remained.

Amy expected cheers of triumph and encouragement – but everyone else was indoors, huddling around whatever warmth they could find.

De Vere lead them on to the next snowman, and the next, and all the others. The Widow Winter, Chill Charlie, Glacé Cherry, the North Pole Cat, Frigid Freda, Sandokan the Snow Bear. With each victory the murder party grew more determined, more relentless. At first they whooped and yelled and insulted the enemy, jeering as faces melted and bodies exploded into fragments. Then, it became quiet, desperate work. The Cold Knights put up a fight, staying standing long after they should have gone down. It took all afternoon. When they were done, no one wanted to talk about it.

Amy had sores from gripping the axe handle with wet mittens.

As a reward for the volunteers, de Vere arranged hot chocolate at teatime. Amy and the others dutifully accepted their treats. She sensed warmth, even burned her tongue, but couldn't taste anything. Her hands and feet were dead – soaked through with sweat and snow-seepage, then frozen solid. Her face was icy rubber and her nose was blue. The snowmen were gone, but the snow was still here.

The next morning, when the girls rose early for Chapel, Captain Freezing was back – hat, moustache and all. The Cold Knight had advanced, as if on a chessboard. He was stationed ten feet nearer the dorms, and seemed to angle his head upwards, glaring at the slit windows of the Desdemona staircase.

Amy and Light Fingers exchanged a grim look.

There were no footprints around the Captain. It had snowed in the night so it was possible the marks of guilt were naturally obliterated. Amy's first thought was that it must have been Gryce, putting her rival in her place… but she couldn't imagine the Murdering Heathens braving Arctic dark to fashion a new Captain Freezing.

As Amy walked by the snowman, shivering from more than the cold, she caught sight of a girl she didn't recognise. The stranger was skipping alone, deftly stepping over the rope, nodding as if hearing a rhyme in her head. Amy recalled the chanting, steeple-hooded monks in her Purple dream.

Was this Mauve Mary? No, it was the wrong spot and the wrong time… and there was no violet glow. But the girl had the aspect of an apparition. Looking at her was deeply disturbing. She made Amy's teeth feel funny.

The skipping girl wore a *sort of* Drearcliff uniform. It took Amy moments to register the differences as if it were a 'can you see what's wrong with this picture?' puzzle in the *Girls' Paper Annual* Uncle Roger – her actual uncle, not one of Mother's bogus beaux – gave her every Christmas.

Instead of grey skirt with black side-stripe, she wore a black skirt with grey side-stripe. Everything else matched: black blazer with grey piping, black blouse with grey buttons, black socks with grey clocks, black straw boater with grey band, and jet-black tie with red-headed pin.

The defier of uniform conventions was short and slight. Amy took her for a Second, though it turned out she was a Third. At first look, she appeared scrawny, undersized, weak... but she was skipping out of doors in a temperature well below freezing so she must be more resistant to the cold than Roberta Hale. She picked up pace without missing a step, face set in concentration, furrows between her eyebrows. She exhaled regular frosty plumes, like a piston-driven engine.

Given that Drearcliff welcomed gill-girls, brain-maggots and junior moth-women, Amy wondered whether the skipping fool was some sort of self-starting automaton – a life-sized wind-up toy with a clockwork brain and a boiler for a heart. Her straight black hair, cut off at her jawline like a helmet, seemed starched. Her boater didn't fly loose as she jumped up and down, crissed and crossed, hopped on one foot then the other, silently counting off. If she was a tin toy, she showed no signs of running down.

This was Antoinette Rowley Rayne. The *new* new bug.

11: An Address to the Whole School

CHAPEL WAS COLDER even than outdoors. Ice-afrits blew through cracks in the window-frames. The pews were ice shelves and the floor was permafrost. Girls huddled together for warmth.

Only whips were allowed cushions. Absalom reported – with some satisfaction – that this sort of injustice set off revolutions in Russia. Even so, most whips looked as miserable as the rest of the suffering masses – hands shoved inside blazers, gold-threaded scarves wound three or four times around privileged necks.

Amy and her pals bent low, praying to South Sea Gods for a volcano to spout in the Quad. Kali flicked her gunmetal lighter – a present from her father on the occasion of his visit to the school – on and off. Its flame was thin and flickering.

The Reverend Mr Bainter delivered a sermon on the theme of mortification of the flesh, illustrated with magic lantern slides. Using details from Hieronymus Bosch, he inculcated night terrors in Firsts and some more sensitive Seconds. Amy thought of the quaking, cracking eggs in her desert diagram dream. Bosch had a Purplish vision, she thought. Someone on the Viola pew sobbed and was sloshed to silence by a whip. The sermon lacked any discernible moral, but Ponce was enthusiastic on its subject. His elongated upper lip quivered like a squid's beak as he talked of bones broken a thousand times and lakes of boiling filth closing over the heads of the unworthy. He miscalculated slightly – just now, boiling anything seemed a pleasant change.

At the conclusion of the address, everyone rose as if to bolt for freedom… but Bainter rapped the eagle-wing lectern with a supple cane. The girls had to stay put a while longer. Digger Downs was stationed by the vestibule doors to prevent unauthorised sneaking out.

'We have a new girl,' he announced. 'Antoinette Rowley Rayne.'

Amy remembered the speech Dr Swan made on *her* first day and felt pre-emptive sympathy for the next victim. This time, it was down to Ponce to curse the rest of a girl's days at Drearcliff.

'Rayne has asked for a moment to address School,' said Bainter.

That was a new one! Was the canny filly going to get her licks in first? A shot across the bows of the witches.

Someone choked in astonishment. Miss Dryden sustained dramatic chords. The cold had not done her organ any favours. Only pained wheezing escaped from frozen pipes.

Amy looked at the mistresses' faces for clues. No help there. The Staff could have been attending an execution or an enthronement.

Wicked Wyke paused in her knitting and paid attention. She habitually knit socks for soldiers throughout Chapel and most lessons, though the War Office had asked patriotic ladies to cease such efforts after the Armistice.

Salisbury Plain must be heaped with unwanted hosiery. Some closer to hand would have appreciated the knitted comforts wasted on ungrateful soldier boys. Miss Kaye smiled sweetly. Fossil Borrodale gripped a hymnal rumoured to be hollowed-out to conceal a hip flask. Miss Bedale snuck a look at her wristwatch.

Headmistress was, on this occasion, absent. A swivelling telescope attachment above the teachers' pew suggested Dr Swan kept an eye on everything. Her study was said to be one of the few well-heated rooms at Drearcliff. Smudge theorised that Keys burned kittens, puppies and confiscated hampers in a special furnace because the secretly cold-blooded Headmistress would slip into a hibernatory state if the temperature in her quarters fell.

'Come up, girl,' said Bainter.

A strange clicking began at the back of the chapel. Like everyone else, Amy twisted around to goggle. It was the girl in the wrong uniform coming down the centre aisle. Her skipping rope was bundled like a belt. The handles clacked, echoing her footsteps. She was in no hurry.

If it mattered to her that all the world was staring, she didn't show it.

The girl replaced Bainter at the lectern. Her head was barely visible over the eagle wings. Nervous laughter. Bainter shoved a stool under her. Now seen by all, she looked straight ahead.

'I am Rayne,' she announced, in a clear voice which filled the chapel. 'In my time at Drearcliff, I shall endeavour to be neat, efficient and cheerful. I shall not indulge in compromise, wastefulness or unnecessary activity. I resolve to be a productive girl. I intend to be a credit to School. I hope I shall be your friend. I have come here to learn, but – as important – to *teach*, by example.'

'I say, chums, have we got a new Headmistress?' FitzPatrick asked out of the side of her mouth.

Rayne slammed the handles of her skipping rope on the lectern. The report was like a pistol shot.

'*I will be heard*,' she said, not louder but more insistent. 'I will not tolerate slacking and joshing!'

FitzPatrick looked sheepish.

Some heads bobbed in assent – disbelieving, but assent.

But there were titters too. Amy swivelled around. Gryce, primly perched on a tasselled cushion, smiled blandly. Her Heathens were open-mouthed in naked astonishment. Buller made big fists.

Kali drew a thumb across her throat. Amy had to agree – Rayne was going to do some hard learning soon. The only 'teaching by example' she was liable to manage would be when her horrible fate dissuaded any other idiot from issuing statements from the pulpit.

Frecks paid attention. Always fascinated by odd specimens, she was a great one for giving benefit of the doubt… until she made her mind up, then she was hard to sway.

What *was* Rayne thinking? Where had she been brought up to have so little idea how School – *any* school – ran? And why on Earth were the Staff letting her go through with this exhibition?

'It is my intention, girls, to…'

'Rayne, Rayne,' drawled Gryce, amused and sympathetic, pausing for the chant to take hold…

'Go away,' shouted a pack marshalled by Buller, '*don't come back another day*!'

Laughter erupted.

The spell of Rayne, with her freakish uniform and unprecedented speaking privileges, was broken.

Amy saw the lines in the girl's brows deepen. She clutched her skipping rope, winding it around her hand until her knuckles were red spots.

The barracking chant continued, louder and louder. Amy found herself joining in. It took greater will than hers to resist – though Light Fingers was silent and Frecks pursed her lips in disapproval.

There was something *slappable* about the new girl. Amy wasn't proud of her impulse, but it ran deep.

'Rayne, Rayne, go away,' she chanted, raising her voice, 'don't come back another day!'

Bainter barged back into the pulpit and the congregation fell silent.

'That will be enough,' he said. 'Dismissed.'

The rush from pews to doors recommenced.

'That silly goose's pasted a target to her own forehead,' said Frecks.

'The Witches will murderalise her,' said Kali. 'Has Nellie opened a book on how long before she lights out over the wall? I give her three days.'

'I might take that bet,' said Frecks. 'Girl's got grit. Maybe nothing else.'

Amy glanced back. Rayne still stood by the lectern, watching the exodus. She unwound her rope, calmly.

Gryce nodded at the new girl, smiling like the cat who's noticed the catch on the canary's cage doesn't fasten properly. The nod was returned with a blank glare. Rayne had very black eyes. Angry, yet purposeful. She didn't know enough to be afraid yet.

No one had told her about the Murdering Heathens. The Crowninshield Sisters had fallen and Paule had wandered off, so Head Girl promoted replacements. Euterpe McClure, a Goneril Fifth who studied the oriental arts of dirty fighting, could twist a wrist *just so* or inflict a Chinese burn that hurt for weeks. Gryce had also wangled a whip's blazer for Vanity Crawford, Viola's flamboyantly vicious leading light. The Murdering Heathens were back to full strength.

Amy had a pang of worry for Rayne. She was ashamed of joining in the chant against her. Of all people, she should have known better than to chuck dead stoats at a new bug who didn't know the ropes yet.

'Did you clock the threads the frail's got on?' asked Kali, as the girls crammed into the vestibule. 'Like a camera negative. How is that legit?'

'It's a new option,' put in Inchfawn, who still wasn't to be spoken to. 'Didn't you read the circular? I think it's smart.'

The whips were usually first out of Chapel. Today they stayed behind, lolling on their cushions, giving the new girl the evil eye.

From the vestibule, Amy looked back at the small figure illuminated at the lectern. The teachers had filed out through the Staff Door, leaving Rayne alone. Amy smelled a set-up.

Gryce leaned forward, grinning like a hungry tiger.

Rayne untangled her skipping rope, seemingly unconcerned.

In the vestibule, Amy found Paule – who was permanently excused Chapel. Religious symbols of whatever denomination set off her vibrations and made her slip into the Purple.

'Interesting times, Amy,' Paule said. 'Watch that girl. Rayne. She's another one. Another *significant addition*.'

III: The Inspection

DESPITE PAULE'S PRONOUNCEMENT, Amy didn't take much notice of the new girl during the next few days. Antoinette Rowley Rayne could take her own lumps.

The purple dreams were growing troublesome. Their afterspell lingered into the waking hours, and Amy worried about slipping into a distracted state. She was afraid of ending up like Daffy Dora. Her friends noticed she was preoccupied, but she couldn't share her night terrors with them.

A persistent, yet hard-to-pin-down story went around that Mauve Mary had been seen again... and spoken to a Second. Every version had the ghost saying something different, but suggestive and enigmatic like 'the caramels are creeping' or 'defy the deniers and doubt the debaters'. The Moth Club looked out several Seconds who were named as the mystery girl. Each hotly denied the story and suggested someone else. Farjeon, at the end of the chain, said it wasn't a Second, but a mistress. Ponce Bainter had ordered that the unknown teacher keep mum about the message from the beyond. Farjeon couldn't explain how, if this were the case, she'd been let in on the truth, and the lead petered out. Did Dr Shade or Shiner Bright have cases like this? Mysteries which dragged on and went nowhere. If so, they never got written up in *Union Jack Monthly* or *Girls' Paper*.

As for Rayne, there was an empty place in Viola.

The girl chosen over Unity Crawford for Lucas Cleeve, the lead role in last term's Arthur Wing Pinero Players production, had not come back after the hols. No one could remember whether her name was Harriet Marion or Marion Harriet. She was at an expensive Swiss sanatorium, recovering from 'complete nervous collapse'. According to Frecks, that was 'medical jargon for being an utter wet'. Amy had thought Harriet/ Marion one of the sturdier Viola gals, given to vigorous calisthenics before breakfast and overdoing the friendly back-slapping and shoulder-punching. She specialised in men's roles and her leading ladies tended to complain of bruises.

Then, without meaning to, the hapless girl crossed Vanity and her fate was sealed.

During rehearsals for *The Notorious Mrs Ebbsmith*, Marion/Harriet suffered. First, red-inked anonymous notes turned up in her Time-Table Book or under her pillow, issuing dire warnings and making unsubstantiated accusations. Then, an unusual series of accidents blighted the production: a minor fire, a mishap with itching powder and unauthorised amendments (in red ink, of course) to costume designs. Following instructions, Light Fingers provided a smart suit which turned out to be several sizes too small. Harriet/ Marion nearly strangled during the first dress run-through. Throughout, Vanity maintained suspiciously unbreakable alibis… though she never could get the red off her fingers.

Come the first night, Marion/Harriet developed serious stage fright. As the curtain went up, she was prostrate in her dressing room with cold compresses on her forehead. Vanity – who had helpfully learned the lines of Lucas Cleeve, on the off chance – went on in her stead. *Mrs Ebbsmith* was not a great success. Amy nodded off well before the last act.

The upshot was that Harriet/Marion was in Switzerland. On the principle of 'one in one out', Rayne was duly delivered to the bosom of the worst House to be in if you were liable to be picked on. Viola had a poor record for protecting their own against even minor persecution, let alone a sustained campaign by the Murdering Heathens. Because of her stage heritage, Light Fingers had many dealings with Viola. She was acidic on the subject of the House's theatrical posing and said some of their 'stars' relished roles which allowed them to suffer prettily… so they went out of their way to invite trouble. They imagined themselves Joan at the stake or Catherine on the wheel, and practised venomous forgiveness as they died in *déshabillé*.

Rayne's unique uniform – if a uniform *could* be unique – stood out, a splash of black in a shower of grey. Therefore, Amy was aware of the new girl's presence in assemblies for meals, indoor games or speeches from Mrs Wyke about the dangers of playing outside in the snow. So she was still alive, at least.

Gryce was stringing it out.

The big story was still the weather. De Vere's duel with Captain Freezing continued. The snowman sprang up anew every time he was battered down, even sporting a replacement shako after de Vere threw his old one into the sea. The whip put a bounty of a cream tea in Watchet on the head of the culprit, payable when information received led to a conviction and a clouting. If anyone knew the identity of the perpetrator who left no footprints, no one was telling. Even Garland of the Second, the Semiramis of Tell-Tale Tessies, couldn't find out who to snitch on. Besides pride in being School's premier sneak, Garland had a particular mania for cream teas and being seen in town in the company of glamorous older girls. Her inability to ferret out the guilty party put her in a vile bate.

Each incarnation of Captain Freezing loomed larger and nearer the dorms, as if he were coming for de Vere. His coal-and-carrot features scowled more exaggeratedly, seemingly growing angrier. That might be fair enough: de Vere demolished him with escalating violence. When she set out to do harm, she braided her hair with battle-beads and striped black and red warpaint on her cheeks. She got frostbite and her hands were bandage-mittened, but she stuck to her Ahab-like mission. At the end of the week de Vere dragooned a party to scavenge driftwood, then built a paraffin-soaked circular bonfire around the snowman and set it alight. The whip led her conscripts in a death-chant as flames ran round the ring. The Captain collapsed in the heat, hissing as his insides melted. He spilled on to the burning wood and doused the fire, leaving the components of his face studded awry on a heap of slush. No one doubted he would be back. Even de Vere knew it was inevitable.

Priscilla 'Prompt' Rintoul, a round-faced Viola Third, was assigned to give Rayne the traditional guided tour. As stage manager, Prompt ruled the wings with ruthless efficiency when shows were running, but was otherwise overly meek even among her feeble sisterhood. Rayne might not be well served by such a model. The pair roamed the highways and byways, with Prompt pointing out features of interest to the solemnly attentive newcomer. The tour extended beyond the look-round Frecks had trotted Amy through. Doors were always being opened by Prompt so Rayne could peer into a room, nod as if memorising useful facts, and withdraw. More than once, chalk sticks were flung at the interloper.

The occasional resounding scream or oath indicated when the expedition ventured into forbidden territory – the Staff room, the Whips' Hut, the QMWAACC armoury. Prompt was uncommonly thorough. Rayne toured School like a diminutive conquering general surveying occupied territory rather than a new bug lucky not to be booted into the sea. Amy remembered Paule said Rayne would bear watching and did flick the odd glance her way – though looking at that wrong uniform made her go cross-eyed and see spots. Purple spots, of course.

On Wednesday afternoon the Third Form endured Double R.I., a lesson legendary for *longueurs*. As Ponce Bainter recited a lengthy list of ancient fellows who begat other ancient fellows, with scarce mention of any part ancient fellowesses might have had in the matter, Amy was distracted by movement beyond the frosted windows.

Two small figures trudged across the frozen tundra which had once been playing fields. The black hat identified the titchier girl as Rayne. Prompt, wrapped in scarves and shawls like a tubby mummy, leant heavily on a vaulting pole, suffering for the sake of her mission. What exactly was the new girl being shown other than a hard time – and why wasn't she in lessons yet? Amy had been tossed into History and Deportment before her trunk was unpacked.

Ponce noticed her wandering eyeline and commanded her to stand.

'You are at hazard, Thomsett.'

Girls sat up straight and paid attention. This, at least, was more interesting than Mizraim begatting Ludim, Anamim, Lebahim, Naphtuhim, Harry Hawke and Uncle Tom Cobley and All. Bainter's dreaded Three Questions trapfall was his way of tormenting an Infractor, often tossed at random because he felt like it. A Minor would go down in Amy's Time-Table Book unless she gave three letter-perfect answers to questions on a random R.I. topic.

'The subject is the Deaths of Bible Kings, Thomsett. Are you prepared?'

'I am, Reverend Bainter, sir.'

'Agag the Amalekite…?'

'…was cut to pieces, sir, by the prophet Samuel, who said to him "as your sword has made women childless, so will your mother be childless among women", sir.'

'Abimelech of Manasseh…?'

'…ordered his armour-bearer to pierce his heart, sir, with a sword because he was mortally wounded by a millstone dropped upon his head by a lady defender of the Tower of Thebaz—'

Cheers from several Tamora girls who had declared this unnamed Thebazite their heroine!

'—and couldn't bear for history to record, sir, that he had been slain by a woman.'

'Adoni-Bezek of Canaan…'

'…succumbed to an infection, sir, after his thumbs and big toes were cut off by Judah and Simeon, in imitation of his own method of humiliating vanquished enemies, sir.'

She sat down, escutcheon unstained, and darted a glance window-wards. Prompt and Rayne had moved on.

Bainter resumed the begatting and somnolence settled on the form.

The next day, Frecks and Amy were ambling to the Chem Lab, when Rayne and her guide appeared in Hypatia Hall, walking very straight down the centre of the corridor.

'Frecks, old thing,' Amy said, 'Rintoul's nabbed your job. She's doing for Rayne what you did for me last term.'

'She's welcome to it. That was a one-time offer, for special customers… like you, my fondest friend and most devoted disciple.'

Amy reached out to tip Frecks' boater off her head. She rose a few inches off the floor to get there and only succeeded in making the hat wobble.

'Hands off the titfer, Thomsett! 'Tis sacred!'

The friends' scuffle meant they blocked Rayne's path. The other girls didn't seem to notice Amy's tiny float. She was always surprised so many failed to clock what Frecks drolly called 'her lighter moments'. People chose not to see things which didn't fit the way they understood the world.

Prompt cringed out of their way but Rayne stopped in her tracks.

It was possible that her eyes *hadn't* missed the levitation. Amy resolved for the umpty-fifth time to be more cautious.

Laughing, Amy said 'don't mind us, ladies… we're an old married couple… the barney never stops.'

Prompt smiled nervously. Rayne's expression changed not a jot.

Frecks stuck a friendly paw out at the new new girl.

'Pleased to meet you, Rayne. I'm Walmergrave and this is Thomsett. Welcome to the asylum.'

Rayne looked as if she were really confronted by two lunatics on the loose while touring a madhouse.

After a few moments, Frecks pumped empty air with her hand and took it back.

'Please yourself,' she said, not taking offence. 'We're off to stinks.'

Too late, Rayne formed a smile. She didn't seem used to the expression. Her eyes remained set and neutral.

Without a hand to shake, the girl bobbed her black-boatered head and did something between a curtsey and a shrug.

She was at least trying.

'Amy Thomsett,' said Amy. 'I was the last new bug so I know what it's like. You'll soon get used to Drearcliff ways.'

'I think not,' said Rayne, calm and cold. 'There will be changes.'

'Drearcliff'll have to get used to your ways, eh?' said Frecks. 'Can't say I hold out hope for that, what with Murdering Heathens on the rampage. But I admire your nerve. Good luck to you, Black Hat. You've no problems with me.'

'I didn't think I would have. But thank you for clearing up the matter.'

Amy wasn't sure about Rayne's manner. She was odd even for an odd 'un.

'What school were you at before?' she asked.

Prompt stepped in, protective yet peculiarly spooked. Her jowls were sweaty, though a chill wind blew down the corridor.

'This is Rayne's *first* school.'

There was a story there, then. Amy and Frecks looked to the subject for further elucidation, which was not forthcoming.

Rayne wore a burnished metal lapel brooch in the shape of an ant.

'Antoinette Rowley Rayne,' Amy said. 'You wouldn't happen to be related to Professor Rosalind Rowley Rayne, would you? The entomologist and eugenicist.'

Now Rayne paid attention to her.

'She is my mother.'

'I have her *A Child's Taxonomy of Arthropodiae*. It's not much on moths.'

'That is her *popular* work. It is inevitably simplified. She'd rather be judged by her twelve-volume *Introduction to Trilobites, Chelicerates, Myriapods, Crustaceans and Hexapods*.'

'I have that on order at the library.'

Rayne looked Amy over as if she were cargo being inspected.

'Your name again?'

'Thomsett. Amy Thomsett.'

Amy was leery of offering her hand, but matched Rayne's semi-curtsey. The new girl nodded... then moved on.

'You've made a friend,' said Frecks. 'New bugs together, eh?'

Amy wasn't sure. She didn't feel befriended. She felt... *catalogued*.

IV: Damocletian Days

EVENTUALLYTHETOURofinspectionconcluded.Rayne had to come to lessons like any other girl. A desk was found and she took her place in the alphabetical order of the Third Form. Amy was five desks behind her, with Rintoul, Sawley, Sieveright, Stallybrass and Thicke in between.

The new girl took notes in a private shorthand. Her exercise books looked as if an insect had escaped from an inkwell and hopped and crawled over the pages. Rayne spoke only if directly addressed by a mistress. If something notionally droll were said, she faked laughter with the rest of the form. Teachers' jokes were seldom genuinely funny, but braying hilarity was a requirement of an easy life – though girls had been Minored for overdoing the thigh-slapping and tears of mirth when Wicked said 'we shall draw a *veil* over your prep' to Morgana Vail or Fossil said '*alimentary*, my dear Watson' to some girl who wasn't called Watson.

Rayne's address to School wasn't forgotten – how *could* it be? – but she made no further declarations of intent. Her resolve to lead by example was apparently set aside. Aside from her uniform, she fit in. It was soon as if she had always been at Drearcliff Grange... along with the semolina, Joxer and the grim weather.

Amy only now realised School had done the same for her. On her first day, she should have looked more closely at the annual photographs. She suspected she'd have found her own face in them, like Headmistress, all the way back to the founding year. Before the Christmas hols, a new photograph had been taken. Amy was in that, with all her friends and enemies and nodding acquaintances. Their whole lives were bound within the walls of Drearcliff. She rarely thought about life before School or life outside School. It was as if she were born fully formed when she stepped off the down train. Home wasn't home any more. School was.

Even Rayne's uniform now seemed less radical. Amy noticed other girls wearing black hats or socks, if not the full kit. Inchfawn had been right – it was now an acceptable option. Few were likely to go fully black until the dust settled. For a start, there was a possibility the dust would be settling on Rayne's grave.

From Light Fingers, who heard it from Prompt, Amy understood Rayne had received the customary visit from the Murdering Heathens. Her trunk contained no contraband – just approved clothes and books. She did not acknowledge Gryce as ringleader of the reception she'd been given in Chapel. She did not whimper when McClure applied a neck pinch that usually raised a high yelp. The puzzled torturer felt around Rayne's shoulder and throat, pressing for nerves she couldn't find. In the end, she slapped the new girl's face and left it at that. Rayne shrugged off the pain like a fakir. Gryce didn't know what to make of her. Lack of terror was a mute challenge. All School – with the exception of Rayne herself – assumed there would be a terrible reckoning.

As Rayne went about unmurdered, suspense grew. Smudge reported vile plans afoot. Even those who disbelieved on principle anything Smudge said nodded sagely. These were Damocletian Days. The Blade of Doom hung overhead. Rats stayed in their holes, Violas slyly practised expressions of heartfelt sorrow in their mirrors, Mauve Mary was unseen and unheard, Nellie Pugh refused further bets on the Dread Day and Antoinette Rowley Rayne was a Walking Dead Girl.

Only Palgraive smiled when Rayne hove in view, and she smiled at *everyone*. Sensible folk scarpered, just in case. Wherever Rayne went, Rintoul tagged along, lagging far enough behind to claim she wasn't with her. As unconcerned as Rayne seemed to be, Prompt was terrified – she shed weight at a time when other girls were stuffing themselves against the cold.

'They'll leave me be,' Prompt told Light Fingers. 'They always have to leave someone alive *to tell the tale*.'

Even as the new girl but one, Amy shouldn't have felt especial sympathy for Rayne. They were in different Houses, different dorms, different clubs. Five desks was a chasm, rendering Rayne a virtual stranger – a Patagonian or a Jainite. If Rayne was of her mother's opinion on moths, Amy could have precious little common ground with her. Professor Rosalind Rowley Rayne dismissed moths *and* butterflies in a mere two pages in her *Child's Taxonomy*... while devoting seventeen pages to uninteresting species of ant.

...and yet, Amy *was* concerned.

She raised the Damocletian issue at a meeting of the Moth Club. Kali said Rayne's forthcoming death was her own business... and besides, she'd probably just get tied to a netball goalpost overnight. Then, the Heathens would crack on with persecuting someone else. Palgraive was overdue for doom and the apostate Paule must be in Gryce's black books – though the chosen victim could as easily be some scrawny Fourth or beanpole Second no one had thought to take notice of before.

Amy still hadn't found a way to share her suspicions about the identity of Red Flame with her friends and was self-conscious about her lack of candour. Kali already deemed her father a rotter of the first water, but Amy didn't know how she'd react if told he was behind the Hooded Conspiracy. She was keeping quiet about Paule and the Purple too, and being vague about her dreams. How did she come to have so many secrets? Even from her closest pals?

'I rather like Black Hat's pluck,' said Frecks.

Was Rayne brave? Or simply acting according to her nature in ignorance of the consequences? The new girl struck Amy as sly and a shade sinister rather than a heroine to rally behind. She had more time for Absalom's futile gestures than Rayne's carapace of uncaring superiority.

'I reckon I'd cut a dash in black,' Frecks said. 'I can see myself in widow's weeds. Or whatever you call mourning clobber when it's, say, a useless brother who's booted the bucket.'

Light Fingers had visited the Viola dorms to take measurements for the Mid-Winter Revue costumes. She reported that, since Rayne joined the ranks, the theatricals were quieter, less tizzy-prone and decidedly off their feed. Amy guessed the new girl's House Sisters were afraid Gryce might decide to make an example by tying, say, Rayne's whole dorm to that goalpost.

'It's not that,' Light Fingers said, 'it's something else. I've never seen Viola like this. It's like they've found something precious and are protecting it, but are afraid of it at the same time.'

'I wouldn't put Viola in charge of guarding the family silver,' said Frecks, 'unless I wanted it half-inched so I could put in an insurance claim.'

Frecks' brother had pulled this swindle as a way of realising fast cash on what ought to be Frecks' inheritance. Doing something about Viscount Ralph was on the agenda of the Moth Club.

'If Rayne winds up in concrete overshoes, Viola ain't gonna do nothin' but shut up about it,' said Kali. 'If Gryce's goons messed with Goneril, they'd land up in the infirmary. Sheesh, if they came round here and pulled that fright stuff, we'd give 'em Italian smiles…'

An Italian smile was a throat cut from ear to ear.

'…and dump the stiffs on the doorstep. But Viola… nah, it'll never happen. Rayne's a goner. Them's the breaks. A solid gone goner.'

If Harriet/Marion had snapped before Imogen Ames, Amy would have been in Viola instead of here. She remembered the dorm rallying around when the Murdering Heathens came to call… she'd only survived her first week at Drearcliff because of her friends in Desdemona.

All Rayne had were the blubbing babies of Viola.

Amy agreed with Kali – she was a solid gone goner. It shouldn't matter to her, but – somehow – it did.

V: Break

WHEN THE SCHOOL Rules were written – if not at the Diet of Worms in 1066, then in secret sessions nearly fifty years ago – each word in each phrase in each sentence in each paragraph on each page was considered. Everything was weighed and debated. Ambiguities were eliminated or enshrined. Rights were established and traps were set. After the final deliberation, the Rules were inscribed in the Drearcliff Grange School Charter. The Founders – often-invoked, never named – ceremonially cut their fingers and shed blood on the document.

Their decisions would stand until the End of Time.

The Last Trump would not sound until the last lesson was taught. Girls would not face Judgement until all books, chalk and pens were tidied away and the desks lined up. An orderly crocodile would be formed. Hats must be worn in the presence of Angels Hallowed or Fallen, but doffed in the presence of Archangels and Above. Whether in Heaven or Hell, a Drearcliff Girl would be a credit to her cloud or furnace. Among the saved or the damned, she would be exemplary.

According to School Rules, girls had Break of forty-five minutes between midday meal and afternoon lessons. Unless it was raining, the period was to be spent out of doors. The word at issue was 'raining'. With a looser definition of precipitation, current conditions might trigger the subsidiary clause which allowed that pupils could take Break in a designated classroom. There, they could play whist for ha'penny a trick, desperately cram up on subjects they should have covered in prep or gossip like washerwomen. As it was, strict interpretation of the Rules meant girls were not excused outdoor Break if it were only snowing.

At the beginning of term, enthusiasm for snowball fights, skating and other winter pastimes ran high. That petered out by the end of the first week. Captain Freezing kept popping up, and de Vere continued her by-now demented solo assaults on his incarnations. Every day, more complaints of chills, colds and frostbite were presented to Nurse. All but the manifestly dying were turned away from the Infirmary. A sudden, unprecedented enthusiasm for second and third helpings of semolina delayed expulsion to the freezing outdoors. Girls volunteered to clear away the meal-things, traditionally a punishment handed out to those whose spirit the whips wished to crush. Only Palgrave had put her hand up for this before. Now, smiling with her mouth and screaming with her eyes, she competed for the chore of scraping leftovers into the foul vats which were carted away to feed pigs or for use in scientific experiments. What unholy life might stir in the depths of foetid custard, rancid bacon rinds, bitter trifle and leathery liver?

For a week Miss Kaye supervised Break. No stickler she for rigorous interpretation of School Rules. Under her merciful regime, girls stayed in the Refectory until the lesson-bell tolled. Provided they didn't get in the way or set fire to benches and tables. Board games were played, Buller retained her status as Arm-Wrestling Champion, and paper aeroplanes sailed the length of the hall. Light Fingers showed Amy how to do cat's cradle, which she said helped her focus and not make involuntary quick moves with her hands – keeping her talent under a bushel, so to speak. Amy saw what her friend meant, but had more than fast fingers to worry about. Intricate string constructs didn't keep her on the ground, so she was back to stones in her pockets. Harmony Meade, a Viola Fourth, reclaimed the long-disused minstrels' gallery. She plucked a lute as the wind blew snow against the long, rattling windows. She knew all the tunes from *Chu Chin Chow* and *The Bing Boys Are Here*.

Then Digger Downs took over as Break Mistress. A fanatic for a literal reading of School Rules, she threw girls out in the cold, cold snow like errant daughters in the melodramas of yesteryear. Scarved and mittened, the whole school had to be herded by literal whips. The prefects used riding crops. Even the hardiest Goneril amazons complained it was a bit much, while the weeds of Viola gave voice to lamentation and wailing and gnashing of teeth. Amy kept her head down and trudged. The Moth Club spent Break in the Quad, which was somewhat protected from icy wind. Many huddled in Mauve Mary's covered walkway, reminding Amy that the spectre had made herself scarce lately. On the playing fields, snow drifts formed around girls who stayed in one place too long.

A rumour went around that Digger was mostly

brass. A miniature coke-burning furnace served her for a heart, the remains of her brain floated in a glass jug in her skull and her mechanical hide was coated with special paint that looked like skin. The story was that she had been caught under an aerial incendiary dropped on Stogursey by an off-its-course Zeppelin, then rebuilt in the Hypatia Hall Machinists' Workshop to combat a shortage of teachers during the Great War. If the leading proponent of the Downs-is-an-automaton theory weren't Smudge, Amy would have believed it. For a start, the teacher stationed herself in the cold too. When Ponce was Break Master, he shooed the rabble outside, then oversaw them from inside his cosy study. The contrast might have earned Digger respect, except no one raised her possible finer points for fear of being throttled. Even the Sixths who enforced her rule looked miserable about it, though they had the privilege of huddling around a stove in the Whips' Hut after the forced exodus was effected.

Everyone had to develop a survival technique. Gonerils practised calisthenics. Tamoras burned Violas' possessions in braziers – diaries, motion-picture fan magazines and woolly nighties yielded the most warmth, apparently. Ariels sported expensive furs and lied about great white hunter daddies shooting snow leopards or dire wolves when anyone could tell they were shop bought. Desdemonas tried it on with uniform variations more inventive than Rayne's black skirt and blazer, generally not caring whether innovations were cited as Minor Infractions.

Under her boater, Amy wore a snug leather flying helmet.

* * *

Happily for the Moth Club, Light Fingers scavenged fur-lined flying helmets from the Viola Dramatic Society's ambitious production of *Captain Skylark vs the Demon Ace*. Amy considered saving hers to add to the Kentish Glory costume, in case she had to float in this weather. However, an urgent need to keep her ears from falling off persuaded her that the prize headgear was best suited to everyday use. Her helmet had been worn by the departed Marion/Harriet, who played Lieutenant Basil 'Goosey' Gander, Skylark's former fag at Uppingham. Goosey was poignantly shot down on his first mission. Half the school wept as Harriet/Marion expired in Mansfield's manly arms, prompting the gallant captain to vow vengeance on the Satanic Hun.

Only Kali – used to walking around with a caste mark/sniper's target on her forehead – was willing to sport the crest of the fiendish Fokker. Frecks tried her uncle Lance's chainmail hood, but the cold metal stuck to her ears. The blessed object might protect her from grievous injury, so long as her cause was just and true, but it was little use when it came to keeping out the bally cold. Also, she heard strange music when she wore the thing and developed a faraway look in her eyes.

Girls huddled on the Quad in knots and cliques, shivering and considering Digger Downs with hostile eyes. At this rate, the teacher would lose a popularity contest even if the other entrants were Hans von Hellhund, Zenobia Aire and Dr Shade's arch-enemy Achmet the Almost-Human. Kali had an idea what First Prize should be...

'Scorpions. In her bed. So when she gets under the covers at night... *sting sting sting*! *Death death death*! I don't care if she's brass or bone, a dose of scorp juice'd lay her on the slab. Yeah, scorpions...'

Kali's father dealt often with Singapore Charlie's, a well-established supplier of exotic flora and fauna on a 'no questions asked' basis firm. When a crimelord installed an alligator pit under a trapdoor in his office, intent on putting errant employees 'on the spot', only one firm sold the requisite hungry reptiles. Mr Chattopadhyay exported Kafiristan's uniquely venomous camel spiders for Singapore Charlie. Camel spiders were Solifugae, a separate class of arachnid from Araneae – as related to camels as horseflies were to horses.

Amy had to tell Kali that scorpions wouldn't survive long in Somerset at this time of year. She couldn't think of any suitably poisonous species indigenous to Arctic climes.

So that bright idea got scratched.

VI: 'Spend Three and Fourpence…'

WEDNESDAY. THREE DAYS into the Digger Downs tenure as Break Mistress.

Amy and her chums shuffled out on to the freezing Quad. The ordeal was almost routine now.

'Lovely weather for polar bears,' said Peebles, ducking to avoid a thumping. She'd said the same thing two or three times a day since term started.

'Great Aunt Gertie's garters!' exclaimed Frecks. 'Look at Black Hat!'

Amy followed Frecks' line of sight.

In front of the Heel, Rayne was skipping again. She wore her normal abnormal uniform – no scarf, no mittens, no overcoat. As Rayne stepped up and down, her boater didn't blow away or fall off. Her pleated black skirt rose and fell, showing knees that weren't blue and legs that weren't frostbitten.

Other girls reported that no amount of healthy exercise kept you warm in weather like this. The hollow shell of Roberta Hale limped around to prove it. 'Work up a sweat and it freezes on you,' said Big Bren Manders, Captain of the Second Eleven. 'You could die of it.'

But Rayne seemed to have conquered the cold.

'What the devil is she saying?' asked Light Fingers.

As she skipped, Rayne rattled off a rhyme.

Skipping was for Firsts and underdone Seconds. Amy hadn't skipped since infants' school. It was a babyish thing she had put aside, along with conkers, off-ground touch and spinning tops. Small as Rayne was, it was unsettling to see a Third skipping. Like catching a grown-up sliding down the banister or riding a rocking horse.

What was skipping? A pastime or a game? Silliness or sport? An innocuous survival of a once bloody pagan ritual? Now Amy thought of it, perhaps Boadicea or the Morrigan skipped a rope made of entrails of fallen foes. Passed down through generations of schoolgirls, along with rhymes whose meanings were long-since obscured, rope-jumping might be a martial tradition... like parade drill, jiu-jitsu or sword display.

Rayne skipped as if she weren't simply (or even) enjoying herself.

Girls got closer to Rayne. Her eyes were open and alert, but her ever-faster and more intricate skips didn't require inordinate concentration. She went through the moves as if by instinct. Every fifth hop was a reverse, every tenth a twist under her feet that somehow didn't knot the rope. On every twentieth skip, she let go of one handle – which flailed out like a bullwhip – then caught it again. It was tantalising, knowing she *must* make a mistake eventually. No one could keep at this without tiring, without missing, without tripping. Rayne sped up and slowed down.

Maybe she *could* go on forever?

She spoke as she skipped. At first, she just moved her mouth, making word shapes but no sound. Then, the odd word of her private rhyme escaped…

'Ants… pants… France… ments… vance…'

Then, phrases, meaningless but distinct…

'Ants in your pants… take another chance…'

Girls gathered in a semicircle. Fascination almost made them forget frozen faces and air which frosted inside lungs. This was at least a novelty.

In the wings as usual, Prompt marked a distance beyond which spectators shouldn't approach. No one wanted to be beaned with an outflung rope handle.

Rayne was speaking confidently now.

> 'Ants in your pants
> All the way from France
> Send reinforcements
> We're going to advance…'

Frecks wolf-whistled. Amy came down with the quease whenever that black hat bobbed in view, but Frecks was inclined to take Rayne's part. Her sneaking admiration for the new bug was blooming like a black rose.

> 'Ants in your pants
> Take another chance
> Spend three and fourpence
> We're going to a dance…'

Repeat… repeat. Two verses, over and over…

A murmuring hum. Other girls took up the rhyme, which grew louder.

Rayne was unaffected by her audience. She skipped on and on, just as she had when no one was watching.

Amy looked at her face. She showed no pride, no enjoyment, no pain.

Again, Amy thought of a clockwork toy. One which would not run down like a self-winding watch. Amy knew Digger Downs wasn't really a brass automaton, but she wasn't sure Rayne was fully human. Did she have a maggot in her brain like Palgraive? Or was she Mauve Mary taken physical form?

Amy shuddered. She had a strange, queasy, yet exhilarating sensation – similar to the stomach-shifts and skin-prickles she felt when floating. She got the same thing from Light Fingers, sometimes – and from Paule, always. It was what happened when Amy met someone Unusual. Someone who was like her.

Being like her wasn't the same as being her friend. Strength-sapping Jacqueline Harper, 'Shrimp' of the *Drearcliff Trumpet*, was an Unusual, but no one's friend. Indeed, she showed a particular, quiet, veiled animosity towards Amy. The *Trumpet* had run mocking, knowing squibs about the Moth Club. Even Gryce wouldn't have Shrimp as a Murdering Heathen. The Tamora Fifth was reduced to battening on to inexperienced Firsts and Seconds, and they caught on after a few days or weeks and gave her the elbow. Shrimp was in danger of wasting away, which Amy reckoned would be no bad thing.

After a few minutes, girls lost interest in the skipping. What Rayne was doing was odd, but not more than that. After a while, her proficiency was tedious – like looking at the insectile innards of a watch ticking off the seconds with repetitive cog-turns and spring-bounces. There was the cold to worry about. If Rayne wasn't going to fall over and break her head, they might as well watch de Vere lay into Captain Freezing with a lacrosse stick.

'Think that'd work for anyone?' Light Fingers asked.

Frecks shrugged. 'Doubt it.'

Light Fingers took off her mittens and stuck them in her pocket. She flexed her fingers and whizzed her hands through the air several times. The ends of her arms were blurs. She stopped and looked at her hands, which were already blue-ish. She sucked her fingers, another futile endeavour.

'Yup,' she said afterwards. 'Still chilly.'

She stuffed her hands back in her mittens and looked at Rayne's thinning audience.

'Good luck to her though,' said Frecks. 'We'll just have to shiver it out till next week. Who's on Break after Digger?'

'Wicked Wyke,' said Amy.

Frecks managed a shivering smile. 'Wicked's a softie. We'll be indoors again…'

'…*if* we survive. Ho, what's afoot now?'

Digger Downs stood at her post by the Refectory doors, whistle poised to shrill at any Infraction. What Rayne was doing seemed within the accepted limits of School Rules. No clause forbade inordinate skipping, though Amy wouldn't put it past the whips to dream one up.

Garland approached the Break Mistress and tugged the end of Digger's cardigan as if it were an old-fashioned bell-pull. The Second needed the protection of the whips and teachers for whom she snooped. The school motto applied especially to Snitcher Garland. Everyone she had told on – which, by now, was nearly the whole school – would cheerfully have shoved her over the precipice or left her in the woods for the wolves.

'Someone's for it,' observed Amy. 'Snitching is in process.'

Downs creakily bent and Garland went up on tiptoes to whisper in her ear.

'There's ways to deal with squealers,' said Kali. 'Some fine day, Garland's gonna be found wearin' a South Side necktie. That's when they cuts your sneakin' throat across and pulls yer snitchin' tongue out through the slit. All the best stool pigeons are wearin' 'em this season.'

Downs expressed annoyance. She took off her whistle and passed it to a whip who happened to be nearby – Sidonie Gryce! – then tramped off, led by Garland, out of the Quad and off towards the woods.

What was Gryce doing out here in the cold? She could invoke Head Girl's privilege and be in the Whips' Hut, warming herself with fags, gin and a picture of Antonio Moreno with his shirt off. Instead, she was out among the cold and desperate. She twirled the whistle idly around her forefinger. Air rushed through it, making a tiny screech.

The other Heathens were in the Quad too, not in their usual gaggle, but stationed at strategic points. Crawford, wearing her flared Hans von Hellhund coat, stood in Mauve Mary's walkway, casually blocking traffic. Though barred from fencing after giving Minty Armadale a Heidelberg duelling stripe, Vanity carried a sabre.

'They're going to get her,' Amy said.

Everyone understood.

Gryce wore calf-length white leather boots and an elegant number with fur-trim and whips' frogging. She looked like an Archduchess at the execution of a commoner.

Amy was tense. She wished she were in her Kentish Glory uniform. But the Moth Club flew by night. Out in the open, they were just... Thirds.

A ripple of understanding went around. Many found reason to quit the Quad. Crawford stood aside to let them pass, encouraging stragglers with the flat of her sabre. It was a good time to get up a game of scratch cricket or form a posse to help Digger pursue whichever outlaw Garland had peached on. The diversion would be detailed enough to include a sacrificial miscreant, whose infraction would detain the mistress... Gryce wasn't an amateur.

Beeke and Pulsipher, Rayne and Prompt's cell-mates, fled. The cowardly custards didn't want to get lynched next to their House Sisters. Viola's reputation for wetness was built on such craven actions.

Amy stayed. Frecks, Light Fingers and Kali did too. A scattering of Violas still watched Rayne, heads nodding in time with her rhyme. Prompt sucked her lips anxiously. Palgraive and Paule floated in their own bubbles, seeming not to notice anything. Crowninshield II skulked, an outcast among outcasts. Even Firsts knew they could get away with pelting her. Their squeezed missiles were more like ice grenades than snowballs. Inchfawn, another untouchable, huffed into her hands and peered through filmed-over specs. Shrimp peeped from behind the Heel, hungry and fascinated. Rayne could keep her going, keep her *warm*, for months, *years...* provided she lived, which was at present doubtful.

Alexandra Weston Vansittart, Countess of Crouth and Kiloyle, Droning of Skerra, House Captain of Ariel, made a rare appearance among the commonality. Amy noticed Sixths from all Houses, as if they'd been invited to observe. Vansittart was so above-it-all she didn't even deign to wear whip's braid – 'who would want to be a species of policeman?' she drawled – but knew how School worked. Gryce, apparently, had obtained scented letters she had written as a foolish Second to one of the mistresses. If the Ariel House Captain ever dared to go against the Head Girl, they might become public.

The other House Captains were present: Matilda Pelham of Desdemona, Helena Mansfield of Viola, Florence Rhode-Eeling of Goneril. With Digger away hunting the wild Infractor, Pelham and Rhode-Eeling risked sneaking crafty cigarettes. Vansittart gulped something eye-wateringly warming from a silver flask which bore one of her family crests.

Now, everyone watched Rayne.

She was still skipping, showing no sign of noticing the circling shark-fins.

'Ants in your pants
All the way from France...'

Ridiculous words, spoken in solemnity, repeated until all trace of meaning was lost.

'Spend three and fourpence
We're going to a dance...'

With a deft reverse, Rayne turned to face the Heel and skipped on. Her back was to the observers.

Henry Buller and Euterpe McClure moved closer.

Buller had her gloves off and was cracking her knuckles. McClure bowed her head and made blades of her hands.

Amy was fascinated by the back of Rayne's hair. Cut straight across, showing her hackles.

Prompt cried soundlessly, tears streaming over her plump cheeks. Amy felt prickles in her own eyes.

Gryce, a field marshal in scarlet lipstick, was at her ease, twirling the whistle on its thong. She waited for Downs to be well away on her fools' errand. Smiling sweetly at the Captains and other interested parties, the Head Girl made a gesture in the air, as if flicking something away from her face.

Buller and McClure went in.

VII: '...We're Going to a Dance'

RAYNE TURNED AROUND again and skipped with her back to the Heel. She rhymed on, face shining, eyes bright.

Amy was queasier than ever.

She glanced aside at Dora Paule. The Sixth had her eyes screwed shut and fingers pressed to her temples. Amy thought she saw ripples of violet in the air around her.

You didn't have to have Abilities to know what would happen next...

Prompt, of all people, stepped in front of Buller and McClure, interposing her quaking body between Rayne and Gryce's myrmidons.

McClure tapped Prompt's breastbone, indicating she should step aside.

For seconds, it seemed a Viola Third would stand up to a Goneril Fifth. That was, in itself, unprecedented...

Then Prompt, sobbing silently, got out of the way.

Rayne didn't show any sign of noticing.

McClure considered the situation, big hands flexing. A sly one, she gave victims a moment to think about the coming pain before flicking the lash. Rayne ignored her.

Buller, less reflective, just ploughed in.

The whip swung a roundhouse right to the side of Rayne's head. A great hollow clap sounded as knuckles impacted against skull. It was a wonder the blow didn't take the skipping machine's head clear off.

Rayne staggered towards a snowdrift, but kept her balance… her head kinked unnaturally, but her legs and arms still worked.

She was still skipping.

A few girls applauded. Gryce's narrowed eyes shut them up. Amy thought she detected the ghost of a smirk on Vansittart's lips.

Buller couldn't believe her first punch hadn't scored a knockout.

Rayne straightened her neck. A few Violas clapped in time to her rhyme.

McClure eyed the situation and kicked Rayne's right knee, hooking her shoe behind the smaller girl's leg and sweeping her off balance.

This time Rayne fell… smashing backwards into the drift. It was at least a cushion for her tumble.

Buller snorted and drew back her size eleven for a nasty kick to the ribs.

…but Rayne was up again, and skipping.

She had leaped up like an acrobat, landed on her feet, and resumed her routine as if nothing had happened.

'Ants in your pants
All the way from France…'

Nasty bruises marked Rayne's forehead and leg. Her blazer, skirt and hair were dusted with snow.

'Send reinforcements,
We're going to advance…'

The clapping was louder, like a war drum.

Enraged, Buller got her head down and charged,

aiming straight at Rayne's midriff. The girl somehow jumped higher than before, three or four feet off the ground, and the whip slammed into the Heel.

Rayne touched down, and skipped on.

'Ants in your pants

Take another chance…'

Now other girls were chanting for her. This wasn't an execution any more. It was more like a prizefight.

Buller turned round, blood on her face. Her boater was crushed. She shook her braids. She didn't know what had just happened…

And neither did Amy.

Had Rayne *floated*? Or simply jumped like a grasshopper.

'Spend three and fourpence

We're going to a dance…'

Buller might be afraid. Awe was stirring in her underused brain.

'No no no no,' muttered Paule, unnoticed by anyone but Amy. The tug of the Purple came. Amy thought the world was about to *shift* again…

But it didn't. Paule scuttled off, hands pressed to her face. Amy thought the Sixth had a sympathetic nosebleed – as if she'd caught Buller's self-inflicted injury.

Paule was not a comforting presence, but Amy had never seen her flee in terror… and worried about whoever was capable of frightening her.

McClure wasn't as headstrong as Buller. She was subtle, cruel, ingenious. And wary. She had no intention of beaning herself.

Crouching, she felt around, naked fingers rooting in the snow. She dug out a chunk of rock from the gravel surround of the Heel. She weighed it in her hand then packed snow about it. School Rules said nothing about such missiles, but they violated the Code of Break, the rules girls made among themselves. You could fling an ice bomb at your best friend or worst enemy and it was all in fun, but a stone in a snowball was not done.

Except by McClure, devotee of the works of the Marquis de Sade.

'That's not cricket,' commented Rhode-Eeling. 'That's not playing the game.'

'This isn't a game,' said McClure, who had the nod from Gryce. 'This is life and death.'

Rhode-Eeling shrugged, unwilling to cross Head Girl. Strictly, Gryce of Tamora should have cleared use of McClure, a Goneril Fifth, with Rhode-Eeling. Then again, Rayne was a Viola weed... and Mansfield wasn't speaking in her defence. Handsome Helena was of Gryce's party and always had been. She hadn't protected Marion/Harriet from Vanity and wouldn't stick up for Rayne. It was as if Captain Skylark flew home safe while Hunnish brutes were shooting Goosey Gander in the tail. Amy shouldn't have confused Mansfield with the heroic roles she played.

McClure showed the stone snowball to the skipping girl.

Rayne had a choice. She could stop skipping or she could take this projectile to the face.

Rayne didn't stop skipping.

The chanting rhyme continued.

Amy longed to do something, *anything*. She had to focus hard to keep her feet on the ground. She badly missed her mask.

McClure, who bowled for the First Eleven, casually walked back a few steps, snowball in hand. Amy recognised her shy smile. McClure liked to begin a match aiming high and straight at the eyes of the opposing opening bat. Most of her victims ducked, sloshed, fled or knocked the stumps to evade injury. Not a move much cared for by umpires, so McClure knew to use it sparingly. She only got one or two out that way per inning, though she had been known to brag that several of her targets slunk back to the pavilion with broken noses and never stepped up to the crease again. When McClure got you out, you stayed out.

Rayne seemed unconcerned.

McClure took a run up and let fly.

…and missed. The stone smashed against the Heel.

'Ants in your pants
All the way from France.'

The chant was triumphal. Amy joined in, though it hurt to shout. Icy inrushes of air thumped her chest.

'Send reinforcements
We're going to advance…'

Frecks was chanting too, and Light Fingers, and Kali. Vansittart nodded in time. Prompt chanted as if in prayer. Rhode-Eeling as a rebuke to the unsporting Goneril.

All Viola House chanted, even Mansfield…

'Ants in your pants
Take another chance
Spend three and fourpence
We're going to a dance…'

With each beat, Rayne skipped. She must be fast as Light Fingers to dodge a Euterpe McClure beamer.

A tide was turning.

Gryce didn't like it.

Prompt produced a rope, and began to skip alongside Rayne. Nowhere near as well as her cell-mate. Rather than jump, she just dragged the rope – which was too long for her – across the ground and stepped clumsily over it. But she joined in. The chant was for her too.

The *wrongness* clenched in Amy's stomach.

McClure signalled. A group of toadying Tamora Seconds unloosed a volley of snowballs at the skipping girls.

Prompt was battered and fell. Rayne dodged most of the balls and kept skipping. Even direct hits didn't faze her.

McClure, angry and forgetting herself, took hold of Rayne's hair and yanked hard. She ripped her hand open as if she had grasped a fistful of pampas grass.

Gryce's Murdering Heathens were hurting themselves more than Rayne.

Beeke and Pulsipher, the Violas who'd run off at the first sign of trouble, came back, barging past an astonished Crawford. They brought armloads of skipping ropes and gave them out to anyone who would take one.

Amy took a rope, but just looked at it. A few were dropped in the snow.

Beeke and Pulsipher began to skip. Better than Prompt, they kept time with Rayne for a minute or so before getting in a tangle… but then they got their rhythm back, and skipped on.

McClure slapped Rayne one way and the other. Her slaps connected, leaving a streak of her own blood on the skipping girl's cheek, but Rayne kept skipping.

'Stop it, you blasted worm, you. Cease…' *slap!*… 'this…' *slap!*… 'impertinent display!'

Unfair punch to the stomach. Sympathisers winced more than the victim did.

Rayne was pushed back against the Heel now, pinned by McClure's blows. She moved up and down, in time with the rhyme.

All around Violas were skipping. And Thirds of all Houses, except Tamora.

McClure left Rayne be – she instantly recovered and, more precise than ever, found her spot and skipped – and careered from Viola to Viola, clouting and chopping and kicking and kneeing and elbowing.

Girls went down and stayed down longer than Rayne.

But they got up and skipped.

McClure's face was red.

Amy, still not skipping, noticed Gryce had toddled off. If this was to be a loss, she wouldn't be around to look defeated.

It wasn't just Violas or Thirds. Amy saw Ariels skipping, now. And the odd Goneril, ashamed of McClure's unsporting behaviour. Keele skipped, along with other Desdemona Sixths who found the ropes too short. Farjeon and her little circle of Seconds had been skipping well before Rayne's arrival, and might wonder what all the fuss was about now. Taking Farjeon's lead, the traditional skippers joined in – abandoning the drowned black babies to their terrible flood and taking up the cause of ants in pants.

And Frecks… Lady Serafine Nimue Todd Walmergrave, *Willow Ermine*… was skipping, long legs bending as she brought her knees up. She must have been a skipping demon when she was younger.

'Ants in your pants
All the way from France
Send reinforcements
We're going to advance…'

It carried throughout the whole Quad now. Amy couldn't bring herself to skip, yet didn't know why she was resisting.

This was a triumph. Rayne was a heroine.

She was an Unusual.

But… Amy's stomach ached acutely. She *wanted* to skip too, but the wanting – a *wanting* close to a *needing*! – was wrong. It wasn't her inclination. It was instilled by an external force. She heard a call her instinct was to resist.

No, she would not join in. No.

Double crumpets! Someone had given Henry Buller a rope. The whip was skipping too, stepping like an elephant, eyes crossed, boater blown away, blood freely spilling.

'Ants in your pants
Take another chance
Spend three and fourpence
We're going to a dance…'

Amy wasn't the only hold-out. None of the House Captains skipped, not even Mansfield – though Amy saw they were resisting a pull, just as she was. Rhode-Eeling tapped her toes to the rhyme. Vansittart clapped daintily.

Some of the spectators had fled.

Shrimp was passed out beyond the Heel, shaking a little. Amy never thought she'd feel sympathy with her.

The racket – rhyming, clapping, the pounding of shoes on snow – brought faces to the windows. Ponce, Wicked, Miss Kaye, Keys.

Joxer walked into the Quad and was surrounded by skipping dervishes.

It lasted until the Break Bell sounded. Then, in an instant, it stopped.

Rayne wound her rope up and walked to her next lesson. The girls she left behind stopped skipping when she did, but were dazed in the wake of their fit… it had been like a craze spread throughout School.

Amy looked at Frecks, so flushed her long-gone freckles had reappeared. Her friend was elated, but Amy was frightened.

'What just happened?' Amy asked.

'I don't know,' said Frecks, 'but I hope it happens again… *soon*!'

VIII: The Coming of the Black Skirts

TWO DAYS LATER, Amy thought she saw Rayne in the library. On the stairs to Entomology, a small, black-blazered girl was ahead of her. Sidling between rows, she passed out of Amy's sight.

Was she ducking away from Amy or just looking for a book?

Curious, she peeped into the narrow, shaded alleyway between tall, dusty shelves. It wasn't Rayne, but Phair – a dark-haired Second. An easy mistake. Phair wore the new Drearcliff kit. Black, with grey; not grey, with black. Perhaps because the uniform *was* new, it seemed shiny, like waxed leather or a beetle's carapace. She'd seen Phair before, of course. Like most Seconds, she wasn't noticeable. A spear-carrier or pageboy in Viola pageants. Light Fingers would call her an Ordinary.

From the top of a set of library steps, Phair was reaching for a book about locusts. Sensing Amy's presence, she swivelled her head like an owl's to stare back. In the gloom, her eyes flashed black as her uniform. The Second didn't much resemble Rayne, really, though she had that same unsmiling expression, at once absent and focused.

Rattled, Amy mumbled an apology and stepped back, leaving Phair to the locusts. She hurried to the cosy nook where the library kept books on moths (and, as she reluctantly had to concede was fitting) butterflies. School had only the standard Lepidopterae texts, but the alcove was Amy's private thinking spot. She came here when she needed to put her mind to something.

One thing private education seldom provided was privacy. In lessons, at Break, in Chapel, at meals, Amy was always among other girls. In her cell, she was liable to be distracted by Frecks commenting on the latest scandals or Kali reading out press reports of machine-gun massacres in Chicago. The dorms rattled with rackets. A cell of Seconds, one floor below, had taken up the ocarina and practised night and day. None of them, as yet, could hold a tune, not even 'Twinkle Twinkle Little Star' – but they had mastered shrill loudness.

The skipping plague had reached Desdemona. A few girls, notably the pariah Inchfawn and gap-toothed Hoare-Stevens, made a ghastly thumping din on bare floorboards. Out-of-time skipping accompanied by out-of-tune ocarina would send anyone into the cold, dark woods. Murder and worse was contemplated, but the Moth Club decided to let the irritations run on… this sort of petty crime was beneath their attention. Amy, however, often fled to the library.

In the lepidoptery alcove, there was a little desk – not much more than a fold-out shelf – and a stool. Amy could work here undisturbed.

To mark her spot, she had carved a moth sign on the underside of the desk with her penknife. The design was too fiddly. Light Fingers suggested she simplify it. Sigils, seals and signals should be bold, striking and easy to draw. Light Fingers said the Moth Club needed instantly identifiable trademarks, like the Scarlet Pimpernel's wild flower or Zorro's sword-carved Zs.

On secret missions, the Moth Club passed coded messages on paper strips left as pretend-bookmarks in Professor Hardinge Oldmead's *Moths of the Midlands* (1867), a book so outdated as to be useless except as a postbox. From instinct, not really expecting a message, Amy pulled down Oldmead and opened it to a cutaway diagram of an anthill. That wasn't right. She looked at the cover and found she was holding Jacob Vereker's sensationalist *Reign of the Ant Queen* (1919). *Moths of the Midlands* wasn't in its proper place. Was this a message in itself?

She looked at the shelves in the alcove. *All* the books were out of place.

Someone had replaced volumes about butterflies and moths with books about ants. Even the card labelled 'Lepidopterae' was gone. A new card read 'Formicidae'. This was officially an ant alcove. Moths were relegated to the general stack.

Amy felt personally attacked!

Irritated, she had a dizzy spell… then found herself floating. She looked down at dust-furred books on the top shelves. Her head bumped the ceiling. She hoped no one chanced to be idly looking up. Phair had gone and no one else was in Entomology. Gripping shelves like the rungs of a ladder, she climbed down and put her feet firmly on the carpet. She had gone *light* for a moment.

And no wonder. This rearrangement was sacrilege.

Scouting around, she found the moth books, all a jumble and out of order, on a lower shelf in the darkest corner of the section. The 'Lepidopterae' card was upside down too. She fixed that. Then she sorted the books, alphabetically by author. All the while, her mind roiled and raced.

Ants?

...as in 'ants in your pants, all the way from France'?

As in '*Ant*oinette Rowley Rayne'?

Amy felt turfed out of her own alcove, though she had no sense Rayne was involved or that the new bug would claim her personal quiet spot.

However, Professor Rayne's books were prominent in the Formicidae alcove. There were multiple copies of her freakishly popular *Formis*. The slender, yellow-covered pamphlet – little more than an essay with photographic plates – anatomised the working of an anthill and set it out as a model for the better ordering of human society. Many who should know better cited this fanciful wittering as profound and important. Amy thought it shaky entomology and dubious politics.

This injustice would not be brooked. Amy would get up a petition in the name of the Moth Club and present it to Dr Auchmuty, the librarian. 'Doc Och' was improbably glamorous. Smudge said she was the model for the 'Beware Female Spies' posters put up around barracks towns during the War. The louche, long-lashed librarian looked the type who could easily beguile a fatheaded Staff officer into passing on the plans for those revolutionary aerial spike-mines which nestled in artificial clouds to thwart Zeppelin raids. Judging by this anti-moth activity, Auchmuty was so unsuited for her current post Amy guessed she must have inveigled her way into it by blackmail. She probably knew fearful secrets about Dr Swan...

The next day, Amy saw two more girls in the new kit.

Then, at the weekend, three girls together in identical black hats, blazers and skirts.

A shower of Raynes.

A week on, the school body was shot through with them.

The Black Skirts.

It was an infection, like the measles. It was only a uniform option. No one told Amy *not* to wear her old grey. But she saw how it would go. At some point, Greys would be in a minority... then decline towards extinction.

Amy would be the last Grey.

Besides anything else, Mother would not open her purse for a whole new kit after only a term and a bit. Other girls wheedled parents or guardians. Ariels even spent their own money. Identical brown-paper parcels from Dosson, Chapell & Co. piled up at the Post Office in town until fetched by a frost-whiskered Joxer and a snowshod Dauntless. Bert Bates, the postman, wouldn't hop out to Drearcliff in this weather. He'd lost a leg at sea and didn't want to risk his whalebone falsie on the grim road to Drearcliff.

Viola went almost completely Black. Other Houses were speckled to various degrees, except Goneril. Rhode-Eeling insisted on traditional Grey and said she'd drop anyone in Black from competitive play. Frecks and Kali received brown-paper parcels, but didn't immediately don dark plumage. They said they wanted the choice. Amy tried not to show disapproval. After all, what did it matter, really?

Kali crimped her new black boater to look like a fedora, but was wise enough in the ways of Drearcliff not to risk a Uniform Infraction by wearing it outside the cell. Few wanted to scrub the Heel in a blizzard.

The first whip to go Black was – no surprises! – Henry Buller.

Buller became Rayne's bodyguard, always ten paces behind the skipping machine, ready to twist arms or slap faces. At first she was busy, enforcing respect for the Queen Ant... then, folk got the message and stopped chucking snowballs or chanting insults at Rayne.

The way Rayne wore her boater reminded Amy of Napoleon's sideways hat.

She remembered what Keele had said about Boney. Was Rayne Amy's own bogeyman, a dark doppelgänger sent to persecute or test or destroy? Rayne was an uncanny creature, but she didn't come from the Purple. According to the note on the dust jacket of *Formis*, Professor Rayne lived in Oxford and lectured at Shrewsbury College.

Gryce wasn't seen much these days. Mansfield, the first House Captain in Black, acted as if she had suddenly been made Head Girl, though there was no system for contesting the position. Even in Viola, the Black tide didn't wash over all. Vanity Crawford remained all-the-way Grey, and kept one or two acolytes. But the Revolution continued.

Handsome Helena cut a dash in black, and was as a consequence admired. She set a style among Sixths – somehow acceptable within the uniform code – for sheer black silk stockings with fine grey seam-stripes. Girls gave up baggy, scratchy grey wool socks for black hose, not caring about the cold.

At Break and before Prep, the Black Skirts skipped together.

In defiance of tradition, girls from all Houses and forms fell in step. A negotiation was effected with

Wicked Wyke, acting for the Headmistress. Skippers were allowed use of the Gymnasium. It was a powerful recruiting tool. The Gym was draughty, but indoors. Rayne might share the freeze tolerance of the flightless midge or the alpine cockroach and be hardy enough to endure the Arctic climes of the Quad and beyond, but most who followed her in fashion and exercise were not so blessed. The winter options of hibernation or migration were denied too.

Passing the Gym after lessons, Amy heard regular clapping over that blessed chant. 'Send reinforcements, we're going to advance.' Advance where? Not to any dance Amy could think of. The skipping *was* a form of close-order drill. Chinese fighting monks were less disciplined than Rayne's Black Skirts. The building shook. The massed jumping sounded like the *crump* of heavy guns on the Western Front.

Amy remembered skipping as *fun*. Years ago, she had skipped with the best of them… until she felt herself coming unstuck with each leap. She gave it up lest she betray her secret. Mother would not have been pleased. Besides, she started getting *light moments* about the time most girls grew out of skipping. For the Black Skirts, skipping was a calling, not a pleasure. It most certainly wasn't a game.

Making sure no one else was around, Amy let herself lose weight and scaled the wall of the Gym alongside the the tall, ice-rimed windows. She found handholds in the brickwork. Peeping in from above a window, she saw the *corps de skip* hard at it. Mansfield and Buller called the rhyme, but Rayne was mainspring of the clockwork parade, dead centre of a square formation. All around, Black Skirts followed her lead. No Greys in sight.

That absent-yet-focused expression was on all their faces. Amy had to rub ice away with her sleeve to get a better look and pick out individuals. The traitor Inchfawn… shut out in Desdemona, but finding a place among the automata. Rintoul, Rayne's first acolyte, now just another ant. Garland, defected along with Buller. Phair, the not-lookalike. Gould, of the hairy cheeks and stubby claws. 'Even' Keele, who'd talked so much sense. She-With-No-Mercy Aire. Thicke, Brydges, St Anne, Gallaudet, so many others.

Swots were skipping. Sloths were skipping. Rolled-stocking flappers were skipping! Hockey hooligans were skipping! Firsts bobbed up and down, higher so they'd fit in. Sixths were skipping like Firsts! Fearsome whips – practically grown women, exemplars to the school – jumped to a tempo set by a new bug Third. It was stranger, almost, than the Purple. Wrong in a way which gave Amy the collywobbles.

This was the Reign of Rayne.

Floating and an upset tummy were a bad mix, so Amy tried to get herself under control. She settled back on the path. She gulped a little, but did not heave. She had spots before her eyes and a copper taste on her tongue. She blew her nose and blood smeared her hankie. She inhaled cold air and the shock settled her.

She kept her head down and hurried on, anywhere but into the Gym.

IX: The Runnel and the Flute

ON THE FIRST Saturday of February, Amy was woken by icy little touches on her face. It was snowing again, and a couple of windowpanes had blown in. Frecks slept on, undisturbed by snow on her counterpane, but Kali and Light Fingers were swiftly stung awake. Amy shook Frecks to make her aware of the situation.

'Not this guff again,' said Frecks. 'We might as well build igloos.'

After breakfast, the Moth Club barricaded their cell against the elements. Kali had scrounged plasticine oddments from the Art Room, pressed into a large, multi-coloured ball. Amy used some of the oily, pliable stuff to fix cardboard squares into the empty spaces in the window, then layered more of it over the hard, cracked putty to forestall further damage. Finally, she squashed thick plasticine ropes into the cracks around the frame to minimise draughty rattling. Every time Amy touched glass, it was like brushing black ice – she was afraid she'd leave raw skin behind.

For once, the Sixths – on the highest floor of Old House – had the worst of it. The weight of new-fallen snow strained the roof and opened fissures in the ceilings of their cells. Joxer went up on the roof – the site of Kentish Glory's debut! – with a spade and tried to shift dune-like humps off the weak spots, but snow fell faster than the old retainer could shovel. De Vere, apparently, was terrified that Captain Freezing, who stood fully eighteen feet tall by now, was going to appear on the roof and crash into her cell.

In the afternoon, Pelham – the Desdemona House Captain – put out a call for volunteers to help Joxer. When only Palgraive stuck up her hand, a press-gang tore through Old House, conscripting everyone who didn't duck out of sight fast enough. Amy and Kali, snug in their newly secured cell, were the first victims. Inchfawn whined that she was expected in her skipping circle, but waving a black hat cut no ice with Pelham and she was on the work party… along with Honor 'Stretch' Devlin of the Fourth and Winifred 'Beauty' Rose of the Fifth. Palgraive fetched them all shovels.

The girls tended to clang spades together too often and get in Joxer's way, but made the best of the Sisyphean chore.

Devlin was tall for a Fourth. She was also an Unusual. As Stretch shovelled snow with no loss of her natural jollity, Amy wondered if she had nerves wired in reverse so she perceived icy blasts as gentle breezes. Then, she noticed Devlin's arms were extended, lengths of wrist showing between her sleeves and her gloves. She got her nickname from her Ability.

The girl must have bones like India rubber. Useful for fetching down balls caught in high branches or fishing out rings stuck in plugholes. By making her arms longer, she could shovel better. Light Fingers' Ability would have been the most use on the snowy roof, but she'd cleverly stepped into a wardrobe when the press-gang hit the Third corridor. Catching Amy looking, Devlin twisted her head round further than she ought to have been able to and wiggled her eyebrows cheekily. She was alarming, but refreshingly natural about it.

By nightfall, the conscripts had done what they could to shift the drift. Even Drearcliff whips couldn't expect anyone to stick to a job like that after dark. Digger Downs' lesson on Great Mutinies of Imperial History, much admired in the Whips' Hut, was that native peoples could be mistreated only so much before they beheaded the missionaries and fired the garrison. Drearcliff girls might put up with more than the average Zulu or sepoy, but there was a tipping point... and whips were trained to stow the cat just before the cry of insurrection rang out across the playing fields.

The shovel party was called in and Keele served hot chocolate and crumpets in her cell. Keele wore her new black uniform.

'I've read that book,' said Devlin, joshing. '*A Fashionable Woman*, by Nathalie Dresst.'

Amy, still not comfortable with Black Skirts, couldn't see that Keele had changed, apart from her clothes. But... part of the Sixth's new kit was an ant badge like the one Rayne wore. Thinking about it, she realised she'd seen more of them lately. Many girls who took the black uniform option sported these tiny lapel brooches. The ants reminded her of the maggot inside Palgraive's brain. Were these metal insects the real invaders and the hosts who sported them their slaves?

Inchfawn, emboldened in black, thanked Keele for the warming treats. She was rewarded with the sort of fond hair-tousling you might give a puppy. Outside the Moth Club, few were aware of the exact nature of Inchfawn's perfidy but word got round that she was – like Shrimp or Snitcher – not to be trusted. But Kali's abduction was last term's hot news, fading in memory. The Black Skirts were the big story this year. Rayne was rising... and Gryce falling.

Kali and Amy sat in a corner of Keele's cell with Beauty Rose. She got her nickname for obvious reasons too. Almost supernaturally lovely, Rose had fair fluffy ringlets, cornflower-blue eyes, a blush in pale cheeks and appealing, dainty features. The official School stunner was always in demand in the Art Room as a model for sketches and watercolours. She was also a tragic case, much pitied in poems by those with literary inclinations – works which would embarrass their authors in a few years' time. Born without a larynx, Rose was mute. When she had to, she communicated with elegant, wrist-flicking gestures. It seemed cruel to put such a delicate flower on the work party and Amy feared she'd shrivel when exposed to the elements... but she proved hardy and deft.

Still, Beauty was easier to look at than to know. She sipped her cocoa and licked her chocolate moustache like a cat.

Light Fingers and Amy had talked about girls who were on the fringes of Unusual... cultivating Talents to such a degree that they might be classed as Abilities or possessed of physical qualities that came close to being Attributes. Rose was one of those.

Amy and Kali both tried to start 'conversations' with the Fifth.

She smiled sweetly and made gestures. She wasn't like Palgraive, who sat vacantly while the maggot took a rest from pulling the wires, but she was hard to follow.

Nevertheless, Amy had a sense that Rose appreciated the kindly effort.

She recalled that sympathy after supper, when she and Kali saw Rose again. Bundled into a grown-up's greatcoat, Beauty was being walked out of the Quad by the Reverend Mr Bainter. Sure-footed while working on the roof, Beauty now dragged like an invalid. As she was pulled past Mauve Mary's shrine, a purplish glow illuminated the pair…

Amy thought she might be about to see the ghost… but this was just a random shaft of violet light.

What she did see was Beauty's face. Her big eyes were bigger and her pretty mouth was open in an O. If she'd had a larynx, she'd have been screaming.

Then she was dragged out of the light.

'Something's up,' Amy told Kali.

'I'll say,' said Kali. 'Ponce's filthy paws are all over Beauty's bod. If he tried them holds on a beerhouse moll, he'd get a slap across the puss.'

'We have to follow them.'

'In this climate? It ain't gonna be no picnic in the park.'

The snowfall had stopped before sunset, but the thermometer plunged even further. Their breath was white mist. Amy and Kali went through the walkway and came out the other side. Bainter and Rose were a way ahead, struggling through driven snow. They were off the path and headed towards the woods.

Knowing they could pick up the trail, the girls went back to their cell and changed. Amy hoped to enlist Frecks and Light Fingers, but they weren't home. There was a Black Skirt after-supper skipping rally in the gym, and the rest of the dorm had gone to watch. Light Fingers, at least, would be inclined to smuggle in snowballs to throw at the skippers.

Amy and Kali changed into their uniforms.

Kali's Moth Club name was Oleander Hawk, after a dramatic arrowhead-shaped species found in Kafiristan. Light Fingers had run up a brown-and-white mask to mimic its wings. Kali wore it with a dark-green trenchcoat and her hair coiled up inside her black faux fedora. She had also assembled a bandolier of implements – a multi-bladed penknife, a sharpened throwing star, several handy tools and her cigarette lighter. So far, Kali had only dressed up in their cell to see how the Oleander Hawk outfit looked. It was judged suitably fearsome.

Kali said she'd like to add a tommy gun to her bandolier, and made a hose-directing gesture and pow-pow-pow noise as if spraying wrongdoers with hot lead. Even allowing for the difficulty of obtaining firearms in England, toting guns wasn't quite the thing. Of course, the Moth Club would be set against desperate characters unlikely to be handicapped by such scruples – so perhaps a *small* tommy gun might be allowed, eventually. The Thompson company must make a ladies' model.

Amy saw Kali was glad of an excuse to put on a mask and hare off into the woods. She had missed out last term, when she was the one tied up and in need of rescue. Amy hoped her friend wouldn't be too headstrong in the field.

'We'll save that dame from a fate worse than death,' Kali said.

'You think Bainter might tie her to a tree and deliver one of his sermons?' suggested Amy. 'That would be dreadful. She can't even scream to drown him out.'

'Yeah, I think he's rotten enough... or worse.'

For winter, the Moth Club added padded coats and wellington boots to their costumes. The effect was more cocoon than imago, but even daredevil adventuresses had to take care not to catch their deaths of cold.

Quietly, they crept out of the dorms. Kali trained a small battery torch on the crisp snow. The trail was plain. Bainter's boot-prints were deep and regular, while Rose's were shallow and scuffed – she was resisting him. She might even have the presence of mind to leave an obvious track.

Because she was pretty and dumb, it was too easy to think Rose empty-headed. Amy knew that wasn't so. Beauty had learned to be wary. She was sceptical of flattery and suspicious of worship. Amy suspected she was a rose with thorns, not a drip like those Yank flicker serial heiresses.

Along with moth masks, they wore earmuffs and scarves. Amy's mask kept the wind off her face. She had goggles, adapted from her Goosey Gander helmet, but kept them up on her forehead for the moment.

Kali trod in Bainter's tracks, trying to make none of her own. A bandit trick her father had taught her. His fiefdom ranged from fertile river valleys to snow-capped mountains.

Making herself light, Amy tiptoed, leaving only the barest impression. The wing-like underarm webbing of her coat caught the air, but she didn't soar. For the moment, she wanted to keep her eyes on the ground.

Soon there were tall trees around them. By day and in other seasons these were the woods. By night and in winter, this was a forest.

Amy had written off Smudge's stories about Bainter being head of a white slavery ring as fables, no more credible than the theory that Digger Downs had brass bones. Smudge had also told Amy three entirely different, contradictory yarns about Mauve Mary – each time, with a quivering, infectious conviction.

Was Bainter's vile villainy harder to accept as fact than Palgraive's brain maggot? She only had Paule's word for that, but believed it. Or the Purple, which she'd visited. If she talked about that, people who hadn't been there would think she was a lunatic.

Far from the lights of School, they only had Kali's torch to go by. She held fingers over the lens so the shining wouldn't be obvious if Bainter happened to look behind him.

Amy remembered Hale's talk of eyes in the woods.

...and those famous wolves.

The high wall didn't run through the woods. The bounds were marked by flags hung from trees, but they hadn't been maintained since the first snowfall. Even in more congenial weather, few abscondees scarpered this way. Braving broken glass on top of the wall or shingle bays which could be cut off by tides were more sensible options.

Everything here was dead, frozen or sleeping out the winter.

Except the things that could hurt you. They never slept, they couldn't die and they didn't care about the cold.

A huge white thing loomed up ahead of them. A face leered down.

Kali played the torch beam up a swollen white body. It was Captain Freezing, remade again. Did the snowman lurk this far in the woods to lure poor, deluded de Vere into danger?

Bainter's tracks looped around Captain Freezing, keeping well out of reach of the twiggy fingers stuck into the bulbous ends of its icy arms.

The snowman's shako was as big as a pillar box.

'Where did he get a hat that size?' Amy asked.

'I last saw that lid on a giant toy soldier in the godawful *Waltzes From Wiener-Schnitzel Land* pageant two terms back,' said Kali. 'No clue how it got out here.'

They hurried on.

Up ahead, between the black bars of the trees, they saw lamplight. Muffled voices came on the wind.

Amy and Kali stopped.

Bainter and Beauty were meeting other parties.

'We get any closer, they'll rumble us,' said Kali.

'Maybe not,' said Amy. 'If there's fuss, chuck some pebbles over that way to distract them. I can get to a better eavesdropping spot.'

Making herself float, Amy rose until she thumped into the lowest branches of a spreading tree. Snow dislodged and showered on Kali, who shook it out of her hair.

Amy sprung from branch to branch, from tree to tree, getting better at it each time. She stopped slamming against branches and began to push herself through the air with some agility. Her wings filled and she was able to glide a little, pushing against the shaking branches to propel herself through the space between the trees.

She ascended, almost to the treetops.

It was colder up here, but snow wasn't falling. She lost feeling in her face and her mask felt stuck to her skin.

This was as near to flying as she had ever managed.

If she let go of the trees, would she drift upwards

until she froze solid and plummeted to shatter on the earth? She extended her mind's grip like an anchor-line and hauled herself on that.

She couldn't deny it. She was flying.

Suddenly she couldn't feel the cold. Exhilaration warmed her. For a moment, she knew what it was like to be literally above it all.

Nothing was keeping her on the ground.

On a moonlit night the view would be spectacular. Now, with heavy cloud cover, she saw only twin funnels of light ahead and the tiny glint of Kali's torch.

She was growing light-headed. Concentrating, she settled on a perch near the top of the tallest tree.

The light funnels were the headlamps of a car. A track ran through the woods, well beyond School Grounds.

Being here was a Major Infraction.

She clung to a tree trunk, fifty or sixty feet up, above the parked car, and heard voices below. She couldn't make out what was being said.

Taking a grip with her knees, she crawled head first down the trunk. She had to take back some of her natural weight, but not too much. She did not want to drop on Bainter's head. Then she'd certainly share whatever terrible fate Rose was being dragged to.

'...the stones are under the snow,' Bainter was saying. 'This is the proper place for the oblation.'

The leafless branches offered little cover. Amy tried not to make a sound so Ponce wouldn't look up. Her frosted breath came back at her face.

She was close enough to see Bainter talking with two other people. He kept a grip on Rose, one big hand around both her wrists. Beauty wasn't struggling. She might have swooned or been drugged. Amy hoped the girl was shamming and biding her time.

'He's right,' said a woman – a woman! – 'this is where we should be. My calculations…'

'Pah,' said a man. 'I believe what I can see. I see snow. Not stone.'

The woman's voice was distinctive – metallic and shrill enough to hurt. She wasn't one of the mistresses.

'I tell you, we are here,' said Bainter.

Ponce's confederates wore hoods. They must have come in the car.

Amy's knee-grip went wonky. She had an uneasy moment, but held fast. She was more stick insect than moth at the moment.

The man who believed only what he saw wore a familiar hood, with a red flame on the forehead. The chief of last term's Hooded Conspiracy…

…and almost certainly her friend's father!

How near was Kali? Would she recognise him from his voice?

The woman was a tubby, barrel-shaped person. Her tweed hood matched her Norfolk jacket and stiff skirt. She didn't seem the sort Kali's father would take for an umpteenth bride.

Bainter had put on a hood – purple silk, with a tassel on top. Embroidered tears dripped from one eyehole.

So, the Hooded Conspiracy reached the Staff Room?

Amy's mind raced. Who else might be in on it? Not Gryce – she'd cast out the Crowninshield sisters for associating with Hoods. Unless that had been a cunning ploy to cast off suspicion. Bainter was in the ascendant this term, with the relative scarcity of sightings of Headmistress. He was very pro-Black Skirt.

Black Skirts and Hood Heads? Together?

Amy felt sick… which, considering her position, was inconvenient as well as uncomfortable. Her tummy roiled.

She missed what was being said.

Red Flame clapped grey-gloved hands. A chauffeur got out of the car.

'Get on with it, Gogoth,' he said.

Gogoth – if that actually was a name – wore a peaked cap over a stiff, shiny black mask which pushed out in the middle like a snout. Something was wrong with the chauffeur's backbone, which seemed to be a zig-zag. He cleared away snow with an entrenching tool.

'Careful, it is forbidden to treat the sacred sites with disrespect,' cautioned Bainter. 'Procedures must be followed. There are consequences for blasphemy.'

The spade scraped flint and struck blue sparks. The chauffeur had uncovered paving stones set in a round pattern, like a clock or an astronomical chart. Looking at it from above, Amy's eye was drawn to spiral grooves she found oddly fascinating – as if she were being pulled towards the centre of the design.

She was reminded of her Purple dreams.

'Good job, Gogoth,' said Red Flame.

'Careful, or we'll all become oblations,' said Bainter. 'One simply doesn't trifle with the Other Ones.'

Amy had never heard of the Other Ones, but didn't like the sound of them. A good rule of thumb was not to trifle with groups who liked to be called the Anything Ones… the Old Ones, the Wicked Ones, the Deep Ones, the Comely Ones. All thoroughly bad lots.

Mrs Tweed had an implement with her, like an upside-down sextant with jewelled lenses. She stuck it close to her eyeholes and surveyed the stones.

'The inscription is clear,' she said. 'This is the Runnel. This is the Flute.'

'Bring over the Girl With the Face,' Red Flame ordered Bainter.

Rose stirred in her swoon and turned over in Bainter's grip. Amy saw she was making herself heavy and awkward to handle.

Clever girl.

Amy fixed her mind on Rose.

It struck her all in a flash that if she could move things without touching them, then she could also *prevent* them from being moved. Just by thinking.

She held Beauty. As she made herself light, Amy made Beauty heavy.

Bainter strained, as if he were trying to pull a nail out of a plank with his fingers. He hadn't expected resistance.

'What's the matter?' asked Mrs Tweed.

'She... won't... be... shifted.'

'Ridiculous,' said the woman. 'You're a milksop. Let me at her and I'll...'

She weighed in and fared no better than Bainter.

'This isn't natural,' she said. 'We're not alone.'

The hoods swivelled as the conspirators peered around. They didn't look up.

Kali must be lying flat in the snow. That wouldn't be comfortable.

'Not out there,' said Mrs Tweed. 'Down here. In the stones. It must be the Other Ones.'

'Why are they hindering the oblation, then?' said Bainter. 'Tell me that, eh?'

He was annoyed with the woman. Amy recognised his snippy, irritable tone from lessons. The chaplain must wish he could force Mrs Tweed to endure the Three Questions just now.

'Priest, if you've misinterpreted the inscriptions...' began Red Flame.

'Everything has been checked, over and over. We have the ideal oblation. This is the sacred site. The night is propitious. The Purple is stirring. And yet the girl won't be shifted a mere *six feet* to the Flute.'

'She doesn't *all* have to be shifted,' said Mrs Tweed. 'Cut off her face where she is and fetch it over. That's all we need.'

Shocked, Amy let go of Rose.

Equally shocked – and with more personal interest in not having her face cut off – Rose made a dash for it. Amy had seen Beauty outpace Goneril's best sprinters at Sport Day. None of the conspirators could catch her if it came to a race through the woods. Provided she didn't run smack into a tree or trip over Kali. As she disappeared into the night, she shrugged out of her inhibiting coat.

'After her, Gogoth,' ordered Red Flame.

Amy twisted Beauty's cast-off coat between the crookback's legs. Gogoth fell face forwards in a tangle.

Mrs Tweed made a sound of disgust.

Red Flame drew a revolver from out of his jacket.

'Don't shoot... she has to be *alive* when we do it,' said Ponce. 'She has to *know* what is being taken from her. It's what she *feels* about her loss of face as much as the physical skin and blood that makes up the oblation. She has to *survive* this for the Flute to stay open.'

Amy decided the Reverend Mr Bainter was worse than a white slaver.

'But I can shoot *you*,' said Red Flame, 'just to make

a point. If I were to take your nose off, you'd feel great loss and we'd have the flesh and blood.'

'I'm not an unspoiled child,' said Bainter. 'I'm not a rare creature, whose shape here and in the Purple is perfection. I'm not the Girl with the Face. And neither are you. Nor is the Professor. I have doubts about Gogoth too.'

'Pah,' said Red Flame – who seemed fond of the exasperated exclamation – as he put his pistol away.

Mrs Tweed – Professor Tweed, to go by what Bainter said – manipulated her strange device, folding and telescoping attachments. It fit over her hand like a spiny gauntlet.

'Gogoth,' she said. 'Here!'

She talked to the chauffeur as if she were calling a dog to heel, but Gogoth unwound the coat from his legs, got up and walked over – shoulders hitching as if his bones were rolling the wrong way – as meekly as any trained pet. Amy had a feeling she wouldn't want to see under his mask.

'Hand and arm,' said the Professor.

Gogoth rolled up his sleeve. He had odd, elaborate tattoos – intertwining snakes or dragons or tendrils or tentacles. Shiny, reflective, strangely positioned eyes might be coloured glass sewn into the skin.

The Professor scratched across his tattoos with her device. Blades sliced almost to the bone and Gogoth yelped.

'Bleed,' she ordered, somewhat superfluously.

Blood – blacker than red – gushed from the ruined tattoo and spattered the flagstone circle. Some fell into the spiral groove – the Runnel – and ran towards a cup-like depression in the centre. That must be the Flute.

Gogoth made a fist of bandaging himself with

a handkerchief. The other conspirators practically bumped hoods over the Flute. They mumbled something like a chant...

The words were different – not English, and perhaps not even human – but the rhythm was all too familiar.

Dum-dum-dee-dum... dumdee-dumdee Dum...

Ants in your pants... all the way from France.

The rivulet of blood reached the Flute and there was a small crackle, like tame lightning...

...and Rose, running full tilt, came out of the night and charged into Bainter's arms! The Professor and Red Flame laid hands on her too.

Whatever ritual they had performed had turned the girl around. Or turned the woods around.

Bainter sat on Rose, pinning her down. Her head was over the Flute. The Professor adjusted her razor-gauntlet again. Amy guessed she was preparing to lift Beauty's face from her skull.

Rose made keening noises in the back of her throat.

'That's right,' said the Professor. 'Make a fuss. We can't hear you, but the Other Ones can.'

Her implement buzzed and crackled. It generated or attracted some sort of electric charge.

Bainter and Red Flame kept up the chanting. The Hooded Conspiracy was on the point of making its ghastly oblation.

Beauty – soon to be the Girl Without the Face – kicked and struggled.

Amy let go of the tree and made herself heavy. She dived at Bainter.

She got her hands around his neck and twisted his hood so he couldn't see out of the eyeholes. She shoved him off Rose and into the shovelled pile of snow. The girls of R.I. would have cheered her for this.

Kicking and twisting, Amy shoved the Professor into Red Flame. The buzzing gauntlet shredded the shoulder of his coat and he shrieked. He went for his revolver again, but dropped it. The Professor, also flailing, kicked the gun away and blundered against the tree. Her glove apparatus sliced bark and lodged deep in the wood. She couldn't easily pull free.

Amy had her feet on the ground – she had pins and needles from hanging upside down too long, but tried to ignore the tingling and rubbery legs. She took Rose's hand and helped her up.

She hoped they could run back to School and out of range of the Runnel and the Flute before the conspirators could recover and work their bleeding trick a second time. Rose didn't waste breath asking who her rescuer was. Then again, she couldn't ask if she'd wanted to.

However, the girls only got a few strides away from the circle.

Gogoth barred their way. He had stopped bleeding. The snout of his mask went in and out. His eyes were fixed on them and his arms were spread.

They would have to split up and run in different directions.

No, that wouldn't work. He'd grab Beauty and the de-facing would be on schedule again.

A branch swung out of the darkness and slammed into the chauffeur's head. He staggered and fell. A triangular, brown-and-white mask loomed in the night.

Oleander Hawkmoth had struck!

Kali tossed away the branch. She applied Kafiristani foot-boxing techniques to the fallen man. In that discipline, the most devastating blows were made with the instep.

Amy and Rose made a start into the woods.

'Stop,' shouted someone ahead – Red Flame!

He'd scooped up his revolver and circled round. He had them cold.

Only his coat was damaged. White shirt showed through the rents. He walked carefully towards the girls.

Amy tried to get a mental grip on him but was too distracted. She hovered a foot off the ground, but her other Abilities were exhausted.

Kali was closest to Red Flame…

…*her father!*

He took aim at her mask.

His hood had come loose and been torn. His chin and mouth showed. He had very white teeth and a very black, distinctive beard.

Kali must know by now who he was.

'You don't understand what you're doing,' he said. 'This has been set down as inevitable, long before any of us were born. It is important. For us, this is religion… a sacred duty.'

'Then why not ask for volunteers?' asked Amy.

Red Flame shook his head and smiled wryly.

'A girl with no voice can't speak up,' he explained.

'You cut off girls' faces,' said Amy. 'That's not religion. That's *poppycock*!'

Red Flame thumbed back the hammer of his revolver.

Kali stood stock still, arms out to her sides.

'You were there before,' Red Flame said to Amy. 'In the tower. You're the butterfly girl.'

She didn't correct him.

'What do you think you're doing out of bounds,

dressed foolishly, wearing *masks*...?'

This was a bit rich, coming from inside a hood.

'Give me the Girl with the Face,' said Red Hood. 'Or I shoot this one.'

Rose, not exactly happy about it, was still prepared to hand herself over. Amy knew Kali wouldn't let that happen.

Slowly, Kali raised her arms – assuming a fighting stance.

'Stop that,' said Red Flame, shaking his gun.

He must recognise what Kali was doing. Amy remembered the bandit rajah had been his daughter's foot-boxing teacher – so he could probably beat her even without a weapon.

The fierceness and bravery of the hawkmoths was well known, but...

Amy tried to get a grip on Red Flame's hand. If only she could hold back his trigger finger. She wobbled in the air and landed... the limits of her Abilities were exceeded.

She might as well have been an Ordinary.

Kali's fingers reached behind her head.

Red Flame seemed puzzled.

'Be still, silly chit,' he said.

Kali took off her mask and hat. Her black hair shook out.

Red Flame, shocked, discharged his revolver... but wildly, up into the air.

He cried out and hung his head in shame. Amy hadn't expected that.

Kali said something to her father in a foreign language...

...and Amy ran, Rose keeping pace with her.

Kali caught up with them.

'Them rats won't be on our tails now,' she said.

They slowed down, not needing to risk slamming into a tree, and walked back to School. Amy grew aware of the bitter cold and the lateness of the hour. They'd missed Lights Out and would be Majored if whips caught them. She ached in her shoulders, her hands, her legs and her head. And still had a troubled stomach.

Outside Old House, Rose placed her open hand on her chest and then on theirs.

Heartfelt thanks.

She went upstairs to the Fifth Floor.

Amy and Kali, masks off, were alone together.

'Kali, I should have said before…'

'Yeah, I know,' said her friend, eyes as dark as her father's. 'But you didn't.'

X: Ugly Winter

LATER IN FEBRUARY, nightly snowfall slacked off…
but the cruel cold went on and on. School no longer
resembled a Christmas card. Merry robins were in
short supply. If any popped beaks out of their nests to
chirrup, they'd be stiff, frosty corpses in an instant. The
jolly round cheeks of Father Christmas fell off to show
the sharp, malicious skullface of Jack Frost.

By day, under thin sunlight, the top layer of snow
melted. Icicle spears detached from eaves, as if aimed
at unwary souls passing underneath. At dusk, the
temperature plummeted. Slush froze into ridged, sooty
ice-crust. Captain Freezing still regularly returned from
the dead, more muck-monster than snowman. There
was no guessing where he'd appear.

Salt winds blew off the sea like razors. Everyone
had red-rimmed eyes, made worse by rubbing. Out
of doors, Amy took to wearing her Goosey Gander
goggles – until she ran into Brydges. The formerly
reasonable Viola whip, now a fanatic Black Skirt,
confiscated the offending item and scratched a stain
in Amy's Time-Table Book. Inappropriate Eyewear.
A Murdering Heathen of *École de Gryce* would have

snaffled the goggles for her own use, but let Amy off the Minor. The new, humourless breed of tyrant lacked the piratical flair of the cutthroats of yesterterm. Amy was forced to concede she preferred the affably corrupt to the horribly moral.

Black Skirts went about in threes – with no more than two from a single House or Form. This meant no two could dispute rulings from on high without the third informing on the apostates. Those who joined because they fancied a change of clothes or thought skipping might see off the cold found themselves buying the rest of the parcel. They weren't supposed to talk about 'the rest of the parcel' with outsiders. Black Skirts on the prowl for recruits hinted at privileges, inner circles and wonders, but Amy understood the top Black Skirts had ruthless ways of keeping the rank and file in line. No one who went Black ever came back to Grey.

The Folk Dancing Society, an obscure activities club populated mostly by Viola Fourths, was first to institute a Black Only policy. Wychwood, leading light of the FDS, couldn't go Black if she wanted to. Her parents stubbornly refused to open the parental purse for non-essential expenses. Amy understood how that worked. Wychwood made a hash of dyeing her blazer and skirt in the Chem Lab, which stuck her with a Major Uniform Infraction. Despite deft figures and flings, she was chucked out of the FDS. Condemned to walk between the winds like a mutilated Red Indian brave, she served as grim warning to those who refused to meet the (climbing) price set by Dosson, Chappell & Co.

After prep one night, Amy went back to her cell to find Frecks sporting full Black. She was looking herself up and down in the mirror inside her wardrobe door. Though cut from the same pattern, the black blazer seemed tighter in the waist than the grey. The glossy material caught the light. Dark rainbows rippled across Frecks' lapels.

Kali lolled on her bed in green silk pajamas, chewing gum and reading *Black Mask*. She looked away as Amy stepped into the room. Since the unmasking of Red Flame, Kali and Amy were on the outs. Amy felt lasting, urgent shame, but was also ticked off with her friend. Kali made no attempt to see things from Amy's point of view. Really, what was she supposed to do? She had only *suspected* Kali's father. It wasn't until the skirmish over Beauty at the Runnel and the Flute that she'd known *for certain* he was up to his beard in the Hooded Conspiracy. Besides, Kali was always going on about how she would bump off the old man when she had the chance. It wasn't as if she didn't believe him complicit in all manner of wickedness, not least the death of her mother. Still, Amy nagged herself, uselessly…

She should have told Kali her father was behind her kidnapping.

Then they'd still be friends.

Frecks going Black wasn't going to help dissipate the poisonous atmosphere either.

Light Fingers sat in her rocking chair, embroidering a green shawl with moth-wing patterns. She rocked harder than usual, repeatedly stabbing the cloth with her tiny needle as if she were doing it harm. The chair had a creak which became a whine if Light Fingers was in a mood.

'It's just new kit,' said Frecks, raising her voice over the rocking. 'Not as if I'm going to take up skipping like a loon. Though I could do with shedding some of this unwanted avoirdupois.'

Frecks had been sold on Black when Martine of the Fourth, one of Desdemona's first converts, said it was slimming. Frecks was infected with the belief she was growing thick in the midriff. The notion had been maliciously planted by the cunning Viscount Ralph. Frecks had spent a martyr's Christmas spurning the mince pies, plum pudding and chocolate bon-bons her brother cruelly scoffed in front of her.

Now, she smoothed her shiny skirt tight across her hips and was satisfied.

'...and, one thing you have to say for the Black Skirts is...'

The whining creak stopped. Light Fingers tossed her embroidery aside and pushed out of the cell.

'I don't know,' said Frecks. 'Some people are getting tetchy-touchy...'

'In spades, sister,' said Kali, glaring pointedly at Amy.

Black might not make Frecks look thinner, but she was more commanding in her new uniform. Amy saw how her friend was changing. After leaving School, she would be reborn. Debutantes didn't have names like Frecks. When presented at court, she'd be Lady Serafine.

A stunner, but cold.

And Kali was a princess. Her people owned palaces and commanded hordes when the forebears of Alexandra Vansittart and Sidonie Gryce were painted blue and living in mud huts. She would be a bandit empress.

Lips red as blood could easily look like lips red with blood.

The cell had been cosy, not just for its small fire, piles of quilts and the scent of Kali's herbal gaspers... but for the warmth of shared friendship. That seemed to be chilling. No daring night-rescue or flight into masked adventure could put magic oil back in a broken lamp. The Moth Club was in danger of dissolving.

'I'll go and see what's the matter,' Amy said.

'As you please,' said Frecks, distracted by the way the sharp shadow of her tilted hat brought out the sparkle in her eye. 'Any de-wettening of the blanket would be appreciated.'

Amy went out into the passageway.

The low, soft patter of the skipping rhyme came from Inchfawn's cell. Surely, there was no jumping in there? She looked through the open door. Inchfawn and Frump sat on a bed, patting themselves and each other in a complicated pattern while reciting the 'ants in your pants' mantra. Both were Black Skirts.

Shivering, Amy passed on.

Light Fingers was at the end of the corridor, by a window, face turned away. In the dark reflection, her cheeks were wet.

'Emma,' said Amy…

Christian names were little-used at Drearcliff – saved for moments of intimacy. This seemed to qualify.

Light Fingers knuckled away her tears and turned.

They hugged quickly. Amy knew what the trouble was.

'They don't even see it,' she said. 'Frecks and Kali. For them, it's just a new hat. They don't mean anything by it.'

'The Black Skirts don't have Unusuals,' said Light Fingers.

Amy was startled. She hadn't thought of that.

Besides, it wasn't altogether true. 'What about Rayne? She started this, and she's… certainly not Ordinary.'

'But is she really an Unusual? Or something else entirely?'

Amy agreed. There needed to be a new phylum for Rayne. She didn't fit into the way things had been. She'd changed School, as she said she would. A terrifying achievement. How had it happened, with the whips and Swan and Tradition and the Rules all against her?

What *was* Antoinette Rowley Rayne?

'There *are* Unusuals in Black,' said Amy, remembering. 'Gould of the Fourth. With the fur and fangs.'

'She wants to be Ordinary, though – the way your mother wants you to be. If Gould could give it up, she would. Before you came, she rowed with Headmistress. From Fourth Form on, Unusuals take personal tuition with Swan. You've heard her talk about her cygnets. We're like an invisible House, spread across the five you can see...'

This was news to Amy. Sometimes, she forgot how much she'd missed by not being at Drearcliff since the First Form.

'Gould denied her Attributes and Abilities and swallowed all the Infractions the whips could stain her with, but still didn't give in. She files her nails and shaves where she can, though there's not much she can do about the teeth. She had an epic bust-up with Marsh last year, which started when she called Marsh a "fish-fluke". Gould trounced her on the beach, scratching and biting, but Gill Girl dragged her into the sea and nearly drowned her. The Black Skirts make Gould Ordinary, the way they make Frecks thin or Inchfawn not a pariah.'

'Frecks *is* thin.'

'Not in her head, where it counts.'

Light Fingers was more rattled than Amy had thought.

'When Mum and Dad got nabbed,' her friend said,

'I saw what Ordinaries were really like. You've heard Headmistress's speech about her cygnets. The Unusual Girls of Drearcliff. Our place in the magnificent century. She's right, in part. Some of us will turn out like the Aviatrix, Ghost Lantern Girl or that prig Blackfist. Biffing rotters, kissing babies and worshipped like little Gods.'

Amy understood why Light Fingers was cynical.

'We're not all *nice people*,' she continued. 'We're no better than anyone. I think even approved Unusuals are just afraid. They make a show of being helpful and vigilant against lawbreakers because they know what'd happen to them otherwise. Jail is just the start of it. My parents didn't do much harm, but got slapped down hard. Swan happily witters on about Lucinda Tregellis-d'Aulney, Grace Ki and Monica Bright. She's less keen on bringing up Ligeia Theleme, Mary Mourdur or the Slink.'

Amy knew who all these women were.

'They're Drearcliff Old Girls too, Amy. They were *cygnets* once. The Slink got the better of Dr Shade when that airship crashed into Mount St Michael – no matter what the papers say. Her real name is Molly Whittle. Desdemona House Captain in 1913. Same year Shiner Bright was Head Girl. They're in the class photograph together. They were *friends*. The Slink slept in our dorm, Amy! Now, she's the Most Wanted Woman in the World. They'll never catch her! She's like Jimmy O'Goblins, Anthony Zenith or Sally Nikola's father. Unusuals who don't try to please anyone but themselves. The ones they're afraid of. I *don't* want to be like them, I don't even want to be like Mum and Dad… but what if they don't give us a choice?'

'Who won't give us a choice?' asked Amy.

'The *Ordinaries*. Seeing inside their minds drove

Imogen Ames out of hers, you know. The vile things she told me... even about my friends, *our friends*. I didn't want to believe her then. Now I know it's all true. Abilities didn't make Ames happy.'

'...and it shouldn't make us miserable! That was her, not us. Besides, like I said, Frecks and Kali only see new hats and socks that pass for stockings. They're not going to take up skipping... and, if they did, what harm could it do? It began as a craze in *Viola*, remember? Something for *wets* and *babies*. As soon as spring comes along, the kerfuff will pass and Rayne'll be on her own again.'

Light Fingers shook her head, sadly wise. 'It's not skipping, Amy. It's *drill*.'

Amy shivered. Light Fingers had seen it too.

'D'you know why armies make soldiers march up and down? Whole regiments of men doing the same pointless thing at the same time?'

'For parades.'

'No. It's so that they can fight as one man. A lot of bodies. One purpose. To conquer, to kill, to devour. Like...?'

'Ants,' Amy said.

'Exactly,' Light Fingers said. 'Like *soldier ants*.'

XI: Becoming a Ghost

EVERY DAY, SCHOOL grew blacker. Those three-girl Black Skirt clusters – or larger groups, six or nine or even twelve – were everywhere, on patrol. The Gym and the Quad were given over entirely to skipping groups. The 'ants in your pants' chant was a constant thrum. Amy didn't even consciously hear it any more, but *felt* it in her stomach, her bones, her teeth. Like the weather, the skipping continued well after its exhaustion as a topic of conversation.

Should Amy number herself among the living ghosts of Drearcliff Grange? Along with Inchfawn, Palgrave, the Crowninshield sisters, Shrimp Harper and Dora Paule? Not expelled, but shunned.

These ghosts had broken the Code of Break. If anything, the unofficial rules were more exacting and merciless. Infractions weren't forgotten after a Heel-scrubbing or ten transcribed encyclopaedia pages. The stain would stay with a girl for her whole school life and beyond. Transgressors were as dead. The Crowninshields knocked about together. Palgrave and Shrimp were so peculiar they'd had no friends to lose. Paule walked her path uncaring and insensible, secretly

Head Girl of the Purple yet ignored on this Earth.

However, Rayne changed even this.

Inchfawn and the Crowninshields went Black and their sins were washed away and forgotten... except by Greys, and they didn't count. Amy saw Inchfawn and a newly Black Smudge together in the library, doing History prep. Smudge *knew* about Inchfawn, knew *for a fact* what she had done, but could now fib even to herself and let the traitor back in. All Black Skirts together and no mention of the past – like in the French Foreign Legion or General Flitcroft's Regiment of the Damned.

The Black Skirts would not take Amy.

Which was as she wanted it, only every day there were more of them. Amy had to give up Miss Borrodale's monthly Arthropod Discussion Group when it went Black Only. Like Digger Downs and Ponce Bainter, Fossil had an ant-badge pinned to her gown, signifying alignment with the Black Skirts. In lessons, the remaining Greys went unnoticed... carelessly marked down on prep, never called to speak. Amy's arm hurt from holding up her hand often and long without being asked to speak.

The ways of the Staff were mysterious and beyond understanding, but Amy sensed the schism had invaded the teachers' common-room. Miss Kaye and Miss Borrodale, youngest of the mistresses, had been friends last term, but now sat apart. Each was brittle when the other was mentioned. Amy reckoned Miss Kaye disposed to the Grey, but feared she was isolated. Eventually, Mrs Edwards would return and Miss Kaye's spell at Drearcliff would be over.

Headmistress was seen only in Chapel and then chose not to speak.

Bainter sermonised often about the bold, electric spirit sweeping School and how fine a thing it was. Amy remembered his eagerness to cut off a girl's face and seethed whenever she saw him. Had he recognised her behind the mask of Kentish Glory? He had seen Kali's face that night and it wasn't exactly a secret that Amy shared a cell with her. Thwarting ghastly sacrifice in the woods hadn't checked the inexorable rise of Ponce Bainter. Red Flame and the Professor – whoever she might be – were still in the game somewhere, and Amy had nightmares about 'the Other Ones'. Bainter and the Hooded Conspirators knew something about the Purple, but she didn't think they'd ever been there – which put her one up on them. She had no one to talk with about her worries. Kali shut up when she tried to raise the matter. Beauty was mute and now wore Black. Was the conversion her way of assuring she wasn't dragged back to the Runnel and the Flute?

Bainter droned on from the lectern.

Dr Swan sat tight-lipped throughout his infernal nonsense. Amy didn't understand the shift of power. Surely, Headmistress was unassailable? Keys – who wore an ant badge – served as gate-keeper, warding off petitions of complaint. Amy felt bitterly let down. Swan was supposed to be High Priestess of the Unusuals. How could she let this Black Skirt thing take hold?

Or was Rayne the Most Unusual of All?

Rayne went around as if she were still on her tour of inspection, as if she'd bought the school. Miss Kaye let slip that the non-Black Skirt teachers referred to the girl as 'demi-Napoleon' so Amy wasn't the only one who had noticed. Rayne was always flanked by short, stout, earnest Rintoul and tall, slim, droll Beeke.

If Rayne was the Queen Ant, Prompt and Beeke were Chancellor and Jester.

Amy thought again about *Boney*. The concept of a personal Boney. It had struck her before that Rayne might be hers.

Queen Ant against Kentish Glory.

Rayne's triad was usually accompanied by a three-girl praetorian guard. The Cerberus. Henry Buller was dog-head in the middle. Either side were Gould and Crowninshield II. Gould let her nails grow out. Crowninshield II did tricks with a skipping rope. Even whips daren't cross the Cerberus. A week after refusing to make the Star-Gazing Society Black Only, Miss Bedale suddenly quit Drearcliff. Word went round that a visit from the Cerberus persuaded her to pack her bags.

One Tuesday in late February, while hurrying down to breakfast, Amy saw de Vere, wearily trudging out to destroy yet another incarnation of Captain Freezing. As the Sixth's lonely campaign dragged on like the Thirty Years War, her supporters had fallen away. Amy assumed everyone had decided to leave de Vere and the Captain to their private duel. Only, this morning de Vere met the Cerberus returning from their own snowman-smashing expedition. Buller had the Captain's shako speared on a hockey stick. Gould gnashed her fangs around his oversized carrot-nose. Crowninshield dragged a prisoner, trussed up with skipping ropes.

Dilys Frost, a Desdemona Fifth. Her cell-mates called her the Frost.

It transpired that the captured girl was an Unusual who had been raising Captain Freezing from the dead every night. The Frost could command snow to stand up by itself and take shape. Apparently, her Ability was for manipulating ice, not making it – so the trick only came into play in winter.

The name should have been a tell-tale, Amy supposed. Tearful at being found out, the Frost claimed the Captain was as much to blame as she. He called to her in dreams, demanding she use her peculiar sympathy with ice and snow to summon him again and again. She tried to say sorry to her House Sister, but was met with a flinty glare. The battle had exhausted them both.

The Frost had begun the term with a white dash in her dark hair. The streak spread with each new incarnation of the Captain. Now her hair was almost completely white, with a dark dash.

The next day, de Vere went Black. Frost – lumbered with a Major Infraction that was almost an afterthought – was shunned even by Greys, even by Unusuals.

'They want us to be alone,' Light Fingers told Amy after Lights Out, whispering so Frecks and Kali wouldn't hear. 'Each of us, alone. Like Shrimp Harper. Like Daffy Dora. Like the Frost.'

Amy lay in her bed, unable to sleep, on the verge of floating. She imagined she was pinned down by tight bands across her chest. Her head ached and she couldn't stop thinking.

She was fed up with Light Fingers going on and on as if pitchfork-and-torch mobs were coming for Unusuals in the next five minutes. But she also hotly resented Frecks' casual assurance that the Black Skirt thing was nothing to fuss over and Kali's meaningful, lazy-lidded cold shouldering. She hated that she and her friends were at daggers drawn. She wished people wouldn't keep doing foolish things which made bad situations worse.

The Black Skirts were smug about their triumph. The Cerberus were heroines, even to girls they had picked on for years. Frost looked like a monster.

The Frost had driven de Vere crackers. Girls like her needed to be reined in before they became the next Slink or Adept Mother Theleme. By being selfish or stupid, Unusuals could make the pogrom Light Fingers was obsessed with much more likely. The ice-witch's explanation for Captain Freezing was generally ignored. Most Ordinaries thought Frost just wouldn't own up, but Amy wasn't sure. An Ability could be like a different creature, nestled inside the mind, forever seeking freedom to run riot. Shrimp couldn't help sucking the air out of a room. Marsh felt the call of the sea in her gills. Though she'd deny it now, Gould's claws sharpened and bled when the moon grew full.

Paule was more and more in the Purple. She wandered about School, muttering as if trying to learn a complicated mnemonic. At Break, she picked up a train of Firsts and Seconds who tried to tease or taunt her with chants or impertinent questions. When Amy saw this, she shooed the pests away. Like midges, they swarmed back again. Paule, poor thing, didn't seem to notice, either her tormentors or her rescuer. With Gryce a spent force, her former pet was safe game for vengeance-seeking victims of the Murdering Heathens. Amy suspected Paule could, if she put her whole mind to it, be more dangerous than Frost or Harper. If she ever woke up angry, she might whisk all the midges off to the Purple to be supper for the realm's unimaginable denizens.

When Amy was older, how would she cope with her insistent Abilities? She envisioned herself trying to keep her shoes on the ground while the voice of Kentish

Glory fluttered in her ear, urging her to take off. The clouds could call too, like the sea or the moon or the Purple or Frost's snowman. Just ask Captain Skylark, the Aviatrix or the Aerial Knights of Avalon. Amy Thomsett might just be the protective colouration of Kentish Glory.

Was she a girl who acted like a moth or a moth disguised as a girl?

Could she become dangerous? She had thought of herself swooping to rescue urchins from burning orphanages. Now, she wondered if she might float over high walls and drop incendiary bombs. If more subtle wrongdoing was her lot, she could eavesdrop from above on secret conversations and sell information to the highest bidder. And there was the other side of her Abilities, the one she dreaded practising because it hurt – making things beside herself float or sink. Could she make people come unstuck and get lost in the sky? Lift treasures out of vaults and tug them along as if they were paper kites?

She didn't *want* to be a death's-head moth, but if the world went Black Only would she have a choice? Such visions terrified her. She drifted in and out of terror-dreams, and was sweaty and sickly in the morning.

'Off your colour, old thing,' Frecks observed. 'You should brighten up a bit.'

Amy hid under bedclothes while Frecks, in her singlet, did her daily arm-swinging, shoulders-back exercises. This rigmarole was supposed to enhance the figure.

'I must, I must, I must improve my bust...'

Another blasted rhyme. Amy groaned until she could bear it no longer and got up to face another dreary, chilly day as a living ghost.

One day, Kali was a full Black Skirt too. She and Frecks needed a third for their triad. They took on Rose.

Beauty might have gone Black for protection against the Hooded Conspiracy, or out of gratitude to Kali. She had thanked both her rescuers... but didn't know who Kentish Glory was under the mask. By showing her face, Kali positioned herself to take all the credit – though Amy didn't for a moment believe her friend had intended that.

Beauty as a Black Skirt was striking. A tide of change surged through the House in imitation. Within days, Desdemona was two-thirds gone. It would have been a worse blackwash, but for the higher incidence of Wychwoodism than in other Houses – girls who would go Black, but couldn't raise the funds.

Amy approached Rose outside the dorm, hoping against hope to bring her back to Grey. It was perverse of Beauty to join the movement Bainter so vocally supported. She tried to frame her argument and opened her mouth to speak, but Rose walked past without acknowledging her existence.

Of course, she didn't recognise Amy out of her Kentish Glory guise.

Her loveliness changed character. The gentleness was gone. Black Rose was strong, imperious, commanding, magnificent. Smaller girls followed her, mouths lolling in awe. Triads nodded respect as if she were Rayne herself. Beauty seemed less tragic – not a girl who couldn't talk, but a girl who refused to talk. Amy hoped Rose was safe now – the Black Skirts should protect her from Bainter, far better than the Moth Club could. But she was disappointed in the girl she had rescued. If this was where Rose went afterwards, what was the point of saving her? Amy was upset with herself for having such a mean, unworthy thought, then with everyone else, for driving her to the point where she let herself down. The poison got everywhere, including into her head.

Light Fingers took to bunking off lessons with ant-badge teachers. She earned so many absence Infractions the House Captain had her up for a stern talking-to. When her friend came back to the cell, Amy asked Light Fingers what Pelham had to say.

'Typical Ordinary bushwah,' responded Light Fingers. 'Letting School down, letting House down, et cetera. Buck up your ways and hold fast to the path of righteousness and whatnot.'

Light Fingers gave a strong impression that she did not intend to buck up or hold fast. So far as she was concerned, the rest of School was wrong. She was the lone martyr of righteousness.

Creepily, this reminded Amy of Rayne.

'We have to be ready for a scrap, Amy,' Light Fingers insisted. 'With anyone, any gang. Think it through, work it out. Don't rely too much on Abilities. They don't make us unbeatable. The Ordinaries are happy to send their pet Unusuals after us. Bloody Blackfist and the like. Dad taught me stage magic is all preparation. So is War. If the Cerberus were set after you, what could you do? If you were pinned to the ground and couldn't float, how would you get away?'

Amy was nervous of thinking like that.

'You know what happens to moths who aren't prepared,' Light Fingers said, jabbing her finger at Amy's chest. 'Stuck through with a pin.'

Light Fingers stalked off.

'What's up with Mrs Huffy Cow?' Frecks asked cheerily. 'The gin run out again?'

At least Frecks still talked to Amy… though being with Kali and Rose took up more and more of her time.

The next day in Chem, Miss Borrodale noted Naisbitt absent. Amy was without a lab partner for an experiment with essential salts. There were no spare Greys to pair her up with, so Fossil had her sit at the back of the room conning the periodic table while the rest of the class made stinks. Kali and Frecks concocted an exemplary explosion. Hoare-Stevens was in the Infirmary with a chest cold, but her lab chum – the deeply Black Peebles Arbuthnot – was permitted to attempt the experiment on her own and even awarded a high mark for her pathetic fizzle. Amy had no doubt she'd be marked down.

She was annoyed with Light Fingers, but was beginning to see her point. Why attend only to be ignored, passed over or discriminated against? Frecks sympathised in a glassy-eyed, cheerily perfunctory sort of way. Amy had noticed a lot of that lately, but it stung worst from her cell-mate.

Light Fingers turned up for English Composition with Miss Kaye, but had nothing to say for herself. She plonked down at her desk and dug out her composition book. She asked for a lend of a pen-nib from Frecks, who opened her pencil box and selected an old one she could spare.

Where did Light Fingers go when she was bunking off? Were other Greys ducking out of Black Skirt-run lessons? Other Unusuals?

Amy felt isolated. Light Fingers had not only proved her point but unwittingly gone along with the master plan she was complaining about.

This was getting ridiculous.

Inchfawn stuck up her hand to ask if the class could sit according to uniform colour rather than register name. Miss Borrodale had set a precedent, reassigning laboratory benches to favour Black Skirts. Miss Kaye shushed the suggestion, declaring herself happy with the arrangement that had served School since its founding.

An insectile chittering of disapproval started. Miss Kaye raised an eyebrow.

'Miss Bedale wouldn't let Black Skirts sit together,' said Inchfawn, loud enough to be heard. 'Now she's not in School.'

'That's quite enough of that,' said Miss Kaye.

Her ruling was accepted. For now.

Light Fingers shrugged in an 'I told you so' sort of way.

Amy felt sicker.

XII: A Summons to the House Captain's Study

WHILE AMY WAS alone in the cell, working on her Book of Moths, Gawky Gifford came to the door. Gawky, a notorious cadger, said she knew something she would share if Amy spared a farthing. Amy paid up and the First told her a letter had been put in her pigeon-hole. Gawky haunted the hallway and knew who received anything. Amy was out of the habit of checking for post, since the service was still irregular.

Another of Desdemona's Stuck-in-Greys, Gawky made herself useful for a price. She was saving up for her Black uniform. Amy was dubious about supporting Gifford's ambition, but the impecunious girl showed the Drearcliff spirit – if only in the way the Slink did School proud during Ascot Opening Week when she stole the Duchess of Cluster's famous pearls, replacing them with a string of boiled sweets sucked down to the proper size.

Amy tossed Gawky another farthing to fetch the letter. The First had anticipated the commission. She produced the letter from behind her back and retreated. Opening the envelope, Amy found a note from Pelham. She was invited to call on the House Captain at her earliest convenience.

Pelham had a cell to herself. It was more like a study, with the bed in a curtained alcove. A decent fire kept the room pleasantly toasty. The House Captain sat in a large wicker chair, wearing a red silk dressing gown and smoking a cig in an ivory holder. Her fringe-curls were in presses and her scarlet lipstick made a perfect heart-shape.

A Russian samovar simmered on rails over the fire. Nancy 'Poppet' Dyall, the Second who acted as the House Captain's bonded servant, served tea and biscuits.

Poppet might be an Unusual. She seemed uncommonly pretty when you looked straight at her, but unremarkable in retrospect. Amy experimented, glancing at the girl and then away. It was true: when she was in view, Dyall was fascinating, even beguiling… but if Amy looked somewhere else in the room, the impression popped like a soap bubble. Out of Poppet's company, Amy wouldn't be able to describe her or draw a picture. What colour was her hair? Was her face oval or round? Was her complexion pale or rosy? Amy wasn't even sure Dyall showed the same face all the time. What did Dora Paule make of Poppet? Maybe the Second's true face could only be seen through the prism of the Purple.

Amy thanked Pelham for the tea, and dunked a finger-biscuit. She left it too long and the biscuit came apart, turning into soggy blobby bits.

'Thanks everso for dropping by, Thomsett,' said Pelham. 'Must have you over more often, don't you know? You're a fine Desdemona gal, and no question about it. We don't rabbit on about tradition and achievement, the way other Houses do, but we're a proud lot, don't you know? Slow to ire, quick to finish and all. Sorts you'd go into the jungle with. Understand the Walmergrave girl took you under her wing last term. Good egg, that one. Will go far. Know her brother and he's a bit of all right and no mistake. Rides with the Blankney Hunt. Dashed rogue, but a good seat. Saw him blooded. Anyway, Thomsett, my dear... thought it was time we had a chat-ette. Nothing too formal. About the Naisbitt lass, primarily...'

Pelham whizzed her hands through the air, indicating that she knew about Light Fingers.

Pelham was a whip, though she'd never issued an Infraction. She preferred these little talking-tos, and had a decent record in setting girls straight. She'd persuaded Smudge to moderate her tale-spinnng, discouraged Knowles from using her Abilities in an underhand manner and convinced Martine not to elope with a bold mountain climber. But she'd not been able to get through to Light Fingers.

She must also be smarting that the Frost had got away with Captain Freezing for weeks without her noticing. De Vere and Pelham were best friends. Their uproarious escapades as Fourths were still spoken of in hushed, admiring tones after Lights Out.

Dyall was suddenly very near Amy, who sat on a stool so Pelham could look down on her. The servant took away her empty cup for refilling. Amy focused hard on her big eyes, small nose and... drew a blank when she was gone back to the fire, face turned away. Poppet's eyes were *huge*, she was sure... but what colour? Her hair was long and lustrous, and... nothing. Amy craned around. Now, Dyall was lit by the fire so her eyes and hair were red.

'...you're great chums with Naisbitt, Thomsett. See

if you can't get her to pull herself together. She's slipping and that's not what anyone wants. If you find out what ails her, all the better. Woes about the Ma and Pa are a distinct poss, though she's not the only Desdemona gal with a parent or two in jug. Poppet's Papa is in the Mausoleum, don't you know…'

Dyall nodded.

The Mausoleum – pronounced Maws-o-*lay*-um, for some reason – was the Special Prison. Amy had only heard of it because Light Fingers was worried her parents would be transferred there. It was on Egdon Heath, girded by dark magics and infernal devices. No one ever escaped from the Mausoleum, and precious few were released.

Who the blazes was Dyall's father?

Only the worst Unusuals were sent to the Mausoleum. Mary Mourdur, the Drearcliff Old Girl whose singing voice drove men to kill. She was gagged except for feeding times, then served only by women, who were immune to her death-siren's song. Valdemar Conquest, whose colossal plan had only been thwarted by the concerted efforts of Scotland Yard, the Splendid Six *and* Dr Shade. Isidore Persano and his Worm Unknown to Science. Potiphar Quesne, the Mad Magus of Liverpool.

'…anyhow, if you could give your chum a spot of talking-to, bring her round a bit… be much appreciated.'

Dyall was distracting. It wasn't just her face. Being around her for more than a minute or two blotted chunks of memory, even of things that had just happened or been said.

Amy worried she'd not heard half of Pelham's little chat.

Still, she got the gist…

Fixing on Dyall, she worried away at it – who was her father? Conquest, Quesne, Persano... the Worm? Some other unknown Unusual? Possibly even someone called Dyall?

Then Amy was outside on the landing, not sure whether she'd thanked House Captain for the tea. Her tongue was scalded, so she knew she'd drunk something hot... but couldn't recall if it was Russian or English, with or without milk.

The gaps were infuriating and unsettling. Was Pelham immune to Poppet? Or driven completely dotty, but somehow able to present a sane, sensible face to the world, don't you know and that's no mistake?

One thing Amy remembered. Hanging from Pelham's hat-hook was a black boater.

Not a good sign.

XIII: In the Playhouse

BEFORE SHE COULD administer the prescribed spot of talking-to, Amy had to find Light Fingers. No easy task. These days, her friend was only slightly more often seen than ffolliott-Absent. She was probably still in a mood to boot.

Amy spent her Breaks seeking admittance to far corners where girls clustered for nefarious purposes. Underground tournaments in dice and cards drew Fifths to the Kitchens, the Herbarium or the Photo Soc's Darkroom. Promissory notes and negotiable items passed back and forth as fortunes were won or lost. Besides taking bets, Nellie Pugh loaned sums of cash at exorbitant rates to gambling fiends. Wary of raids, the gaming hells were unwelcoming. Poking her head round doors earned Amy cold stares and pellet-peltings, as if she were Snitcher Garland spying for the whips. Warily and wearily, she stuck to her quest. She even floated a little, peeping through the occasional window.

Other secret places drew other categories of Infractor. Absalom and her disciples – the Ariel Seconds Frensham and Dace – met in the Sewing Room to plot the overthrow of capitalism by embroidering quotations from Marx and Kropotkin on handkerchiefs. Rather improbably, they had become a Black Skirt Triad overnight. Absalom claimed they were practising Trotskyist *entrisme*, though Amy was disappointed to find them skipping to the same rhyme as the rest of the ants. Phillips of the Fifth sold sweets, make-up and racy literature from her cell in the Tamora dorms. All Phillips' contraband was smuggled into School by baggy-trousered beaux she cultivated in town. Lately, with the snow, supplies were running low. Sally Nikola's Arcane Science Circle performed illicit experiments in makeshift laboratories, giving off loud bangs or puffs of foul-smelling, bright-coloured smoke.

Light Fingers wasn't in any of these hidey-holes.

After lunch, Amy tried the Drearcliff Playhouse. Traditional Viola territory, the theatre was now a Black Skirt nest... but Light Fingers knew the building intimately. She might seek sanctuary in the prop storage basements. It was worth a peep under the stage.

In the foyer, posters for the Mid-Winter Revue depicted Mansfield and Crawford as Scott of the Antarctic and Nanook of the North. The show was called *Poles Apart!* Judging from the illustration, it featured dancing penguins, the late unlamented Captain Freezing and something like a goggle-eyed cuttlefish exploding out of a husky's head with musical notes dotted all around. 'You'll shiver and shake – with merriment! Your teeth will chatter – from laughter! Nurse will be in attendance to sew up any split sides. May not be suitable for Firsts and those of a Nervous Disposition.'

The auditorium was empty and dark. Amy felt her way down the side-aisle towards the stage. She heard a humming, deep underground, and felt a vibration...

as if vast dynamos were whirring in the depths. A light moment came on her. Unable to see the floor, she found her feet weren't on it. Panic took hold. She staggered through the air, arms flapping... and fell badly, jarring her knees and the heels of her hands. She made a racket, which resounded in the theatre. Her heart raced and she took long moments to overcome her terror.

She *was* alone in the big, dark space. But not in the building.

Her eyes adjusted and she saw a little better. Just in front of the stage was a trapdoor. Amy took hold of the brass ring set in the floor and, lifting with her mind as well as her arms, raised the door a crack. Sound came out of the basements, and a rush of warmth...

Dum-dum-dee-dum... dumdee-dumdee Dum...

Ants in your pants... all the way from France.

Her heart sunk. She wasn't likely to find Light Fingers under this stage.

...but she felt compelled to lift the trap further, to see what was going on. She squeezed under the heavy door and took its weight on her shoulders, then went down a flight of steps, lowering it after her with a minimum of noise. Inadequate electric lights were strung over the stairs. The understage area smelled of paint, sawdust, stale make-up and dead flowers.

Lately, Amy kept her Kentish Glory mask about her at all times. She couldn't wear the whole uniform under her clothes – though she had thought of it, especially in this weather – but the mask rolled into a soft tube and fit into a customised inside pocket. Pulling her mask on, Amy felt instantly braver.

She also had to watch her step. Before its (temporary?) breakup, the Moth Club had experimented with eyeholes. Too small, and they severely limited peripheral vision (those Hooded Conspirators must be almost blinded); too big, and they gave away your identity – in which case what was the point of a mask? She wished she still had her confiscated goggles.

Spend three and fourpence… we're going to a dance!

Amy went towards the noise – the chanted rhyme and the beat of skipping.

The main cavern was hosting a Black Skirt rally. She kept to the shadows.

Clutter was tidied away or got rid of, changing the character of the vault. It was more like the hold of a warship than the innards of a theatre. Spotlights shone bright beams which cast stark shadows.

An unrolled backdrop hung on a rear wall. A painted plain of blasted trees and burned-out huts represented the aftermath of battle. The canvas was still stained with the arcs of stage blood overenthusiastically sloshed by Handsome Helena in her controversial *Grand Guignol* production of the Scottish Play. Girls still had nightmares about Vanity's Lady Macbeth, who – in an added business intended to 'beef up' the Bard – clawed out her eyes during the mad scene and tossed two poached eggs slathered in raspberry jam at the front row.

The skipping and chanting stopped dead. Amy thought she was discovered, but heads did not turn her way.

The Black Skirts were assembled before the Queen Ant.

Rayne sat on a huge throne used in history plays. Her feet dangled. Thirty or forty girls, mostly Violas, stood to attention in the cleared space. Arranged in order of size, titches at front and beanpoles at back.

Once ordinary girls – friend or foe or indifferent – but now part of the Black-Skirt army. Lapham, St Anne, Phair, Hone, Pulsipher, Stannard, Vail, Sundle, Dungate, Acreman, Brydges, Aire, Inchfawn, Oxenford and Frump – apostates of Desdemona. Pelham, *House Captain* of Desdemona. Mansfield, daringly in black *trousers*. Skipping done, they wound their ropes around their middles like belts.

The ranked silhouettes on the backcloth looked like the trees of Birnham Wood, ready to march. One of the smudge pots was lit. Greasy smoke pooled.

Amy couldn't make out what Rayne was saying. Her audience nodded, as if agreeing. Rintoul and Beeke flanked the throne like handmaidens. Besides black uniforms and ropes, they wore black shoulder-sashes pinned with ant-shaped clasps. The Cerberus had their own bench. Gould of Goneril, of the talons and teeth, sat alert, like a good dog. Garland, an expedient defector from the Murdering Heathens, was on her knees in front of Buller, polishing her shoes and smiling like a convert.

Three hooded grown-ups also stood near the throne. Amy recognised them. Ponce Bainter wore his hood tucked into his dog-collar. The Professor was still all in tweeds. Kali's father had a new hood, with a bigger Red Flame.

The Black Skirts had a hierarchy. Orders of rank were denoted by brooches, sashes, clasps, badges, ropes and pins. The insignia must be manufactured on the premises. By Viola costumiers? Rayne's ant brooch was copied over and over, in simplified form. The design impressed Amy. She remembered Light Fingers' advice. The ant emblem was more striking than her moth sigil. She had seen it chalked up around School, inked on exercise books and scratched in snow.

Some Black Skirts thought it a great jape to daub black treacle ants on the backs of gray blazers. Greys were Minored for unknowingly sporting sticky insects on their uniforms. Black Skirts weren't punished for putting their mark on someone else's kit.

A canvas sheet was spread on the floor before the throne – a backdrop face-down. On it was traced a design in black paint. Amy recognised the Runnel and the Flute, and recalled the strange traceries and plain of hatching eggs of her Purple dreams. The spirals drew her eye in. She felt dizzy looking at the Runnel to the Flute, as if her mind were pouring out and circling a plughole.

Down the drain was the Purple.

She crouched, making herself small, wishing her Moth Club friends were with her. Being alone among the Black Skirts felt less like an adventure and more like dangerous foolishness.

Rayne kept talking, as if leading a prayer. The rhythm was different from the skipping rhyme, but the words made no more sense...

'Hierophant elephant sycophant phoo
Antelope antedates Antony Stew
Cormorant coruscant celebrant mites
Antimony antipathy antagony bites...'

Amy got the message... ant, ant, ant, ant, ant!

She tried to listen and her head hurt. She tried not to listen and her head hurt more. She tried to understand... but the words weren't to be understood. They were like music... to be felt.

And she felt stark fear.

Her Purple dreams bubbled up, intruding into her waking mind. She looked at the blasted heath backdrop and saw it as the Purple, extending into the far distance. Littered with bloodied corpses and cast-off armour, the plain was vaster than the space under the Drearcliff Playhouse. Ugly birds flew slowly through skies she had thought painted. Beyond the purple horizon, dark fires burned.

She stood and was drawn towards the ranks of the Black Skirts. She walked in a curve towards them, as if entering the Runnel…

Despite what Light Fingers said, there *was* a place for her in the anthill… she could shed her wings and join the reinforcements who were going to advance. She could get the three and fourpence and buy a ticket to the dance.

She wanted to be part of *something*. This was bigger than the Moth Club, than Desdemona House, than School… this was, in the end, *everything*. The Purple and the Back Home. She could be a part of it all.

She was close enough to see Rayne's smile. A tiny insect crawled across her face and she did not twitch. There were ants in her eyes!

…Amy was horrified by Rayne's face, and more horrified by the lull she had been in.

They had *nearly* had her. She had nearly given in.

She had been following the Runnel and forgetting the Flute.

The Black Skirts didn't even want her. Because of what she was. Because, when she got close, when she saw Rayne's smile, she knew what was wrong with this picture. The farmer had two left feet. The kitchen window was upside down. The wind was blowing in one direction and the weathervane pointing in the other. The cat had too many eyes. She would always see what was wrong… and she would never completely give in. She could be unmasked, unwinged, made to skip, made to chant… but inside would always be an uncrushable, persistent bud of resistance… of glory.

Kentish Glory.

'Queen Ant, Queen Ant,' recited Rintoul, 'you sit in the sun,

As fair as a lily, as white as a wand…'

'I send you three postcards,' Beeke took over, 'and pray you read one.

You must read one, if you can't read all…'

'So pray, Miss or Master,' said Rayne, clearly and loudly, looking straight at Amy, 'for down will you fall!'

She was noticed!

'Down, down, down will you fall,' said the Ant Queen and her Princesses in unison. They all pointed at Amy.

'I spy strangers,' said the Professor loudly. Heads turned en masse.

The lines of perspective on the backdrop changed… the birds froze, painted again. A spell had been broken by Amy's presence.

Again, she had interrupted the Ritual of the Runnel and the Flute.

The Professor pointed at Amy and screeched. She still wore her mandibled gauntlet. Arcs crackled between the talons.

Who was under the hood? A mistress? A tall, stout Sixth?

Amy backed away, fast… up the stairs and through the trapdoor. A rush of Black Skirts jammed together as they came after her. The ants were swarming. They clacked their mouth-parts, jumbling their rhymes.

'...hieroph*ant*, eleph*ant*, *Ant*ony Stew... down, down, *down will you fall*!'

She let the trap drop on them with a bang. She hurried through the auditorium and foyer and out of the theatre.

Blinking in the sunlight, she realised she still wore her mask.

She tore it off and stuffed it back in its secret pocket.

The trapdoor wouldn't keep back the Black Skirts for long.

XIV: The Viola–Goneril War

JUST OUTSIDE THE Playhouse, Amy ran into Frecks' triad. She started chattering about wanting to borrow something from Light Fingers and wondering where she was.

Frecks shrugged. Kali looked away. Beauty was blank.

Beeke and two other Black Skirts came out of the theatre. They looked around purposefully.

Had Amy been recognised?

She went on about the book she needed a lend of, trying to seem as if she'd been with Frecks and company for ages. She flapped her hands in an exaggerated 'silly me' manner and was breathless with jollity... rather than terror.

'Sisters Dark,' Beeke addressed the triad. 'Did you see a foolish girl running just now? A Grey pest who's shoved her snout where it's not wanted?'

'Running? No,' said Frecks – not lying, since Amy had *walked*.

'Keep an antenna out,' said Beeke. 'You know how things are.'

She went back into the theatre. The other Black

Skirts stood by the doors. They unwound their ropes and began skipping slowly.

'I say, pal-o-mino, you've gone scarlet,' observed Frecks. 'Been doing anything you shouldn't haven't oughtn't to have been?'

'Not I, sir.'

'You don't say so, sir.'

'Say so sir, I do.'

'Thought as much. Any notion what Nosey Beeke was on about?'

Amy shrugged.

'Another of life's mysteries,' said Frecks.

Frecks, Kali and Rose had no sashes or badges. Amy hoped that kept them out of any inner circles of sinister Black Skirt intent. They hadn't been at the meeting under the stage – though Desdemona was represented by Pelham, Inchfawn and other feckless Gone-Blacks.

Something was up among the 'Sisters Dark'. Amy didn't think it would be cheering to know what it was. It had to do with the Purple.

She wanted to confide her worries to her friend, but a voice in her head – very like Light Fingers' – cautioned against it. She couldn't tell whether Frecks had covered for her with Beeke or just not realised Amy was the pest the Black Skirts were after.

Not realising things was becoming a Frecks trait. It was unlike the old her. Last term, her keen perception fringed on the borders of Ability.

'I'll keep looking for Light Fingers,' Amy said.

'Please yourself,' said Frecks.

Amy walked on. She happened to look back and saw Frecks' triad ambling towards the theatre. Were they invited to the meeting after all? If so, they were late.

Being late wasn't a Black Skirt sort of thing. Rayne had spoken about being 'neat, efficient and cheerful'. She was most likely always on time. Or early, in order to catch you out. It was impossible to tell whether she was cheerful or not. By her own strange standards, she might be. And being cheerful wasn't the same as being happy.

Crossing the Quad, she saw Wychwood – blazer still streaked with black – and a few other Greys milling about in the cold. Black Skirts were suddenly in short supply. Usually, they were all over the show. They couldn't all be under the stage, surely? There wasn't room, even in the scenery vault. Like so much else lately, this struck Amy as ominous.

Wychwood was heading towards the Gym. Amy hadn't thought of checking there for Light Fingers. It was skipping territory. With Black Skirts in session elsewhere, Light Fingers might have found refuge between wooden horses and climbing ropes. Amy followed Wychwood out of the Quad.

Outside the Gym, Goneril House was gathered. Captain Flo Rhode-Eeling, proudly Grey, was flanked by stars of the cricket elevens and netball teams, plus the outstanding runners, jumpers and chuckers. Some wore cricket caps and scarves and held bats as if they meant business.

The javelin champion Kat 'Shoshone' Brown wore the Red Indian headdress she affected on Sports Day and shouldered her favourite spear, Strikes-Like-an-Adder. The shot-put virtuoso Helen 'Overwhelming' O'Hara juggled miniature cannon balls. Euterpe McClure represented the Murdering Heathens.

Amy was brought up short by the Goneril Gang. All were still in Grey.

They were preparing for War – or, at least, serious scrimmage. Shoshone Brown wasn't the only girl flying martial colours. Sharpshooter Jemima Sieveright wore a trenchcoat inherited from her Victoria Cross-winning brother, with darned bullet holes and slight singeing. She had an air-gun, not the wooden rifle issued by the QMWAACC.

The school falconer Netta Kinross had Polyphemus, her one-eyed prize bird, perched on her leather armlet. Amy was wary of Kinross. She hoped never to have a falcon set after her while aloft.

Roberta Hale, still nervous in the open, had showed up, hands mittened and a muffler around her face.

Pinborough, who fought under the soubriquet of the Blonde Bruiser, wore singlet, shorts and big red boxing gloves. She jabbed the air to keep the circulation going. Smaller girls kept heads well away. Smudge said Pinners strung the knocked-out teeth of former opponents on a necklace. Ker, whose father was a rebel general in Formosa, sat on the steps with her knees up under her chin. The least-bullied Second in School, Ker was proficient in Chinese Boxing. She could (and did) floor girls twice her weight. Her family were headhunters, which made Pinborough's string-of-gnashers seem tame.

Even Nellie Pugh wouldn't take bets on a match between Ker and Pinborough, and neither was inclined to take on the other. Indeed, Amy would worry about anyone who went up against the both at the same time... assuming they could get close enough without being impaled by Brown's feather-tipped spear, brained by one of McClure's beamers, ripped apart by Polyphemus or catching a discus in the throat from Rhode-Eeling.

Amy was surprised.

Tamora was the warlike crew, but they stayed home. Aside from the odd maniac like McClure, Goneril was known for ritualised, formalised, good-humoured competition... not extremes of violence. Generally, they got on with their games and chose not to intervene in other business. Wary truce between Rhode-Eeling and Gryce kept Tamora and Goneril, perceived as the strongest Houses, from outright hostilities. The usual Goneril girl was jolly if on the dim side. They had a few Unusuals, like Marsh and Gould, but generally relied on the tiresome, demanding business of exercise and practise to maintain their reputation for being top at sport.

Relying on Abilities wasn't quite playing the game, old thing.

Marsh, scarf around her gills, was here. Her sport, of course, was swimming – which was only held in summer term. To keep in trim, she took a dip in the ocean every day, even when it was stormy or freezing. She was pop-eyed and fish-lipped, but sleek as a seal in the water.

Gould, one of Goneril's few Black Skirts, was under the stage with the Cerberus. She was School champion at Hare and Hounds and an accomplished huntswoman. Her cell was decorated with heads, furs and antlers. She brought back broken-necked rabbits for midnight stews, though softer-hearted girls baulked at eating bunny-wunnies.

Seeing the massed ranks of Goneril – down to Firsts and Seconds with cricket stumps and huge boxing gloves – ready for battle didn't make Amy queasy the way the Black Skirts did. But she didn't care for the implications either.

'...it's *Viola*,' Rhode-Eeling said, contemptuous.

'Have you forgotten what *babies* they are? New bonnets don't change that. Goneril can't let the affront stand, can't let this rot go on. Skipping is not a sport... it's a bally *pastime*.'

A Viola advantage, Amy realised, was that Mansfield had memorised acres of *Henry V* and would deliver more stirring addresses to the troops. They'd still get a battering, though. A stage-trained swordswoman accustomed to blunt tips and opponents primed to bleed and fall down and die on cue would come off worst against a sporty duellist who cared more about winning than looking pretty as she fought. This was likely to mean more Grand Guignol. The Violas would get a chance to play the death scenes they so loved.

Despite herself, Amy felt a surge of hope.

The battle Light Fingers had worried about, that she had herself dreaded, would be fought and won and the Black Skirts broken before any more damage was done.

And Amy didn't even have to be in it.

...then she remembered the way the *Macbeth* backdrop had shimmered into the Purple, and had dreadful premonitions.

Rhode-Eeling had the heartier Ariel Greys – like Haldane and Manders – on board. The Goneril mob even took in a lone Desdemona Sixth – Hern, School's best yachtswoman.

But Amy wasn't invited into this army, and nor were any of her intimates. Despite Frecks' urging, she and Light Fingers hadn't gone up for netball.

'Girls,' continued Rhode-Eeling, 'one of our own has fallen into *black* company...'

That was about as clever as it got in Goneril.

'...and it's down to us to rescue her, to show her the

error of her ways, to bring her back to our side and the right track.'

So this was about Aconita Gould, of all people. The right head of the Cerberus.

Amy didn't see how this was going to work. Did Rhode-Eeling expect her House to march across to the Black Skirt rally like the Greeks intent on reclaiming Helen of Troy? That had lasted ten years and no one came out of it terribly well. Even if they got Wolf Girl back, what then? They could hardly strip her kit and force her into Grey. Perhaps there would be an intensive talking-to, with Rhode-Eeling appealing to Gould's House pride. If so, she'd missed the latest news… Black and Grey cut across the whole school, and meant more than Houses or anything else.

Ker leaped up and flexed, doing light bends and passes to show off her limberness – then flat-palmed the wall with enough force to crack a brick and shake a rind of ice off the lintel. Pinborough punched the air and, in her signature gesture, flicked her fringe out of her eyes before launching her knock-out blow. Now Amy came to think of it, that mannerism was a dead giveaway. If the Blonde Bruiser were ever matched with a fighter who wasn't a Dim, she'd regret that tell.

Light Fingers would be proud of Amy. She'd just worked out how to duck the best boxer in school. But Light Fingers wasn't here and staying to watch a punch-up wasn't helping find her.

Still, Amy couldn't walk away yet.

Lucretia 'Lungs' Lamarcroft, a Sixth who had seriously tried to persuade Miss Dryden to let her compete in archery with one breast bared like an ancient Amazon, raised a curly hunting horn. The tooter usually hung among trophies in an overstuffed cabinet in the Goneril dorm. A deep yet shrill *view halloo* sounded… and echoed mournfully, like Kali's *mi-go* moanings.

Goneril began to march towards the theatre.

Lungs tooted her horn again, and a ragged war song was raised…

> '*Stickses and stoneses and broken boneses,*
> *Heed our dreadful warning!*
> *Thumpses and blowses and bleeding noses*
> *You'll ache tomorrow morning!*'

Amy had heard that before. Goneril sang it before every game of everything. Including tiddlywinks and Old Maid. Always, they played aggressively, but within the rules. And they always won.

The girls' breath plumed like snorting cavalry horses. They stamped across the snowy Quad. Digger Downs stood, somewhat surprised, in a doorway. She covered her black ribbon with her hand and let Goneril pass unmolested.

Amy tagged along, well behind the army. A few other girls – Gifford, Harper, Jones-Rhys – were similarly interested. Gawky and Taff, Desdemona Firsts, knew enough to shun Shrimp Harper. Amy made sure she kept well away from the mind-leech too.

Shrimp had her notebook out, though Amy doubted the *Drearcliff Trumpet* would cover what happened next. Apart from anything else, there had been a slight coup at the paper. The long-serving Tamora Fifth was demoted to 'Our Correspondent in the Remove', with a cabal of Viola Thirds – Pulsipher, Stannard, Vail

– elevated as the new editorial committee. Now the *Trumpet* had ants on the masthead and took a Black Skirt line. A 'review' by the lepidopterally illiterate Stannard fawned over Rayne's mother's latest outrage against entomology *What We Can Learn From Our Insect Chums: Eugenics in Nature and Progress Towards Human Perfection.*

It was impossible to feel sorry for Harper, but the girl hadn't had much – besides being the sort of Unusual no one wanted to be around – outside of being editor of the *Trumpet* and now she'd lost that.

Like camp-followers, Amy and the others trod in the trampled slush footprints of an army which expected to be all-vanquishing.

The two Black Skirts left as skipping sentries didn't miss a step, even as the mob – bristling with bats and projectiles – swarmed across the Quad. Rhode-Eeling, a discus in each hand, cried halt and the Gonerils formed battle lines.

The song continued…

'*Stickses and stoneses and broken boneses!*
Thumpses and blowses and bleeding noses!'

The Black Skirts skipped, unconcerned.

'Antoinette Rowley Rayne,' hollered Rhode-Eeling, 'come out to play!'

Pinborough punched her gloves together and hopped on the spot. Her arms and legs were goosefleshed. Presumably, she hoped to warm up while punching some girls' heads for them.

The last time Rayne had won against the odds just by not staying down.

Now, she was up against athletes, not bullies. The average whip relied on fear and tradition to prevail against girls who only had to stand their ground to see them off. Ker and Pinborough were used to fighting people who fought back... and the Gonerils weren't all good sports. McClure's beamers were deadly.

'Look, up on the roof!' gasped someone.

The Playhouse had a pretentious frontage, with columns, an arch and large masks of crying tragedy and laughing comedy. Rayne perched on the apex of the arch, black skirt flapping in the wind, the Queen Ant looked down on the crowd. Amy wouldn't have been surprised if cauldrons of boiling tar were at hand, to tip on the army of Goneril.

Polyphemus flew up from Kinross's armlet. Rayne didn't so much as flinch. The bird halted in mid-air, making kites of its wings, and flapped off altogether, spooked from the field of battle by Rayne's stare.

Kinross whistled but her bird didn't come back.

'Give us Gould and we'll say no more about it,' shouted Rhode-Eeling.

This wasn't about the Wolf Girl, not really. Before all this, Rhode-Eeling wouldn't have had the hairy, toothy Fourth round to tea. Goneril was, of all Houses, least happy with Unusuals in its midst. Marsh's swimming cups were hidden at the back of the cabinet.

For a moment, Amy was sure Rayne was about to jump off the theatre.

The Queen Ant couldn't fly... though ant queens generally could.

Amy realised she was several feet off the ground and reached out to grab the Heel. She scrabbled and settled on the broken-off ankle. If anyone noticed, they'd assume she'd climbed up for a better view.

The only person who might have seen her in the air was Rayne. The Queen Ant was so wrapped up in herself Amy doubted she'd have noticed.

'...or come down and take your porridge, Wet Blanket Rayne!'

Pinborough jogged up the theatre steps and punched very near the head of one of the skipping Black Skirts without intending to connect.

'We can settle this right now,' Rhode-Eeling continued.

Rayne raised her arms above her head, and made fists. The signal looked like the extended antennae of an insect. She waved her arms from side to side.

'What's she doing?' Gifford asked, looking back to where she thought Amy would be and then craning up to see her on top of the Heel. 'Cor, what a climb!'

Then, from everywhere, the Black Skirts swarmed in. Like ants.

XV: Under the Black Skirts

VIOLA TROUNCED GONERIL, but it wasn't about Houses. Black prevailed over Grey.

No one – least of all, Amy, who saw it from the Heel – could say how the battle was lost, but numbers told. And the element of surprise, and ruthless commitment.

In games, Goneril always won... but the Black Skirts weren't playing games.

Despite the crowing about broken boneses and bleeding noseses, the sportists marched on to the field as if already celebrating victory. They were prematurely of a mind to console not-yet-actually-vanquished opponents with back-slapping, warm congratulations for putting up a bally good show under the circumstances and mugs of strong sweet consolation tea.

The Black Skirts weren't the match-conceding sorts Goneril were accustomed to bowling out, scoring against or running past. They didn't put up with having their backs slapped and they spat strong sweet tea back in the faces of anyone foolhardy enough to offer it.

Skipping, as the Black Skirts did it, was not a pastime. As Amy and Light Fingers had perceived, it was prep for war.

The Black Skirts were quick, harsh, and *everywhere*.

The next day, Rhode-Eeling – powder over her bruises, crushed hand in plaster – showed up for breakfast in a black skirt and blazer. After the ruckus, her grey kit wasn't wearable. Even the laxest whip would notch her for rips, bloodstains and general dilapidation.

By the end of lessons, Goneril was virtually Black-Skirt Only.

Inevitably, the other Houses fell. Desdemona, to Amy's disgust, followed Pelham's lead and quietly went Black. Ariel managed with tiresome nonchalance. It might have been that they were thinking of going Black for some considerable time but only now happened to get round to making the switch. If they deigned to notice lesser Houses had beaten them to it, they were too well-bred to care. Then, Tamora got changed in an undignified hurry, as if there were a wooden spoon for Last in Black.

The next Monday, as the full register was called in Chapel, Marsh was marked absent. According to Smudge, the Gill Girl swam out to sea after the Fall of Goneril and was sulking on the bottom among the wrecks and skeletons.

'Good job too,' snorted Bryant, a Tamora Third Amy didn't know well. 'No place for *flukes* here. Not at all at all.'

Amy had an urge to slap Bryant's face for her, but the comment provoked mutters of agreement from all sides. Hot rage turned cold. Bryant just said what most Ordinaries thought.

She had heard the term 'fluke' before. Since the rise of the Black Skirts, it was commonly used… and never in an approving manner. Talk of Unusuals gave way to jibes against *flukes*. In two minds about being classed among Swan's cygnets, Amy still bridled at being called a fluke. The word was always bitten down on like an unpleasant pill, uttered with venomous contempt… the way 'shirker' or 'Hun' were during the War… or 'sneak' and 'wet' were in School.

Bryant's remark was loud enough to be heard beyond her pew. Bainter, who was calling the register, issued no rebuke. Talking in Chapel ought to earn at least a Minor. Were Dr Swan at the lectern, the impertinent chit would be quartered by steam engines and the bloody parts buried in salted earth at the four corners of the grounds.

Headmistress was absent again. Did the coup extend all the way to her study?

Ponce Bainter all but wore the Black Skirt himself.

Amy remembered him saying 'she has to be *alive* when we do it.'

Rose sat with Frecks and Kali, seemingly unconcerned that the man at the lectern had wanted to cut her face off.

The oblation had been about 'opening the Flute'.

…Amy worried that their action that night hadn't kept it closed. What had gone on under the stage before the battle was another ritual of the Runnel and the Flute, and had presaged spilling of blood.

An oblation had been made, Amy realised. More important than cuts and bruises sustained by individual girls was the overturning of the established order. Bainter said cutting off Rose's beautiful face wasn't enough – she must be alive to understand her loss. Now, Goneril had lost face and felt it keenly. Their status as Sport House – their *pride* – had been slaughtered on the altar of the Quad. Going Black was more than an admission of defeat, it was a total submission. The fall of Goneril meant all Houses were lessened. The Black Skirts superseded them. A few Gonerils and Ariels were bitter that *Viola*, of all Houses, had prevailed... but Amy understood Rayne had eaten away at Viola from within. It was the Ant Queen's first conquest. Viola, for all the foolishness and blubbing, had stood for something which the Black Skirts now threw away. *Poles Apart!* was cancelled without explanation. The Black Skirts had stolen Viola's theatricality. Frivolity aside, they were *all about* dress-up and performance. Now they took what they needed from other Houses. Goneril's pride, Ariel's hauteur, Tamora's violence and Desdemona's... well, Desdemona's distinctiveness, its not-like-the-others-and-happy-about-it attitude. Among Houses, Desdemona had been the Unusual, the fluke. Now, it was All Black Skirts Together and never mind the rest. House Spirit was at an end.

Amy thought more and more of the Other Ones. She sensed their silent, invisible presence in School.

She missed Mauve Mary – the comparatively harmless ghost hadn't been seen lately – and even wondered whether Captain Freezing hadn't had his good points.

Light Fingers sat glumly beside Amy on the pew, fists in her pockets.

The talking-to Pelham had prescribed didn't seem relevant any more. Things had gone too far South.

Pelham was spiffy in black. A fashion-setting ant-head hatpin was stuck through her boater. She had banished Poppet Dyall and taken the puddingishly Ordinary Dottie Fulwood as her new familiar.

Light Fingers nudged Amy and directed her attention to Poppet.

Dyall sat on a wonky bench to one side of Chapel, well out of the light, lumped in with Harper, Palgrave and other awkward, unlovely Unusuals. From time immemorial, or at least the founding year, the far pew was reserved for the Leper Colony. Here sat the Remove, a floating form of girls who didn't fit in their years on account of being held back, sprung forward, arrived late or destined to leave early. The extraordinarily gifted and the terminally dim alike gravitated there. The Remove had lessons with whichever mistress drew the short straw in a former potting shed called Temporary Classroom Two. Temporary Classroom One was not on current maps, having gone over the cliff in the Landslide of '08.

All the Remove were in Grey, except Shrimp Harper. Trotting up in her new kit, the canny little leech suffered a severe disappointment when it transpired that the crucial ant emblem couldn't be bought but had to be bestowed – by Antoinette Rowley Rayne, of course. In Shrimp's case, the ant was withheld. Just wearing a black skirt didn't guarantee acceptance into the Black Skirts.

Light Fingers nodded at the Remove and then at Amy. Her meaning was clear. She expected they'd eventually be transported to the Leper Colony.

The only House Captain still in Grey was Gryce. The terror of last term cut a sad figure and tried to avoid the public eye. Her craft had run out when Goneril lost her battle for her. Unlike Harper, she had been issued with an ant badge. She wore the insect speck on her grey lapel… not as a way of fitting in, but as a sign of giving in.

Tamora was otherwise Black as an ace of spades down a coal mine. The Murdering Heathens had defected to join the Soldier Ants. They showed no particular malice to their former patron, but their indifference must be devastating.

Dora Paule was daffier than ever. One Break, she had gone barefoot in the snow – an unthinkable Uniform Infraction – and had been packed off to the Infirmary with frozen feet. Amy had tried to visit but Paule had been babbling, and Nurse had said she needed her rest.

There were still dwindling pockets of Grey resistance. Knowles of the Fourth proved an object lesson when she tried to present a list of grievances to Dr Swan.

Charlotte Knowles could speed-read and learn by heart reams of information. The knowledge she gobbled only stuck in her head for a short time, but her bursts of expertise were a great advantage. Given a half-hour in the library, Know-It-All could be fluent in Portuguese, master tapestry-weaving, follow complex algebra, sail a dinghy well enough to compete with Hern or play harpsichord to a professional level. She didn't merely stuff her head with facts but could *use* what she knew. Whatever her current craze was, she was a prodigy at it... for four to six weeks. Then, it poured out and she was virtually a Dim. Knowles came top in every test, provided she had forenotice of what she'd be quizzed on. When her crazes were wearing off, she grew clumsy and suffered fainting fits and crippling migraines. Like Amy, she got nosebleeds if she pushed her Abilities too far – by cramming two or three subjects at the same time.

Knowles was in Martine's cell. The two were great chums before the Black–Grey divide. Amy had looked up to them and wondered if she and Frecks would be as worldly and glamorous when they were a whole year older. Know-It-All was Desdemona's most prominent Unusual. Though her looks were changeable, depending on her current hobby horse, she always seemed impossibly mature, poised and confident. Just the sort to form a committee of action and carry the day with eloquence and righteous determination.

The little rebellion in the Fourth began when Miss Borrodale took Knowles aside and told her that from now on she would sit tests on her own. She would not know the subjects in advance. Without her Abilities to rely on, she was a mediocre scholar. A level playing field was mentioned. To the delight of the Dims, Not-so-Know-It-All Knowles was no longer always top of the form. Martine advised Knowles against complaining and Pelham flat out told her not to, but she gathered a deputation of Unusuals and tried to get a hearing with Headmistress. Amy guessed Knowles had been given Swan's speech of welcome too, and felt betrayed that she was back to being treated as a fluke.

Joining Knowles to present her petition were Devlin and Paquignet. Stretch Devlin, another Desdemona Fourth, was always using her Abilities to help girls out when reach or long fingers were needed. Green Thumbs Paquignet, a rare Ariel Unusual, had a sympathy with nature which meant she could make anything grow in flower garden, vegetable patch or greenhouse.

Without a glance at the document, Keys turned the deputation away. Her Lee–Enfield happened to be assembled at the time. And loaded.

Headmistress was indisposed… which might mean imprisoned. She'd not been seen for weeks. The sense of always being watched didn't go away, but Amy thought that might be because the Black Skirts had eyes everywhere, more even than Dr Swan. Every ant shared what they saw with the Queen.

Over the next days, Knowles and her cronies were Minored for hitherto-undreamed-of Infractions. Paquignet raised snowdrops and was punished for defiance of nature. The Cerberus shut Devlin in a disused dumb waiter as 'an example to others'. She escaped, only to be written up for 'resisting discipline'. Knowles attempted to cram the entirety of Drearcliff School Rules and several shelves of Board of Education reports, in the hope of finding loopholes. Blood vessels burst in her nose and she was cited for 'impertinent bleeding'. Black Skirt whips insisted these persecutions had nothing to do with the deputation's temerity in crying injustice. Few believed them. The sorry trio replaced Blacker-than-Red Absalom on the Heel-brushing party. Which ought to be lesson enough for anyone.

Then, inevitably, Knowles, Devlin and Paquignet were Removed.

Smudge sat next to Amy at Supper and spun yarns about life in the Remove... more swede and fewer crumpets, extra prep upon extra prep, regular visits from Crowninshield II and Aire, Minors treated as Majors, painful inoculations...

'Know where they find sparring partners for Pinborough to knock down? The Remove. Know who they send into the woods as hares when Gould is leading the hounds? The Remove.'

Smudge went on and on, shamming pity.

Amy noticed that Smudge shifted from describing what it was like for Knowles and company in the Remove to explaining what it would be like for Amy when she was sent there.

When Smudge went Black, her modus operandi changed. Formerly, her wild tales were almost endearing and few took them seriously. Frecks said Smudge couldn't help but make things up. It was almost an Ability, a way with words to make dull reality more exciting. Now her exaggerations were nasty and sly, more threat than fable. Smudge knew exactly what she was saying. Every whisper was a poison pinprick.

'I shall be awfully sorry when you are Removed, Thomsett,' she said. 'I shall miss our little talks.'

The new Smudge made Amy's skin crawl.

But she was just a single ant. It was the whole army that made Amy fear for the future.

Rayne's antenna-arms hail caught on. Black Skirts did it all over School, especially if the Queen Ant hove into view. Rayne's shoulders must ache from returning so many salutes. In purposeful moments, the waving included odd, double-jointed hand-flapping that mimicked the twitching of feelers. It wasn't a trick Amy wanted to learn. The circle of priests in her dreams of the Purple made similar gestures.

Between lessons, Black Skirts patrolled in triads, hexads and enneads. Triads had six legs, of course – as many as an insect – and functioned as composite creatures. Each group had – or seemed to have – its own duty. They were always doing something. No wasted effort in the anthill. Amy stopped thinking of Black Skirts as girls, and started perceiving insect patterns in their movements. It was obvious the Black Skirt movement was modelled on ant behaviour... if only as described by Rayne's mother.

Many Black Skirts carried Rosalind Rowley Rayne's *Formis* like a pocket testament, consulting it as if it were an almanac or book of wise saws. One evening, Amy caught Kali reading the wretched yellow thing, hidden inside an Edgar Wallace.

'Why are you rotting your mind on such tosh?' she asked.

'Dunno, doll,' Kali responded, turning a page. 'Some say it's got all the answers.'

'All the answers to *what*?'

'Everything, doll. Everything.'

This was Amy's longest conversation with Kali since that night at the Runnel and the Flute.

'Give us a read of it, then,' she asked. 'I'm always open to answers.'

Kali handed the booklet over. Amy had tried to get through it but given up halfway. The new edition – the *eleventh* impression in the year since publication – bore enthusiastic recommendations from authors, politicians and journalists Amy made a mental note not to trust in future. Mr Wells, Mr Chesterton and Mr Shaw should know better than to provide endorsements willy-nilly to any fathead who wrapped a tenner around a presentation copy of their book. And Mr Roderick Spode – whoever he might be – could do with a long lie down and a cold compress, judging from his statement that *Formis* 'set my veins a-throb and expanded the old brain matter as if it were a turgid sponge!'

'Note none of this praise comes from entomologists,' she said, tossing *Formis* back.

'That's because it's not about insects,' Kali said.

She caught the thing and affectionately smoothed its pages as if it were a ruffled kitten.

Amy sputtered. 'Of course it is – it's about *ants*!'

'Think about it,' said Kali, tapping the ornament in her nose. It wasn't a gold snail any more, but an ant in amber. 'Think about it.'

Kali looked at Frecks, who was lolling on her own cot waiting for nail polish to dry. They exchanged knowing, in-on-the-secret smiles and manufactured identical simpers of pity to direct Amy's way.

Amy was outnumbered by Black Skirts.

Light Fingers was doing her prep elsewhere these days, coming into the cell just before Lights Out.

Amy felt more and more isolated.

XVI: The Exorcism of Mauve Mary

WORD RAN ROUND that the Black Skirts were going to 'do something' about Mauve Mary.

What with the other to-do, Mary had slipped off the front page of the *Trumpet*. The Hypatia Hall Psychical Investigation Soc, informally known as the Spook-Spotters, regularly tramped through her haunted walkway with plumb-bobs and anemometers – which seemed to scare the spectre off. Besheeted jokers tried to sub for Mauve Mary, but were quickly found out. Impersonating a ghost was inflated from Minor to Major Infraction, and the ragging stopped.

Then, Mauve Mary popped up again…

Ellacott, a Goneril Third, was hurrying through the covered walkway on the way to some secret Black Skirt activity. She was, as usual, not on time. Ellacott had earned the handle 'the Late Miriam Ellacott' through chronic tardiness. With use, the soubriquet transmogrified into 'the L.M.E.' or 'the Ellemy'. Thiele and Meade, her irritated triad partners, were waiting in the foyer of the Playhouse. On hearing the story, Amy was relieved to learn that not all Blacks ran like clockwork. Rayne didn't have *everything* her way.

When Ellacott passed Mary's shrine, she was dazzled by purple light. As she reported it, the ghost girl loomed out of the wall and *clutched*. There was an attendant crackle, like lightning. Ellacott saw Mary's face clearly, but didn't recognise her. A glowing bump on the spook's forehead threatened to open like a third eye.

The fright put salt on Ellacott's tail. She ran into the Playhouse and gabbled her story at her triad partners. They first took it for the latest in a long line of sorry excuses. Thiele in particular was near the end of her patience with the Ellemy, who persistently held them back. Unless Ellacott pulled her socks up, they'd never earn their next ant badges. Meade, more sensitive than most Sisters Dark, realised quickly that the Ellemy was genuinely upset. Before they went Black, Meade was a Viola Fourth and Ellacott and Thiele Goneril Thirds. The younger girls still deferred from habit.

What struck Meade and Thiele most was that, uniquely for March, Ellacott seemed to have caught the sun. Normally, she had little colour... but now her complexion was bronze, with reddish skin flaking on her forehead and cheeks. Amy had heard of apparitions frightening folk so much their hair went white, but never of ghosts giving people spots. Just what manner of ghost was Mary? The Ellemy must have thrown up her hands at the *clutching* creature. Her palms were nut-brown while the backs of her hands were pale.

Thiele, formerly of the Spook-Spotters, was irritated that Mauve Mary failed to appear to qualified persons with proper scientific equipment but put on a show for a rank amateur. She insisted they hurry to the shrine to test for ectoplasmic residue. Ellacott took some persuading, but was dragged across the Quad. She had begun to doubt her own senses. An idea formed that she might have been the victim of a rag involving a more elaborate deception than a sheet with eyeholes. Stage lights, Chem Lab fizzling potions, magic lantern slides... rigged up by smugglers or counterfeiters. Meade later admitted she found the rational explanation harder to credit than ghosts.

To the triad's shock, they entered the walkway to find Mary still manifesting. She sank back into the wall. Her arm stuck out for moments, then withdrew – leaving no ripples in the brickwork. There was a smell of spent matches. With her battery torch, an essential instrument from her Spook-Spotters kit, Thiele cast light around the walkway. Mary hadn't just given the Ellemy a tan. The paving stones and the opposite wall were faded. A poster for the cancelled *Poles Apart!* was bleached nearly white. An outline of Ellacott, cringing in terror, was burned onto the ground. Thiele was excited by the physical evidence. Past experience with practical jokers made her test for paint before she listed the effect in her Diary of Parapsychological Phenomena.

The musically inclined Meade drew her partners' attention to a ululation audible under the winds that blew through the walkway. The eerie sound continued for a minute or so after Mary's departure, then quieted as if the procession had turned a corner. Meade couldn't say whether the music had been an unknown instrument – something like an aeolian harp, perhaps – or the voices of an unearthly choir. There was something eerie and skin-prickling about the sounds.

In her detailed report for the *Trumpet*, the main source for the story, Thiele theorised that Mauve Mary was a wailing spectre, like the Irish banshee or the Mexican llorona. In a footnote, Meade suggested the song was more enrapturing than terrifying, which might make her an ondine, like the classical Greek siren or the German lorelei. In either case, she was an ill omen. Wailing spectres presage disasters and ondines lure sailors onto the rocks. The fact that Joxer and Ponce Bainter were the only men on School Grounds limited the pool of suitable victims, though there was discussion as to whether girls and women could succumb to the lorelei lure or siren song if no men were about. Hern, after all, was a sailor. So far she hadn't seen or heard Mary and claimed to be tone-deaf.

Having won a war with Goneril over Gould, the Black Skirts were ready for another with Mauve Mary over Ellacott's suntan. The victim wasn't much damaged by her hair-raising experience. Indeed, she quite enjoyed her celebrity and went around without mittens showing off her varicoloured hands. Her normal colour soon returned and the blotches cleared up. Her shadow – a tourist attraction, even for sceptics – remained on the flagstone path, despite Joxer's attempt at scrubbing it off.

The precedent of Captain Freezing and the Frost, an earlier Black Skirt victory, triggered a witch hunt that raged through School. Amy saw the reasoning. Was there a Frost-like unknown Unusual who could summon or create Mauve Mary and set her on unwary souls? The Mystic Maharajah could depart from his body in astral form, so Mary could be the wandering soul of someone very much alive.

Equally, Amy remembered the Runnel and the Flute and could envision a Hooded Conspiracy ritual to allow angry intrusions from the Purple. Mary, with her neither-Gray-nor-Black uniform, might be the Purple's idea of how to pass for normal in what Paule called the Back Home. Thinking like Light Fingers, Amy could even imagine the Hoodeds and the Black Skirts conjuring Mary as an excuse to root through School in search of fresh flukes to pick on. Frost was in the Remove along with Harper, Dyall and Palgraive. Their Grey blazers might as well have 'Leper' written on them in luminous paint.

Black Skirt Triads were about everywhere. Anyone who had seen Mauve Mary was put to the Question. Then, *not* having seen the ghost seemed even more suspicious and the investigation widened.

Amy was cornered in the Library by Sundle, Ker and Pinborough.

This triad was called the Chimera, second only to the Cerberus when it came to Black Skirt violence. It was all round that they had given Susannah Thorne a beating for being a fluke. No Infractions were marked against the Chimera, but Thorne was Minored for having her blazer misbuttoned after she'd taken her lumps.

'What do you know about the Walkway Ghost?' asked Sundle, a curly-haired, rather pretty Viola Fifth. She had three ant badges on her lapel and another on her hat-brim.

'Mauve Mary?'

Sundle shook her head. 'We don't like that name,' she said. 'It's misleading.'

'She's *not* mauve?'

'More violet.'

'There's a difference?'

'To the discerning eye, yes.'

Amy shrugged. 'I've not seen her, whatever her name is. All I know is what I read in the *Trumpet*.'

Sundle put the questions, while Ker and Pinborough radiated menace. Kicker Ker played with a pencil, giving the impression she could snap it with her eyelids if she had to. The Blonde Bruiser's hands were knotted into fists.

'Do you *know* anything about the Walkway Ghost?' asked Sundle. 'Think carefully. If you omit or conceal anything now that later comes to light, there will be consequences. You want to be a credit to School, don't you?'

'Of course. But I don't know any more than you do. I've heard far-fetched yarns, but if you're going around asking all and sundry about Mau... about the Walkway Ghost, I suppose you've heard the same fairy tales. I wouldn't put a farthing on any of 'em. For what it's worth, I doubt it's smugglers in phosphor-treated sheets.'

Sundle gave her a hard looking-over. This was part of the Treatment. Amy tried not to be flustered.

She was not fidgeting. But was being calm more suspicious than being nervous? Her soles tingled and she pressed her toes down. She did not float.

Four ant badges was suggestive. A clever Black Skirt, on the rise in the anthill. Sundle wasn't overtly threatening. With Ker and Pinborough to back her up, she didn't need to be. The Chimera wasn't as showy as the Cerberus, but Amy guessed they'd be around longer and do more damage.

'I'll tell you a secret, Thomsett,' confided Sundle. 'We don't think it's smugglers either.'

Ker took Amy's boater off a library desk, looked at it from several angles, and put it back down.

'Thank you for your co-operation,' said Sundle, half-turning away.

Amy didn't want to sigh with relief.

'One more thing,' said Sundle, turning back again. 'You seem a clean, healthy, productive sort. Why are you, ah...?'

Sundle gestured towards Amy's boater.

'Still in Grey?' Amy shrugged. 'I only came here last term. This is still a new uniform. Mother is a fiend for economy, and won't replace it till it's worn out...'

'Say no more,' said Sundle, patting her arm.

'I could help you go Black,' said Pinborough. She had a strangely high-pitched voice. 'Part-way, at least.'

The Blonde Bruiser flicked back her hair, as she did before launching her best punch. Amy flinched, but bit.

'How?' she asked.

Pinborough leaned forward into Amy's face and bared her teeth.

'...*by blacking your eyes for you!*'

'Leave off, Pinners,' said Sundle. 'We've more to see.'

Sundle raised her arms and did the antenna-wave. After being breathed and snarled at, Amy was too unnerved to laugh at the ridiculous salute.

She didn't return it either.

Ker reached over and felt the material of Amy's badgeless lapel. Amy held her breath, expecting a blow. Ker smiled sweetly, then pinched and pulled. There was a rip, and a flap of cloth hung loose.

'Grey wears poorly,' said Sundle. 'That could be an Infraction. Watch out for the whips.'

The Chimera turned in unison and walked away, skipping at every third step as if to the rhythm of the ants in your pants rhyme. Amy breathed again.

Amy examined her torn lapel. She needed to find Light Fingers – who was still keeping out of sight and earning too many absence Infractions – and get repairs done. She was luckier than Thorne, in that only her blazer was damaged... but that could change.

She wrapped a scarf around her neck and arranged it to cover the rip.

On the Library Steps, she was accosted by Dora Paule, who was in a flap. Amy hadn't known she was out of the Infirmary.

'Amy, Amy, you must come... they're going to break the Purple!'

The Sixth was wild-haired and big-eyed, though at least wearing shoes. The gold piping was gone from her blazer, signifying the loss of whip status. Loose threads showed where the braid had been unpicked.

Paule had come down in the world. Only her unofficial status as Holy Fool saved her from being plastered with multiple Infractions whenever she set foot outside her cell. She was still beset by midges. Three annoyances – the undersized Third Pest Merrilees and the overgrown Seconds Joan Hone and Dottie Fulwood – had trailed Paule to the Library.

'Daffy Daffy Daffodil,' they chanted. 'Daffy Daffy Daff-o-dil!'

Pest chucked a pebble at Paule's tilted boater. Instinctively, Amy warded off the missile with her mind. Pest's mouth hung open as the stone changed direction in mid-air. Amy wished she could pop the pebble into the chit's gaping gob... but let the thing go.

'Daffy Daffy Daffodil,' chanted Hone and Fulwood. 'Daffy Daffy Daff-o-dil!'

'Push off, you perishers,' said Amy.

They ignored her and kept up the barracking.

'Daffy Daffy Daffodil,' Merrilees joined in again, 'Daffy Daffy Daff-o-dil!'

'Is this really how you want to spend precious time?' Amy asked.

'Yes, miss,' cheeked Hone. 'Yes it is. Daffy Daffy Daff-o-dil!'

'Most certainly, miss,' echoed Fulwood.

Last term, this rabble of Dims would have been cowed by a Third, but Black Skirts thought they didn't have to pay attention to anything a Grey said.

Paule was too worried about the Purple to notice her mocking retinue.

Amy thought of floating Merrilees, Hone and Fulwood up into the air and dropping them from a height. But she didn't do it. She shouldn't get in a bate. Pest was a pest, that's all. Not worth wasting her Abilities on.

In the Back Home, Paule was still a popular ragging target.

When the whips stripped her piping, season was opened. Even the most meagre could go at her. Titches sought respite from their own torments by persecuting Paule, hoping to cosy up to horrific harpies like Aire or McClure.

It depressed Amy that girls who should know better would pass on the hurt others ladled on them. For one thing, the tactic didn't work. Trying to mollify monsters was useless. They got bored easily and would lash out at anyone within reach, including their own toadies. The Black Skirts didn't discipline their rogues, even in the way whips did. Rayne, once the most put upon of putupons, gave out badges for bullying.

Dr Auchmuty came out of the Library. At sight of her,

the perishers scarpered. Merrilees turned back to shoot Amy a nasty look and tripped over some frozen snow that happened to shift into her way. Doc Och lectured Pest about self-endangerment. The edict against not running on slippery ground was still in force.

'Amy, Amy, they're at the shimmer,' repeated Paule.

Amy tried to pay attention.

Paule grabbed Amy by the scarf and yanked. Which hurt.

'The shimmer, Amy…'

'Slow down, Paule,' said Amy. 'And don't throttle me. What, where, when, how and why?'

Paule blinked as if answering in Morse.

She was more in the Back Home than usual, capable of recognising Amy and seeking her out. But she was straining herself to stay focused.

'The wreckers are tampering,' she said. 'They've found one of the shimmers… the places where the Purple comes closest to the Back Home.'

'Like the Runnel and the Flute, in the woods?'

Paule nodded. 'Yes, but that place is locked. It needs an oblation to open. For most, not me. I can get to the Purple from anywhere. I can *make* shimmers. The wreckers are at one of the thin shimmers, where the barrier between here and there is wavery. They're shutting her out, but that's not it at all. They're making a breach!'

'Her?'

Paule pointed towards the Quad. Amy realised there was activity in the covered walkway.

'Mauve Mary?'

'That's not her real name.'

'You know who she is?'

'Have you ever thought it was funny ghosts are called "presences"? Because they're not present, are they? They're not all here. They're mostly there. Remind you of anyone?'

'Is she *you*, Paule? The other part of you?'

The Sixth shook and nodded her head at the same time – which Amy wouldn't have thought possible – and didn't clear up the matter.

Paule kept tugging at Amy's scarf as if it were a dog's lead.

It was just after dark. Mauve Mary's favourite time of day.

Amy gave in and let Paule lead her towards the walkway.

The all-too-familiar rhythm of jumping up and down to that blasted rhyme sounded. Black Skirts rarely said the words out loud any more. Most didn't even use skipping ropes. They just hopped and stamped. It was like an eternal drumbeat. The pulse of the anthill.

'There's no going through at the moment,' said a Black Skirt whose triad barred the way. It was Keele. 'You can take the long way round if you need to get to the Quad.'

Paule yanked on Amy's scarf again, exposing her torn blazer. If Keele, a whip, Minored her, she'd be annoyed. At the moment, the Sixth overlooked the infraction.

'The wreckers, Amy… the wreckers.'

'She's upset, Keele,' Amy pleaded.

Keele had looked after Paule before she went Black. She was still the same person. She understood more than most.

'You know she's not just mad. She sees things we don't. If she's worried, we should be too.'

Keele paused, as if out of the habit of thinking.

'Boney?' she said, at last.

'Yes, she knows about Boney. *Boneys.*'

Amy was encouraged. Keele was at least listening.

In the walkway, by Mauve Mary's shrine, a Black Skirt ennead circled, hands joined, jumping while turning. Rayne was in the middle of the ring, arms antenna-waving. Braziers burned foul-smelling stuff. The circling Sisters Dark all had metal ants stuck to their faces. Others crowded into the walkway, blocking off both ends. Amy guessed this was a ritual of summoning or exorcism.

The Black Skirts had a down on Mauve Mary – the Walkway Ghost.

A grown-up triad was there too, keeping to the shadows. Ponce Bainter, Red Flame, the Professor. The Hooded Conspiracy was a part of the Black Skirts or the Black Skirts were a part of the Hooded Conspiracy or they were all parts of the same horrid thing.

'Paule feels this is *dangerous*, Keele,' said Amy.

The Sixth looked sceptical. She glanced over her shoulder at the jumping circle and shrugged.

'I'm more worried that it's *ridiculous*,' she said. 'But ridiculous today is often common sense next Thursday. It'll be over soon. Then you can get through to... to wherever you're going.'

The scarf was getting tight around her neck.

'Incidentally, where *are* you going?'

Now Keele was suspicious.

Amy thought she saw a ripple on the wall of the walkway, as if it were a liquid surface. Was this what Paule meant by 'a shimmer'?

'It can't be mended, it'll never get fixed,' said Paule, insistent.

'Keele, please, listen to her,' said Amy. She's your *friend.*'

The Sixth looked as if Amy had slapped her.

Amy felt very, very cold – inside and out. She couldn't feel her hands or feet or face or heart.

'She's not my *friend*,' Keele said, as if astonished by the notion. 'She's a *fluke*!'

And *that word* was as if Keele had slapped Amy.

She was strangling now, the scarf knotted tight.

Keele's eyes widened as she looked up.

'...and so are you, Thomsett!'

Amy was three feet above the ground. Her scarf was taut as a balloon string. Her Kentish Glory mask was tucked into its pocket, and no use at all.

She was exposed as an Unusual.

Keele's triad partners – She-With-No-Mercy Aire and Black-at-last Wychwood – stared and pointed. Amy stretched her arms out for balance and wobbled. She had a headache coming on.

Whips often Minored distracted girls for having their head in the air or not having their feet on the ground. Amy was guilty of these vague Infractions in a terribly specific way. She could be Majored for this.

At the moment, too much else was happening.

Looking over the heads of Keele's triad and into the walkway, Amy saw the skipping circle more clearly. The ripples in the air pulsed to the beat of the rhyme. On the paving stones, where Ellacott's shadow was still marked, a design had been made with chalk and pebbles. The Runnel, again. Rayne, skipping higher than the surrounding ennead, was the Flute. As the

Queen Ant jumped, she saw Amy floating. They looked at each other, as if no one else were present... and an electric thrill passed between them.

Paule screamed!

A dazzling light. A vile smell. And change...

XVII: Purple and Black and Red All Over

WHEN PAULE FIRST transported Amy here, the Purple was weird beyond her previous experience... but calm, a respite from the turmoil of Back Home.

This time, the turmoil passed over with them.

Paule hadn't brought them here. The Black Skirts had, by performing the dance of the Runnel and the Flute.

Paule said wreckers might break the Purple.

Amy itched with the *wrongness*.

Was this place broken? Or just its natural state?

Insect cacophony sounded – metal clashing on metal, steel-capped boots stamping on stone, vast war engines in motion, grinding and chewing and crushing. The ant army marched.

The atonal music Amy had heard before – the banshee ululation – was louder, more strident. Agitated tendrils rippled and lashed. Infinite eels or airborne seaweed. The music came from them. The tendrils vibrated like disembodied vocal cords.

Amy's scarf came undone and she was floating freely. Her antennae stung – not a new sensation, but a new sense.

Perhaps she had not been transported but transformed? The Purple wasn't entirely another place, but another layer of the place she knew. It was always there, but only in this shape could she perceive it – and could its denizens perceive her. Below her dangling feet was an almost familiar landscape.

The cover was off the walkway and a desert had risen to engulf School. The sea had receded. In the Purple, you could walk from Somerset to Wales without wetting your shoes. Buildings were fallen down or built on to, as if the Drearcliff that was and the Drearcliff that will be were tumbled together and left to fight it out. The masks on the Drearcliff Playhouse were as big as sphinx faces. The tumbled Tower still stood, though it floated high above the shingles, the cliff eroded away from under it.

Amy's wings, rooted again, flapped and she held steady in mid-air. It was an instinct, like breathing. She did not have to concentrate to flutter, though wondering about how her wings worked made her waver and fall a few feet. She caught the wind and held steady.

On her previous trip to the Purple, time stopped for everyone but her and Paule... now – because the shimmer had been opened by the skipping circle? – they had company.

The wreckers.

Keele's triad was frozen. So were most of the Black Skirts at the periphery of the circle, including the Hooded Conspirators. Amy saw them more clearly under the violet light of three moons. The masked chauffeur, Gogoth, was with them. This side of the shimmer, he was even more misshapen.

The skipping circle still revolved, but at quarter time – as if they were asleep but still hopping. Their faces betrayed no alarm, so they couldn't be seeing what

Amy was seeing. They were Back Home, mostly.

Rayne didn't have wings, but rose from the Flute anyway.

The Queen Ant could fly. She was fully in the Purple, alert and aware. She was still looking at Amy.

Should they dogfight, like Captain Skylark and the Demon Ace? Amy didn't think she was up to aerial combat just yet. She'd need a catapult or something.

Beneath them, Paule was stricken and writhing. Half her head was swollen out of proportion. One eye filled with blood, as if on the point of bursting like a boil. Her scalp stretched thin over bulbous skull-bones. Previously in the Purple, she was grotesque but lucid. That compensation was gone. Paule shrieked like a loon, mind scattered between Back Home and here.

Amy and Rayne floated upwards at the same pace.

As they rose, Amy saw more and more of the land below. The contours were familiar. There were the woods, as winter-leafless as Back Home, but with trees twisted out of shape. Twig-limbed, yellow-eyed dog-shapes detached from the trunks. The wolves of the Purple, neither animal nor vegetable, creaked as they loped along spiral paths.

There was no snow here, but fine sand drifted everywhere. The air was full of it, and Amy's wings pins-and-needlesed. She tasted a vileness worse than Drearcliff swede... worse than the cigar she had once filched from Uncle Peasegood's humidor and shared with Lettie, which had made them both sick for days. The dust clung to her antenna. She knew it was slow poison.

The wall that bounded School still stood, with a few breaches of spilled brick and broken glass. Where Watchet should have been an inferno raged, pouring thick dark smoke into the sky. Two of the moons were blotted out. Things with beating wings hid inside the cloud, disturbing the smoke into eddies and puffs. Were the things animals or aircraft? She suspected a ghastly commingling of gigantic insect and fighter plane.

Amy saw that the Runnel extended beyond the space it covered Back Home and spiralled through the woods and around School Grounds and across the landscape, scored deeper into the dry earth and becoming ever more branching and elaborate. The Flute here was a black sinkhole. Sand poured into it as if it were an earthy whirlpool. Wood-wolves squatted around the Flute like guard dogs. One missed its footing and was sucked into the maelstrom, then flew to pieces as the throat of the hole ground it like grain.

Rayne looked into the clouds. She waved her arms in that silly salute, which was returned by the things in the smoke. They had eyes, carapaces and scythe-like mouthparts.

Rayne's mouth opened and she exhaled insects.

Ants, Amy supposed. In pants.

...clouds of them. Not pants as in knickers, but pants as in breathing.

Rayne was a living Runnel and her mouth an open Flute. The ants poured through her, swelling the clouds. The smoke was alive with them.

Cross-currents lashed Amy and she flew lower to avoid being torn apart. The stinging, foul-tasting sand-dust made her unsteady.

She couldn't blink. She had no eyelids here.

Folding her wings, she set down. The ground was spongy and pulsating. In the Purple, was the earth – the Earth? – *alive*? Any warmth came up from the world's skin not down from the violet moons.

She saw the skipping circle through a small dust storm. The rest of Back Home was less clear. She could make out a few floating figures – Keele and Aire, Gogoth and the Professor – but they were transparent. In the Purple, the denizens of Back Home were ghosts.

Keening cut through the other din.

Dora Paule was in pain.

Amy saw her on the ground, struggling against purposeful tendrils wrapped around her. She was fully ten feet tall or long, but not strong in limb. Three wood-wolves – with the carved and painted faces of Pest, Hoan and Fulwood – worried at Paule's shrivelled legs and feet. They nosed her great bulk along a path – the Runnel – and took an occasional nasty bite, embedding splinter-teeth in her spindly calves. The tendrils dragged her.

If the Runnel and the Flute Back Home led here, where did the Runnel and the Flute of the Purple lead?

Not Back Home, she was sure.

Amy stretched her wings and zoomed towards Paule. She took hold of her friend and fought the tendrils. The wood-wolves came at her. She crushed their throats with a mental pinch, popping their eyes and snapping their necks. A deep crack ran across the Pest mask. Sappy green pus dribbled through. Heads lolling wrongly, the wood-wolves scarpered.

Paule, unknowing, fought Amy.

Taking handholds on gigantic blazer-buttons, Amy hauled herself up Paule's body and put her face in front of her friend's handspan-across good eye. Recognition flared. Paule stopped resisting and Amy dug her heels in.

The tendrils snapped and flapped.

Paule could sit up, though that meant rearranging

her huge head so it didn't crush her ragdoll body. Amy saw her friend was struggling with herself.

Amy looked up and couldn't see Rayne any more. The clouds of smoke and insects whirled into a great Runnel pattern. The third moon was obscured and night fell in the Purple.

'Paule, Paule,' she shouted. 'What's wrong here? What can we do?'

'Knowles should read the big book,' said Paule conversationally.

'Knowles of the Remove? Miss Memory. What book?'

'In the Swanage. That book.'

The Swanage was called Tempest Keep on the maps. It was the building where Headmistress had her office and rooms. In the Purple, a windmill with mottled silk sails stood in its place. Dr Swan had shelves of books.

The pull of the Flute grew. Amy felt it too. It tugged at her wings, and a pain – a new kind of pain – burned in their roots. She flapped, trying to fight. She tasted rotten tangerine with her antennae.

The tendrils seized Paule again, winding more thickly around her.

Rayne was engulfed by the black cloud.

Were the things inside the Other Ones?

Amy held Paule's wrists and wouldn't let her be drawn back onto the Runnel.

Both girls were coughing. The dust was whipped up by the winds which stirred the clouds above. In the dust, tiny insects swarmed and bit. Amy choked on them. This wasn't like house dust Back Home. More like fine gravel or the shingle on the beach. It was partially composed of fragments of eggshells. She remembered the plain of hatching eggs.

Dust shapes rose to form tubby torsos, football heads, broad shoulders and thick arms. They were like Frost's snowman, not alive but ambulant. Three of them – like the wood-wolves or Black Skirt triads. Hulking, malign dust-golems of the Purple. They stumped towards Amy and Paule in formation. Gold eyes glittered and third eyes, in the foreheads, began to glow. The arrangement was the same as the moons above. And matched Ellacott's description of Mauve Mary. The recurrence of threes persisted.

Amy flat-palmed the air, fingers slightly curved, and pushed out with her mind to block the lead dust-golem. A hole punched through its chest, but it kept on walking. Bugs swarmed in its bulk, eating each other and spitting out pulp that wove together to fill in the hole.

'Let me go, Amy,' said Paule. 'You can get Back Home. I'll have to go on from here…'

Behind the dust-golems appeared a tall, slender figure. She strode through the storm.

It was a girl in Drearcliff uniform, but fully present in the Purple. An inner light spilled through her own forehead-fissure. She struck a dust-golem from behind with a hockey stick…

…and the creature flew apart, a ball of yellow energy slammed out of its head, dissipating like a dandelion clock. Its fellows stopped in their tracks. Their heads revolved away from Amy and Paule.

The new girl smote them both and they collapsed. The insects crawled away from their heaps. She swept through the bugs with her stick. Small fires erupted where she scythed – burning blue, like a Bunsen lamp. Tiny scraps of creatures flared into nothingness.

Amy looked at the girl's face and didn't recognise her. But she knew who she was.

Mauve Mary.

She wore a whips' blazer, in Drearcliff Grey. An Ariel tiepin.

Amy wondered if their rescuer would say anything...

Then, there was a lightning crack and the stink of spent matches.

It was very dark and Amy and Paule – the girl-sized Paule of Back Home – were in a small, sticky place. Someone had hands on them, a firm grip. They were hauled through oily stuff. Amy was her normal self, without wings or feelers. She felt the loss acutely, as if suddenly struck deaf or blind... but a moment later couldn't describe even to herself what her moth-senses had been.

Another lightning strike and they were tumbling across paving stones.

Back Home.

'You, girls,' shouted someone – Keele! 'What are you doing?'

Amy and Paule rolled into the skipping circle, like a ball into skittles.

The ritual disrupted, the ennead got tangled up with each other. Ropes were underfoot. Gould growled, fangs bared, and Crowninshield II spat oaths which would have earned her a Language Infraction in less chaotic circumstances.

Keele waded in to sort things out.

The walkway was covered again. Rayne was here too, standing stock-still on the Flute. Insects crawled on her face and lapels. No, they were just badges...

'You came out of the wall,' said Keele.

There was still a purple glow. The shimmer.

'Look,' said Keele. 'There...'

Amy untangled herself and looked above the shrine. She saw Mauve Mary. The ghost had been in the Purple. Mary had saved her and Paule from the dust-golems and whatever raised and commanded them. She had sent the girls Back Home. Mauve Mary was guardian of the thinning spot between the worlds. An anti-wrecker.

Apart from the glowing spot on her forehead – as much like Kali's castemark as the bud of a third eye – she looked normal. She had thick eyebrows and dimples. She solemnly sank into the wall, waving goodbye.

She was gone and so was the violet light. Someone turned on a torch.

There was a great deal of milling-about as Black Skirts tried to tell each other what just happened. The Hooded Conspirators stepped back into the night.

Amy felt her own face and Paule's, finding no injuries. The Purple left aftertastes and lingering images.

Torchlight swung across Keele's face. She was astonished.

'Enid,' she said. 'That's Enid. Mauve Mary is...'

'Who?' asked Amy. 'Enid who?'

'ffolliott. Enid ffolliott.'

'ffolliott-Absent?'

'No,' said Paule. 'ffolliott-Presence.'

XVIII: Sisters Light

'THIS IS WORSE than last term,' said Light Fingers. 'Then, the Moth Club were strictly outside School Rules, but so were the Hooded Conspiracy. The Black Skirts *are* School Rules. Nothing hooded about them. Moth masks are no use any more. So few of us are left in Grey that even the dullest of the Dims could tell at once who we were.'

Amy was forced to agree.

This inquorate meeting of the Moth Club was convened in the Biology Lab annexe. In autumn, before the Black Skirts were dreamed up, Miss Borrodale had supposed that Amy might be interested in the Calloway Collection. The most exotic specimens were in the annexe, stuffed under glass domes, floating in jars of brine or arranged in drawers. Loosely interpreting casual invitation as actual permission, Amy had let Light Fingers pick the lock. If they approached Fossil now and requested the key, they would have no joy. The science teacher only bestowed favours on the Sisters Dark. Inchfawn was restored as Fossil's pet, which made Amy all the warier of the six-eyed sneak.

It had been a mistake to think Inchfawn permanently

sent to Coventry. Going Black was a way back.

Light Fingers lit a Bunsen burner. Adjusted to burn pure blue, it gave off enough light for the girls to see each other's faces and enough heat to warm their hands.

'You know what we are,' said Amy. 'Moths around a flame.'

'...which is supposed to be dangerous. For moths.'

Amy had tried to tell Light Fingers everything. Having lost Kali's friendship by keeping uncomfortable truths from her, she didn't dare chance it again. She did her best to explain Daffy Dora Paule and the Purple, the true identity of Red Flame, the unholy partnership of Hooded Conspirator and the Black Skirts, and that Mauve Mary was ffolliott-Absent. A lot to take in. Light Fingers had trouble following it all – especially when it came to wood-wolves and dust-golems. Amy knew she sounded like the old Smudge. Indeed, her story was more far-fetched than Smudge's wildest exaggerations.

Her friend seized on the oddest things to fuss over. Told about Amy and Kali saving Beauty Rose from the Runnel and the Flute, Light Fingers was miffed she hadn't been included in the rescue party – which was entirely her own fault for making herself scarce. She was so aggrieved to have been dropped from the team that she forgot to be appalled by revelations about Ponce or horrified by the dread shadow of the Other Ones.

'...and, in this Purple place, you have *feelers*? How can you keep your hat on?'

Light Fingers put her hands up to her forehead and waggled her forefingers.

Amy couldn't help but laugh at that.

'I don't understand where Dr Swan is in all this,' said Amy. 'I thought she was for us. She went on and on about

Unusual Girls. I can't see how she's let this happen.'

She detected a whininess in her own voice which she disliked, and resolved firmly to change her tone... though it was difficult to complain cheerfully.

'I told you how the Ordinaries are,' said Light Fingers, crowing a little too much. 'Headmistress couldn't stand against all of them. I'm not surprised Bainter and the rotters have got her out of the way. It was bound to happen.'

'What should we *do*?'

'We can't do anything, Amy,' said Light Fingers. 'Too many of them and precious few of we. I'm giving it until the snow melts enough that I don't leave tracks, then I'm over the wall. Will you come with me? There's nothing for us here.'

'The Moth Club,' Amy said, searching for a hope.

Light Fingers shook her head. 'Frecks and Kali aren't with us this time. Even if they weren't Black Skirts, they're not like us.'

The other half of the Moth Club left off talking whenever Amy came into the cell, but were elaborately polite. Kali started speaking proper English, with a musical Kafiristani accent. Frecks sounded more and more grown-up and stopped taking crafty naps in Double Geog. It was as if they'd been fetched off by the fairies and replaced with well-mannered changelings.

Beauty Rose was often in the cell, occupying Light Fingers' rocking chair. Since the Runnel and the Flute, she and Kali had become friends. They were always passing notes back and forth between them, with smiles and smirks and strange little giggles that had a razory touch on Amy's skin. For a girl who didn't talk, Rose filled silence with a great deal of meaning.

Once, Amy came back to the cell to find Frecks, Kali and Beauty waving their arms like a proper Black Skirt triad. When Amy hove in view, they all three quickly folded their arms and tried to look innocent. Their simpering lasted only a few seconds before they collapsed into laughter – Beauty laughed by tapping her chest and nodding her head at the same time – directed at the Grey interloper.

'Too difficult to explain, old thing,' said Frecks, wiping away tears of mirth. 'Just take our word for it, it's *funny*.'

That set them off again. Amy withdrew and went to the Library – angry and hurt and sad.

...and yet Amy still wasn't ready to give up on her friends. Or on School.

But Light Fingers was persuasive.

'Schools are like prisons,' said Light Fingers. 'I know that from my parents. Jails have cells, lights-out, Chapel, flicker shows, bells, slop, stains, whips – just like here. Modern schools and modern prisons are built on the same model, Jeremy Bentham's panopticon. Old ones just turn out the same, like Drearcliff Grange and the Mausoleum. Look at the bottle-topped walls. Patrolling guards in black. Your wood-wolves are guard dogs. I'd rather pick oakum or sew postbags than brush the blasted Heel. I've been working out escapes. Wherever you go, you should think how to get out if you have to. Every building, every room, every friendship.'

Amy's heart hurt. She had heard this doctrine from Light Fingers before, but it had seemed like a game rather than a serious way of life.

'Even without snow, Gould could track you.'

Light Fingers shook her head. 'I'm prepared. You

know the perfume Peebles got from her uncle for Christmas. That pongy stuff she hates and never uses? I can take it off her hands. I'll sprinkle scent on my bed and some clothes I'll leave behind, then douse a fox or a rabbit so it'll leave a false trail while I nip off in the other direction. I'm quick, remember. It's an advantage.'

Amy saw Light Fingers had thought it through.

Had she dreamed up tricks to deal with *anyone* who might go against her? Was that level of distrust sensible, or dangerous? Amy knew what being alone was like and didn't want to go back to it. At Drearcliff, she had found friends.

Light Fingers saw her hesitating.

'Amy, even without you, I'm going…'

The door was opened. Light flooded the annexe.

'Going where?' asked Miss Borrodale.

Snitcher Garland had gone to Fossil, of course. A Black Skirt triad came with them – Inchfawn, Bryant, Vail. With skipping ropes wound round their fists, they tried to look like a Wild West lynching party. The effect was somewhat spoiled by them being titchy schoolgirls rather than rangy cowboys. The black hats helped, but not enough. Ants were only fearsome in a horde… as individuals, or even in small groups, they were just *bugs*, the lowest, dullest, meanest sort of insect.

'The lock's been tampered with, miss,' said Inchfawn, holding a magnifying glass to show the tiny scratches Light Fingers had left.

Occasionally, Amy had felt sorry for Inchfawn. Never again.

'Naisbitt, Thomsett. Major Infractions. The Heel. Naisbitt – this comes as no surprise. The apple, in this case, does not fall far from the poison tree. But

Thomsett… I have to say I'm disappointed. I had thought more of you.'

Inchfawn's excited smile was terrifying. She was close to wetting herself.

Vail, to whom Amy had never paid attention, was blank-faced, not even relishing petty victory or advantage as Garland or Inchfawn did. What did Vail get out of the Black Skirts? She had always been among Viola's 'courtiers, attendants, guards, clowns, & co.' An ant crawled down the side of Vail's face, like a tear.

'This, girls, is what grasshoppers look like,' Fossil lectured the Black Skirts. 'The lack of industry, the slyness, the arrant sabotage. We are *not* grasshoppers.'

She tapped her ant brooch.

The Black Skirts' arms shot up in the antenna salute. Hands waved and fingers flapped like agitated antennae.

Amy felt more ashamed than aggrieved, but Light Fingers was sullen. She expected no better from the Ordinaries.

'Mute defiance, eh?' said Fossil. 'Not a seemly attitude, girls. I trust you'll improve your conduct in your new form. You're to report to the Remove.'

The Remove

I: To the Leper Colony

BEING 'REMOVED' DIDN'T just mean hiking to Temporary Classroom Two for lessons. Now Houseless persons, the lowest form of living ghost, Amy and Light Fingers were booted out of their Desdemona digs.

If Amy *could* have gone Black, she would have done – to keep her cosy place in Frecks' cell, to stay well in with friends who now pretended not to know her or solicit the approval of teachers who'd gone cold on all Greys. She'd have skipped and antenna-waved and marched with the other ants... if the option were open to a fluke like her. She'd have turned on others, too, happy to march in step with the Black Skirt majority and scorn the pale dregs of the Greys.

Realising she was no better than Inchfawn made her tears hotter.

Mother would take the news with an exasperated sigh and sham pity. She was used to Amy humiliating her. A favourite expression was 'what your poor father would have said I don't know', which truly meant she knew *exactly* what Father would have said and that it would have been withering. Amy had her own ideas about what Father would or would not have said. She resolved not to write home about her removal.

What happened at Drearcliff could stay here.

To put the old tin lid on it, Fossil had characterised them as grasshoppers. *Caelifera*! As a science teacher, Miss Borrodale should know *Aesop's Fables* was an unreliable entomology text. Grasshoppers were as active and ferocious as ants. In battle, flight-capable, voracious grasshoppers would prevail over nest-building, cowering ants. *Locusts* were grasshoppers, and they numbered among the Plagues of Egypt. The Lord God didn't bother visiting *ants* upon Pharaoh.

Removal was supervised by Digger Downs, who was more pro Black Skirt even than Fossil. An insect badge crawled up and down her jacket. A giant ant, over an inch long (*Dinoponera australis*?). One of its legs was tethered to a black thread pinned to her lapel. The living brooch strayed as far as the ruffle of Downs' blouse but couldn't reach the skin of her neck. The insect must want to give the teacher a nasty nip.

Ranks of Black Skirts gathered to watch Amy and Light Fingers laid low, antenna-arms raised and stiff. The skipping rhyme and the repetitive crunch of stomping feet came from the Quad. Those sounds were heard everywhere these days.

The disgrace meant she wasn't permitted to fetch her own things from the cell. She had to make a list of her possessions and give it to Bryant. It wasn't easy to remember everything off the top of her head. Some items she didn't want on record. She had trophies of her night-time exploits, including a conspirator's hood retrieved from the broken tower and broken-off pieces of tile and chimney pot collected while floating. Her Kentish Glory togs were in with the rest of her kit.

Bryant went up to Amy's former cell to collect everything on her list. Amy supposed Frecks or Kali would hand over anything she happened to forget – or just chuck it out of the window.

The condemned girls waited outside in the cold. Fulwood came out of the dorm to take away their enamel Desdemona badges. Amy hadn't remembered to wear the thing half the time, but giving it up was like having her head shaved in the market square. Light Fingers was required to unwind and hand over a House scarf. She made a point of shivering. At least, they didn't have epaulettes to be ripped off or swords to break. If anyone tried to snap a hockey stick over their knee they'd do themselves an injury.

Bryant's triad came out of the dorms with Amy's trunk held up over their heads, as if demonstrating the proverbial ant knack of carrying many times its own weight. Another triad, with Pulsipher on point, followed with Light Fingers' trunk – a family heirloom plastered with stickers from theatres where her parents had performed. Her rocking chair was left behind, classified as furniture rather than a personal possession.

Amy looked up and saw Frecks' face at a window.

She stuck her hand up to wave at her friend. Frecks exhaled, misting the glass to opacity.

Another arrow to the heart.

Light Fingers was almost smug. Having her worst fears proved warmed her a little.

Frozen slush was cleared from gravel paths. Green grass showed through the thinning snow. In other circumstances, Amy would have delighted in the approaching thaw. Now, she felt as if she were at a hasty funeral for a double suicide.

Downs tooted a whistle. Amy trudged along after the removal girls.

'My old man said "foller the van" and don't dilly-dally on the way,' said Light Fingers. At Drearcliff, doing a midnight flit was less of a disgrace than being removed. Anyone could be short of funds. It took effort to fall short of expectations.

Kindly, Light Fingers took Amy's hand and squeezed.

As they passed, the Black Skirts chittered and waved their arms in agitation. That was new.

The Black Skirts were becoming less like girls, more like bugs.

The exorcism of Mauve Mary had sped the process along.

'Ignore them, Amy,' said Light Fingers. 'Ignore them and they'll go away.'

'We're the ones who're going away, Emma.'

Some Black Skirts had specks crawling on their faces and hands. Ants crept out from collars and cuffs. Into eyes and mouths.

This was wrong. Ants weren't like that... lice or mites lived on the human body, but were mostly too small to see. Even Professor Rayne didn't go so far as to say ants could colonise *people*. Had Rayne *fille* brought these ants back from the Purple? The Flute was open and the Purple was exhaling through it... breathing out bugs, *ants in pants*.

'Courage,' said Light Fingers, helping her along.

Purple or Purple-ish things were all around these days... wood-wolves, dust-golems, insects unknown to science. Not yet in the open, but in thinning shadows, gaining confidence. The ants weren't in pants any more... they were everywhere. School was turned into a giant anthill.

Rayne didn't show up to witness their removal. Did the Queen Ant even knew who they were... or who anyone was? She had divided School into Black Skirts and Ghosts. In Rayne's world, there were no individuals. Even queens were replaceable.

Amy and Light Fingers followed their luggage across the grounds. Black Skirts on all sides waved and shrilled. Unremoved Greys made themselves scarce, for fear of being further lumped in with *flukes*. Amy bitterly regretted not speaking up when others were being kicked.

The Auxiliary Dorm, known as Remittance Man's Rest, was a former stables. Even Dauntless wouldn't put up with it. The horse shared a cottage with Joxer.

Devlin met the new arrivals with something like a welcome. She stuck out her paw, knobbly wrist extending six inches from her sleeve. As they shook hands, Amy felt Stretch's pliable bones shift.

The Remove wasn't a House, so it didn't have a House Captain. Devlin was stuck with the responsibilities but benefited from none of the privileges.

Incidentally, who'd be Desdemona Third Captain now Light Fingers was gone? Probably – uck! – Inchfawn.

'Welcome to the Fluke Show,' said Stretch, not unkindly. 'Sorry, but you've to put up where we can fit you and there's only one cell with two free berths. Far end on the right. Thought you'd rather bunk together than be prised apart. Your chests have been dumped already, just outside your cabin. Do what you can to get stowed away. We're short on shelves and wardrobes. Not much on home comforts at all.'

Amy and Light Fingers, still holding hands, passed under the lintel.

Inside, the dorm still smelled strongly of horse.

Duckboards were laid over a beaten earth floor. Ill-fitting doors let in draughts. Each pen had four cots shoved into it. There was no electric, but oil lamps hung from posts.

Palgrave stood under a light, smiling as ever. Little flames danced in her eyes, as if her maggot were fascinated by fire. Frost sat on a stool in the corner. She looked up at the newcomers eagerly… then slumped, disappointed. Who had she expected to come and rescue her?

Lamarcroft – who knew *she* was an Unusual? – stood by a music stand and practised scales on a miniature bugle. Lungs wore her untidy black hair clipped short and had a Grecian fringe. She was – *had been* – Goneril's archery champ. She paid no attention to the newcomers.

Like orphans abandoned in a wood, Amy and Light Fingers ventured cautiously down to where their trunks were dumped. Amy's was open. Her belongings were jumbled. Books dumped on clothes. Brushes in with pens and pencils. Roly Pontoons' floppy feet stuck up from the mess.

They looked into their assigned cell. It had dusty windows at horseneck-height.

Two small girls sat in the gloom, playing Old Maid. Harper and Dyall.

Amy and Light Fingers looked at each other and – through strength of will – didn't burst into tears.

'Hullo, new chums,' squeaked Harper. 'Come in and make yourselves at home. We won't bite.'

11: A Different Form

TEMPORARY CLASSROOM TWO was a former greenhouse, converted from horticultural use by painting thickly over the panes – except for a few left clear so they could pretend to be windows. Previous convicts had scratched hieroglyphics into the glass walls. Sunshine beamed through the arcane signs, so mystic lights crept across the floor like an alchemist's clock. TC2 was heated – if not well – by a smoky stove. Mismatched furniture was salvaged from all over School. The chairs had wonky legs and skirt-piercing splinters. The desks were nailed shut and inscribed with the names of long-gone girls. The blackboard was new, but the room so damp chalks crumbled before much could be written up on it.

Amy and Light Fingers found places near the front of the class. Amy's too-high chair jammed her knees up under her too-low desk. After a night in the same room as Poppet and Shrimp, she was exhausted *and* befuddled… Was this what one of Mother's 'heads' was like? She hoped that curse was not hereditary.

Harper was bright and sparkling this morning.

Light Fingers had taken Amy aside and said they had

to get out of the leech's cell or else they'd be skeletons by the end of the week while the sharp-toothed Shrimp would be plump, pink and blooming. At least, Amy thought she remembered Light Fingers saying something like that. With Dyall around, she couldn't be sure.

She had either not slept or suffered night terrors. She couldn't have had *both* conditions, but this morning her memories of the night were vague and ill-formed. She had aches from the lumpy cot and the impression of a hungry, ballooning face looming over her.

The rest of the Remove were too concerned with their own woes to be sympathetic. Why didn't Poppet and Shrimp cancel each other out? Would their peculiar Abilities affect Palgraive? She might not have a mind left to cloud.

Lamarcroft, a Sixth, had been a whip. Her piping was unpicked when she was removed. She still tried to wield authority and came over to tithe the new girls. She said it was customary to pay rent on desks in TC2. Arrant extortion, but there were no real whips here to stop such piracy.

Unfortunately, Amy came impoverished to the Remove. She had no tribute to yield. She pulled out empty pockets.

The Amazon Archer glared and cracked her knuckles.

'I shall make an example of you.'

'To whom?' put in Light Fingers.

'It speaks,' said Lamarcroft.

'It speaks, and it spits!'

Light Fingers pressed her lips together but did not spit. Lamarcroft backed away, though.

'Made you flinch.'

Light Fingers passed her hands in front of the Sixth's

face very fast, making her cringe again. In the Remove, there was little point in keeping Abilities secret...

'We shall resume this discussion later,' said Lamarcroft, striding back to her desk.

A cracked bell sounded. Miss Kaye came into the room, carrying a stuffed briefcase and the register. A small potted plant stood on the teacher's desk. A winter-flowering polyanthus.

'Thank you, Paquignet,' she said.

Green Fingers stretched out her skirt in a seated curtsey. She seemed to thrive in the Remove. Amy supposed she'd been ill at ease in Ariel, most toffee-nosed of Houses. And TC2 retained enough of its former atmosphere to suit the gardening girl.

Amy would not thrive. Plants were hardier than moths.

'We have new girls today,' said Miss Kaye, examining the register. 'There has been an influx lately. I can't think why.'

At least the Remove was taught by someone who'd never wear a black ribbon or an ant brooch. Amy always thought Miss Kaye the fairest and most humorous of the Staff.

'If you please, would you introduce yourselves to the Remove. Naisbee and, ah, Thompson.'

'Close enough,' said Know-It-All Knowles dryly, from the back of the room.

Miss Kaye frowned. She knew she'd mistaken the names, but couldn't call the proper ones to mind. She'd known who Amy was last term. They'd had long conversations.

Front and centre in class sat that menace Poppet Dyall.

Miss Kaye was uncharacteristically distracted. Her

hair-band was awry and she had chalk marks on her blouse. She was thinner, paler and more fluttery than Amy remembered. Removal affected teachers too.

Amy stood and announced, 'Thomsett, Amanda,' then stopped herself before she proudly added 'Desdemona'. 'Third Year,' she concluded weakly. She sat.

'Nais-*bitt*,' said Light Fingers, without standing.

'Bless you,' said Knowles. She paused for titters, which didn't come. Miss Kaye didn't upbraid her, either. Know-It-All slumped, unsatisfied.

'Today, we have…'

It was on the tip of Miss Kaye's tongue, but she couldn't produce the words.

'Ancient History,' prompted Lamarcroft.

Miss Kaye smiled, gratefully.

'Arctic Geography,' piped up a voice from the back.

'Aramaic Composition.'

'Advanced Thinkology.'

'Black Marketeering.'

'Murder.'

'Mayhem…'

'…and Magic Beans.'

Miss Kaye was distressed by the ragging. No one laughed, not even the jokers. The suggestions were tossed with venom rather than in play.

Amy looked at Light Fingers, who shrugged.

Things were different in the Remove. It was like the jungle.

'If you will open your exercise books,' Miss Kaye suggested.

Amy raised her hand.

'Miss,' she said.

'What is it, Thompsomething?'

'I don't have an exercise book with me. We weren't told what to bring…'

Howls of crocodile sympathy.

'Pretend you have one and try to keep up, there's a dear.'

Amy realised she was unlikely to prosper academically in the Remove. Thorn openly read *Girls' Paper*, Frost raised a sparkling black stalagmite from her inkwell and Lamarcroft sharpened a pencil with a penknife as if making a shiv. Palgraive, Dyall and Paquignet smiled vacantly, keeping quiet rather than paying attention. Devlin craned her neck, her extra vertebrae creaking, so she could look at drawings Knowles was making in her exercise book.

Lessons were baffling and pitiful. Miss Kaye got into more and more of a tizzy as she struggled to keep a train of thought. She snapped at the form, though few maintained the energy to snap back. When Light Fingers dozed off during a discourse on the obliquity of the ecliptic, Harper leaned over and snuffled, inhaling her victim's breath. Was that how she did it? Amy shooed the pest away and Shrimp showed her teeth. Light Fingers jolted awake and fell off her chair. Miss Kaye didn't even tell her to sit properly.

While Miss Kaye dealt with a dispute between Frost and Knowles, Amy felt a finger poking between her shoulder blades. There was an empty desk behind her. She turned round and just caught Stretch Devlin pulling back her long arm.

'What can you *do*, dearie?' asked Devlin.

Amy knew what she meant, but shrugged as if she didn't.

'You're a fluke like us. Your pal's fast, but you're…

311

a mystery of the sea. Come on, Thomsett, out with it…'

Trapped by her desk, Amy wasn't in a position to float, even if she'd wanted to show off. But there was the other thing.

Amy popped her pencil into the dry inkwell of the empty desk and left it there. Then, inviting a headache, she concentrated, feeling for the pencil with thoughts, stretching her mind as Devlin could stretch her bones.

The pencil flipped from one angle to another.

Devlin's eyes widened. 'Stap me vitals,' she said, admiring.

The pencil stirred, like a teaspoon gripped by invisible fingers. Round and round.

Amy was getting better at this, but there was a catch. When she was floating and in her Kentish Glory guise, her Ability was off the leash. She could expertly shift all sorts of things within eyeshot. But, if she were just her ordinary self with her feet on the ground, she could only move small items which were within reach anyway. There was no point getting a headache turning the pages of a book or picking up an apple when she could manage perfectly well with her hands.

She took her pencil back by reaching for it.

Devlin gave her a salute, though. At least, no one took against you here just for being a fluke. She wasn't really an Unusual in TC2. Everyone had Abilities or Attributes… though having a brain-maggot puppeteer like Palgrave or being a tick like Harper or Dyall removed them even within the Remove.

Her head wasn't aching and her nose wasn't bleeding. She was finding it easier to use her Abilities without suffering.

By the end of the day, Amy was bored as well as

absent-minded, sick and dejected. Miss Kaye dismissed them without even assigning prep. Cause for celebration in any other form, but here just another sign that they were abandoned and outcast.

Trudging back to Remittance Man's Rest, Amy found the next exile waiting outside the old stable, sat on her trunk.

'Ashes, ashes,' said Paule. 'I've fallen down.'

III: Remittance Men

PAULE WASN'T THE only fresh removal. Marsh came over at the same time, back from the sea but turfed out of Goneril. Devlin greeted her like a long-lost shipmate, but she wasn't cheered. Marsh muttered darkly of 'surface-dwellers', the rising of sunken cities and dreaming squid-gods in the depths. The Gill Girl couldn't have spent *all* her time away under the briny since she returned to School newly marcelled. Having her dark hair set in stiff waves might be a declaration of allegiance to the tides, but also made her look like a flapper from the flickers.

With no whips to stop them, Amy and Light Fingers changed their sleeping arrangements. Light Fingers worked her magic on a rusty lock – exciting admiration from Lamarcroft and Knowles, who evidently had larcenous ambitions – and opened a disused tack room which smelled of leather and liniment. A two-tier rack could pass for a bunk. Amy shifted two sets of bedding from their cell and Light Fingers dragged along two trunks.

'Moving out so soon?' asked Harper.

'No,' said Light Fingers. 'You are.'

For the first time in her life, Amy was in a position

to push around girls smaller than she. She felt guilty about exercising the power, but desperate measures were required. Another night with Shrimp and Poppet and she'd be broken in body and mind.

Lamarcroft stood by as Harper and Dyall were forced into the tack room. Light Fingers had bribed her before striking. This, it seems, was what it took to get by in the Remove. Ruthless practicality… and boiled sweets. Lungs was a slave to gob-stoppers. Light Fingers advised Amy to spend her tuck ration on placatory offerings. So long as the Amazongeld was paid, they'd be left alone.

In the Remove, there was more freedom than in dear old Desdemona. A dizzying, daunting prospect. Even if you bridled at some School Rules – official or off-the-books – there was comfort in knowing what was expected. Beyond the law were delights and terrors, but a girl had to make choices and live with the consequences.

Shrimp yelped as she was shoved into her new cell, but Poppet went quietly. Amy didn't know whether Dyall's eagerness to be useful was a pose. The ticks couldn't help their Abilities, any more than Amy could help hers… but Harper's predatory inhalations were slyly malicious, while Dyall seemed not to notice the befuddling effect she had on others. As Light Fingers shut the tack room door on the menaces, Amy saw Shrimp getting angry and ready to complain then lose track of her thoughts and seem puzzled, almost afraid. So she wasn't immune to Poppet.

'Emma, are you sure…'

'Let 'em drain each other empty,' said Light Fingers. 'Do us all a favour.'

Amy was uncomfortable with that sour thought.

This wasn't Desdemona and this wasn't the Moth Club. Girls did not look after each other in the Remove.

Drearcliff was more and more like home every day. Amy's home, that is, where Mother's moods were like the weather and she was always a disappointment... not that ideal idyll some meant when they said a place was like home.

The freed-up cots in Amy and Light Fingers' cell went to Paule and Marsh.

The Gill Girl took to her bed immediately, a net protecting her precious and slightly whiffy hair. She was still in a sulk.

Amy tried to talk with Paule, but the Sixth was too much in the Purple. She spoke about violet lights and spring storms and something she called the Scrambling. Light Fingers listened to her, for the first time... for confirmation of what Amy had told her. She had to admit things were happening at School beyond mortal ken. With ants crawling all over girls' faces, it was impossible for anyone not in Black to pretend this was a normal term – but Light Fingers wasn't quite ready to swallow Amy's whole story.

Also, she remembered Paule as a Murdering Heathen and wasn't as inclined as Amy to forgive her part in the *ancien regime* of terror.

Just because the Queen Ant was worse didn't mean Gryce wasn't bad.

Would Gryce wind up removed? She wasn't a fluke and had made a token concession to Black, so the Sisters Dark might keep her around the way potentates paraded defeated enemies in court or held rivals' children hostage to make a point.

Amy couldn't believe Head Girl had just given up.

She was almost disappointed in her old enemy. But also in herself. Rayne had done what she said she would – changed Drearcliff. She had never said change would be for the better, though in whatever she had for a mind she doubtless believed the present situation an improvement on the old ways.

Amy had taken things as they were and *not* tried to change them.

Rayne's example proved her wrong. The Moth Club should have done more. Their original charter was too limited… from the first, they should have acted for change. Once Kali was saved from the Hooded Conspiracy they should have found new crusades, rooting out larger ills, righting accepted wrongs. If they'd made School a fairer place, then Rayne – who had stood up to bullies and whips, after all – might not have got so many to follow her.

How would the Aviatrix or Dr Shade deal with the Queen Ant?

Amy considered posing this question to 'Stargazy', editor of *Girls' Paper*, acknowledged expert in the field of modern-day heroes and heroines. A new rule meant all letters had to be handed to Keys, unsealed. She read them before they were sent on, and blacked out anything deemed 'inappropriate or unhelpful'. School set up the system after a petition requesting vigilance over outgoing post was handed in by a Black Skirt deputation. Light Fingers said they'd ask for longer detentions and harsher beatings next. After all, good little girls wouldn't object to rules that only applied to bad little girls.

The Remove didn't have meals in the Refectory, but had to sit in a basement known as the Crypt. By the time food got to the Crypt, it was barely warm. Sometimes, their fare was partial because supplies ran low. If all the roast spuds were scoffed by Black Skirts, the Remove got extra boiled swedes instead.

Drearcliff boiled swedes had a well-earned reputation for vileness. If too many were scraped into the tub Joxer hauled off for swill, farmers complained their pigs turned their snouts up at the feed. Most girls would rather scrub the Heel with their own toothbrushes than eat extra boiled swedes.

In the Crypt, Amy and the others could hear the rhythmic crunch of Black Skirts at their troughs in the Refectory proper. The horde ate to the same rhyme as they skipped, stamping under the long tables. It wasn't a human sound.

For lessons and meals, the girls of the Remove were escorted to and from Remittance Man's Rest by Downs and an ennead of Black Skirts. A register was taken over and over again to make sure flukes weren't roaming free. Marsh, after her little dip in the sea, was on a short leash. Amy noticed key positions around School were always occupied by triads, skipping together like figures on Swiss town clocks. They stood guard in shifts, all through the night. Sometimes, Downs or Bainter supervised. Mostly, they got on with it by themselves.

It was plain now who ran Drearcliff Grange.

IV: The Invisible House

WITH NO PREP and shut out of Black Only activities, the Remove had to amuse themselves of an evening. Lamarcroft tooting scales on her horn offered limited entertainment. Thorn's *Girls' Paper* was passed around. Amy had read the number already. All that was left was chat.

Reluctantly, the flukes got to know each other.

The consequences of having Poppet Dyall nearby were well known, so she was told to stay in the tack room. Uncomplaining, she retreated to her cupboard-sized cell with a candle and *Uncle Satt's Miscellany for Boys and Girls*. Amy felt a twinge of pity, but hardened her heart. Poppet seemed perfectly happy with her lot… unlike everyone else in Remittance Man's Rest.

The girls found perches in the common area, as near as possible to a stove. Most draped coats and blankets around their shoulders.

Amy and Light Fingers huddled up on three-legged milking stools left over from when School had its own farm.

'I shouldn't be here,' said Thorn, not for the first time. 'It's a mistake. I'm Without an E. They were supposed to remove the Other One. With an E.'

Susannah Thorn, formerly of Tamora, was often mixed up with Susannah Thorne, of Viola. They were stuck with each other's exam results, assigned each other's prep and received each other's post. The Chimera had even duffed up Thorne – not, apparently, a fluke – by mistake. Though both Fourths, they looked nothing alike. Understandably, they weren't the best of friends.

'With an E should be here, and I should be…'

They had heard this song before. Misjudging her audience, Thorn was affronted by a lack of sympathy from the *justly* removed.

'Come off it,' said Devlin. 'A body doesn't get here *by mistake.*'

Stretch prodded Thorn with an eight-inch finger.

'What colour is your skirt?' asked Amy.

Thorn had to look down, but her uniform was still grey.

'And what colour's hers? With an E?'

Since the beating, Thorne was Black Skirt in good standing.

'You've a "party piece", like the rest of us,' said Devlin, wagging her extended digit. 'Give us a demonstration.'

Thorn sighed.

'No use pretending,' said Knowles. 'You can't pretend here.'

'It's all right,' said Amy. 'We're all Unusuals.'

Amy understood Thorn's hesitation. In dark moments, she still thought Mother might be right about the floating… especially now Drearcliff agreed that Amy's Ability was unnatural rather than Unusual.

'A pin to see the peepshow,' said Devlin. 'Come on, Thorn.'

Thorn gave in. She stood up and took a deep breath. 'Keep well back,' she said, rolling up her sleeves.

Amy moved her stool. Thorn made shooing motions and everyone shifted further until she nodded for them to stop. She now had room to swing a long-tailed cat.

'This better be a blinder,' said Know-It-All.

Clicking her fingers, Thorn made sparks. They lingered for moments like dying fireflies. Rubbing her hands together, she birthed a flame between her palms. A fire shape rose, illuminating Thorn from below, giving her face an infernal cast. Kneeling, she set her flame free on the floor. It whirled like a top. Thorn took some twists of paper – sweet wrappers – from her pocket and fed the fire. The twists went up in flashes like magnesium in the Chem Lab.

Girls cooed and clapped.

Puppeteering with her fingers, Thorn made the fire shape dance like a pixie ballerina, leaving a scorch-mark across the duckboards.

Amy applauded. Thorn was sweating with the effort.

'You and Frost even each other out,' said Devlin.

Angrily, Thorn made the ballerina puff and disappear.

'I'm *not* like anyone else,' she said, face dark. 'I'm Thorn, without an E.'

'Don't bust a boiler,' said Devlin. 'All flukes together in the Remove, remember?'

It was hard to get House Spirit going in the Invisible House.

'So, Frost, can you meet the Thorn challenge?' said Devlin. 'Want to make a dancing snowman?'

Frost shook her head. Since *l'affaire* Freezing, she'd buried her Abilities. She was afraid of them. Amy could understand that too.

Devlin, on the other hand, wasn't averse to showing off. She could make her fingers grow and twist. When she did, her face elongated as if her chin were being pulled.

'There's no part of my back I can't scratch,' she said. 'I can scrape my own barnacles. I still don't see what the fuss is about. I can do things other people can't. Other people can do things I can't and no one seems bothered. I'm so clumsy I couldn't skip in time if I wanted, and it seems *everyone* can do that.'

'They *are* bothered, though,' said Light Fingers. 'Knowles could come top in anything, if she had a mind to. So they stopped her.'

Knowles scowled at the reminder.

Rules had been changed to prevent Know-It-All from profiting from her Ability, so she was particularly aggrieved. It would be difficult to frame a rule barring Devlin from fetching down balls stuck in trees or fastening her own hooks if she wore a dress that did up at the back. Difficult, but not impossible. That might come next.

'They chucked Green Thumbs out of the Horticulture Club,' said Knowles.

'Don't mind,' said Paquignet. 'Not much for clubs. Clubs girls too noisy. Happier just with plants. Know where you are with plants. Quiet, are plants. Calm, too.'

Paquignet was another odd one – not all there. Perhaps she inhabited a Green the way Paule lived in the Purple. Her Ability was also her enthusiasm, but Green Thumbs didn't have an easy time of it. She had weals on her hands and splotches on her face. In the sort of perverse twist Amy had come to expect among Unusuals, Paquignet – her Abilities must run in the family or her parents wouldn't have called her Fleur

– suffered from year-round hay fever. She was allergic to almost everything vegetable. Green Thumbs made plants healthy, but they made her sick.

In a further irony, Paquignet's thumbs actually had taken on a greenish tinge… which Amy worried was the beginning of gangrene.

'Lungs,' said Devlin, 'what's yours?'

No one had asked the intimidating Sixth straight out before. Lamarcroft was sheepish.

'I'm quite strong,' she said.

'Can you straighten a horseshoe?' Thorn asked, presenting an old one which was lying around.

'I can try,' said Lamarcroft.

She tugged on the ends of the horseshoe, seemingly with little effort. Instead of straightening, it snapped in two.

'Behold, the Amazing Amazon,' said Thorn, impressed.

'Is that it?' said Light Fingers. 'You're only *strong*?'

Amy thought Lamarcroft might thump Light Fingers. Back when she was a Goneril Sixth and Light Fingers a lowly Desdemona Third, that tone of voice would have earned an instant Minor. And a cuff round the ear.

But Lungs didn't bristle at the scorn.

'I also… have dreams,' she said. 'The same dream, over and over. Most nights. You know the poem "and we are here as on a darkling plain, swept with confused alarms of struggle and flight, where ignorant armies clash by night"? I dream of *that*. Exactly that. I've had that dream ever since I can remember.'

'"Dover Beach", by Matthew Arnold,' said Knowles. 'It's still in my head after the Eng. Lit. test. Did your nanny read it to you in the crib? Rum choice for an infant, if so. My *ayah* barely ran to "Fairies in the Dell" and "Grumpy Goat's Half-Holiday".'

'I hadn't heard of "Dover Beach" until I had the same lesson you did, with Mrs Edwards when she was here. But as soon as Mrs Ed read it out, I knew Arnold was writing about my dream.'

'The poem's really about the rise of agnosticism,' said Knowles. 'Not beaches and battles. It's symbolism.'

'I think he had the same dream,' Lamarcroft said, 'and tried to tidy it away by making up a reason for it. No one dies of not going to church. Or perhaps it's just a coincidence. But that darkling plain is real. I'm in that war. A long-ago war or a yet-to-come war. I think it's why I was made strong.'

'What colour is the sky in your dream?' asked Paule.

Even Lamarcroft was surprised her fellow Sixth had spoken. She seldom asked direct questions.

'Dark,' said Lungs, shaking her head. 'Dark *purple*.'

Amy hadn't realised how afraid Lamarcroft was. That made her more afraid than she had been. Even before the Black Skirts penned them in a stable, the girls of the Remove had worries beyond the ordinary. Abilities seemed to come with curses attached, like Amy's nosebleeds or Paquignet's allergies.

'Perky, what of you?' asked Stretch, cheerfully. 'What occult talents do you harbour?'

Devlin was trying to lighten the mood. For all her jollity, she was mindful of others' feelings. She ran into a brick wall with Palgraive, who smiled back as if she hadn't heard the question.

'Yes, I wondered why you were here,' put in Thorn.

'To learn… my lessons, of course,' said Palgraive. 'And… be a good girl.'

Palgraive's voice was high-pitched, as if it came

from a much younger girl. Maggots are the larval stage of flies. The one nestled in Palgraive's brain might be young in the terms of its species. The strain of working a human body – vast and complex equipment for so small a grub – sometimes told. Putting sentences together was a colossal effort.

'Why else… should girls go to… school?'

'There's something about you, though,' said Knowles. 'You're one of us, all right.'

'If they chopped your arm off, would it grow back?' asked Laurence, an intense Second who'd only just been removed.

Palgraive smiled but didn't answer.

'Can you walk through walls?' asked Thorn.

'Talk to animals?' Amy ventured.

'Commune with spirits?' suggested Knowles.

'Conjure up the dead?' elaborated Frost, trembling.

'How about fetching *Rudolf Valentino*?' said Knowles.

General laughter broke out. Stretch draped a sheik-like towel over her head and rolled her eyes as if contemplating a fresh conquest in the harem.

'Rudy's not dead,' said Shrimp quietly. 'He's in California.'

'Same thing,' said Marsh, who – Amy only now realised – was American.

'Rudy's not dead *yet*,' said Paule definitively.

That stopped the laughing and joshing. They all looked at Paule askew and shocked. Why would she say Valentino – a youthful film star who played sheiks and bullfighters – was not dead *yet*? In the sense *everyone* alive was not dead yet? Or had she private, ominous insight gleaned from the Purple?

Paule was caught up with counting her fingertips. It seemed she couldn't make the sum add up in her head, though her hands looked perfectly normal.

Devlin turned back to Palgrave. 'Come on, 'fess up. What makes you a fluke?'

Amy wasn't sure Palgrave counted as an Unusual. Possibly, the brain-maggot was entirely ordinary and unexceptional as brain-maggots went. The girl-shell it wore wasn't all that unique. Palgrave had long pigtails and a wonky front tooth.

'I can tell you what's special about Perky,' said Light Fingers. 'She's still smiling. If that's not an Ability, I don't know what is.'

'We all know why they call you "Light Fingers", Naisbitt,' said Knowles. 'You have larcenous hands. Do you steal things in your sleep?'

'Yes... so watch that long nose of yours doesn't get mysteriously pinched.'

They were laughing again.

Like Amy, Light Fingers had shared some Abilities but kept others quiet, even in this company. Only Amy knew Light Fingers was *quick* as well as dexterous. Just as only Light Fingers knew Amy could float herself better than she could float a pencil.

'And Larry's trick is famous,' said Devlin.

Amy had heard about Laurence, formerly of Ariel. She sent small items away and brought them back – buttons, pencil-stubs, playing cards.

'Lungs,' said Stretch, 'bung Old Larry the broken horseshoe.'

Lamarcroft handed over the two lengths of metal. Laurence held them up for all to see and then disappeared them... not like a conjurer, with a distracting flourish, but casually. She made a hole in the air as if she were pulling open a drawer, popped the shoe pieces into it, and pushed it shut.

'We're in the pocket. Gone.'

She reached into the hole, which had a slight mauve tinge around the edge, and brought the pieces back.

'...and here we are again.'

The purplish caste objects had when fetched from Larry's 'pocket' suggested where they might have been.

If Paule was Queen of the Purple, was Laurence the Princess?

'Can you pull Valentino out of your pocket?' said Knowles.

'The lass has Rudy on the brain,' said Devlin. 'The only thing she doesn't forget after a month. It's in the bones and the blood, not the grey matter.'

'The pocket's not big enough for a person,' said Laurence. 'And I tried it with a mouse once, at home... it wasn't well when it came back. Cyril had to squash it with a brick. I don't think the pocket is for living things.'

'Shame,' said Marsh. 'I can think of a fair few who could be shoved into your pocket and not brought back without anyone missing them at all.'

'Things sent away have to be brought back,' said Laurence. 'Or else I get pains. The longer they're in the pocket, the worse the pains. I put a book away for a whole day, but it was like having a toothache in my hand. When I brought it back, the print had faded. You could hardly read it. In the pocket, it's not like it is here. I'd just as soon not put things away, but – after a while – if I don't send *something*, it's like an itch. Not as bad as a pain, but you know what itches are. No matter what Nurse says, you end up scratching. In the end,

I have to find something and put it away. I think the pocket needs to be *fed*.'

'Does the pocket travel with you?' asked Light Fingers. 'If you put something away here, you could bring it back in, say, the Refectory or – if you could stand the pain on a train journey – Plymouth or London or Dieppe?'

Larry nodded.

'You'd be the best diamond smuggler who ever lived,' said Light Fingers. 'They'd never catch you at customs.'

'Or you could be a secret agent and carry letters,' suggested Amy.

Laurence, youngest daughter of a Marquess, hadn't made an impression in Ariel, even with her pocket trick.

'At home I'm supposed to sit quietly and let my sisters show off their gowns,' Larry said. 'In the playroom, I have to be the Germans so Cyril can charge my lines. My brother charges everywhere, on his hobby horse. He pokes me with a wooden sword and calls me "Fritz der Schnitze". Once I put his sword in my pocket and he screamed until I brought it back. He got a new sword and doesn't use the purplish one any more. I thought everyone could put things in pockets and bring them back, because no one paid attention when I did. Not until I came to School. I wouldn't need to smuggle diamonds, though. Mummy has enough of those to begin with.'

Amy saw Laurence was coming to life in the Remove.

'I could get uncensored letters past Keys,' Larry said. 'The Black Skirts could search me all they like, at the gates. But I could take letters into town and post them. If I had the stamps.'

There was enthusiasm for the proposition, though

passes for Greys to leave School Grounds were in short supply these days.

'Abilities aren't enough,' Light Fingers said. 'Swan told me that, on my first day here. She said that what I needed was Application.'

It turned out that they had all heard variations on this speech.

(Where *was* Headmistress?)

Suddenly, they were thinking and talking about Applications.

It was like being in the Moth Club again.

Devlin and Lamarcroft held together the ends of the broken horseshoe while Thorn made flame and tried to join them by melting. It didn't work because the shoe pieces became too hot to hold with bare fingers.

'Thomsett, you try holding the bits up,' said Devlin.

'And burn my fingers too? No fear.'

'I didn't mean with your fingers.'

Amy tried to take a grip on the pieces with her mind, and she lifted them off the duckboard a few inches before they dropped. She shrugged an apology.

'I think you need an anvil and hammer, not just flame,' said Thorn.

So that was a wash-out.

Paquignet coaxed a tulip bud open and Frost flash-froze it into a sparkly, stiff ornament... then Thorn made a flame near the shoot and droplets of water fell from it before it began growing again.

Pretty, but useless. Still, there was enthusiasm for the enterprise.

Something like House Spirit.

Marsh and Lamarcroft competed to see who could hold their breath longest. Lamarcroft won, but Marsh said it'd be different if they were underwater.

'Then it'd only be fair if you held your gills too,' said Thorn.

Marsh's eyes popped wider than ever. Generally, people were too intimidated to mention the gills to her face. Even when Marsh was removed, no one had said it was because of her fishy Attributes.

After a moment, when Amy was worried Marsh would fix shark-sharp teeth in Thorn's neck before Without an E could whip up a flame, Marsh expelled air through her gills and made a dribbly raspberry.

It was unexpected, and everyone laughed. Amy, closest to Marsh, got a close look at her gills. Inside, the flesh was crimson, liverish. Usually the slits weren't even noticeable.

'It's okay,' said Marsh. 'You can touch them.'

Amy put her fingers out and brushed the slits. Marsh rippled her gills, giggling through them.

'All my folks have them,' she said.

She had an unusual accent too.

'Where are your people from?' Amy asked.

'Innsmouth, Massachusetts,' she said, 'or the South Sea Islands… or all the oceans.'

Devlin wanted to touch Marsh's gills, too. A queue formed. The Gill Girl had always been standoffish. Among flukes, she was more congenial, or at least weary of the effort she had to put into sulking.

Even Palgrave put her hand on Marsh's neck, imitating the others rather than following her own impulse. The maggot was trying to fit in.

'They've made a mistake,' Amy said tentatively.

The others looked at her.

'The Black Skirts,' she went on. 'They shouldn't have

put us here together and they shouldn't have left us alone. If they had Unusuals, they wouldn't have done it. They'd have expelled us... or worse.'

Someone coughed 'Gould.' Someone else said 'Rayne.'

Amy shook her head. 'Rayne isn't an Unusual. No matter what she's done. She's something else again. And Gould's given up on herself... but it won't be enough. Ants can't abide difference. It's why they're so successful. But this isn't an anthill and this isn't a prison. This is a school.'

A sarcastic snort from Light Fingers.

'Yes, Emma, there are similarities. But there are differences. Schools are about changing. We change... we learn, some things in lessons, other things just by being at school. School is like a tunnel through a mountain. We go through it and come out on the other side. We don't stay here.'

'The Black Skirts want to spread,' said Knowles. 'I've heard them talk about it. I went Black too, until they removed me. Rayne plans to send enneads to other schools, to spread their rhyme... *and everything else*. Boys' schools as well as girls'. It's like the measles. Soon, everyone will have spots and hop up and down with ants in their pants.'

Amy shuddered.

'We *can* stop them,' she said. 'Ants don't really work together like we can. They just all do the same thing. Like when they lift things – lots of identical ants doing one job. We can be different. Like Stretch said, Frost and Thorn even each other out... their Abilities are distinct, and would be useful in different situations. And our Applications can mesh. Like with the ice flower.'

Even Light Fingers was paying attention to her now.

Amy tingled... then wondered what she was doing. This was silly. She sounded like *Rayne*. Moths don't have queens. They're not really social animals.

'Go on, Amy,' said Frost.

'Oh, I can't... don't listen to me. I'll probably get us all expelled. It's what they'll do anyway. We're only here till we're got rid of.'

Light Fingers got up and went into their cell, then came back with something.

'Put this on and keep talking.'

It was a moth mask. Light Fingers had improved the design and sewn a new, sleeker domino. Amy hadn't had a chance to wear it.

She slipped on the mask.

'This is the real Amy,' said Light Fingers. 'Kentish Glory.'

Amy looked through the lenses Light Fingers had put in the eyeholes, which gave a slight magnifying effect. She felt stronger again, thought more clearly. She wasn't as self-conscious.

The rest of the Remove paid attention.

Kentish Glory could say things Amanda Thomsett couldn't. Light Fingers knew that, the way she knew she couldn't command attention the way Amy could. Her attitude was all wrong. Though she understood what needed to be said, she wasn't the one to say it.

'This isn't just the way things are, the way they're supposed to be,' said Amy. 'This is Wrong. The Black Skirts are Wrong. They've tried to make us feel guilty for not being able to join in. We have nothing to feel guilty about...'

With Shrimp in the circle, that was pushing it. And the maggot probably ought to feel guilty about eating

Palgraive's brain. But this wasn't the time to think of that.

'...but they've tried to make us ashamed of not being them. When we should be *proud* not to be them. You know who we're like? The Splendid Six. They started out like us – people with Abilities and Attributes, who saw Wrong things and came together to do something about them. We're The Splendid Six – Girls' Auxiliary Version. And more than six of us. We aren't *flukes*. We are Unusuals. We should do *something*.'

Everyone agreed and a certain amount of comradely back-slapping put off the inevitable moment when the next question – the one Amy couldn't answer – was asked.

'But what?' said several people. 'What should we do? What *can* we do?'

'Rayne,' said Harper, certain in herself.

Shrimp had sat at the edge of the circle, keeping quiet, watching – not coming too close to the others because she knew she'd be shut up with Poppet if she battened on to anyone. Now, she stepped into the light. A Fifth, she was a foot shorter than Amy. Even Laurence was taller than Shrimp, who might have stopped growing. At first glance, she seemed frail and fragile but – when well-fed – she was wiry and strong.

Shrimp was a test for Amy's invisible House Spirit. No one was more of a fluke than she, more outcast and despised... and for good reason. But Amy had said they *weren't* flukes. She needed to stand by her words, even as looking at Shrimp made her feel tired.

'Harper,' she said. 'What about Rayne?'

'We have to stop her,' Shrimp repeated. 'We have to stop Rayne.'

V: Fair Copies

WHEN THE REMOVE pitched up at TC2 the next morning, Miss Kaye was absent. In her stead, a Black Skirt triad held the register. Martine, Wool and McClure, known as the Ghidorah. None were whips, but they assumed authority. Two large boxes sat on the teacher's desk.

Knowles tried to greet her old chum Martine. McClure got in the way and gave Know-It-All a calculated wrist-pinch, smiling at her yelp. One of the worst Murdering Heathens was now one of the worst Black Skirts. Amy thought Rayne wouldn't approve. Soldier Ants weren't supposed to *enjoy* their duties.

Martine, point of the Ghidorah, motioned for the girls to sit. After a token show of defiance, the Remove complied. Were Black Skirts taking lessons now? Amy put her hands on her desk and faced front.

'Miss Kaye is indisposed,' Martine announced.

She still had smile-lines, but the Fourth was no longer humorous. Three or four ants crawled on her face. Amy itched in sympathy. How could Martine not scratch where the bugs were? Wool was infested too, and had red swellings where she'd been bitten.

Most ants weren't truly venomous, but *Solenopses* (fire ants) and *Myrmecia* (bulldog ants) had nasty, poisonous bites. Of course, the *Formicidae* of the Purple, *the ants in pants*, might be unknown to science. In *Formis*, Professor Rayne wrote wildly of the Ideal Ant, an imminent super-species. She said it would evolve to fit a post-war environment, thriving on the quantities of mustard gas, cordite and atomised human matter which had been discharged into the atmosphere.

Some Black Skirts reacted badly to ant bites. Girls like Wool sported obvious stigmata – red-rimmed eyes, glittering pupils, visible traceries of dark veins. The victims didn't seem to notice their condition and carried on as usual, though in a somewhat somnambulist manner.

Wool and McClure took a box each and opened it. They went up and down the rows, dropping new books on desks. Amy loved the paper-and-ink smell of new books but knew she would be disappointed in these.

'You are not permitted to slack in your teacher's absence,' Martine went on. 'You will copy, in your best hand, the foreword and the first three chapters of the book, including charts and figures. Your fair copies will be collected at the end of lessons. If any girl has not completed the assignment, the Remove will forego supper and remain in class until the work has been done. There will be no talking. Girls will stay at their desks.'

Thorn, Paquignet and Light Fingers stuck their hands up.

'No questions will be taken,' said Martine. 'No exceptions will be made.'

Wool came to Amy's desk and dumped the book in front of her.

Social Order in the Anthills of Northern Europe,

by Professor Rosalind Rowley Rayne.

A triangular ant face stared out from the dust jacket.

Books thumped on more desks. Some girls groaned.

'Exercise books have been provided and your inkwells filled,' Martine said. 'Take out your pens and commence.'

'You're a Fourth,' said Lamarcroft. 'We don't take orders from you…'

McClure was behind Lungs in an instant, arm crooked around her throat. The Black Skirt held for a moment, as Lamarcroft fought for breath… then let her go.

'The assignment does not come from me,' said Martine.

She did not go on to say Miss Kaye had set the lesson. Amy didn't believe their teacher had anything to do with this. She detected the hand of the Queen Ant. The pointlessness of the task was deliberate. It was supposed to be demoralising.

The Ghidorah gave out exercise books.

Some girls – Dyall, Harper, Palgraive – began to do as they were told. They opened *Social Order in the Anthills of Northern Europe* to the foreword, dipped their pens and started scratching away in their exercise books. Amy couldn't bear to follow suit. She didn't even want to *read* Professor Rayne, let alone transcribe lunatic entomology in her spidery approximation of copperplate.

'Remember, you will all remain here until you have each copied three chapters.'

The Ghidorah raised their arms in the antenna-salute. A few of the Remove – Light Fingers, Knowles, Marsh – made mocking responses, exaggerating the waving from side to side and the chittering, clicking sounds.

'You show improvement,' said Martine. An ant

crawled into her mouth, and she neither spat nor bit. 'Carry on.'

She left the room, followed by McClure and Wool toting the empty boxes. As the Ghidorah walked off, their skipping ropes clacked. Black Skirts had a distinctive gait, almost a scuttling. The pleats of their skirts shifted in rhythm to the rhyme.

'Ants in your pants, all the way from France…'

Amy looked at the new book she had been given. It rose from the desk without her touching it. The dust jacket ripped across. Another ant face looked through the rip. Focusing, she snapped the spine and tore out pages. Paper leaves fluttered around. It was barely five past nine and she had ruined her day's lessons. She resolved to sit here until doomsday, without copying a single word. Even if it meant the whole Remove were punished with her – another blatant attempt to set them at each other's throats.

Only after the book was ruined did it strike her that she had more control of her floating-other-things ability today… and, for the first time, had used the trick to destroy something. If pushed, she was dangerous…

Some girls whistled in admiration. Laurence might have been frightened.

'Good show, Thomsett,' said Devlin. 'I can't be doing with this either.'

She stretched out her arm and dropped her book into the waste-paper bin.'

Thorn and Knowles moaned about their lost supper, but didn't join the copiers either.

When it was certain that the Ghidorah did not linger to spy, the Remove got their heads together. Only Dyall and Palgraive kept at the copying.

'Do you suppose they've set watch on us?' asked Knowles.

'Not likely,' said Light Fingers. 'We're low down the Black Skirts' list now. They're getting on with other things.'

'What?' Laurence asked.

'Being evil,' said Light Fingers.

'We shouldn't have to do this rot,' said Lamarcroft. 'Making fair copies. It's babyish. Only Firsts and Seconds have copying in lessons.'

Firsts and Seconds in the room complained.

'Sorry, but you know what I mean,' said Lungs.

'Even if they send someone to check up on us, they won't examine the copies until this evening,' said Light Fingers. 'Even then, someone'll just look at every page to see there's writing there. No one is going to *read* the things. We're not going to get marks out of a hundred for this. So long as they get fourteen copies at the end of the day, they're off our backs.'

Light Fingers opened her exercise book, and dipped her pen. Knowles happened to be nearest Light Fingers' desk, so she was recruited.

'Know-It-All, turn the pages, as if I were playing the piano. Amy, ready with the blotting paper. Frost, see if you can keep the temperature chilly around the desk. I wouldn't want to set fire to anything.'

Amy guessed what Light Fingers was going to do, but others were puzzled.

At a nod, Knowles began turning the pages. Light Fingers copied what she saw, lightning-fast. Her hand disappeared in a blur as it passed over the page. Words appeared in her exercise book – and figure drawings of ants and anthills – as if she were doing a brass rubbing. When each page was done, Amy leant in with blotting paper. Half-way through the first chapter, Light Fingers' nib broke and Lungs handed over her own pen. Devlin craned like a cobra to get a better look.

'Lawks a' mercy,' she said.

Within five minutes, Light Fingers had completed her day's work.

'Now, let's try it with a different handwriting. Thorn, you're left-handed, right?'

'Righteously left, right.'

Light Fingers switched hands and, with Knowles turning pages and Amy blotting, completed another fair copy. It looked different enough from the first. Then, Light Fingers tried right-handed but slanting left and with a thicker nib. Marsh and Paquignet took over page-turning and blotting duty.

Devlin fished her exercise book out of the basket.

Dyall, catching on late, abandoned her copy. As gently as possible, Amy led the girl to the farthest corner of the classroom.

'Could you sit here, Poppet?' she asked. 'Just till we get things sorted.'

There was an irregular niche, partially screened from the rest of the room, just big enough for a chair and desk. Dyall seemed happy to make this her hidey-hole. Amy gave Poppet one of Lamarcroft's gob-stoppers, which she slipped into her mouth. Her cheeks hollowed and her eyes widened. It would take her a while to dissolve the big sweet.

Even brief proximity to Dyall gave Amy the beginnings of a head. What day was this? Why was she in the abandoned greenhouse with such a strange assortment of girls?

Getting away from Poppet brought on a dizzying

rush of relief. The spots of forgetfulness filled in and Amy remembered everything.

Light Fingers had produced another copy, with a different nib and slant.

'Harper,' said Light Fingers, still writing away. 'What you were saying last night... you're right. We have to stop all this. The Black Skirts, Rayne, everything.'

Shrimp was still nervous about talking with the others. She was so used to girls wanting to get away from her that she had forgotten how to be direct.

'I tried on my own,' she said shyly, 'but my Ability – I call it *breathing in* – won't work on Rayne any more. When she came to School, I might have managed it... made her so weak we could have done something about her. She was just like *y-*... just like *everyone*, except Palgraive and Paule. I caught a *breath* from her when she was first here. But when I tried again, after the Black Skirts caught on, it was no use. I can't *breathe in* from any of them now. It's like they're all one animal, too big to get a hold on. *Breathing in* is like sipping hot tea... sometimes, if I've gone a long time without, gulping down a whole mug at once. With the Black Skirts now, it'd be like trying to drink a boiling lake. Their level wouldn't go down and I'd do myself an injury.'

Amy wasn't the only girl disgusted with Shrimp.

'Good gravy, Harper,' said Thorn, 'but you really are *dreadful*. I remember when you tried to "interview" me.'

'And me,' said Marsh. 'I was parched.'

Panicked and squirming, Shrimp looked at the hard faces and pleaded 'It's not something I can help!'

'Yes, but you *enjoy* it, you witch,' said Knowles.

'Leave her alone,' said Frost, who understood runaway Abilities. 'We can't afford to be like this.'

'The Frost's right,' said Light Fingers. 'It's what *they* want. The Ordinaries love it when we fight among ourselves. It means they don't have to go to any bother to keep us in hutches.'

The air around Thorn simmered with heat haze. Amy wished she'd been in Thorn's cell this term – it was probably the toastiest place in School.

'Sorry, Shrimp,' said Thorn. 'I spoke out of turn. I was forgetting... I set light to my grandmama's wig once, without meaning to. I know what can happen.'

'You *should* be sorry,' responded Harper, with her old spite. 'You should *all* be sorry.'

'*Shrimp*,' said Amy, sternly.

Harper calmed down, took a deep breath – which made girls back away from her – and fixed a simper on her face that adjusted into a smile.

'It is fine,' she said, with a curtsey. 'Thank you, Thorn. Thank you, Thomsett.'

Amy accepted the apology, though – like everyone here – she would remember what Shrimp had said about *breathing in*.

'One thing, Shrimp,' said Amy. 'Your Ability works on everyone. Even Poppet?'

'What she does is like what I do, I think. But not the same. When we're stuck together, it's *awful*. Neither of us could stop. It was like we were puffing up and running down at the same time, over and over. Keep us apart, please.'

There was no denying the little Unusual's desperation.

'...you said "except Palgraive and Paule",' said Amy. 'What did you mean?'

Shrimp put her hand up to her mouth and whispered 'I don't think Palgraive's *alive*, really. She's like an empty cup. With *something* wriggling in the dregs. It keeps her walking and working and smiling, but *nothing else*.'

Palgrave paid no attention and continued copying in a measured hand. The Remove all stared at her. Even Amy, who knew more, shuddered. As she worked, Palgrave kept smiling.

'And Paule?' asked Amy.

Harper paused, reluctant to say anything... which, after the confessions she had made, was alarming. Finally, choosing her words, she said, 'If the Black Skirts are like a lake, Paule's like an ocean. There's just *so much* there. You can't see it, but I can. And it's *terrifying*, chums. You all have *fringes* you can't see but I can. Like second shadows. Wavering, transparent fringes around you all the time. Paule has more than a fringe. It's like a storm, around her all the time, with lightning. And it's...'

'Purple,' said Light Fingers, looking at Amy.

'Like the skies in my dream,' said Lungs.

'I see *fringes*,' said Green Thumbs. 'Around plants, not people.'

'Anyone else?' asked Amy.

'I see my pocket,' said Laurence. 'And things have fringes when they come back. Not purple, but purple-ish.'

'Paule?'

Paule seemed to have heard nothing, as immune to being talked about as Palgrave.

'It's snowing upwards in the Purple,' she said. 'Thinning on the ground and thickening the clouds. Things are moving under the drifts. Holes with other holes in them are opening everywhere. Dandy and fine and safe as houses.'

'That was terribly helpful,' said Knowles, who got

impatient when things didn't make sense. She could put concrete information in her head, but contradictions and ambiguities annoyed her. 'But what's it got to do with the price of tea in China?'

Light Fingers was on to her sixth copy. She was even speeding up. She went through nibs and ink and tore pages occasionally, but kept at her task. Only Palgraive was still working on her own copy. She hadn't finished the foreword.

'Know-It-All has a point,' said Lungs. 'We might be pals now but we're still in a prize pickle. The Black Skirts have the whole school. We've just got what's in this room, and some of us are not up to much. We're hard put to be any earthly use with these blasted Sisters Dark marching about like they own the place.'

'Is it just us, though?' asked Devlin. 'What about the Staff?'

'Miss Kaye's been dealt with somehow,' said Frost. 'And remember Miss Bedale – she spoke up and was degowned. The rest of the beaks are Black Skirt to the bone. Ponce and Digger have their arms up in the air all the time doing the wavey-wavey dance.'

Mockingly, several girls did their own ant salute.

'I'm not thinking of them,' said Amy. 'I'm thinking of Headmistress. Aren't we supposed to be her cygnets?'

VI: Golden Rules for Detective Stories

CONVERSATION TURNED TO Dr Swan and her Unusual Girls.

Everyone present, except fluke-among-flukes Palgraive, had received an invitation to Headmistress's study when they first arrived at School. Only Marsh – who attended a Young Ladies' Academy in Massachusetts before coming to England – shared Amy's experience of being singled out as a Third. The others had all been titchy Firsts, overwhelmed by their new school, let alone personal attention from the imposing Dr Swan.

Some, like Frost and Thorn, were puzzled by the cygnets speech; they hadn't yet twigged they were responsible for the occasional cold spots or smoulderings around their childhood homes. Laurence hadn't realised her party piece wasn't something everyone could do if they had a mind to. Dyall, gently questioned, *still* didn't seem to understand what she did and looked like she'd cry if pressed on the matter.

Not everyone paid much attention to Swan's speech. Some resisted any suggestion that they were different. They didn't want to be flukes. In the Remove, they owned up. Here, they'd be flukes if they *weren't*

344

Unusual. Laurence, Frost and Paquignet told stories like Amy's – their parents disapproved of and discouraged their Abilities.

Only Devlin, whose parents thought she was smashing no matter how far she stretched, was *encouraged* at home. The indulgence had limited her to trivial good deeds like fetching things down from high shelves. Marsh's family were all like her and Light Fingers' parents passed on suspicion of Ordinaries as well as their Abilities – which, it now transpired, included rapid-fire forgery.

Lamarcroft's father was a Conservative Member of Parliament. 'Dad told me not to break so many things and keep mum about the battle dreams,' she said. 'He was worried that if word got round I was cuckoo, Mr Bonar Law wouldn't put him in the cabinet. Judging from the Ministers he's had round our place, a cuckoo in the nursery shouldn't be disqualification for high office... most of them are round the twist.'

Shrimp admitted her mother came down with a rare wasting disease just after she and her brother Jacques were born. Mrs Harper had been travelling abroad for her health ever since, leaving the twins to the care of a succession of nannies, all of whom got tired and quit after a few months. Even considering Shrimp's slyness, Amy hadn't the heart to say outright what everyone thought... Harper *must* realise she'd come close to killing her mother. She might not be able to own up to it even to herself.

Amy supposed that whenever Dyall's family suspected something, they'd suffered bad headaches... then wondered what they'd been thinking. Prolonged and repeated proximity to Poppet might wipe her permanently from their minds. They would see family pictures on the mantelpiece and wonder who the little girl in them was.

Paule couldn't remember if she ever had parents. Amy noticed the others were as wary of Daffy Dora as menaces like Harper and Dyall. They were hard put to remember her ever *doing* anything to them. It's just that sometimes she said things which upset people.

'Dad still thinks I'm only clever,' said Knowles. 'If he knew my trick, I'd be for it.'

Know-It-All lived in dread of her father catching on to her. Carleton Knowles wrote complicated detective novels in which impossible crimes turned out to have sensible solutions. *The Body in the Belfry*, *The Cadaver in the Cabriolet*, *The Head in the Hat-Box*. In a newspaper article, he had listed Thirteen Golden Rules For Detective Stories. The First Golden Rule was that a mystery should not have a supernatural explanation. His daughter worried he'd be no happier with her Ability than with a fictional murderer who could strangle a victim in a locked room and seep under the door in ectoplasmic form.

'Anything that can't be made sense of is not playing the game, he says, and not playing the game is a gross breach of trust.'

This prompted the Remove to spend a happy hour devising ways each could commit murder in a locked room and get away with it. Amy couldn't distinguish between who was making conversation and who was thinking seriously about future homicidal enterprises. At first, it was agreed Frost and Thorn would make the best culprits – freezing or boiling victims from outside the window – though, of course, Larry Laurence could stash a bloodied blunt instrument or a just-discharged revolver in her pocket and pass the most thorough police search.

'Amy, you should be able to lock and unlock doors by making the tumblers move,' suggested Knowles. 'You could leave the key in the lock and turn it from the other side of the door.'

That had never even occurred to her. Now, of course, she wanted to try it.

Not necessarily for murder. But not necessarily for anything noble and moral either.

Eventually, the topic of locked-room murders ran dry, and they came back to the matter at hand.

Headmistress.

Whatever their families thought of them – whatever they thought of *themselves* – the Unusuals were dear to Dr Swan.

'We have a tradition of Unusual Girls at Drearcliff,' Headmistress had said to Amy. 'I like to think of them as my cygnets… My eye will be always on you. We shall see what can be done with your Abilities.'

Amy did not believe Swan's eye had strayed.

She remembered that face, over and over in School photographs, back to founding day, unchanging with the years. Swan was an Unusual, too. It was the only explanation. If she had a choice, she would not have allowed the Rise of the Black Skirts. Rayne went against everything Headmistress professed to believe. Like her cygnets, she had been *removed*. She was put away, like a small object in Larry's pocket.

It was down to the Remove to fetch Swan back.

VII: Protective Colouration

'THERE'S SOMETHING WE have to do, or – rather – *pretend* to do,' said Amy. 'We have to go Black.'

Hisses rose. Marsh showed shark-teeth. Devlin pulled her face out of shape.

'It won't work,' said Knowles. 'I've tried it. So have most of us. They won't take us. We're flukes, remember.'

'They don't have to take us,' Amy continued. 'It's protective colouration. We just have to look like them. To get about freely. Knowles, do you still have the black kit? They didn't strip you of it?'

Know-It-All nodded. 'It's in my trunk, back at the stables.'

'Between us – and Light Fingers' sewing when her hand's better after being wrung out from all the copying – we should have enough black uniforms to put up a false front. You've noticed how dull they all are, the Soldier Ants. Even duller than the Dims. The Queen Ant thinks for them so they don't pay attention to anything but their allotted tasks. They should be easy to fool. We need to get about School without being marched back here… or locked up. That's what they'll try next, if we give them an excuse.'

'Three into fourteen doesn't go,' said Paule.

Outside the Purple, Amy was rarely sure whether Paule was talking to the point. She sometimes said things which made sense the way patterns in the grain of wood can look like the face of a frog.

'Twelve is four threes,' Amy said. 'So we're a duodecad, with a secret weapon – a thirteenth girl – and a mystery member – the fourteenth. It'll be different secrets and mysteries at different times. I'll work out your moth names when we have the time to think.'

Not everyone was keen on having a moth name, so Amy let it go. Thanks to Rayne and her pest of a mater, entomology was in bad odour. Reason enough for revolution.

Light Fingers got into the home stretch on her thirteenth copy. Palgraive was still on her own.

At Break, Knowles and Shrimp went to the stables to collect black uniforms while Amy and Light Fingers led a raiding party to the theatre. The under-stage area was padlocked and chained. The Queen Ant's sanctum was secured against spies – presumably since Amy's previous expedition. Looking at the trapdoor, she rattled the chains without touching them. She tried to feel inside the locks for the tumblers, but couldn't really concentrate.

'I could open that with a bent hairpin anyway,' Light Fingers said. 'No need to strain your mentacles.'

The material they needed – yards of black cloth – was no longer under the stage anyway. Much that had been stored there was piled up in the auditorium, shifted out of the way.

Carrying scavenged material, the party left the theatre.

...and ran into a triad. Stonecastle of the Sixth,

Duchess of the Dims, with a brace of weedy Seconds, Lapham and Finn. The Triceratops.

'What are you doing, germs?' bellowed Stoney – whose black boater didn't fit properly on her large head.

'Punishment for Minor Infractions, Prefect Stonecastle,' said Amy. 'Removal of rubbish to the school tip.'

There was such a place and whips often had girls haul unpleasant items there on a whim. It was not unknown, under the Gryce regime, for a whip to dispose of the sticky paper which had been wrapped around a bun she had just scoffed by pinning a dreamed-up Infraction on a random passing girl who then had to trudge out to the tip with the single item of refuse.

Stonecastle, no brighter now than when she'd worn Grey, slapped the nearest girl – Green Thumbs, who staggered but otherwise wasn't bothered.

'Get on with it, germs. Double time. Rubbish don't shift itself, you know.'

'Except in the case of these *rubbishy* girls,' said Lapham.

'Yes, they do *shift* themselves,' said Finn.

Stoney was irritated. The tiny brain marooned in her thick-boned skull sparked. There was a joke and she hadn't got it. An ant crawled on her eyelid.

She gave out a sound that was supposed to be a laugh.

Before she went Black, Stonecastle was the whip girls could make fun of. As mean and ferocious as the others, she was easy to dupe... and driven to tears of frustration when she sensed she was being made a fool of but couldn't see how. An exemplary Tamora in the question of violence, Gryce hadn't taken her for a Murdering Heathen. Even Henry Buller deemed Stoney an utter Dim.

Amy and the others hurried off, counting themselves fortunate not to have come up against a shrewder Black Skirt. Lone ants were squashable. Even a few were nothing to worry about.

Amassed, they became a trickier proposition.

VIII: A Wolf, New to the Fold

AMY'S RAIDING PARTY made their way back to Temporary Classroom Two.

Black Skirts were everywhere, formed into skipping circles. Their lessons seemed to be suspended. They all jumped at the same time, shaking the ground. The rhyme was carried by the whole school. It took an effort *not* to walk in time to 'ants in your pants all the way from France' so she gave in to it. The tripping gait was more protective colouration.

At regular pauses, the Black Skirts left off skipping to give the antenna salute and chitter en masse. It was a periodic burst of ritual insanity. With each wave-and-chitter, her skin crawled and she had to fight panic. Amy and the others tried to join in with these spasmodic eruptions, but always started too late and carried on too long. Luckily, the ants paid little notice to anything outside their circles.

In the Quad, Prompt Rintoul stood at the head of a triangular wedge of thirty-nine girls, solemnly leading jumps as if they were a tribal rite. The Sisters Dark were dervishes warming up for a whirl or berserkers getting into the spirit for pillage. In the tridecennead,

Frecks and Kali skipped with the rest of them, bereft of expression. Frecks wore her chainmail balaclava, relic of her gallant flying uncle – with a black boater on top. Was its spell tarnished now her cause was no longer just and true?

Regret welled up for something lost. Light Fingers saw her pausing and tugged her sleeve.

'They're gone, Amy,' she said. 'Into the Black.'

Reluctantly, she allowed Light Fingers to pull her away. They left the Quad, though Amy flicked a backwards look. Frecks's rattling headdress shone amid the black-and-blank crowd. Silvery coils caught winter sun. Amy was determined her friends in Black should be freed and forgiven. Every day School got blacker and that duty seemed harder. Light Fingers thought Frecks and Kali were lost forever. Amy didn't. The Moth Club was a stronger idea than that.

They were near an end of it. The Black Skirt takeover was complete. Triads were making new paths everywhere, with the equipment used to mark the cricket pitch. The Runnel now extended throughout School. The Drearcliff Playhouse was a new Flute. With Mauve Mary banished, the Purple was swelling into the Back Home. Malign purpose was being achieved.

More than anyone else in the Remove, Amy was resolved to stop Rayne.

Knowles and Shrimp were already back at TC2 when Amy's party arrived. Palgraive was on Chapter Two of her fair copy. Paule was talking with Dyall. It was impossible to tell whether they were making up nonsense rhymes or having a profound conversation. If *anyone* were immune to Poppet, it was Daffy Dora.

Light Fingers took stock of the wardrobe material.

'First, how many black boaters have we? I've a pot of creosote, so we can make our own but they won't be as good. And they'll whiff something awful.'

Knowles began counting boaters…

…but was interrupted by a growling from the darkest corner of the room.

It was low and scrapey. Amy had the queases again, badly.

A shape loped out of the shadows.

A curtain of hair fell over a grubby face. Big eyes glistened between lank strands. Dog-teeth showed, sharp and yellow.

Marsh hissed and adopted a fighting stance.

'Don't mind me,' said the newcomer. 'I'm one of you now.'

Aconita Gould had been removed.

Her black blazer was torn, her skirt muddy. A fresh bruise rose on her lightly furred cheek.

'You were right, Jan,' she told Marsh. 'The ants never meant to keep me.'

Marsh wasn't disposed to be forgiving.

'We should chuck furface out of the room,' she said. 'She's a turncoat and a spy.'

Gould, whom Amy had always been a bit afraid of, hung her head like a whipped dog.

'I've read that book,' said Devlin. '*In the Wolves' Den*, by Claude Savagely.'

'You're part of the Cerberus,' said Frost. 'I still have scratches.'

Thorn's hands smouldered.

Gould was disturbing the Remove.

'Brown's got my place,' said Gould, pulling her blouse aside to show a scabbed-over shoulder wound. 'The spear-thrower. They kept me as long as they needed, but not as one of them. I know that now. Thought I could be tame, but I'm just not.'

Goneril and the Sisters Dark had gone to war over the Wolf Girl... but they were all one thing now, and Gould was out. The world was broken. This was not the Drearcliff way.

Marsh rolled up her sleeves. Her hair slicked down like sealskin. She was ready to resume the fight, fish-fluke against wolf-witch.

Amy looked at Light Fingers, who shrugged. So far as she was concerned, Gould could take a battering and like it. Amy saw the justice, but...

'We don't have time to do this again,' said Amy. 'Gould, welcome to the Remove. I expect you, more than any of us, know we're in a desperate position. Most of us can pass for Ordinary. Those of us who only have Abilities. But you have Attributes. You're undeniably Unusual.'

Gould's dog-eyes were sad.

'If you don't mind me asking,' said Lamarcroft, 'are your Attributes a family thing? All Marsh's tribe are spawn, she says. Do you come from... what, a pack?'

'My folk took a Carpathian motoring holiday while the Lady was expecting. The Laird's a fiend for motoring holidays. Call of the wild, he says. Which is what he got. Something bit the Lady. Just a scratch. Only a wee cub. She wanted to take the beast home to Inverglourie Glen... as a pet. What was in the scratch skipped the Lady and got in me. I came out hairy. I don't have a pack. I just have me, and a small fur rug. The Laird's a fiend for shooting, too. Potted the cub. Tricky shot, he says.'

'You're a Lone Wolf,' said Thorn.

'No one here is a Lone Wolf,' said Amy. 'Gould, Marsh, shake…'

Neither were keen. Amy wondered if she should put the Kentish Glory mask on.

After shuffling, Marsh deigned to stick out a hand. Gould briefly held it.

That was over. They could get on with important matters.

The Wolf Girl caught up quickly with the plan. She had her own Black kit – though it needed mending. Light Fingers took up her sewing basket – which Knowles had fetched from the stable – and set about making speedy repairs. Gould's eyes bulged like the Big Bad Wolf's in the fairy tale as Light Fingers demonstrated her Ability. Devlin parodied that look, but girls protested when Stretch popped out her eyeballs so she put them back in.

Reluctantly, Gould coughed up her story. At Break, the Cerberus were sent off into the woods to run down a straying Staff member. Gould didn't know who they were after. Given a perfumed handkerchief to smell, she picked up an obvious – too obvious – trail. Bounding ahead, she followed the scent into a copse… where Brown was waiting with Strikes-Like-an-Adder. While Gould was pinned at javelin-point, Buller tore off her ant emblem. Then, they all gave her an unsporting kicking. Afterwards, she was dragged to TC2 and unceremoniously dumped. She still had earth and snow on her.

'Minnie Crowninshield said my shooting badges had been taken out of the trophy case and melted them down for bullets.'

'I doubt they use much real silver in those awards badges,' said Know-It-All.

Unless other unknown Unusuals hid among the

Black Skirts, Gould was the last addition to the register of the Remove.

'Divisible by three,' said Paule. 'Fifteen.'

There was that. Multiples of three were versatile, strong, handy. Threes had significance among insects. Triangular heads. Three stages of life. Six legs. Amy didn't quite see the point. Paule was looking at it from the Purple, which might make the view clear as glass or opaque as fog.

Light Fingers worked a miracle kitting out the whole Remove in convincing Black. She blackened white boaters and twisted bits of tin into fake ant badges.

After discussion, everyone agreed they should get on and find Dr Swan before they lost what little freedom they still had. Tomorrow, Miss Kaye might be back, or – worse – a Black Skirt teacher could be in charge, watching them as they did their own copies.

'We might be *expelled*,' said Knowles.

'At least we'd be away from the Sisters Sinister then,' ventured Devlin.

'They won't stay just at Drearcliff for long,' said Light Fingers, in her Prophet of Doom voice. 'They want to spread. If they aren't stopped here, they'll get *everywhere*. We won't be in a disused greenhouse then. It'll be the Mausoleum... or *a* mausoleum... or piled in a ditch with dirt shovelled on top.'

Light Fingers was very good at impressing the seriousness of the situation on people. What she wasn't very good at was suggesting what they could do about it. In a funny way, she liked it when things were as bad as she said they'd be. A fast friend, she was not someone girls would look to for inspiration.

For that they needed Kentish Glory.

Amy knew she *was* Kentish Glory, but she could only say and do some things from behind the mask. It stripped away the self-consciousness which hampered Amy Thomsett.

It was getting that she didn't even have to put the mask on. She just had to imagine it and she became the Moth Girl. The Remove paid attention, even Sixths like Lamarcroft and Paule and formidable Unusuals like Marsh and Thorn.

'It's important we get to Headmistress now, *this afternoon*, before the end of lessons,' she said. There was general agreement.

A Black uniform was put together for Amy. Knowles' spare blazer fit her reasonably, though Amy itched when she put it on.

'Don't worry,' said Know-It-All. 'I've not got fleas.'

'Not even ants?'

Knowles smiled tightly and pinned her ant badge on Amy's lapel.

'I kept this back when they removed me,' she said. 'I knew there was a reason for that.'

Amy didn't ask how she looked.

IX: The Swanage

THOUGH A RELATIVELY recent addition to Drearcliff Grange, Tempest Keep was tarted up with functionless crenellations and gargoyles to match the character of the rest of the pile. The Swanage was authentically defensible against armed attack, as had been proved in the boiled swede riots of '88.

Amy had only been inside the Swanage twice: welcomed on her first day and interrogated in the aftermath of Kali's abduction. Neither occasion was comforting. Early this term, Burtoncrest had dragooned Amy and Frecks to clean gritty snow from the wings of the stone eagles flanking the mock-mediaeval entrance. The whip had Minored them for not thinking 'buffalo' when she called 'moose', then stuck them with the chore. Brushing the Budgies wasn't as arduous as scraping the Heel, but was a wasted Break when she'd rather have been inside somewhere warmer doing something less dull.

Approaching the Tempest Keep, Amy realised she was in the habit of avoiding this part of School, even walking a long way round so as not to pass before the hawk-eyed Budgies. She remembered her uncomfortable sense that Headmistress saw all... though surely that wasn't so this term and she rather wished it was. The Budgies' glass eyes were gouged. The telescope above the doorway was twisted, lenses blacked over. Funny how things which seemed oppressive turned out to have been a comfort once they were gone.

The Remove had assembled ten black uniforms. Since Black Skirt patrols had to be divisible by three, they could only use nine. The ennead included Light Fingers, Paule, Devlin, Laurence, Knowles, Gould, Marsh and Dyall. Amy made Poppet rear guard and had her follow at a distance. They needed clear heads.

Lamarcroft held the fort at Temporary Classroom Two. She had the fair copies to hand over when Martine came for them. To pass the time usefully, she offered to train Paquignet, Frost and Thorn in sword-fighting, using rolled-up tubes of paper as harmless weapons. Knowles piped up that in *The Stabbing in the Scullery*, her father used a rolled-up tube of paper as a particularly gruesome murder weapon. That led to another bloodthirsty discussion. The left-behinds were probably still happily exploring lethal applications of stationery.

The skipping moved indoors to the Gym, but the rhyme was still heard all over School. A constant background noise, like the crunch of waves on the beach or the whistle of wind in the trees. Everything shuddered to its beat. Amy even felt it in her teeth.

> *'Ants in your pants, all the way from France,*
> *Send reinforcements, we're going to advance...'*

It got in your head, the way Dyall's Ability did. Unusuals weren't as susceptible as Ordinaries, but even Amy wasn't immune. Of the Remove, only Palgraive was completely unaffected by the damnable rhyme.

You forgot what you were supposed to be concentrating on and found yourself not thinking. Eventually, you were just repeating the couplets over and over in your head as if reading the words from a spiral strip of paper, an inscribed ribbon on which words marched like a long line of – what else? – ants. You pictured the spiral turning in the dark of your mind, becoming the Runnel, drawing you towards the Flute.

For Amy, the Flute was a flame... and Kentish Glory was just a moth, drawn to bright, hot immolation.

> *'Ants in your pants, take another chance,*
> *Send three and fourpence, we're going*
> *to a dance...'*

The words had long since lost meaning. It was no longer a human sound. It was the din of ants, chewing and building, spreading like a writhing carpet.

The Runnel was completed. Fresh white tape was pinned to the ground, winding across lawns, playing fields and the Quad. Amy imagined quaking eggs at the nodes. Paule kept tip-toeing along the Runnel like a tightrope walker. Amy detailed Devlin to pull her off the line lest she be drawn inexorably to the Flute and lost.

She understood how it worked. The *you* in your mind – the core of your person – was hooked like a fish and gaffed along against the last scraps of your will. Dancing sickness had struck in the middle ages, compelling unwilling pilgrims to jerk and caper along unseen paths till they dropped dead. More recently, a craze for using little pendulums to follow mystic lines in the earth had taken hold among a certain spinsterish breed of madman. Professor Rayne wrote about – and dubiously encouraged – the craze in *Formis*, making spurious connection between ant pathways and more efficient ordering of human society. The whole world could become the Runnel and the Flute.

The faux-Black Skirts gathered outside the Swanage. Amy half-expected to find a triad posted by the Budgies, but the stone eagles were left to themselves. They hadn't been brushed lately.

Amy unrolled and put on her mask.

With Amy Thomsett put away, she had a keener sense of her Abilities. She had prickly feelings in her back and forehead, where wings and feelers sprouted in the Purple. When she was Kentish Glory, the Remove listened to her properly. They squabbled less and followed orders. A responsibility, but also a thrill.

Light Fingers wore her Large Dark Prominent mask too. Devlin rearranged her face, making her nose pointy and twisting her eyebrows up to turn her eyes into slits. She was trying to be scary, but it came out comical – she looked more like Roly Pontoons than a wicked witch. Gould shook and strained and made herself hairier and toothier. And, most unexpected, Marsh peeled off false eyebrows and wiped away make-up from her temples… she had the beginnings of scales.

'This is who we are,' said Marsh. 'Thank you, Thomsett… Kentish Glory.'

'Hurrah for the Anti-Black Skirts,' said Devlin, a little too loudly.

'I want a Miss Memory uniform,' said Knowles. 'A mortar board and a burglar's mask. An academic cloak with Greek letters around the hem.'

'A *black* cloak?' objected Devlin.

'I *like* black,' said Knowles. 'We mustn't let bally ants spoil black for everyone.'

Knowles had decided she'd rather be Miss Memory than Know-It-All.

Amy looked up at the Swanage. They'd come this far, so they must press on...

The ground floor was Keys' domain. Above the reception room was Dr Swan's study, and a suite where files on all present and past pupils were kept.

In a lucid moment, Paule told Amy that Headmistress knew so much that Old Girls were obliged to serve School for the rest of their lives. It was in the Grand Plan. Now women had the vote and could sit in parliament, it was inevitable – by Swan's lights – that Drearcliff girls would eventually hold high offices of state in Britain and overseas, control great industries and fortunes or stand at the head of mass movements. Headmistress intended these women should dance on her strings. Dr Nikola or Val Conquest couldn't have come up with a more insidious scheme to hold sway over the twentieth century.

Dr Swan lived in heavily curtained apartments on the top floor. The décor was cause of much speculation. Factions argued whether her nest was characterised by monastic austerity or unparalleled decadence. A saintly hermit's pallet or a fleshy sultana's divan. A bucket of icewater or a marble bath filled with goats' milk. Maybe a combination of both extremes – a military cot piled with gold-tasselled pillows.

Smudge once said she'd seen picked-clean human bones tossed from Swan's window. Even credulous Firsts didn't believe that. Among the Sisters Dark, Smudge was no longer a whimsical fabulator but Ant

Minister of Propaganda. Amy had another pang. Last term, Smudge had been a colossal nuisance – especially when she'd made her one disastrous attempt to tell the truth. Now, Amy remembered the old Smudge's fibs as splashes of entertainment during a long week's wait for the next flicker show. The Black Skirts weren't much for films. They had extra skipping on Saturday afternoons instead, though it wasn't as if they neglected the pursuit throughout the week.

If she came back from Black, Smudge might end up assisting 'Stargazy' at the *Girls' Paper*, embroidering the exploits of the Mystic Maharajah or Frecks' Uncle Lance. Amy hoped there was a way out for most, if not all, Soldier Ants. They might be in a big, regimented shared daze, but their brains hadn't yet been eaten from the inside like Palgraive's.

Gould and Marsh had ropes out and were ready to lead the skipping if anyone came by.

'I *think* I still remember the rhyme,' said Gould. She was joshing – up until the morning, she'd skipped with the rest of the Black Skirts.

Devlin poked her tongue out six inches and wagged it like a finger.

Even Light Fingers laughed. Stretch the Clown.

It was twenty past three and gloomy, but not dark enough for Amy to float up the side of the building. Even Flightless Ants would notice so ostentatious a display of Abilities.

So they had to get into the building and up the stairs. Which meant tackling Keys, who was not easily got past.

Peeping through the window, Amy saw Keys at her desk, mechanically taking envelopes from one pile, gumming them closed, and shifting them to another pile. There was no real point in censoring letters from Sisters Dark. They must all write the same things, to keep families and friends from prying too much.

Since the new Rules came in, Amy hadn't bothered with letters. Mother blanked out anything she read which might upset her, so censorship was redundant in her case. The Frost had written a frank letter about the Drearcliff Situation to her folk and tossed it over the wall with a sixpence stuck to the envelope in the hope a passing charitable soul would find and post it. The letter had come back to her pigeon-hole, opened and entirely blacked out – with the sixpence gone too.

To complete a triad, two Firsts were in the reception room. Gawky Gifford, in Black at last, and Quilligan. Were they Keys' pets or her guardians? They skipped in silence, mouthing the rhyme.

Amy signalled for Dyall. The Second trotted over dutifully. The others backed off, but Amy held her ground.

'Poppet, you must *concentrate*,' said Amy, knitting her brows and *willing* away the ice-cream headache which began when Dyall got near. 'You must get close to the lady inside, Keys. You must concentrate on *her*. Do you understand? When you're near her desk, think about her. How she looks, the mood she seems in, what she's doing. It's very important.'

'I say, shipmates, why aren't we in lessons?' said Devlin, who hadn't backed away far enough. 'It's still light out.'

Knowles hauled Devlin back and slapped her, leaving a hand mark in her cheek.

Devlin shook her face out and snapped back together. 'Did I go off again?' she asked. 'Poppet, you *pilchard*!'

Dyall tucked in her chin and stuck out her lip.

'Don't frighten her,' Amy said. Needles stabbed into her brain. 'She can't help it and we need her.'

'Yes, but hang it all, I… oh never mind. As you were.'

Devlin smiled, forgetting what she was annoyed about. Poppet's chin relaxed. She had done it again.

Amy hurt behind the eyes. She wanted to shut out the world and not think about…

What she had to think about. Nancy Dyall. *Poppet*.

'What you just did,' said Amy. 'That's what you must do to Keys. You understand, don't you? What it is that you do, your Ability. You can *point* it?'

Shyly, Dyall nodded.

'This is how monsters are born,' said Gould.

No one bothered to say 'you can talk' to the Wolf Girl.

'We shall come with you as far as the front door, then you'll be on your own for a bit,' Amy told Dyall. 'Here, take this.'

She gave the girl a letter marked 'Important: For the Personal Attention of Headmistress'. It was two pages torn from an exercise book stuffed into an envelope sealed with melted crayon. They hadn't had matches, so Thorn had obliged with a fiery finger. They'd used Knowles' ant badge for a seal.

Poppet marched up the front steps, between the Budgies and through the door. Amy and Light Fingers, notionally the other points of a triad, followed, but stayed outside. They could see and hear what went on in the reception room, but hoped they were out of Dyall's range.

If Poppet could *point* her Ability, could she turn it off? Harper didn't have to *breathe in* all the time. She could choose when to drain her victims – usually when girls let their guards down. Amy hoped Gould was wrong. Learning to control her Ability should make Dyall less of a monster.

Poppet walked across the room with the letter.

Keys got up from her desk. She wore heavy black boots and a long black coat with brass buttons shaped like ant-heads. Towering over Dyall, she blinked and shook her head. The first stabs of brain-ache. Amy winced in sympathy.

'It's for Headmistress,' said Poppet.

'I shall take it and give it to her,' said Keys.

'It has to be handed over personally. It is *important*.'

'Dr Swan isn't seeing petitioners. She is always busy.'

'Then I shall wait.'

Any other girl would have been turned out of the office, but Keys just forgot Poppet was there. She sat on a chair near the desk, and stayed there, letter in her lap. Her feet dabbled like a duck's under water. She put the gob-stopper Amy had given her back in her mouth. It would last all day... probably longer than anyone could with Poppet around. She looked sideways at the custodian.

Keys pressed the heel of her hand to her brow and her eyes watered.

Light Fingers nodded, smiling.

'See how you like it, Keysie,' she said bitterly. 'Bit of a throb in the old grey cells, eh? How about a nice cup of arsenic and semolina to make it go away?'

'Hush,' said Amy. 'No need to gloat.'

Light Fingers, weirdly, hugged her and kissed her ear.

'Good old Kentish Glory,' said Light Fingers. 'Without you, we'd be lost. You are our moral compass.'

It was as if Light Fingers were giddy with excitement. Or some other intoxicant.

Amy shushed her again.

Poppet sat quietly, holding the letter, sucking the sweet... and invisibly *pointing*.

At her desk, Keys frowned greatly and was distracted. She didn't look at Dyall and wouldn't have noticed her if she did. Poppet was, in some circumstances, an invisible girl.

Gifford and Quilligan kept skipping, but slowed and started missing their step. Poppet got to them too. She must have been *radiating* her Ability, filling the room like a leaky gas jet. Gifford swooned and Quilligan made a hash of catching her. They went down in a jumble. Keys looked at the fallen Black Skirts, but couldn't focus. A tiny tear of blood dribbled from her eye. She might have been thinking about what was for supper... though she was more likely wondering what it was she'd been thinking before she lost her thread with the start of this terrible headache.

Stretch shoved her face up to the door, at the end of an eighteen-inch neck, just to see what was going on.

'Cor lumme,' she said. 'Dyall's a flattener!'

Devlin was in high spirits. Amy felt the overspill of feeling. Finally, they were *doing* something. Being on the fringes of Poppet's range was giddy-making, too... as if an exhilarant were discharged when she did her party piece.

A glass pane in the door cracked across, loud and close and startling. Keys fell forward on her desk, asleep.

Poppet got off her chair and walked over to open the door.

'Thank you, Poppet,' said Amy. 'Now, can you *hold in* the way you *point*? Turn off what you do?'

Dyall looked down, doubtful.

Amy knew what she was doing, all too clearly.

Poppet wasn't affecting her at the moment. But she didn't know how long that would last.

'It's safe,' Amy said. 'Well, safe enough.'

Amy led the others into the reception room. It was crowded, what with an ennead and a triad in the same space. There was no way to back off, so she hoped Dyall had run out of fluence.

'Did I do well, Kentish Glory?' Poppet asked her.

'You did splendidly. What county are your people from?'

'Wiltshire.'

'Your moth name is Scarce Forester. Distinguished by silvery-green wings.'

'Can I have a mask like yours?'

'Large Dark Prominent will make you one.'

'Yes, of course,' said Light Fingers. 'But for now, perhaps you could go outside and hide behind the Budgies. Keep a look out for Black Skirts.'

Poppet smiled at the responsibility.

'Yes, go on, Poppet,' Amy said.

They were relieved when Dyall left, and felt ashamed about that. Poppet was, as ever, eager to be helpful.

Marsh and Gould checked Gifford and Quilligan.

'Sleeping the sleep of the conked-out,' said Gould, snuffling Gawky's hair. 'They smell like plum duff, though.'

'Heel, girl,' said Devlin. 'Eating Seconds is against School Rules.'

Gould giggled at that, which made her fur ripple. Like Marsh, she was in no sense conventionally pretty… but Amy suspected they'd not go short of beaux. Wolf Girl and Gill Girl were stunners, all right – weird, but no stranger than the perfect doll face of Beauty Rose.

Devlin lifted Keys' head and dropped it on the desk.

'Out cold,' she said.

Keys' rattling breath shifted letters across her blotter.

'Look at this,' said Laurence, holding up Quilligan's specs, which had fallen off. One lens was broken.

'And there,' said Knowles, pointing at the wall of photographs. Some hung crooked. Smashed glass had fallen out of a few frames.

'What will Dyall be like when she's too big to be called Poppet?' said Light Fingers, impressed. 'A Scarce Forester who can fell trees?'

Amy suppressed a frisson.

She looked again at the photographs. Rows and rows of Old Girls caught in time, and always Dr Swan in the middle. Paule was in the pictures too, mostly half-hidden behind others.

Paule joined Amy. So many were gone from School but she stayed.

'I don't like having my picture taken,' she said.

Amy wasn't surprised. The camera sometimes saw more of Paule than she cared to show. In the 1915 photograph, her face was blown up by a purplish imperfection in the plate and seemed a yard across with extra eyes and noses.

A rattle made Amy's heart pause for a long moment but Keys hadn't come round. Devlin was holding up the famous ring of keys, detached from the custodian's belt.

'These could come in handy,' said Stretch.

'My dad says you should never lift anything on impulse,' said Light Fingers. 'Always plan ahead, take what you mean to and leave all else well alone... no matter the temptation. If you crack a safe to pinch a duchess's diadem, you don't take the packet of scented letters you happen to find there.'

'Remind us again where your dad is these days?' said Devlin.

Light Fingers shrugged, not offended. 'Fair point,' she conceded. 'But the keys will be missed. School will be turned upside down until they're found and we'll most likely get found out. Besides, you don't need keys to open locks... if Thomsett can't tumble tumblers with her mentacles, I can wiggle most things open with a bent nail and a hairpin.'

Amy wasn't sure Light Fingers should be so confident. Some of the keys were unusual – more like implements of torture or the solutions to puzzle-games.

Keys' keys are totemic objects,' said Paule. 'They can open locks that don't seem to be locks and close doors so they can never be opened again.'

The others looked at Paule askance. Used to ignoring her daffiness, they were starting to guess she made sense more often than a stopped clock's twice-a-day.

'Have a care, Stretch,' said Amy. 'Don't open anything by mistake.'

The ring rattled by itself, as if the keys heard what Amy said.

'Lob 'em my way,' said Laurence. 'I've a notion.'

'I've read that book,' said Stretch. '*A Bright Idea*, by Ivan Ocean.'

Devlin, suddenly eager to be rid of the keys, reached out and dropped them in Larry's hands.

Laurence sat cross-legged and shut her eyes. Now, *she* was concentrating on her Abilities.

A purple fold opened in the air. Larry popped the keys into the pocket. Normally, this seemed easy as posting a letter. Now, she looked as if she were forcing down a second helping of boiled swede.

'Paule's right,' said Laurence, grimacing. 'They're not just ordinary keys. They're…'

She gulped, as if about to be sick.

Amy was concerned.

Then, Laurence reached quickly into her pocket and pulled out the keys. She dropped the ring on the floor.

'Careful,' she said. 'One's hot.'

She was right. One of the keys – a long, spindly metal rod with an adze-like head – glowed as if pulled from a furnace. The others were just cold metal. The hot key visibly cooled.

'Put the realies back now,' said Laurence.

Slightly doubtful, and extending her wrist to keep the keys away from her body, Devlin did as she was told – hooking the bunch back on to Keys' belt.

'We should at least have tried the tuck cupboard first,' said Knowles. 'And the armory where Fossil keeps Sieveright's rifle.'

'It's only an air gun,' said Light Fingers.

'Say "only an air gun" after you've been shot with one,' commented Gould.

'Shush,' said Amy. Laurence was still concentrating. She wasn't finished yet.

Larry reached into the pocket and pulled out another set of keys. These were bright purple.

'Voy-lah!' she said.

Light Fingers took the keys and examined them against the originals.

'They're the same,' she said. 'Except for the colour. The weird one's even a little warm.'

Laurence stayed sat down. She was woozy and drawn. Her new trick took a lot out of her.

'Have you done that before?' Amy asked.

Laurence nodded. 'Just with… little stuff.'

'Good luck spending purple half-crowns,' said Devlin.

Laurence shook her head, smiling a little. 'Not money,' she said. 'Stamps. I tried it with stamps. The extras came out purple. Exactly the same, but purple.'

'That's an amazing Ability,' said Light Fingers. 'Even more than smuggling and spying.'

'Seems useless to me,' said Larry. 'Whenever is it handy to have two identical things with the extra being purple? What you did this morning would be beyond me. My fair copies would come back purple. Besides, you never get anything you don't pay for somehow. I may be only a Second, but I know that.'

'You lack imagination, my dear. And your stubborn moral streak holds you back.'

'Leave off her, Naisbitt,' said Knowles. 'Thanks to Larry, we have the Keys to the Queendom. We can get in anywhere we want without them knowing we can…'

'…providing we can match the keys to the locks, yes.'

'Which shouldn't be beyond *your* Ability. You can try every key very fast can't you?'

'Just because I move quickly doesn't mean everything else can keep up. A stiff lock is still stiff. If I try to open a door fast, I'll most likely pull the handle off. I used a typewriter fast once. The works got tangled like string. Speed turns into force – good for hammering nails, bad for stroking a cat.'

Laurence stood up now. She had been faint – 'you never get anything you don't pay for somehow' – but pulled herself together.

Poppet could point or radiate. Larry could copy. Devlin could stretch her face. Light Fingers could probably flick a nail through a brick wall.

The Unusuals were learning Applications for Abilities. Dr Swan ought to be proud of them.

Which reminded Amy...

'Come on, girls. Let's get upstairs before Keys wakes up.'

She led the way. The telescope fixtures drooped, unattended. No remote eyes were on them.

At the top of the stairs was a door. Normally open, now shut. Light Fingers sorted, quite swiftly, through purple keys and found the right one. She opened the door, slowly so as not to break the lock.

'Thanks, Larry,' she said.

Amy hadn't even considered this door might be locked. Her plan wasn't well-thought-out, even for something thrown together in haste.

Eight girls crammed into the corridor leading to Headmistress's study. It was lit by stuttery electric light. Amy didn't remember it being as long on her earlier visits as it was now. Not being invited made this place more forbidding.

How many School Rules were they breaking?

Now was not the time to think about that. The others wanted Kentish Glory in the forefront, not Amy Thomsett in a dither.

At the other end of the corridor, a dead end was covered by a bas-relief of savage, magnificent Britannia, girded by the flag, sat on the White Cliffs of Dover looking out to sea. On her trident points were stuck pop-eyed severed heads resembling Phillip II of Spain, Napoleon and Kaiser Bill. The personification of Great Britain looked a little like Lungs Lamarcroft. She even had half her chest showing.

As Amy led them towards Headmistress's office,

Britannia's trident shifted. Her gory trophies shook.

Gould let out a high-pitched, whiny yelp.

Amy was suddenly floating a foot above the floor, hair fanned out and prickly, eyes fixed on Britannia's red-white-and-blue-painted face.

'Thomsett, you're *flying*,' said Devlin, in awe.

'She only floats,' said Light Fingers. 'It's not the same.'

The bas-relief had not come to life. A hidden door was opening outwards.

Amy moved forwards, swimming through the air.

Gould was on all fours, snarling. Marsh reared up, glaring. Devlin's fists were the size of pineapples. Knowles shut her eyes. Laurence took a catapult out of her pocket – the one in her blazer, not the one in the air.

'Here's something you don't see every day,' said a familiar voice from the dark beyond the door. 'A Kentish Glory with black wings.'

Frecks – Lady Serafine Walmergrave – stepped into the corridor.

Amy's old cell-mate wore an immaculate Black uniform and her Uncle Lance's silver snood. She hefted a cricket bat.

'Gould, go for the throat,' shouted Light Fingers, as if letting slip a dog of war.

The Wolf Girl bounded along the corridor. Frecks batted her aside effortlessly. Gould slammed into the wall and fell, howling, to the carpet.

'Light Fingers, dear,' said Frecks, bat straight as if she were commanding the crease, 'perhaps you shouldn't be so eager to send others to get your cloutings for you.'

'Amy,' said Light Fingers, '*fly*!'

X: Just and True

ALL AT ONCE, Amy realised that if she could shift other things, she ought to be able to shift *herself*. When floating, she was practically weightless. She could lift herself up and throw herself forward like a paper plane. She wrapped what Light Fingers called mentacles around her own body, latching on to that *core* which was where she lived. It was different from picking up a book or a pencil without using her hands, but was – she found – something she could do. It was even a pleasant, bracing sensation. Airborne, she felt stronger, clearer. Some of the senses she had tasted in the Purple came back.

Now, she *thought* herself forward. Not flying, but close to it.

Frecks was impressed. Her jaw dropped and her eyes goggled.

'That's new,' she said. 'Removal has its perks.'

Amy reached out, *stretching* the way Devlin extended her arms, trying for a hold on Frecks' bat. Her phantom fingers brushed wood. Frecks must have felt the tiny pull and yanked it back.

Laurence let fly with her catapult. A pebble bounced off Frecks' shoulder.

'Ouch,' said Frecks. 'Pax pax!'

She dropped her bat and put up her hands.

'I'm not with the Black Skirts,' she said, rattling her chainmail hood. 'Not since I put on this blessed thing.'

Gould growled. She had recovered but was still on all fours, fur bristling and teeth bared.

'Down, girl,' said Frecks. 'Sorry I sloshed you, but you came at me with your scratchers out. We're on the same side. I'm creeping about where I shouldn't ought to be just the same as you shower.'

'You're a fluke?' said Knowles, incredulously.

'I'm something, all right. I don't think it's me. It's Uncle Lance's mail coif. When I said "blessed thing" I wasn't just being euphemistical. The wire wool balaclava makes the skipping rhyme goes quiet. Do you lot *really* not hear it?'

Amy descended and settled her feet on the carpet. Her weight came back.

'Of course we can hear it,' Light Fingers said. '"Ants in your pants, take another chance…"'

'Not like that,' said Frecks. 'I mean the rhyme in your head, even when you're alone, even when you're sleeping. Like ringing in your ears after a loud bang. Not a sound out loud, but something inside.'

Amy and Light Fingers looked at each other.

'It dislodges everything else,' Frecks went on. 'Like when you hear a song and the words get stuck in your head for days… only it's more than the words, it's the *rhythm*. It stops you thinking. If you try, it *hurts*. Like a Portuguese man o' war wrapped round your brain. To make the hurt go away, you have to stay in step, keep skipping, follow instructions, do what… what *Rayne* wants.'

'Like ants,' Amy said. 'They wiggle their antennae when they're getting orders.'

'If you say so,' Frecks said. 'I wondered if it was like Marconi waves and Morse signals. Go full Black Skirt – not just by putting on a dingy boater, but by taking the full package – and you turn into a wireless receiver. Part of you's still there, but keeps in its kennel – no offence, Gould. You do what is expected, what Queen wants. It hurts if you don't, but that's not why you do it. You *want* to serve Rayne – for what she is, not who she is. She's against you lot because she says you're broken. You can't get on the path.'

'I don't think we're broken,' said Amy. 'I think we're hardy. Like people who don't catch colds when everyone else has the sniffles.'

'That's how I see it too,' said Frecks. 'Wearing the coif is like having a bandage on a cut, not like not bleeding. If I took it off, I'd skip with the rest of 'em. My lugholes don't half chafe and it's useless for keeping warm. These metal rings are like ice.'

'Why did you put it on?'

Frecks shrugged. 'It seemed to want me to. The way Rayne wanted me Black Skirt. That started with girls having a notion to change their stockings. The idea came from *somewhere*. When I gave in and went Black, the chainmail woke up and wasn't having any of it. Near the drawer where I kept the coif, I felt it calling – stronger than the skipping rhyme, at least at close range. I took it out. Touching it was shivery. Maybe there was a woman's voice, telling me to don the armour. Perhaps I imagined that bit – I don't know.'

'You make things up to fill in gaps where you don't understand,' said Paule.

'That's about the size of it, Daffy,' Frecks went on. 'Donning the old coif was like a bucket of ice to the phizz. Woke me up properly. I realised I must look a right clot, hopping up and down like a clueless First, marching about on Godfrey Knows What mission. I went along with the charade as long as I could, reckoning I had a rare opportunity to spy on the Black Skirts from within. Espionage is in my blood, remember. British Intelligence, that's me. It's deucedly hard to fake being in their gang, though. Get a stitch and stagger out of a ranks and they turn on you. If they weren't so dim, they'd have cottoned on sharpish. It takes three of them to tie a shoelace. They aren't good at noticing things which don't fit their anthill. Rayne is the cleverest and even she's missing something.'

'Insect queens are slaves as much as rulers,' said Amy.

'I thought you *liked* her,' said Light Fingers, accusing.

'I liked what she did... standing up to the witches,' said Frecks, frowning. 'I doubt if anyone could like *her*. It's as if there's no *her* to her, really. And when there was only one of her, she *was* admirable. You have to admit that. But when she was *everyone*, when the Black Skirts were everywhere, she just replaced a bad thing with a worse one.'

'Come back, Sidonie Gryce, all is forgiven?' crowed Light Fingers.

Frecks shrugged.

'I tried to find out what the Black Skirts are up to by remaining in the ranks,' said Frecks. 'But they don't know themselves. They march and skip and don't ask questions. They're marking those lines all over the show, like putting out flares for a night landing.'

'It's called the Runnel and the Flute,' said Amy.

'Our hooded friends are involved in that.'

'Yes, I saw them creeping about,' said Frecks.

'You'll never guess who Red Flame is,' said Light Fingers, delighted at knowing more than British Intelligence. 'Kali's father!'

'What a turn-up for the books,' said Frecks. 'I spotted Ponce Bainter and the other one, the woman…'

'The Professor,' said Amy.

'Rayne's mama,' said Frecks, as if everyone knew already – and Amy realised she had sort of worked it out.

'A veritable termagant,' said Frecks. 'Spotted me in the crowd and wanted to stain me with a Uniform Infraction. I knew what that meant. Off with the silver coif. Skipping in step again. Ants in the blooming pants. Not for I, no fear. Do you know how *boring* it is, being a Black Skirt but awake at the same time? Worse than Double R.I. So I ditched my two watchdogs – Kali and Rose, both far gone – and took trouble to vanish. Word'll be out on me now. What one ant knows, the whole colony knows.'

Amy was happy her friend was her friend again. She and Frecks hugged. Frecks lifted her off the floor.

'I missed you,' she whispered in Frecks' ear.

'Good old Amy,' said Frecks, setting her down.

Light Fingers was still suspicious.

'You could still be with them and spying on us,' she said. 'You said it was in your blood.'

'They don't *understand* spying,' Frecks replied. 'It's how I lasted as long as I did. Red ants can't paint themselves black and go undercover in an enemy hill. You're either with them or you're furniture. The Black Skirts despise Unusuals, but don't take you seriously either.'

The rest were convinced. Frecks apologised to Gould

and ruffled her behind the ears. Amy remembered Frecks was a doggy sort. Her family had hounds.

'Welcome aboard,' said Devlin, pumping Frecks' fist.

'I'm Larry,' said Laurence, looking up at the taller girl. 'I am very pleased to meet you. I have a purple pocket.'

Frecks raised an eyebrow at that.

'She'll explain later,' said Light Fingers. 'Just now, we're here to see Swan. Are you with us?'

Frecks nodded. She scooped up her bat.

'Just in case we run into any of the blighters. They're not getting me back without taking blows to the bonce.'

Devlin, in a whisper, introduced Frecks to Marsh and Knowles.

Of course, she already knew Paule – and was wary of her. Amy didn't have time to disabuse everyone of their notions about everyone else.

Light Fingers picked the lock to Swan's office so Larry's purple keys weren't needed. She pushed the door open and they all piled in.

Disappointingly, Headmistress was absent.

Her apparatus was covered with a dustsheet. Her desk was too neat, as if she hadn't worked here since the place was last tidied. The grate was clean of ashes and cool.

Gould took some kindling from a rack and lit a fire. There was bickering about whether it was wise to send smoke signals announcing where they were. Advocates of an immediately warmer environment ventured that the Black Skirt gaze tended to be fixed on the ground where they were walking rather than cast upwards at telltale chimneys. By the time the wood caught light, the argument that a pound of comfort was worth an ounce of risk had won the day.

They weren't sure what to do next, anyway. Amy hoped Frecks could tell more about life under the Queen Ant's spell... and whether there was a way to wake up anyone else. The original charter of the Moth Club was about rescuing Kali. Now, their friend – and the whole school! – was captured again... held fast by something more insidious than ropes and harder to float over than high walls.

The others wanted to know about Frecks' chainmail coif. Seen close, it was curiously fascinating. The links knit together strangely, like tiny silver snakes, and had their own odd, cold light.

'Uncle Lance was in Pendragon Squadron,' Frecks explained. 'When they broke up after the War, he passed on this bit of kit to me. The Aerial Knights are supposed to be at rest under Avalon, pledged to return in England's Hour of Greatest Need... but Uncle Lance actually runs a garage in Lewisham. He spends his time tinkering with motors that ran better before he improved him. He's one of those fellows who's splendid during a war, but a bit of a liability any other time. Terribly decent, though. And canny enough to give me the chainmail, rather than waste it on my rotter of a brother. When the Aerial Knights gathered to receive the benison of the Lady in the Lake, they all got chunks of armour which would protect them from grievous harm in battle so long as their cause was Just and True.'

'I've read about Pendragon Squadron in *Union Jack Monthly*,' said Laurence. 'Didn't one of them die in the War? Why didn't *his* magic armour protect him?'

'Sir Percy Welsh,' said Frecks. 'Shot down by boring ground guns, not any famous ace or flying witch. One of those deuced war things. High Command gave orders to bomb a German airfield as a diversion for a ground advance somewhere else along the lines. So, the Aerial Knights of Avalon took off to flatten this behind-the-lines target – only some Staff officer got the map upside down. Instead of the airfield, they blew up a hospital. Evidently, the Lady of the Lake is a stickler for codes of chivalry. Bombing the wounded – and some French nuns working as nurses – isn't "just and true" enough. But orders is orders... and poor Sir Percy was brought down in flames. Suddenly, bullets and shells could do their job properly on him. Major Roy said the War would have been won years earlier if not for tactics that were called "expedient" if our side used them and "atrocities" if the Hun did.'

Amy supposed Frecks had a right to be cynical about the War. Her parents got killed in it, leaving her to the mercy of the odious Ralph. But Amy's father had died as well and Mother had never really got over it – and Amy still believed in causes that were Just and True. Frecks did too, really – though her own causes, not any country's. No one was firmer in her dedication to the ideals of the Moth Club. Frecks had been tested. She could have stayed a Black Skirt, but chose not to be. Most of the Remove would have gone Black Skirt if they could, no matter what they said now.

Headmistress' study was cosy. Girls found perches or idly searched through drawers and cupboards while Frecks caught up with the doings of the Remove. She clucked in sympathy at stories of persecution and exclusion, but wasn't surprised. Despite the fact that she wore magic armour, she cooed in amazement when she learned about the Aptitudes of the Unusuals. She insisted Larry demonstrate her pocket and was jolly enthusiastic when the Second put away a glass paperweight shaped like an ammonite and brought it back along with a purple copy. She chimed in with goshes and crumpetses when told tales of Thorn, Frost, Harper, Dyall and the rest.

Amy and Light Fingers searched the office while the others gabbed. Gould sniffed around locked cabinets, but they were disappointing when opened – plenty of ledgers and bills and registers, but nary a trace of explanation for the Rise of the Black Skirts.

And no clue as to where Headmistress was at present.

'We assumed Swan was locked up,' Amy told Frecks. 'This was supposed to be a rescue.'

'You were acting on limited intelligence,' Frecks said. 'Headmistress's not a prisoner. She's flown the Swanage and is hunted. The Black Skirts have standing orders to bring her in.'

'I should have *known* Swan was Quarry One,' exclaimed Gould. 'The prime purpose of the Cerberus is Quarry One. They gave me a gown for the scent but it didn't smell like Headmistress... more like carbolic.'

Light Fingers looked smug. 'I know what she did,' she couldn't help saying. 'It's what I would have done. Laid a false trail, put you off the scent... I say, I suppose that's where the expression comes from!'

'Carbolic, yuck,' said Gould.

Amy suspected Gould's failure to run down Quarry One was the immediate reason for her removal. The Black Skirts might have thought she wasn't really trying.

'Why do the Black Skirts want Swan?' asked Knowles. 'I'd have thought they'd be happy she was out of the way.'

'Bainter and Downs are as Black Skirt as it's possible for a grown-up to get,' said Frecks, 'but they can't run

School. The Professor gets annoyed when they don't know things. Headmistress slipped out weeks ago. Left her false trails and went to ground.'

'She's abandoned Drearcliff Grange?' said Devlin, appalled.

'Not her,' said Frecks. 'She'll be last to give up. But she's abandoned this position and slipped into the walls. I was looking for her when I heard you girls clomping about like a herd of elephants.'

'What's in the walls?' Amy asked Frecks.

'Secret passages,' Frecks said.

'Of course,' said Larry, who had a tiny crush coming on Frecks, 'all old places have secret passages, and School is very old.'

'This building isn't that old, young Larry,' said Frecks, not at all bothered by the adoration of new pets. 'But it fits the rest of the ruin. I knew there must be a secret way up here because Dr Swan never had snow on her shoes. She got from here to assembly without going outside. Once I put the coif on and could shut out the rhyme, I started using the hidden doors. There are quite a few if you know the signs. We've heaps of secret passages at Walmergrave Towers, escape routes and priest-holes… and a few nooks only I know about, where my parents left materials to do with their work. They taught me to look for things people aren't supposed to find. They'd have loved to have your pockets, young Larry.'

'Amy said I should be a spy,' said Laurence. 'And Light Fingers said I could be a diamond smuggler.'

'Or diamond-*maker*,' suggested Frecks. 'Purple diamonds are rare and valuable.'

None of them had thought of that.

Of course, Laurence would need an ordinary white

385

diamond in order to manufacture a fabulous fortune in duplicated purple ones. And they weren't easy to come by, though Light Fingers had an idea where one might lay hand on a jewel or two.

'That would be *stealing*,' said Gould, shocked – she hadn't caught up with what Light Fingers' parents did.

'No,' said Frecks, 'it would be *borrowing*. When Larry has made a spare, the first diamond could be put back. Can you make many spares of a thing?'

'I've never tried,' she said, suddenly eager to give it a go to please Frecks.

She pulled out another purple paperweight, and looked off-colour.

And another – which wasn't quite an exact copy, but lopsided and with misshapen coils. Now, she was definitely green.

'I think I'm going to be sick,' she said.

'You said, "you never get anything you don't pay for somehow",' Amy reminded.

Clutching her tummy, Laurence nodded.

In her rush to impress Frecks, she had forgotten.

'Would putting your spares back help?' Devlin asked.

Laurence nodded again, eyes watering. She put the two purple paperweights into her pocket.

'They won't need to be brought back. Nothing that comes from the pocket does.'

'Your pocket is like the secret passages,' said Frecks. 'Only the space doesn't have to fit into the walls or the architect's plan. Where do you suppose the extra room comes from?'

Amy thought Paule might be able to answer that.

'I've been looking for the secret doors ever since I came to Drearcliff. Just out of interest. Cupboard handles that bend the wrong way, carved fleur-de-lys with push-buttons, false book-spines attached to levers. But I only started exploring behind the walls since the Black Skirts got on to me. Those portraits of Dr Swan in gown and mortar board in all the hallways have removable eyes. If you pull out these little plugs with painted eyes on, you can peep through the holes from the passages and keep abreast of the latest news.'

'So Headmistress prowls the place by night like a wraith,' said Light Fingers. 'Seeing all, doing little.'

'Where is she now?' asked Devlin.

'I thought I'd found her a couple of times,' said Frecks, 'but Swan takes precautions. I nearly stepped in a pit with spears in, and I saw other booby traps. There's a whole world in the walls and under School. Not just passages, but rooms. There's an underground river, flowing to a cave on the beach – with a smugglers' jetty. I've barely explored a fraction of it. Headmistress could hide for *years*.'

'But we need her *now*,' said Amy.

Amy and Light Fingers found a locked roll-top desk which seemed significant. The smallest purple key opened it. Inside was a large book, like a monastery Bible. Too heavy to pocket, it was chained to the desk, which was bolted to the wall. Intrigued, Amy ran her fingers over the thick cover. It was bound in leather with stiff fur. Opening the book, she saw lists and charts, hand-written and drawn. Some in code.

She remembered Paule had said 'Knowles should read the big book.'

This book? It was big enough. It couldn't be taken out of the study. Maybe what was in it could be borrowed, though.

'Miss Memory, over here a mo,' Amy said.

'What's up?'

'This weighty tome. I think it's the full map of the School Buildings and Grounds, with secret places marked and instructions on how to avoid pits of spears and the like.'

Knowles looked through the pages. Others craned around.

'Some of this is Double Dutch,' said Knowles.

'Can you get it all in your head, though? Double Dutch or not?'

'I learned Single Dutch once, so I should be able to cope about half-way. Do you want me to cram?'

Amy nodded. 'I think that's why you're here.'

'Knowles should read the big book,' said Paule.

'Okey-dokey,' said Know-It-All. 'Here goes...'

She narrowed her eyes and began turning the pages.

XI: Into the Walls

KNOWLES HAD BEEN a dedicated Spook-Spotter before they went Black Skirt Only. The society had later disbanded. As per their treatment of Mauve Mary, Black Skirts were militantly anti-ghost. Amy supposed Rayne didn't like competition when it came to being terrifying. Thanks to her one-time enthusiasm, Know-It-All had a Psychic Investigator kit in her satchel. Most usefully, a battery torch. That – along with details of Drearcliff's within-the-walls and under-the-basements byways now crammed into her head – equipped her to guide an expedition into secret passages.

Amy remembered Dyall was tucked behind the Budgies and decided it probably best to leave her there. In enclosed spaces, she was as dangerous to allies as the foe. The conscience twinge Amy had about this went away when she looked out of the window and saw Poppet wandering off across the Quad. She thought to call down, but decided against it. Dyall could take care of herself. She was reminded that the Remove – Unusual though they might be – were still a rabble of schoolgirls. She couldn't expect them to be Royal Marines, holding a position under fire until orders to stand down came.

She wasn't Major Arthur Roy or General Flitcroft. She could only make suggestions. It was a wonder they'd come this far without mutiny.

Having paged through the whole of the big book, Knowles showed the strain of swallowing so much information. She had to blot blood from her ears with a hankie. Amy was concerned, but Know-It-All claimed she was all right.

'Does it hurt?' Frecks asked.

Knowles shook her head. 'It's like being stuffed after extra helpings of Christmas pudding,' she said. 'Only behind the eyes rather than in the tummy. It'll settle in a moment.'

'Where should we go?' Amy asked.

'I can only tell you what's in the big book,' said Knowles. 'If you want the wine cellars of the Old Grange or the underground Museum of Curiosities or the Staff Turkish baths, I know the ways to get there. I can't say whether Headmistress is in any of these places. It's not as if she put a marker to lead us to her. That would be too easy.'

'So that whole procedure wasn't much use?' said Devlin. 'Boning up on the maps and doors?'

'Information is always useful,' insisted Amy. 'Just in case.'

'Do you know where the traps are?' asked Frecks.

'The old ones, yes. The ones you said Dr Swan rigged up recently *ought* not to be charted, but I think they are. There's something about the big book. It changes of its own accord. If you knocked down Hypatia Hall, the labs would disappear from the map. If you put up a tea-tent on the cricket pitch, it would appear. It's not so much a blueprint...'

'...as a purple print,' said Paule, clapping.

Everyone except Amy looked at her suspiciously.

'She's not mad,' said Amy. 'She's like School. There's the part we can all see and walk around and then there are secret passages.'

'What's all the persiflage about purple?' asked Devlin. 'It keeps coming up.'

'I don't know how to explain,' said Amy. 'I don't think it *can* be explained. Having a map or book of instructions isn't possible... though having a Dora Paule helps.'

'I know what the Purple is,' said Laurence. 'My pocket is there.'

'Yes,' said Amy, patting Larry's head. 'I think so too.'

'Let's ask Paule where we should go, then,' suggested Frecks. 'We've got a sane person with maps in her head and she's – sorry to say, Know-It-All – of limited use... so why not consult the oracle? She can gaze into chicken innards or a crystal ball.'

Knowles was stung by that. Amy knew she had to stick up for her.

'Paule told us Knowles should use her Ability,' she said. 'It's important to her.'

'Knowles should read the big book,' said Paule.

'She's done that,' said Amy, trying not to be irritated. 'What next?'

'Into the walls and down the well,' said Paule.

They all looked around Headmistress's study for a well or clues to a well.

'Should we go back to the Britannia door?' Devlin suggested.

'That wardrobe is a more direct way down,' said Knowles, indicating an unexceptional item of built-in furniture.

Devlin tried to open the wardrobe. It was locked.

Light Fingers, custodian of the purple keys, picked out the correct implement and unlocked the doors. Black gowns hung inside, like curtains. Light Fingers parted them and disclosed a polished fireman's pole. For sliding down. A ladder was fixed to the wall. For climbing up. Amy wasn't the only girl who giggled. It was comical to imagine Headmistress using the pole or the ladder.

'It leads to an underground crossroads,' said Knowles. 'Seven passages converge. It's in the big book as Seven Dials.'

Devlin stretched her hands around the pole, taking a grip.

'*Don't!*' said Knowles. 'There's a trick.'

Devlin looked puzzled… if she got caught up in something, her expressions became exaggerated. Her quizzical look practically turned her eyebrows to question marks.

She didn't let go of the pole. A mechanism sprung with a whoosh.

Amy peered into the chimney-like space. Razor-edged blades sprouted from the walls, a little below the level of the wardrobe. Anyone sliding down the pole would get to the bottom in pieces.

'I've read that book,' said Devlin. '*Cut to Ribbons*, by Will B. Gutted.'

Knowles showed Light Fingers how to twist the key the wrong way in the lock to retract the blades. They ratcheted into the interstices of the brickwork.

Devlin admitted that Know-It-All's boning-up *was* useful after all.

The retractable knives made the enterprise of venturing into secret passages seem less like a lark.

'It's safe now,' said Knowles, with authority.

Gould volunteered to go first and disappeared into the dark hole. The others crammed around the wardrobe and tried to look down.

Gould called up that she was still alive.

Amy went next…

Gripping the pole lightly with her hands, elbows and knees she made herself light. She didn't plunge like Gould, but floated down, past the folded blades, into a well of darkness.

The light from above dwindled.

The pole went down much further than the ground floor of the Swanage. Brick gave way to rock.

Eventually she landed, light on her feet, in Seven Dials.

Gould had found a switch. Dim lamps glowed in sconces. There were seven passages leading away. Seven paths to death in the dark, she supposed.

Knowles came down next. She shone her torch into each of the passages, demonstrating that two were dead ends.

Frecks gave out a *yaroo!* as if on a ride at a funfair. She arrived, and gushed about the sensuous joy of sliding down poles.

'Better than spooning with Clovis,' she exclaimed. 'Much!'

Light Fingers, Paule and Marsh joined them in Seven Dials. Laurence came down last and needed a lot of coaxing. Even without the ring of daggers, she wasn't keen on sliding. Eventually she gave in, but screamed all the way down… then had to be detached from the pole and cajoled into opening her eyes. She was surprised not to be dead.

Paule wandered off into the largest of the tunnels. Knowles kept the torch aimed at the errant Sixth. One of the things Know-it-all knew was not to lose sight of Daffy Dora. They didn't have time to waste wandering through a labyrinth looking for her, even if Knowles had the maps and instructions off by heart.

Light Fingers looked to Amy for orders. That was happening a lot.

'We follow Paule,' said Amy, trying to sound sure of herself. 'Knowles, good thinking with the torch. Gould, keep track of her. Frecks... take up the rear and holler if anything nasty comes after us. Everyone, watch your step... and listen to Knowles. Especially you, Stretch.'

'I'm not opening an envelope unless Miss Memory says it's safe so to do,' said Devlin.

Knowles smiled slightly. 'The way Paule's gone is clear, just so long as you don't walk too close by the knight at arms...'

A crash came from the passage.

They rushed there to find Dora Paule sat on the ground – rock with wooden planks laid over the more uneven stretches – with a disassembled suit of armour scattered around and a long-handled battleaxe in her hands. She'd caught it falling towards her head. It would have done more than parted her hair.

'Before you get killed, perhaps you could tell us where we're going,' said Amy.

'...to the seaside,' said Paule.

'The whole school is by the seaside,' said Laurence. 'Before I saw it, I reckoned there'd be sand and Punch and Judy and ice cream at the end of the pier and bathing machines. Then it turned out to be shingles and seaweed and sudden tides and breakers you can't paddle in. Mouldy chiz, I thought.'

'One sympathises, young Larry,' said Frecks.

Marsh was appalled by Laurence's idea of the seaside, but didn't start an argument. Amy gathered the American girl had definite views about bank-holiday excursionists who went for a quick dip then drank beer and ate fish and chips on the pier before chucking their waste paper in the sea. She sometimes spat out 'surface-dwellers' the way Light Fingers said 'Ordinaries'.

'...to the *underground* seaside,' said Paule.

'She's off again,' said Gould. 'Awa' wi' the faeries...'

'No, hang on,' said Knowles, shutting her eyes and pressing forefingers to her temples as if picturing pages turning to the one she wanted. 'Daffy Dora's on the money! At the end of this road there's a cavern with tidal waters. A hidden harbour.'

'Smugglers?' asked Amy.

She had known smugglers would come into it eventually!

'Pirates, more likely,' said Knowles. 'Or sea-raiders.'

'There's a difference?' asked Amy.

'Pirates prey on ships from ships, sea-raiders prey on coastal settlements from ships,' put in Devlin, who was up on nautical matters. 'Many believe Sir Wilfrid Teazle, Squire of Drearcliff in the 1750s, was the masked sea-raider Cap'n Belzybub, but no one has ever proved it. The Cap'n hated the Welsh. He plundered the Severn Estuary in his fast frigate the *Johanna Pike*, named for the Bristol lass who threw him over for a poet from Pontypool.'

'Ouch,' said Frecks. 'Hellish heartbreak!'

'Cap'n Belzybub ran through the parson of Llantwit Major in a cutlass duel,' said Devlin, 'and sank the Navy brig *Glendower* off the Mumbles. Sir Wilfrid made the

Grange a retreat for retired sailors, supposedly out of the kindness of his heart – though no one ever noticed him doing anything else kindly. The magistrates thought he was Belzybub because the old salts knocking about the estate very much resembled a crew of ruthless sea-raiders. But Sir Wilfrid seemed to have nowhere to dock any vessel larger than a rowing boat. The mystery of the Home Harbour of the *Jo Pike* stands to this day.'

'It might be solved now,' said Knowles. 'The big book shows a ship in the cavern.'

'The *Johanna Pike* was said to have sunk with all hands in a storm. Neither Cap'n Belzybub nor Sir Wilfrid were heard tell of thereafter, so conclusions were drawn. The retired sailors disappeared too, though few thought to look for *them*.'

'Should we go to the ship?' Amy asked. 'It sounds like a place a person might hide if they weren't too fussy about getting their stockings wet.'

'The underground seaside,' repeated Paule. 'There's a Flute.'

'Are we to expect jolly sea shanties?' asked Frecks. 'Ralph knows all the rude verses of "What Shall We Do With the Drunken Sailor?" and "Off to Philadelphia in the Morn-Eye-Ing". Most of them have to do with bottoms.'

'Paule doesn't mean a musical flute,' said Amy. 'She's talking about the hole at the middle of all those spirals the Black Skirts make. The holes they're all drawn to. The entire pattern is called The Runnel and the Flute.'

Frecks and Gould – the ex-Black Skirts in the party – looked at each other and shivered. Amy didn't point it out to the others. In this case, knowing more wasn't helpful. She didn't want everyone to be like Laurence faced with a pole and a drop into darkness.

Paule picked herself up and kept hold of the axe.

Frecks had her cricket bat. Amy took up the sword from the pile of armour. The blade was rusted to the scabbard, but it could fetch a nasty slosh. She still felt a need not to do too many permanent injuries. Most Black Skirts would wake up eventually and be sorry for being Soldier Ants, she believed.

They followed Knowles along the passage.

'I can smell the sea,' said Laurence.

The air down here had a damp, salt quality.

They were walking on sand. The tunnel expanded to be more like a natural cave. Torchlight flashed off shallow pools. Crustacean eyes blinked back on stalks. Seashells glistened.

'Did you memorise a tide-table?' Amy asked Knowles.

'No. Why?'

'Because when the tide comes in this tunnel fills up with water,' said Amy.

There was an obvious tide-line on the rock wall.

'Ah,' said Knowles. 'Could be tricky. There are steps ahead. Probably best if we hurry up them.'

Amy agreed.

They quick-marched the rest of the way, bunching up a bit. Only Marsh was casual about the prospect of a dip in the drink. Amy suspected she'd be least likely to drown. Stretch admitted she couldn't swim, but experimentally extended her neck like a sinewy eel to see if she could keep her head above water. Her crown brushed the passage ceiling. Her head bobbed from side to side.

'Has anyone ever told you how unnerving that is?' said Frecks.

'Not really. It's just my bones.'

'Upstairs, in bright light and good company, having a four-foot neck is a party trick. Down here in the dark and damp, it's flesh-creeping. I'm only telling you so you know.'

Hurt, Devlin pulled herself back in shape. Marsh's pop eyes rolled sideways at Frecks. She wasn't directly included, but knew she fell into the flesh-creeping category.

Amy worried they'd fall out with each other before they could take on the Black Skirts. It wasn't even that Rayne was a master tactician. The Remove could divide themselves and become conquerable without any outside influence.

'Frecks, in the Purple I have moth wings and antennae,' she admitted. 'You might find that "flesh-creeping" to behold. You're wearing an enchanted hat which only works if your cause is *Just and True*. Remember Sir Percy and take care not to tick off the Lady of the Lake by letting a stray unjust or false thought sneak through. We're all flukes here. We all make flesh creep.'

In the dark, Light Fingers took Amy's hand and squeezed.

'Swipe me but you're right,' said Frecks, rattling her chainmail. 'Stretch, apols… you're all right in my books, and always have been. I spoke out of turn and – as is tragically my wont – without thinking. Pals and quits?'

She stuck her hand out and Stretch extended her arm, kinking around Larry who was between them, to shake.

'Quits and pals,' said Devlin.

Amy trusted that was settled.

An iron door in the side of the tunnel opened with a wrench. A dazzling light was aimed into Amy's eyes.

They were found out and caught!

'Time to make a fight of it, Remove,' she shouted.

Her invisible feelers extended. She rose a little off the ground and tensed for an attack.

'What ho, girls,' came a voice.

It was Lamarcroft, longbow and a quiver full of arrows slung over her shoulder.

She'd brought the rest of the Remove – Harper, Paquignet, Thorn, Frost, even Palgraive, who smiled and ambled along as usual.

'Lungs led the way,' said Harper, the one with the torch. 'She was in a trance or something.'

'No one showed up for our fair copies,' said Thorn.

Light Fingers pouted – hacked off to have wasted the effort on forgery. She'd been fagged out ever since.

'School is deserted,' said Frost. 'The Black Skirts have gone to ground. The air's heavy and tangy, as if a storm was coming... or some other big event. We thought Lungs might be leading us to her last battle.'

'I've trod these passages in dreams,' said Lamarcroft, who didn't seem in a trance to Amy. 'There's a ship here.'

'Know-It-All said that too,' said Devlin. 'We think Cap'n Belzybub's Hidden Harbour is just ahead.'

'Cap'n Who's-a-my-flip?' asked Frost.

'A former squire of Drearcliff who turned to piracy,' explained Amy.

'Sea-raiding,' corrected Know-It-All and Devlin together.

'You don't need to know the difference,' Amy said.

The pedants didn't give her argument. Amy didn't need a tide-table to know second high tide of the day was due around teatime, and the afternoon was nearly over. She heard water trickling in and the sand under her shoes was soggy.

She suggested they get a move on.

'I say, it's jolly good we're all together again,' said Shrimp. 'When we were split, I felt weaker.'

Thorn's eyes fluttered. Harper was next to her.

'Cut the breathing in, Shrimp,' said Amy. 'We need everyone at their best.'

Harper *let go* somehow and Thorn shuddered to wakefulness. She made a puff of flame.

By the light of the fire, they saw the steps Knowles had expected. They led up to a dock, hacked out of stone. Iron posts were hammered in at regular intervals. Their torch-beams were too feeble to illuminate the whole cavern, but Amy had an impression of rocky roof a hundred feet above them. Thorn sent up puffs of fireball, which gave a better view. A body of black water rippled below the dock.

Dying flames from Thorn's conjurings plummeted past rotten sails.

'Here's the Good Ship *Jo Pike*,' said Stretch. 'Though, all things considered, it might be classed as a Bad Ship.'

Amy didn't know enough about ships to say how old the *Johanna Pike* was or what kind of a vessel it had been in its prime. Devlin had said it was a frigate from the 1750s. Two masts still stood, but the third had fallen like a tree and lay broken on the dock. The black snouts of cannons poked out of gunports.

'Drearcliff has its own fighting ship!' exclaimed Devlin. 'I was impressed the school had a fives court! I claim right of salvage.'

'You can only claim salvage if nobody alive's aboard,' said Marsh, darkly. 'It's why wreckers killed shipwreck survivors.'

Amy remembered Marsh's fishy family were

sailors. She was up on the law of the sea.

The hulk sat low in the water and listed, probably holed in the hull and resting on the bottom. *Johanna Pike* was written in flaky gilt on the side. A figurehead might once have represented a fickle Bristol lass. Seaweed had swarmed up over the bows and taken hold, turning her into a frond-frilled, bladder-benighted grotesque. No bard of Pontypool would be composing verses about her rosy cheeks these days.

'The harbour entrance was over there,' said Knowles, gesturing with her torch at a fall of rocks. 'It collapsed hundreds of years ago. I doubt even a submarine could get in and out nowadays.'

'I can't see how a ship could have sailed from here, even with an opening,' said Frecks.

'They hauled down the masts and rowed,' said Marsh. 'Then put the masts up again, like a ship in a bottle.'

'Very ingenious,' said Frecks. 'Hats off to Cap'n Belzybub.'

'You don't suppose there's treasure down here?' asked Frost. 'Spoils of sea raids and such?'

'The harbour and the ship are in the big book,' said Knowles. 'Headmistress knows about the cavern. She'll probably have had any treasure away.'

Amy thought another mystery solved.

'That explains how she came by funds to found Drearcliff. Welsh doubloons, if they made any.'

'Belzybub mostly stole sheep, I understand,' said Devlin. 'But he must have had *some* treasure.'

'Rustling's a decent crime,' said Light Fingers. 'If the plods get close to feeling your collar, you can cook and eat the evidence.'

The ragged remains of human skeletons hung in

iron cages from the masts, two still aloft and one spilled on the dock. A grinning skull with a three-cornered hat lay nearby.

'Is this the two-faced Cap'n?' Gould asked.

'That's not real,' said Light Fingers. 'The skeleton is plaster and the hat's from the Drearcliff Playhouse. They were in *The Flying Dutchman* last year. I reckon the Viola Black Skirts have tarted up the cave to make it more picturesque. The original raiders wouldn't have put the masts up inside the harbour. This has all the hallmarks of being a lair of villains. Real villains usually take trouble to live in places that look misleadingly innocent. Like a school.'

Devlin was disappointed, but strode towards the ship. A gangplank led from dock to deck. Amy wouldn't have trusted anything wooden which had been down here in the wet for two hundred years, but supposed Stretch could bounce back.

'I still claim salvage,' said Devlin.

'You can't,' said Gould, sniffing the air. 'There's somebody alive aboard. I *smell* them.'

'Dr Swan,' said Amy, excited.

'No,' said Gould. 'Not Headmistress. *Rayne!*'

There was a fizzing and a sudden stink of sulphur... and a cannon discharged with a mighty roar and a flash of blinding flame.

Something black and round flew straight at them.

XII: The Last Battle of the *Johanna Pike*

'POCKET,' SHOUTED LIGHT Fingers.

Laurence – smack in the path of the onrushing cannonball! – swiftly pulled her hands apart as if drawing out a cat's cradle. A purple gap opened in front of her midriff... a pinafore pocket!

The projectile disappeared into the rip.

With an audible plop, the cannonball was *pocketed*. Larry immediately pressed the seams closed. The missile hadn't torn through her middle, but she was unsteady on her feet...

Speed into weight, Light Fingers had said.

'Quick thinking, Light Fingers,' said Amy.

She'd noticed Light Fingers gaining confidence with a newish Application. She could literally *think quick*... forming logic strings as deftly and speedily as she stitched a hem. She'd seen *all in a rush* that Laurence's Ability had a uniquely useful Application when a cannonball was zooming at her.

Larry sat down with a bump, holding her tummy as if she'd eaten a bowl of green apples.

Long unmaintained, the cannon had rolled back as it went off and done damage inside the ship. Cries and complaints issued through the gunport. People were in there.

Girls.

Amy rose. She hung in the air, ten feet above the jetty. From this vantage, she could look down through decks of the *Johanna Pike*. The planking was badly warped by time and water, and much had fallen in. There was movement in the ship's insides. A *lot* of movement. Churning and chewing and grinding.

Then... *they* swarmed out through the gunports and hatches, over the bows and across the gangplank.

At first, Amy wasn't sure what *they* were.

They slithered on four limbs, but had the faces of girls. Some even still wore Drearcliff boaters. Black, naturally. Spines kinked alarmingly as if hinges had been fitted. They crab-walked on elbows and knees, chittering and keening as they came. Wave after wave of Black Ants.

It was hard to take in.

She recognised faces... Beauty Rose, Prompt Rintoul, Pest Merrilees, Damaris Gideon. Their crawling bodies were bent out of true, but they still wore their skins. Their eyes were black and their bodies aswarm with ants. But they were still girls she knew, some her friends. Surrendered completely to the Ant Queen, they were just a mass of bugs.

Amy was consumed by horror and pity. And was angry.

If it weren't for Larry's pocket, she'd be dead... and so would most of the Remove, caught in the blast.

Instead, the Remove met the Black Skirts with defiance. Numbers might tell in the end, but the Unusuals would go down fighting.

Frecks fetched mighty whacks with her cricket bat and the others fought the horde with scavenged weapons or teeth and claws. Gould twisted around, throwing off half a dozen girl-bugs. She met chittering with war-howls.

Devlin pounded heads with ham hands and caught four or five throats with an outstretched arm slam. Light Fingers had altered her blouse, adding in pleats and folds which gave her the freedom to exercise her Ability to its limits without compromise.

Light Fingers' gentlest taps, *repeated swiftly*, were hammerstrikes. Speed into mass.

Marsh dived off the jetty and slid into the water, floundering Black Skirts on her tail. She turned and dragged them under one by one, letting them go only when they passed out. Most floated face up.

Had this been a trap?

Or had Paule brought the Remove here because here was where they needed to be?

Amy was twenty feet in the air now, steadying herself with her arms.

There were bursts of flame and blasts of cold icy air as Thorn and Frost put up a spirited defence. Spars of ice crashed through the rotten wood of the *Johanna Pike* and cobwebby sails caught fire.

Lamarcroft was in a battle now, even if it wasn't *her* battle. Her arrows fixed Black Skirts to the timbers, spearing through clothes and soft flesh. She was accurate enough to immobilise rather than kill, but there would be painful unpinning to do before her targets were freed.

Before she could nock another shaft, Lungs was rounded upon by Pinborough and Ker. They came in kicking and punching and ducking and dancing. Soldier Ants, dauntless and deadly. Lamarcroft wielded her bow like a quarterstaff, knocking both their heads for them... but they came back at her. An Amazon beset by Ants. Girls would be talking about this fight for generations, though it was but a small part of the mêlée.

Even Paquignet made seaweed rattle and pop under the foe, tripping a wave of ants and dragging them into the water – where Marsh struck without mercy. The long-calm harbour was afroth with the battle.

Palgrave stood a little way off, uninvolved – somehow the Black Skirts didn't bother her, as if they saw her as a post or a rock rather than a person. Amy wasn't sure bringing her – and her brain-maggot – was a good idea, though she was happy that the full force of the Remove was at this scrap.

They were outnumbered massively, but fought for glory.

'Just and true!' shouted Frecks. 'Just and true!'

The foredeck of the *Johanna Pike* was in good repair. It had been fixed up recently – by the clever carpenters of Viola? The planking was inscribed with the now-familiar spiral.

Rayne stood on the Flute.

Though her followers crawled, the Queen Ant was upright. She took out her rope and began skipping, looking up at Amy with that blank expression.

Lights sprang from firepots placed around the foredeck.

Through rifts in the ship, Amy saw Black Skirts swarming over each other. Some were entwined like rat-kings, elbows hooked together to make bodies into barrel-staves, braids tied in a tangle to lump heads together like a bunch of coconuts. A choir-like section raised their arms and chittered, attempting to imitate the ululation of the Purple.

Another oblation was to be made!

Hatches raised and shock troops appeared. The Cerberus and the Ghidorah – together! Brown, Crowninshield II, McClure, Martine and Wool shinned up the masts, coming for Amy. She floated back, out of their reach. Missiles flew up. Chunks of wood torn from the ship. A marlinspike. A hammer. Tennis balls. She easily batted away the volley, using her mentacles like lacrosse sticks. In the thick of the fight, with her blood surging, she was enough in command of her Abilities to be accurate at twenty or thirty feet.

Shoshone Brown reached a crow's nest and took a careful aim.

She hurled her javelin at Amy. Strikes-Like-an-Adder slipped past Amy's tries at getting a hold with her mind... but she struck it aside with her sheathed sword. She felt the jarring impact in her arms and shoulders, but was not impaled. The deflected javelin spanged against rock, but the sword fell and she was left holding a hilt with a blunt, useless two-inch tang stuck out of it.

Brown raised her arms and did the antenna wave.

Amy flew over the crow's nest and grabbed Brown's wrists, pulling her up into the air. Her shoulders hurt as Brown's weight dragged. Amy dropped the girl, and she plunged, long legs kicking, into the harbour. A great splash was raised. Amy saw Shoshone floundering, squirting water through her mouth and nose.

Black Skirts swarmed about Paule, who kept a circle free by scything around with her long-poled axe. Light Fingers zigged and zagged, whooshing audibly, beaning bonces with fast, heavy knuckle-taps. Knowles protested that the map in her head was changing and that it *hurt*. Frost and Thorn formed a protective ring around Knowles, singeing and icing off attackers.

Rayne kept to her skipping.

> '*Ants in your pants,*
> *All the way from France...*'

And so on.

There were Hooded Conspirators on the foredeck. The Professor – a proud parent? Red Flame. Ponce Bainter. Gogoth was there, bent over almost double. And newcomers to the coven, Fossil Borrodale and Digger Downs – with discreet veils rather than full hoods. Amy couldn't tell who had volunteered and who was just drawn into the spell.

That rhyme was in her brain, throbbing painfully.

> '*Send reinforcements,*
> *We're going to advance.*'

The firepots flared and burned sickly violet.

The tug of gravity, which Amy felt differently anyway, *shifted*. The water *tipped*, as if in a jug being poured out.

She remembered a riddle heard in the dorm. 'Have you heard about the Dim who wanted to try water-skiing? Gave up because she couldn't find a sloping lake.'

Well, here was one. A sloping lake.

An iceberg slid into a patch of fire and steam hissed. Frost, scalded, screamed. At that, a white bulk gathered from seawater and took golem form – Captain Freezing was back! Huge snow fists pummelled Black Skirts who came near.

As water climbed the cavern wall, the harbour bottom was revealed. Amy saw a rusted anchor, a discarded chest (treasure?), fish bones, a mass of glistening weed with girls struggling in it, Marsh dripping wet and panting through gills, Brown scratching her head as if she'd just woken up and wondered how she got here, long-sunken stones carved with runes and signs.

There was a spiral in the sea, a Runnel underwater. Amy found herself pulled through the air in wide circles, struggling against unseen currents. Water rose up to splash her. She got wet shoes and socks. Squelchily uncomfortable, and a drag on her flying.

The *Johanna Pike*, long grounded, shifted with a vast creak. Water poured in through its sides, washing more chittering Black Skirts out on to the wet jetty. Timbers strained and broke. Another mast snapped and crashed down on top of the skirmish around Paule. The battleaxe was lost and Paule went under a human surge, only to bob up on top of the crowd. Many hands supported her struggling body and bounced her from perch to perch, carrying her towards the ship as an army of ants might convey a leaf across their many backs as an offering to the queen.

The roof of the cavern was glowing now. Purple.

Amy fell upwards.

Rayne skipped back from the Flute, which was opening at the centre of the Runnel. A bright Purple circle grew there, as hard to look at as the sun. A hole in everything. Beyond were the things Paule was worried about and Mauve Mary had guarded against, the tendrils which yearned to reach through into the Back

Home, into the place Amy lived, and take an inhuman, cruel grip. She saw what was to come and knew it was her place – her *purpose* – to put a stop to it.

She took hold of herself, refusing to be blown and batted hither and yon by swirling winds or the siren call of the Purple. She ignored everything and found her place in the air.

Calm, she had control.

She fixed on Rayne and swooped.

Red Flame – Kali's father – took a revolver out of his pocket and thumbed the hammer. He drew a bead on Amy. The hole in the end of the barrel was her own Flute. Her death would issue from it.

She veered to the side but – a practised marksman – Red Flame kept his arm steady as he swung round, keeping his aim true. He didn't fire. The nearer she was to him, the better his chance of potting her. She hoped his hood impaired his vision more than her mask did hers. She was close enough to see he had one eye closed and his thumb was tensing.

A blur slammed into Red Flame and pitched him off the foredeck. Light Fingers, running faster than Amy had ever seen. She and Red Flame slammed against a rotten railing. Both went over the side, though Light Fingers skimmed the surface of the water and was back on the dock in a trice. The gun went off but fired wild. Red Flame fell into the water and floundered – the Kafiristani bandit chief couldn't swim! He had to be pulled to safety by a couple of Firsts barely out of water-wings.

Amy had no time to think.

Paule was being anthandled over the Flute. Her middle stretched as if she were Devlin – though it was

410

different, a warping effect of being caught between a here and a there.

This time, she was to be the oblation. A creature partly of the Purple, sacrificed to bring the Other Ones here.

Amy got her hands around Rayne's throat and pulled her up into the air.

She was close enough to see the girl's face. No trace of expression, even at this impertinent interruption.

The Professor howled a protest. Bainter chanted – ants in your pants backwards?

Amy's hair whipped her face. Rayne's boater came off and her fringe flapped.

Amy whirled around and around, fighting against the spiral. Rayne took hold – not of Amy's wrists, but of her face. She pulled off Amy's mask and let it fall. No longer Kentish Glory, Amy blinked and tried to adjust her vision. Rayne opened her mouth, wider than Amy thought possible, and made a tube of her throat. Tiny crawling things poured up from her gullet, over her tongue, between her teeth.

Ants spewed into Amy's face, getting in her mouth, her eyes, her nose. The insects bit and stung. A thousand pinpricks of venom.

Amy's face was on fire. She had no sense of what was up or down.

Together, Amy and Rayne collided with the last standing mast of the *Johanna Pike*.

They fell out of the air in an embrace of enemies, and hit the deck.

Amy felt something break – it was only wood!

Purple lightning struck, making glass clusters in the sand and jagged streaks on the cavern walls. Some Black Skirts were shocked by the flail of electric discharge.

The smell of burned hair and baked skin!

Rayne, queen demoted to worker, crawled towards Paule and the Flute. Amy hung on to Rayne's blazer.

She was still choking on and spitting out ants.

Rayne shrugged off Amy's hands but couldn't get away from her mental hooks. Amy was dragged across uneven planks, scraping her knees. She pushed herself up until she was on her feet, but kept invisible reins on Rayne, trying to hold her back. Inch by inch, Rayne got away from her.

Paule's legs were pulled into the Flute, but she held fast to a chain. Below her waist, she trailed off into a shimmer.

The Professor and Bainter struggled to get to Paule, but the spiral swirl pushed them away. The maw of the Purple closed around what it wanted and Paule was stuck. She wouldn't be swallowed but she couldn't escape.

'Gogoth,' shouted Professor Rayne. 'Stop that girl!'

Amy realised the 'that girl' was her.

The chauffeur loped across the deck with an ape-gait. He seemed expert in getting about in high winds and with topsy-turvy gravity. She couldn't let Rayne go *and* turn her mind to the problem of him.

So that was it then.

The brief, inglorious flare of Kentish Glory!

Gogoth picked up pace, but stalled as three girls jumped on him, gripping his knees, his arms and his chest and toppling him over.

Frecks, Light Fingers… and Kali!

The spell, apparently, was lifting. This close to the oblation, the Queen had cast off all the inessential workers… Amy had a sense that, all around, Black Skirts were coming to their senses, then losing them again as they discovered they were in a deep dark cavern where the world tilted and all around were monsters.

Only a few recovered presence of mind to do anything.

Kali was whipping Gogoth's swollen skull with her skipping rope.

'Go away, *mi-go*,' she shouted. 'You're not wanted, *yeti*.'

Evidently, she recognised the chauffeur and knew what he was.

Kali, awake, was in a righteous fury. Gogoth was beaten down. A sodden Red Flame, hood torn away, loomed up.

Kali uttered a long stream of insults in several languages.

'*You* did this to me,' she said. 'You're the dirty rat that killed my ma! And you tried to kill me!'

Mr Chattopadhyay's face was stretched and pale. His eyes were watery. Amid all this, he was shocked and upset...

'Kali, no,' he said. 'I tried to spare you this. I tried to get you away from this place before this started. You are my best beloved, and this – what I do here – is for you. I will give you an empire, an empire on many worlds. You should not stand with them.'

Kali turned her back on her father, and slammed two Black Skirts' heads together. She started kicking Gogoth in the hump, tears running down her cheeks, more ashamed of her father now than ever, more ashamed even than angry.

'Kali,' pleaded Red Flame weakly. He lost his footing and fell back into seaweed.

'I don't want an empire,' said Kali. 'I want my mother.'

Amy focused *everything* on Rayne and Paule. Her temples throbbed.

Rayne had crawled up on to the foredeck and was within grabbing distance of Paule. She was still muttering...

'Ants in your pants, take... another chance...'

She got her hand on Paule's forehead and *pushed*...

It was as if she were shoving the girl underwater. Paule lost her grip on the chain and slid into the shimmer, her body trailing off and twisting like a hundred-foot scarf. Amy ran over and tried to take hold of Paule's hands, but was too late. Paule's fingers brushed Amy's palms as she was sucked downwards by a powerful undercurrent.

Paule looked up, eyes infinitely sad, and her face sank through the shimmer. The Purple light closed over her.

The oblation was made.

'No,' Amy shouted. 'No. This will not happen.'

The Flute was whirling, irising wider open. Through the hole in everything, she saw Dora Paule tumbling away like a rag doll.

Like Marsh diving into the water, Amy dived through the shimmer.

Into the Purple!

XIII: A Reunion of the Moth Club

DREARCLIFF GRANGE HAD gone to War. The cricket pitch was a dig-for-victory potato field. A tarpaulin was battened down over the Heel. A poster outside the Playhouse read 'be like Dad – keep Mum!' Sandbags were packed around the Budgies and the Swanage windows blacked out.

Everything was smaller than Amy remembered… though she knew that was because she'd been small herself when she was first at School. The place hadn't changed much but she had. An Old Girl rather than a girl. A Sixth in a braid-trimmed blazer sauntered past and Amy went tight inside, worrying whether her seams were straight. Then she remembered she was grown up… and relaxed. Whips couldn't notch her. No prep, no swede, no Removal. Things she'd hated she now thought of fondly – except Sidonie Gryce, of course.

The smell from Hypatia Hall was an acrid mnemonic, taking her back to scrapes, stinks and the time Francesca Stone sent half the Fifth to the Infirmary by concocting mustard gas 'by accident' in the Chem Lab. Three children – Firsts? – skipping in the Quad chilled her to the bone. Good grief, there was that rhyme again…

…ants in your pants, all the way from France…

It had been extinguished, for obvious reasons, after the Fall of Rayne, but must have lingered in the collective memory of Drearcliff to be revived by girls who had no idea what it had once meant. A whip with an ARP armlet – she looked twelve – came along and broke up the skipping circle, which was a relief. Amy trusted the words had lost their power. Without an Ant Queen, the rhyme could no more breach the Purple than 'Ring-a-Ring-a-Rosy' could spread the Black Plague.

Walking from the car park – School had a car park! – she had strayed near the woods and found no trace of the Runnel and the Flute. That was done with three or four wars ago. It wasn't even in Kentish Glory's Top Five Worst Perils. Since then, they'd all been busy… the Wizard War, the Dawn of the Kali-Yuga, the Water War and the Current War…

It was late afternoon, night falling fast thanks to the blackout. Girls walked by in groups, chatting and joshing. Their short skirts, smart-fit blazers and rakish berets were more stylish than the scratchy, baggy uniform stuck on her generation by the long-out-of-business Dosson, Chappell & Co. Drearcliff kit was now supplied by Tanqueray – For Girls, who streamlined skirts and padded shoulders.

As was proper, the girls didn't know or care who Amy was.

Had she even noticed Old Girls when she was a young one? Ex-convicts must have pitched up at School on missions like this, grown women invisible to growing girls. Even in her day, there were reunions and state visits. Some of these children might be the daughters of her contemporaries. She knew Hannah

Absalom, Charlotte Knowles and Marigold de Vere had girls in School… was there a new Radical Rita or Miss Memory, defacing the Heel or coming top in every scheduled test?

She'd motored from London in her Riley Falcon, blowing six months' coupons on the one trip. Past Exeter, road signs were taken down or turned around in case there was an invasion and the enemy needed to be fooled. She still knew the way…

Driving from Watchet to Drearcliff brought back a memory. Joxer at the reins and dear old Dauntless clopping along. Serafine Walmergrave cocking snooks at horn-honking motorists.

Her car had been garaged for three years while she was busy on the home front and in France. Kentish Glory had gone to war too. Officially, Amanda Thomsett was a Second Officer in the Women's Royal Navy Service, seconded to Naval Intelligence. Her cover job was shoving model ships around a huge map with a modified snooker cue. But she had other duties.

She wore her Wren uniform… mask rolled up in a concealed pocket of her greatcoat, a trick learned from Emma Naisbitt all those years ago.

She resolved not even to think the words *all those years ago* ever again.

They were all in uniform these days. A new Pendragon Squadron flew Spitfires in the Battle of Britain, without help from the Lady in the Lake. Don Conquest, atoning for his interned father, was Captain Conquest of the Conquering Commandos, hero of lightning raids into the occupied territories. Kentish Glory had gone along with them on a jaunt in Norway, striking against a dark physics facility in the lea of a glacier – preventing the

Nazis from reviving a rhedosaurus from the ancient ice. Connie Hern showed up at Dunkirk with her racing submersible *Silver Sprite* and rescued dozens from the beaches. Dennis Rattray, disgraces set aside again, was with Monty in North Africa. Facing a squadron of Tiger tanks controlled by the bottled brains of dead Afrika Korps commanders, Rattray used his Fang of Night gem to blacken his fist once again and halted the enemy advance in its tracks.

Even Jonathan – Dr Shade, *her* Dr Shade! – had rejoined the Royal Army Medical Corps. Long shifts among the wounded of the Blitz didn't stop him zipping about London during air-raids, tracking down (and terrifying) Fifth Columnists. Hans von Hellhund was back, with a sulphurous swastika burning on his Stuka. The Demon Ace called out Dr Shade as his only fit opponent in this war. Poor old Sidney Skylark – whom Amy had met at Gatherings of the Circle and couldn't help but feel sorry for – was in a deep sulk. Thanks to his infernal pact, von Hellhund still flew, but his original arch-nemesis was grounded by arthritis and tummy wobbles.

Now the Yanks were in the big show, whole divisions of mystery men, boy geniuses, night-avengers, circus daredevils, muscle maniacs and machine marvels were storming into the fray. Overpaid, oversexed and over here wasn't a tenth of it. It'd be a miracle if the Allies got through the War without a major falling-out among their Unusual Combatants. A section of the Mausoleum called the Glasshouse was a military prison for Infractors with Abilities, the No-Stockade-Can-Hold-Me Brigade. It already needed to be expanded.

Sometimes, Amy missed Antoinette Rowley Rayne and the Hooded Conspirators.

Hitler's favourite British books were *Tarka the Otter* and *Formis*. When she'd first seen newsreels of marching Nazis, she'd thought them a comical imitation of the Black Skirts. They didn't seem so ridiculous now.

Sometimes, Amy felt everything in her world – in *the* world – had started at School.

After all, for her, it had.

She passed between the Budgies and stepped into the reception room of Tempest Keep.

The display of class photographs was bigger. She was in four of them. But the wallpaper hadn't changed and the furniture was the same.

Keys was still at her post.

No, *a* Keys was behind the desk.

The Keys was gone. Near the end of her time at Drearcliff Amy had learned the custodian's name, Hilda Percy.

'Amy,' exclaimed the new Keys, smiling.

She came out from behind her desk, working the wheels of her chair with her hands. A tartan blanket was tucked around her dead legs, which were twisted and fused together from knee to ankle…

'Paule,' said Amy, tears in her eyes. 'Paule.'

Several more white streaks ran through Dora Paule's cloud of hair, but her face was unlined. She didn't look old enough to be Keys. She seemed, in fact, much younger than Amy.

A bunch of keys, mostly purple, was hooked over the arm of her chair.

'Those are Larry Laurence's copies,' said Amy.

'We buried Miss Percy's set with her.'

'Of course you did.'

The original Keys was still on the grounds, in a

small, well-tended cemetery. It was also the last resting place of Ponce Bainter – interred face down with an iron spike through his head, if there was any justice – and a number of former Staff and old girls.

Amy understood a few asked to be brought back and buried here because later life had disappointed them. School really had been the best days of their lives. Spanish flu in '19 and an outbreak of beri-beri in '32 added clusters of small, sad stones.

Soldier Ant casualties whose bodies were found this side of the shimmer – Priscilla Rintoul, Bryony Burtoncrest, Gladys Sundle – were buried elsewhere, but a plaque listed their names… along with those lost in the Purple. The unrecovered were only presumed dead. No new Mauve Mary loomed out of the thin shimmer in the covered walkway. Officially, that had been an epidemic – the Purple Plague.

Some girls were taken out of School for months afterwards, but most came back. The uniform rules were amended. Black was no longer an option. Former Black Skirts remembered little of the craze, and didn't care to think too deeply about time spent skipping along the Runnel after Antoinette Rowley Rayne.

Amy bent over and hugged Paule, which was slightly difficult…

…but only with her arms. An old trick came back, and she entwined Paule with her mentacles, lifting her out of her chair. She caught her blanket and tidied it away. Paule wore a long skirt in Drearcliff grey and shiny shoes.

At first, she'd had to puppeteer Paule. Then, they learned better. Her Ability supported her friend's weight as if it were a body of water. Paule swam in it of her own accord. Amy had sworn she'd never leave the Unusual girl to be stuck in her chair... but, of course, she'd left School in the end, as Paule insisted she should.

'Am I first?' she asked.

'No, you're nearly last. We're not sure the fourth can make it. We had only a formal acknowledgement of receipt from the Diogenes Club, with a PS blacked by the wartime censor. I sympathise. I have to read the girls' post and blot out strategic or demoralising information. Sneaky Steff Seelan makes up paragraphs about troop movements and death-ray projects just so I have to use up ink.'

They danced around the room, without touching. Both floated.

'Baby Fa-a-ace,' they sang, adopting shrill little-girl voices, 'You've got the cutest little baby fa-a-ace...'

Then they collapsed in giggles.

'We had the best songs,' said Amy. 'Have you heard the rot girls listen to nowadays? *Doodly-acky-sacky want some seafood, mama.* What does that even mean?'

Paule hung in the air, momentarily melancholy.

'You always forget, Amy. I was old and young when you first knew me and I still am. I don't have your songs the way you do. "Baby Face" and "Yes, We Have No Bananas" and "Ain't We Got Fun?" I have the songs that were silly when I was first a girl *and* the songs that are silly now... and all the ones in between. I get "Ta-Ra-Ra-*Boom*-De-Ay" and "Der Feuhrer's Face" mixed up.'

Amy wanted to hug her friend again.

Paule drifted back into her chair and settled herself. With her blanket on, she looked like a mermaid in disguise...

...thinking of mermaids: Janice Marsh grew up to be

a real Hollywood film star, despite (or because of) the fish-lips and pop eyes. She'd been in *Nefertiti*, *Down Ecuador Way* and *Salome in the WAVES*. She'd also fallen in with the very fishy Esoteric Order of Dagon in California. Not all of the Remove stuck with *Just and True* as a motto. Amy couldn't always blame them – even if Kentish Glory had to send Frost and Thorn to the Mausoleum after their wheeze of freezing and firing their way into the Bank of England.

'You trot upstairs,' said Paule. 'Headmistress knows you're coming. The all-seeing eyes are still there.'

Amy looked to the portrait of Dr Swan. Its eyes were crystals.

'Television?'

'Something like,' said Paule. 'Welcome to the Marvels of Futurity.'

That gave Amy a tingle. Also *déjà vu*.

After the downfall of the Splendid Six, the Mystic Maharajah's Sordid Seven challenged Dr Shade and Kentish Glory to a duel in the ruins. Mystic Marge had tried to slap the fluence on her and this tingle felt oddly like that...

Why, after all, was she here?

There was a war on. Didn't she have more important things to do?

The spell passed and she climbed the stairs to Dr Swan's study. There were more of them and the walls stretched and contracted.

She had an urge to pull on her mask.

Outside the Swanage, what colour was the night?

Then, she was on the landing. Britannia still commanded the corridor, brandishing heads that looked like Hitler, Mussolini and Hirohito.

The door of Headmistress's study opened by itself. The mechanism was smoother than in her day, but the trick was the same.

Dr Swan, unchanged, stood by her desk, with a glass of something violet in her hand. She wore her academic gown over a silver evening dress. It was if she'd been standing there for twenty years, waiting for Amy to come back.

Two women got up from chairs and rushed at Amy.

She was embraced, simultaneously by Inspector Naisbitt of the Women's Auxiliary Police and the Ranee of the Kali-Yuga.

Amy knew Kali was still on WAP's Most Wanted International Criminal list. Emma must be prepared to overlook that... for the evening.

The scent of Kali's herbal cigarettes was still heady.

The three former cell-mates hugged.

At least her friends had the decency to get older at the same rate she had. They had little lines around their eyes and mouths.

Amy had seen Emma only a few weeks ago, at the site of the Clerkenwell Beheadings. They tended to run into each other at scenes of the crime. Together, they had settled the hash of the Fiend of the Fifth Column, put an end to the Blitz Butcher, saved St Paul's from the Mjolnir Bomb, solved the Riddle of the Xenoglyphs and broken up the Black Quorum.

Officially, the WAP looked askance at the likes of Dr Shade and Kentish Glory... but Amy and Emma worked well together. Jonathan, she noticed, was a smidge jealous of the old school tie. When the women dug up some deep-buried scrap of Drearcliff lore or laughed at something impossible to explain to a non-

Old Girl, Amy sensed his eyes narrowing behind the Dr Shade goggles and saw his slouch hatbrim angle to convey irritation.

'Oof, no strangling,' said Emma. 'Especially not from you, Ranee Kali.'

So far as Amy knew – and who could really tell? – Kali hadn't set foot on English soil in ten years. She'd been active in China when the Japanese invaded. The mysterious deaths of five particularly brutal officers who held high rank in the Blood Banner Society were credited to her. There was a fanciful movie about the case, *She-Strangler of Shanghai*. She'd also been in the Deep South around the time Dudley Hogg-Pidgeon was assassinated. If he'd lived, the demagogue might have united several American fascist parties into an effective movement. Kali was more likely to be in bad odour with Emma for robbing the Sub-Continental Stronghold of Box Brothers Bank in Calcutta.

The Kali-Yuga – the Age of the Demon – had influence in every corner of the world. Its queen had proved herself much more than the mere thief her father had been. To some, Kali was a distaff Dr Mabuse... to others, a female Gandhi. It was said Hitler and Churchill only agreed on one thing – that Kali Chattopadhyay should be hanged.

'Looking aces, kid,' Kali said.

She wore a crimson sari with gold trim. Her nose-stud was a ruby. Her other jewellery was a choker of black pearls and a diadem with a snarling, fanged face – emblem of the Demon.

Emma wore plainclothes, with a WAP tiepin. She was so excited by the reunion her hands were a blur... she rarely showed off her physical speed, concentrating instead on the other aspect of her Ability that had suited her for her profession.

Charlotte Knowles' book about Emma was called *The Quick-Thinking Inspector Naisbitt*. Given a puzzle or a room full of clues, she could make lightning connections and have a workable hypothesis in her mind before the first fingerprint was lifted. Amy knew it frustrated Emma that she had to wait for everyone else to catch up before she could get on with the job.

'I left a message with your service,' said Emma. 'I'd have come down from London with you...'

'I was in...'

She really shouldn't say.

'Copenhagen,' deduced Emma, 'near the Tivoli, in the red-light district. You brought out a rabbi and his wife and daughters. The middle daughter is the one the Navy wanted. An Unusual. Something like what's-her-name, Imogen Ames. A brain-peeper. She'll be with a recording angel in Whitehall now, giving names, addresses and lists.'

'Still in the loop, eh?' said Kali. 'Light Fingers keeps an ear to the ground.'

'No, she *thought it through*,' said Amy.

'You're wearing the coat you wore on the trip,' said Emma. 'Coats tell stories.'

Emma was too impatient to explain in detail how she knew what she knew. Amy was too polite to mention it was the *youngest* of the rabbi's daughters who had drawn battle plans out of a German clerk's head. Anna Taub wasn't quite like Ames either. She didn't just *read* thoughts, she sucked them out. What she knew, the clerk no longer did. The process was painful too, but there was a war on and this was important.

'She's already told me stuff that'd get her throat cut if she tried her jazz where it wasn't wanted,' said Kali. 'And my outfit's fresh on today.'

Amy took her coat off and draped it over a chair.

Kali saluted her uniform.

'Don't the WRNS have a Fightin' Fluke already?' she asked.

'Yes,' said Amy. 'Jenny Wren. She's an unsinkable Unusual. I'm not.'

'Shouldn't you hang your lid in the WAAF?'

'I dislike flying... in aeroplanes,' said Amy, smiling. 'Besides, it's not as if I spend much time at sea. I'm seconded on the hush-hush to...'

'Be like Dad,' interrupted Emma. 'Loose lips sink ships. Ranee Kali's an enemy of the Empire, remember.'

'I'm the enemy of *every* empire.'

'Except your own.'

'The Kali-Yuga isn't an empire, Em. It's a *movement*. A philosophical venture. A little bit of a religion, maybe – but not too much. It's just a thing, you know. An *our thing* thing. I don't hear any complaints when I mix it with the *Japanese* Empire. Or the Nutzi Nazis... have I told you how much I hate them mugs? Heel-clickin' heels and goose-steppin' gooseberries. Know what they remind me of?'

Emma and Amy did.

'What's said in Headmistress's study stays here,' said Amy. 'That's always been the Drearcliff way.'

Dr Swan raised her glass in approval. She was proud of her cygnets, even when they bickered in front of her.

With the world of nations you could find on maps again locked in a Great War, the underworlds were also in flux. Territories were abandoned or occupied, unlikely alliances were formed and old partnerships riven. Interests quietly shepherded over centuries ticked over even as spectacular battles settled nothing very much. The Kali-Yuga was likely to come out of this turmoil as the dominant factor in the secret cabals which ran much that was illegal and more that was dangerous around the globe.

Did Kali ever wear her father's old Red Flame hood? She was adept in the mastermind's practice of getting other people to fight her battles for her. Amy was sure the tip-off which set Emma on the trail of the unutterably vile Stepan Volkoff came from Kali. The Master of Mutilation was now clapped up in the Mausoleum, shunned by even the worst of the other inmates. No one complained about that, but the Kali-Yuga benefited from Volkoff's downfall by taking over his profitable Archipelago of Atrocities.

Amy looked around the room, again and again.

The big book was here – chained to a lectern, under a glass case. Its secrets must have faded from Knowles' mind by now. The cupboard that was the entrance to the maze inside the walls was newly varnished. Amy trusted the fireman's pole was polished. The sound of the ticking clocks and other apparatus was the same.

Only the Moth Club were different, really... and if she closed her eyes, they were still Thirds.

Amy had another tingle moment.

'What ho, fillies,' boomed a familiar voice.

'You came,' Amy exclaimed, turning.

'Couldn't miss this... reunion of the reprobates.'

The last of the four stood in the doorway, posed in dramatic flared trenchcoat, lilac dress and black beret.

Lady Serafine Walmergrave, Codename: Seraph.

Her oldest friend – Amy had met her a full hour before she was introduced to Kali and Emma. Having shared tiny cells with stockings hanging from the bedposts for three years, they had still roomed together (in Lamb's Conduit Street) when they first moved to London. Amy had stuck by Serafine when she was wrung out and vindictive after Clovis threw her over for the little marchioness, then put up with the ups and downs of her tempestuous love life. She had held Serafine's head over the bucket when she was in a despairing swoon over gallant Captain Geoffrey Jeperson, who was never going to notice her (until he did). She frankly told her friend what she thought – leading to a two-month freeze dissolved with tears when Serafine admitted Amy was right – while she arbitrarily experimented with treating the gall. Capt. appallingly by running off to Gretna Green with Roddy Poulton-Jones. When Serafine came to her senses at the last moment, she telephoned Amy, who flew up to Scotland and rescued her from the altar. It was hard to go through all that – plus a great deal more comedy and tragedy – and remain impressed with someone, but Amy was astonished by and proud of what Codename: Seraph had done for British Intelligence. Without her efforts, the country would be occupied territory, its capital city Birmingham (renamed Hitlerdorf) and the King bolted into an automaton exoskeleton with a mechanical sieg-heiling arm. So long as secrets stayed secret, there would not be a biographical film called *The Woman Who Won the War* – with Deborah Kerr or Googie Withers – but there jolly well ought to be.

Seraph sauntered into the room.

Another habitué of the shadow world, her name was

on the members list of Britain's least-known intelligence and investigative outfit, the Diogenes Club. You could be clapped in the Tower of London for even knowing where she bought her hats. Even Jonathan was wary of the Diogenes Club, dwellers in deeper darks even than Dr Shade. Serafine had been put up for membership by one of their old teachers, Catriona Kaye, and seconded – with superhuman decency, under the circumstances – by Captain Jeperson.

After Mrs Edwards reclaimed her rightful place, it turned out Miss Kaye had been at Drearcliff to keep an eye on Dr Swan's cygnets. She had been scouting for long-term potential recruits. Amy, Kat Brown (Olympic javelin Silver, 1936), Lu Lamarcroft and Venetia Laurence had done odd jobs for the crown under the aegis of the Diogenes Club, but only Seraph earned full membership.

Dr Auchmuty, the librarian, had also been looking to recruit girls for unusual endeavours, but on a mercenary basis. Her employment agency specialised in adventuresses, seductresses, assassins and deceptively decorative body guards. She had placed the De'Ath Sisters, Bizou and Angela, with the Haghi Circle in Berlin. Doc Och had also made overtures to Gould and Marsh, but they hadn't been interested.

The others pounced on Seraph. They linked arms and jumped.

'Ants in your pants,' said Seraph... who then ducked to avoid the general head-sloshage that came her way.

'Ouch, ouch, pax pax,' she said.

'Not one of my favourite memories,' said Emma.

'In spades, sister...'

'I've not thought of that... of Rayne... in... how many years?' said Amy. 'Not since...'

She found it hard to concentrate, to fit memories together.

It was like looking through to the Back Here from the Purple. Paule had said you could skip ahead in the playscript or riffle backwards, but you never saw the whole thing properly.

So much had happened... so much.

'It ended down below, on that pirate ship,' said Light Fingers.

'Sea-raider,' corrected Amy.

'The *Johanna Pike*,' said Frecks.

Seraph wore a plain necklace of silver links. Amy realised they were unpicked from her uncle's coif. Much more stylish and practical than the balaclava, but... just as effective?

'We stopped the Hooded Conspiracy,' said Amy. 'All of us in the Remove...'

Knowles was a writer now, like her father – though she concentrated on true-life crime. She had been 'Stargazy' at *Girls' Paper* before paper shortage killed the publication. Aconita Gould was whatever you called a lady laird. A lairdess? No, probably just a lady. A strike team of German saboteurs who recently landed near Inverglourie Glen with orders to blow up coastal defences were found badly scratched and blubbing on the beach, so Amy knew Gould was contributing to the war effort. Thorn and Frost, on parole, were undergoing tests at a weather research station in Sutton Mallet, to see whether their Abilities had military application. From what she knew of the army's Unusuals division, Amy thought they'd be better off in jail. Laurence was tucked under Seraph's wing, travelling between neutral territories with pockets full of experimental fuses and crown jewels. Lamarcroft was in Burma, serving in the Regiment of the Damned. General Flitcroft took anyone tough enough into their ranks, no questions asked, even if they wore petticoats. The Japanese, apparently, were terrified of Lieutenant Lamarcroft, V.C., and called her the Tall Demon Archer Lady. She was still looking for her battlefield.

The others of the Remove, Amy wasn't sure of… Harper, Dyall, Paquignet, Palgraive. She hoped they'd found places

…even thinking of Dyall made her lose track of things and ponder gaps in her memory… and she was even more discomfited when Palgraive's smile crossed her mind. There had been a *scene* with Palgraive and Rayne, she knew, but the details were lost in violet haze…

The Purple, again…

'Paquignet's at Kew Gardens,' said Emma. 'Superintendent Bright had her in for questioning on the Strangling Vine Case. She didn't do it, though. Some Aztec Nazi cult was behind that.'

Amy didn't even bother to ask her friend how she had known what she was thinking.

'Did you see that gangster picture Jan Marsh made with Humphrey Bogart?' said Kali. 'Who'd a thunk?'

'You have picture palaces in the Hindu Kush?' Seraph asked.

'We have motion picture *studios*,' said Kali. 'We could throw over all the smuggling, blackmail, gambling and jewel-snatching and make more dough legit with musical pictures.'

'But you won't?' said Emma.

Kali shrugged. 'Where'd be the giggles without deviltry and daring? You'd be out of a job, for a start.

It's not like you can stay home and bake cakes...'

Emma laughed.

A not-always-happy girl, Emma Naisbitt had become a serious, purposeful woman... but Kali could always make her smile. Amy was sad for a moment, because she couldn't.

This was why the whole Moth Club was needed.

Amy's antennae buzzed.

She had to resist an urge to touch her forehead, to make sure her feelers hadn't sprouted. Her back itched too, where once... long ago and in another place... she had grown real wings.

Her friends' faces wavered. Layers peeled away and she saw them as girls.

It was as if they had returned after years away but only minutes had passed.

'Dr Swan,' she said. 'Something's always bothered me...'

Headmistress nodded, allowing her to ask a question.

'Rayne... why did you let her go so far?'

Dr Swan angled her head to one side but said nothing.

'You knew what she could do... what she was. You knew about the Runnel and the Flute, and Professor Rayne, and the Other Ones, and the Purple... Mauve Mary and Mr Bainter and Kali's father. You knew what was happening in School, but you left us to deal with it. Us. The Moth Club. The Remove. Everything you had worked for, all the girls you had invested so much time and effort in... you let it all be at hazard. Just... why?'

Headmistress's eyes opened wider and purple light reflected.

'I think you have answered your own question,

Thomsett,' said Dr Swan. 'I have always had confidence in my cygnets.'

Amy was a little queasy – she remembered that, too, from the rise of the Black Skirts, the ways that Rayne and all her works had made her sick.

'It was an exam?' said Emma. 'An exercise?'

'And you passed.'

Amy was still appalled. At the time, and all these years on, it hadn't seemed like anything you could call educational. More than just the school had been put in danger.

It had very nearly been the day the sun rose purple.

The Black Skirts might now rule the world, ants swarming over the face of the globe.

And they might all be dead or changed or lost in the ranks.

But Headmistress always had confidence in them.

Her Unusuals had proved themselves. The Remove had come together, even flukes among flukes like Harper and Dyall, and had learned how much more effective they were playing as a team, finding Applications in their complementary Abilities, helping each other overcome handicaps, embracing and celebrating their unique natures.

Afterwards, Amy hadn't cared what Mother thought of her – *she could fly*.

Light Fingers stopped worrying about what Ordinaries thought or her parents said and came to her own decisions.

Kali – like others pulled into the Black Skirts – overcame what had been imposed on her, and shrugged off the remnants of her insect carapace.

And Frecks kept their cause Just and True.

So much had happened since... too much to remember, so much more than Amy had expected or imagined as a girl.

...the Creatures from the Serpentine, Colonel Slaughter and the Slaughter Boys, the Adventure of the Crooked Thumbs, the Burrowing Behemoths, the Wizard War, the Jollity Plague, the Wrath of the Onion Men, the trial of Olivia Gibberne, the Gorilla of Mile End, the Last Ride of Dick Turpin, Spring-Heel'd Jack and Razor Strop Reg, the Gibbering Doom, Biffo the Crime Clown and the Circus of Carnage, the War That Never Was, Bunyip Nowlan, the Abdication Abomination Crisis, the Last Will of Decimus Dexter, the Bristol Burglaries, the Vengeance of Madame Maupertuis, the Haunting of Hellespont Hall, the Philately Will Get You Nowhere Affair, the Loss of the *LS908*, the Reign of the Sordid Seven, the Green Obscenity, Mr Eius and the Murder Memoranda, the Poisonings at Judas Cross College, Lord Piltdown's Final Innings, the Miscalculation of Primrose Quell, the Centurion of Caerleon-on-Usk, the Daughters of Dien Ch'ing, Stepan Volkoff's Enthusiasm for Atrocity, the Unlikely Bicycle, the Calderon-Munster Prizefight, the Appearance of the Hole, the explosion at Winnerden Flats, Emma's unfortunate but short-lived marriage, the persistent problem of Moria Kratides, the Rot in the Gideon Family Tree, the Frinton Fascisti, the Girl With the Ghost Lantern, the Overground Moles, the Electric Uberman, Tom B. Idle, the Hydes of March, the Buggleskelly poltergeist, the Boat Race That Vanished, the Burning of Parsimony Dell, the Lilac Monk, the Slink (again and again, the Bloody Slink), the Spawning of the Slithards, the Tea Exchange Scandal and its Remarkable Aftermath, the Duel of the Seven Stars, the Clockwork

Churchill, the Monkey-Gland Monstrosities...

...through it all, she had *flown*.

The others didn't use their moth names any more, but she was still Kentish Glory.

Jonathan – Dr Shade! – had come into her life or she had stepped into his world... which was not anything she could have imagined when reading about him and the Aviatrix and Shiner Bright in *Girls' Paper* and *British Pluck* in her cell at Drearcliff.

It had been a long, exciting, challenging night.

And she was giddy from it.

She remembered it was here, at School, where she first put on a mask... where she first admitted to herself that she couldn't just float, where she had learned to reach out with her mentacles like Devlin with her arms...

Stretch was married to a bank manager and had five pliable children. She called herself Plump Devlin now. She was the one who settled down.

The Hooded Conspiracy.

The Black Skirts.

The oblations to the Other Ones.

The Yettymen.

Kratides of the Sixth.

The Sisters of De'Ath.

All of it...

Jumbled up together in her mind, swirling round and round, in a spiral, like the Funnel and the Lute...

No, the Runnel and the Flute.

...Dora Paule pulled through the shimmer, into the Purple. She had reached after her, fallen in...

'Are you all right, Amy?' asked Emma.

It was as if photographers' bulbs were flashing and popping around her. Flashing *purple*.

Now, nails were driven into her forehead – where her feelers were rooted.

Seraph took her shoulders and held her up.

Headmistress stepped back, against a bookcase, which revolved and took her into the secret passages.

'Whaddya know whaddya say?' said Kali.

Frecks looked at her with concern, then recognition.

'It's you in there, Amy,' she said. 'Not the you you... the *young you*.'

The walls of Headmistress's study dissolved.

Everything had been... what? A dream, an illusion, a peep at the last act of the play?

Amy was falling through purple twilight.

No, she was *not* falling.

She was *flying*.

XIV: Where the Ants Stopped

Dora Paule was below her, tumbling towards a desert plain. The sands were shifting, a swirling wind erasing the lines of the Runnel.

Things swam under the ground. Things big as whales.

Amy flew fast – here, wings burst through the back of her blazer – and circled around Paule's straight plummet. She closed in and snatched Paule, gripping her around the waist. Paule flung her arms about Amy's neck and held tight.

In the Purple, gravity was upended and inconstant... but, for Amy, that was normal.

They wobbled alarmingly as Amy tried to account for the added weight and awkward shape of Paule. She had to extend her wings like glider-planes to regain stability.

Above was the shimmer... the Flute from the other side.

Amy had been thinking of something, but it was gone like ice in hot tea.

She descended gracefully and set down on the sands, letting Paule go.

The Purple was spinning dizzily, like water circling a whirlpool... everything preparing to drain into the Back

Home. The Other Ones – whose shapes made Amy's feelers throb with pain – would be washed into the world.

A strange automobile, boxy yet streamlined, was half-buried nearby. She recognised it as *hers*.

…no, that couldn't be. She didn't know how to drive. *Girls don't drive*, Mother said. But that contraption was *hers*, she knew. Was it just a car, or could it burrow into the ground or run underwater? It was called a Falcon, but didn't have wings… she guessed it couldn't fly.

Other things were strewn across the plain… some girls had been sucked into the Flute and deposited here. A few weren't moving.

A grown-up woman, about fifty, walked over. She wore a black boater.

Ignoring the sandstorm and the hole in the sky, let alone the three moons and burrowing behemoths, the woman took hold of Amy's lapel.

'Grey wears poorly,' she said. 'Uniform Infraction.'

It was Gladys Sundle. An *old* Gladys Sundle.

An ant the size of a human hand was pinned to her jacket, legs writhing. It leaked yellow ichor. Mandible-pincers nipped the soft fold of Sundle's throat, making red, inflamed punctures.

Sundle didn't seem to notice the ant… any more than she noticed she was years, *decades*, older than she should be.

Where had her life gone?

Amy had barely noticed the Fifth before she went Black, so didn't know whether Sundle was naturally a cold, nasty piece of work or had just given up and gone along with Rayne like so many others. She had seen Sundle's charcoal sketches in the Art Room and thought them quite good. Her speciality was contemplative portraits of Viola 'stars'. Sundle gave Crawford, Mansfield and Upton her own curly hair, heavy eyelashes and bee-stung lips... so the sketches ended up looking more like the artist than her sitters.

After putting a Black Skirt on, she stopped sketching and led the Chimera.

'Watch out for the whips,' said Sundle.

The woman walked on. Five or six more giant ants were stuck to her back. Holes were chewed in her clothes. Mandibles were embedded in her flesh. Dried blood and ichor stained the back of her blazer and skirt.

'Come back,' Amy shouted. 'We can help you home.'

'Wherever would that be?' Sundle said, over her shoulder.

She disappeared into the dust-swirls.

How many like her were in the Purple? Stuck or changed or dead?

'This is a pretty pickle,' said Paule.

Amy couldn't tell how *compos mentis* Paule was. If she was now daffy in the Purple, that was bad.

It meant *nothing* was reliable.

'I was in School, but here... a lot happened, *years* of it, and I was... a grown-up, I think? Or dreamed I was. Like Sundle, only not as ancient... and without the ants in the pants.'

'That happens to me sometimes too,' said Paule.

'I met you... a you of the future. There was a war on. Another one. Or the same one, started up again. See that car? It's from then.'

'What car?'

The Falcon was buried. Then the sand moved on, and uncovered the car's skeleton – engine, frame, wheels, all polished like chrome. The rest of it was eaten away, consumed by the desert.

The shifting sands weren't sands.

'Did you meet my husband?' asked Paule, cheerily. 'He's someone like me... doesn't get old. Gavriel Skinner. We'll be a dance team, like Vernon and Irene Castle... only with funny-sounding music that's like fireworks going off in an orchestra.'

Amy had a flash-image of Paule sitting down. In a wheelchair.

'I didn't think you danced,' she said.

Then she remembered *dancing* with Paule... or at least shaking her all around the room – a room with class photographs on the walls – to music.

Doodly-acky-sacky want some seafood, mama.

What did that even mean?

With a clanking, the last of the Falcon fell apart. Cogs and rods melted as sand-things swarmed over them.

The desert was made up of tiny insects, dead and alive. Mites, not motes. In the air, midges.

Sand-coloured ants swarmed around Paule. She didn't seem concerned.

'Can you take us Back Home?' asked Amy. 'Like before.'

Paule was wincing now. Half-deflated, she was becoming a wriggling scrap of herself... she couldn't concentrate, the compensatory clarity of thought she had in the Purple was torn away by ten thousand little bites.

Amy looked around, hoping for help.

Enid ffolliott – Mauve Mary – lay nearby, face up, arms crossed on her breast, sand-ants slowly piling over her. The guardian of the shimmer had been brought down by the Hooded Conspiracy's allies in the Purple.

The Other Ones.

Amy lashed out with her mentacles, and scattered the bugs off Paule's legs. They reformed at once and redoubled their swarming. Living winds – zephyrs – funnelled cruel clouds of them at Amy.

Her face was numb from stings. Now, she felt sharp bites in her wings.

'Paule,' she pleaded. 'We can't take this much longer.'

Paule wore a mask of ants, like writhing ochre mud. They stayed away from her eyes and mouth, but grew thick on her face.

Her eyes were panicked.

Amy wiped away ants with her hands, but they came back.

She didn't even think the insects here were properly alive. They were little sand golems in the shape of ants. Tiny Black Skirts with pincers and poison.

'Ants on your face, what a great disgrace,' she said. 'Spend two and sixpence on cleaning up this place.'

Paule heard her and closed her eyes.

She was part of the Purple, living in two worlds. She could no more be consigned here than she could be kept Back Home.

Amy felt the changes coming.

Paule didn't need mentacles. *Everything* here was connected to her.

ffolliott sat up, eyes alive. Bugs poured away from her, clearing a circle. The bare ground was more like bone than rock.

Amy heard water and shouts and fire. An air-raid siren went off.

A newspaper seller shouted '*Starnewsnstandard Starnewsnstandard Starnewsnstandard!*' Headlines floated…

MAGISTRATE DECAPITATED – HEAD STILL
MISSING! KENTISH GLORY CAPTURES DIAMOND
GANG! A NATION MOURNS – DR SHADE FEARED
LOST! A NATION CHEERS – DR SHADE RETURNS!
WHO IS THE KENTISH GLORY?

She was dizzy from it all.

A phantom ship, a broken hulk, appeared around them. On every deck, phantom girls were scrapping, silent and see-through and juddering. It was like the flickers when the projector went wonky and Miss Dryden ran out of music to play… pale ghosts in Black and Grey, swimming through mud or slipping on ice, mouths open but mute.

The figures became more solid, recognisable.

Lamarcroft knocked out Pinborough and wrestled with Ker.

Frecks had Bainter on his knees, crooking her arm around his neck from behind. His bald pate was going red.

The Purple faded. Amy and Paule were Back Home.

It was noisier here.

Amy held Paule, who was exhausted. By force of her will, she had withdrawn the oblation. The shimmer was gone. The Runnel and the Flute were ruined.

'I might not be able to go back, Amy,' said Paule, terrified.

Amy tried to comfort her.

'…oh, and I can't feel my legs.'

Paule was heavy in her arms. Amy set her down on a coil of old rope and arranged her as comfortably as possible.

'Wiggle your toes,' she said.

'I *am*,' insisted Paule.

Amy looked – the Sixth's feet were like dead fish.

They were on the foredeck, the most solid part of the ship.

Kali's father sat nearby, sobbing. Tears soaked through his hood, making damp sticky spots over his cheeks. Kali stood over him, his revolver in her hand… she didn't shoot him in the hood, though Amy could tell she was in two minds about it. She wanted revenge, but not to be an orphan.

Amy looked around, wondering how the pieces had fallen. She stood up, to try to get a better view.

Rayne, furious, ran at her – charging along the deck. Dead ants fell from her clothes and hair. She had compound eyes and mandibles. She shrieked and chittered, mouthparts working weirdly, ropes of spittle flying.

Amy tensed, ready to fly at the deposed Queen Ant and join battle.

Someone – Palgraive! – got in the way, and Rayne was slammed aside. The fight was knocked out of her.

Palgraive, head lolling like a hanged man, held Rayne up. Inside her brain, a maggot was hatching.

Into what? A fly?

Rayne hung limp, an empty suit. Palgraive's head shifted, with a crack as her neck settled back in place. Something looked out through her eyes and into Rayne's slack, vacant face.

'Good girl,' she said – rather, the thing in her brain said. 'One should be a good girl.'

Palgraive let Rayne go. The girl crumpled on the deck and the Professor – her mother – snarled in disgust. No tears from the author of *Formis*.

A Queen falls, and a Princess rises.

Amy really really hoped they wouldn't now have to go through this whole thing again with Palgraive's brain-maggot instead of Rayne's skipping rhyme.

The fight was mostly gone out of the Black Skirts. Captain Freezing had cooled a lot of them off before dissolving in the harbour. But they had a last ditch – what was left of the Cerberus and the Ghidorah, and a few others. Most – like Brown, Ker, Pinborough and Manders – woke up and laid down arms, wondering what on earth they were doing in an underground inlet with the remains of an old-fashioned ship and a lot of other soggy girls. But Euterpe McClure, Henry Buller, the Crowninshields, Angela De'Ath, Snitcher Garland and Stheno Stonecastle had no better senses to come to… they'd gone Black entirely of their own accord and come into themselves as Soldier Ants. Together, they held the deck of the *Johanna Pike*, and could still do an awful lot of harm.

Amy and Paule were not alone on the foredeck. Kali fired wild, emptying the gun. Then she threw it in the sea. Her father bowed, thumping his hooded head against the deck in submission or worship. This was the dawning of the Kali-Yuga, the Age of the Demon. Frecks let Bainter go. He gargled and slumped, making strange gestures he couldn't get right. Light Fingers' hands were invisible because she couldn't stop buzzing – if she touched wood, it flew into splinters. Gould and Marsh stood back to back, fur bristling and gills flaring. Devlin made big stretchy fists.

From the ruins of the Black Skirts, Beryl Crowninshield rose – a pretender to the throne. She rallied the diehards.

'We can still win this, Black Skirts,' she said.

'I've read that book,' shouted Devlin. '*Ridiculously Overconfident*, by Victor E. Gloating!'

Crowninshield can't know what this had really been all about...but her lust to *win*, defined as giving the flukes a right drubbing, was strong as ever.

Amy was exhausted.

Crowninshield's Corpse Corps advanced across the deck.

An explosion in the side of the ship scattered the Black Skirts. Stonecastle and Garland went over the side, flopping into a shallow pool. Buller yelled rage in the middle of the mess. Another explosion went off.

Amy, astonished, saw Gogoth lope across the burning deck, snatch Buller over his shoulder, and scale the remains of the rigging to get her safely to the dock. Even more astonished, Buller made 'my hero' eyes at her surprise saviour.

Another explosion.

'Look,' said Light Fingers, pointing at the jetty.

Amy saw where this was coming from.

Lamarcroft and Knowles held Larry Laurence's shoulders. A shimmer, with visible violet lips, was open in front of Larry's chest, held apart by her fingers.

A purple-pink cannonball burst out of the pocket and popped amidships.

When Larry's duplicate cannonballs went off, there was no shrapnel... just a popping of energy like lightning. The ship was further damaged, but people were just thrown around.

Crowninshield tossed back her fringe, showing both eyes.

It was her way of signalling surrender.

Amy raised her hand and accepted pax.

Relieved and worn out, Laurence stopped firing.

'Hurrah for the Remove,' shouted Frecks. 'Hurrah for Amy!'

'...and everybody else,' Amy said, not sure she could be heard over the hearty, if ragged cheers.

The water was back where it should be and what was left of the *Johanna Pike* was sinking under it, coming to bits. Cap'n Belzybub's ship was going down at last.

Amy floated over the drink. Others got their shoes and socks wet.

Frecks had more hurrahs to stir up, but Amy thought it best they get out of this cavern before they all drowned.

Luckily, Knowles knew the escape passages.

Limping, bedraggled, bloodied, puzzled, elated, wet and aching girls made their way through hewn rock. Some started to ask questions. Some were already making excuses. Not a few had complaints.

Frecks started on her brother's version of 'Blow the Man Down, Bullies' but her sacred coif didn't feel the ditty qualified as Just and True and got very hot. Frecks took the thing off before it burned her ears.

Some were lost, some left behind.

When the register was next called, who would be Absent? Rayne, Sundle, ffolliott... others?

But most were in reasonable shape.

'Hurrah for Kentish Glory,' whispered Light Fingers.

'Hurrah for a mug of tea, a hot bath and a good night's sleep,' responded Amy, 'then Nurse in the morning to get scratches ointmented and sick notes signed.'

'Amen to that,' said Light Fingers.

The secret passage came out in the cricket pavilion, where a whole wall pivoted on a hidden hinge.

Dr Swan was waiting for them, with a deputation of other teachers.

XV: The Start of a New Term

ASIDE FROM A chilly weekend with Mother and Uncle Nugent, Amy spent the Easter hols at Frecks' family home in the Lincolnshire Wolds. Walmergrave Towers was a greater pile than Drearcliff Grange, with enough secret passages, abandoned chapels and fairy dells to keep the young explorers occupied. Light Fingers and Kali were unable (Light Fingers) or unwilling (Kali) to spend time with their own parents, and also came along... so the Moth Club ran riot throughout the Towers, across the grounds and over half the countryside. In a hidden chamber, they found a cache of British Intelligence 'gadgets', which Light Fingers tried to get working. Several went off at once. Fortunately, only one under-butler was hurt and him not badly. The Moth Club made up for it by nudging the tweeny he was sweet on into noticing he was much more dashing and romantic than the strapping yet obviously cloddish groom she'd been walking out with.

Frecks got quite ticked off with her friends when all three of them met Viscount Ralph and didn't at once perceive the double-dyed rotter she'd told them he was. He had quite a nice smile and a funny way of talking to them that led to a certain degree of swooniness that Frecks was appalled by. But that didn't last. Amy added *seventeen* new species to her Moth Book – more than in two whole terms at Drearcliff.

They didn't talk much about the last term, but a lot about the next.

Grey was back to being the only uniform option, but new designs from Dosson, Chapell & Co. were smarter. Light Fingers had ideas for small, within-the-rules alterations which made the kit more chic. It was all to do with smart lines, apparently. And sheerer stockings.

Amy exchanged letters with Knowles. Know-It-All's father had agreed to write a book about Dennis Rattray, but called it off because he thought Blackfist was a bounder when he met him. Light Fingers, who still harboured resentment against the Captain, was glad to hear it. She asked Amy to pass on the suggestion that Knowles' father stick with the book but expose the heroic adventurer as a brutal hypocrite.

When time came to go back to Drearcliff, Ralph was persuaded to drive the pack of them across country. His Bentley was racing-green and the fastest thing in three counties, except for Light Fingers on foot (not that she mentioned it – she was more interested in thinking quick than moving fast these days). Ralph insisted on having the top down, because some of the girls – naming no names, but he meant Kali and Amy – had rather overdone experiments with scent. They'd found Frecks' mother's stock of intoxicant perfumes, and other tricks of the espionage trade. The lesson of the exploding fountain pen hadn't sunk in enough to prevent them sampling posh pongs.

It was possible, Amy conceded, that Viscount Ralph

was the Complete Cad Frecks made him out to be... but the back of his head was perfectly formed, and when he turned back to talk to them, his eyes twinkled with attractive mischief. He would bear watching, of course.

The Remove was, for the moment, dissolved, though the girls who had been consigned there – with the exception of Palgraive and (for no reason Amy could see) Devlin – were expected to take special lessons with Dr Swan from next year. This term, an afternoon a week was set aside for an introductory course to prepare for this honour. Frecks and Kali were expected to attend, as were several other non-Unusual, non-Removed individuals – Shoshone Brown, Muyun Ker, Jocasta Upton, Zenobia Aire (!), Sally Nikola, Winifred Rose and Hjordis Bok. Headmistress evidently saw qualities in them.

The Moth Club stirred up some excitement when they arrived at School – mostly because of Ralph's Bentley, though also because of Ralph. A crowd gathered and had to be dispersed by Miss Borrodale with a whistle. Fossil was one of those who could barely remember being Black Skirt, though Amy would never forget what the teacher had been like in Rayne's thrall. Ralph radiated his charm at Miss Borrodale, who shot him down. His 'I like a challenge' smirk punctured girlish hopes and made Amy suspect the Viscount really was a rat after all. She hoped Fossil crushed his heart like grapes in a press.

Girls were everywhere, all in grey, chattering and flocking. A few faces were missing – some parents heard rumours about last term and didn't want to send their darlings back into danger. Several prominent former Black Skirts couldn't bear to return to the site of their defeat and had manipulated parents or guardians into sending them to other schools on flimsy pretexts – though plenty who'd skipped and rhymed like automata had managed to forget the whole thing and went about being as matey as you could like.

Amy thought that was for the best.

She wasn't even sure if poor, lost Rayne could be blamed.

Outside the Desdemona dorms – to which Amy and Light Fingers could now return – they ran into Smudge, Peebles and Inchfawn.

'Have you heard?' began Smudge. 'Ponce Bainter popped his clogs over hols. Massive blood vessel exploded while he was on the pier at Brighton. He wasn't coming back, anyway... but this saves Headmistress the trouble of sacking him.'

'She is actually telling the truth,' put in Inchfawn. 'It was in *The Times*.'

After last term, it seemed silly holding Inchfawn's crimes against her. So much worse had happened... and, as Amy understood it, the first phase of the Hooded Conspiracy had been Kali's father's attempt to whisk his daughter out of harm's way. So they were at least talking to Inchfawn again.

'Funny thing,' said Smudge. 'Witnesses said he seemed to be running away from something, but no one saw what it was. Dashed the whole length of the pier and dropped just as he reached the railing at the end. Nowhere else to go.'

'There's a new chaplain,' said Peebles. 'Wait till you see him... a real Latin lover type. Valentino in a dog collar. The Reverend Luca Rinaldo. His wife, if she is his wife, is a stunner... Ariadne. She's so fair her hair looks white, and she plays funny, oriental music on the organ. You've not heard the likes of it. They're thick with Headmistress. I'd volunteer for Double R.I. if it meant gazing into his eyes and listening to his voice all term.'

The last weeks of last term, Bainter had been in School but not at lessons or chapel. He'd looked worried and harassed, as well he might be. Sometimes, he had glanced over his shoulder and up into the sky as if a predatory bird were stalking him. Had he imagined Kentish Glory had his number? If so, he'd been wrong – she couldn't be bothered to keep tabs on him, believing him a spent force. Amy had assumed Dr Swan would get rid of him at once, but he had stayed on, ever flimsier, as if his days were numbered – which, it turned out, they were. That blood vessel must have been swelling all the while. Paule told Amy the botch of the Runnel and the Flute would have *consequences*, and Professor Rayne and Kali's Father had already been paid back with the literal (the Professor) and in effect (Red Flame) loss of their daughters. Invisible tendrils from the Purple were hooked into Ponce and would tear him apart for the failure.

Dora Paule was more in her own mind, now... but her legs were dead. Amy was resolved to help. Paule assisted Dr Swan in teaching her class of Unusuals and Others. It was a way of finally leaving the Sixth but staying on at School. She had become Staff.

Amy looked out for Paule – she was becoming adept at getting around on crutches – but didn't see her in the milling crowds.

A poster outside the Drearcliff Playhouse advertised a Summer Revue entitled *Balmy Daze!* and an Arthur Wing Pinero Players production of *Dandy Dick*. By the Heel, a whip was notching Absalom before the anarchist had even prised the lid off her new tin of red paint. Firsts who might once have skipped were playing hopscotch instead. Frost and Thorn palled about together, having discovered hot and cold made tolerable partners in crime. They brought out the mischief in each other.

Dauntless clopped up the drive, pulling the school cart with Joxer on the box. A woman Amy didn't know got down. She wore an old-fashioned long coat and a hat with a gauzy veil and a dramatically stuffed bird attached to it.

'That's Mrs Edwards,' said Light Fingers. 'Back in harness. Watch your split infinitives around her. She likes to bruise your knuckles with the ruler.'

So Amy had that to look forward to. What had happened to Miss Kaye? At the fag-end of last term, she'd rallied round – taking up slack as other teachers got over their Black Skirt moods. Now, she was back where she came from – though she'd left Amy and Frecks her card, which she said bore secret messages under the right light. They hadn't cracked that yet, but probably would.

'*Bonjour mes filles*,' came a chillingly musical voice. 'I do so hope we've enjoyed our hols, for *beaucoup* improvement is required to spruce up School. *Toujours gai*, remember, *toujours gai...*'

Sidonie Gryce, large as life and twice as objectionable, was back in office. Head Girl and Boadicea of Bullies. She had a new pack of Murdering Heathens, drawn from several houses and years – an All-School Rogues Gallery. Her coterie included Beryl Crowninshield, Euterpe McClure, Netta Kinross and Polyphemus, and – in Snitcher Garland's old role of general toady, spy and informant – Shrimp Harper. A formidable bunch.

'You still here, Sid?' said Frecks. 'Weren't you last seen hiding under a pew during the Battle of the *Jo Pike*?'

'One doesn't have to be *at* a battle to win it, Walmergrave. *En fait*, it's preferable to be elsewhere as the *têtes* get *blessé*.'

Amy burned and concentrated so as not to float.

Had they gone through all *that* for *this*? Gruesome Gryce back in power?

Gryce's boater lifted up and was torn in half... by a freak wind, they all agreed. Amy was becoming as dexterous with her mentacles as her fingers. In the hols, the others had challenged her to perfect her paper-folding and -tearing skills.

Light Fingers made very quick movements with her hands, to distract the Heathens.

Gryce went cross-eyed with fury. She had a deep well of resentments after last term, and – in the absence of Rayne – others would suffer for it.

But Amy and the Moth Club would be ready.

'*Au revoir, mes enfants*... toodle-pip and -oo.'

The Murdering Heathens sauntered on, in search of other girls to put the frighteners on.

'Look, that's *him*,' said Smudge. '*Them*. Mr and Mrs Rinaldo.'

Outside the chapel stood a tall, dark fellow in a long black robe. He had a thin moustache and wore dark glasses with sides. His wife was, indeed, so fair as to be almost ghostly. She wore a cream dress a shade darker than her skin and hair, and another pair of those sunglasses. She held a parasol which shaded both their faces. They must be night people. The only colour about them was the rich redness of their lips. They smiled sweetly at the girls passing, accepting nods of greeting.

Amy had a *feeling* about them.

Behind those glasses, eyes were fixed on passing faces. They had already made their pick of pets, though Amy wasn't sure what that meant.

'And *that's* their servant,' said Inchfawn.

Shambling out of the chapel came Gogoth, wearing a verger's frock rather than a chauffeur's uniform. His shaven head had grown out, and he sported a shaggy, greyish beard.

'Ah nertz,' said Kali.

With Gogoth was Henry Buller, less stocky this term and with a clearer complexion. No longer a Heathen, no longer a Black Skirt. There was no telling where she fit in. Gogoth, it seemed, was devoted to the maiden fair he had rescued from a burning ship…

…now she thought about it, Amy was envious of that lump Buller. She could think of other much worthier candidates for rescue. She even fancied sometimes that it might be nice to be rescued herself – say, by Viscount Ralph or Uncle Nugent's surprisingly decent son, Patrick, or, strange to admit it, Dr Shade. She'd read a lot of Dr Shade adventures lately, and started collecting pictures and clippings about his career. It was said that he had a secret headquarters inside Big Ben.

'Don't think like that, Amy,' said Light Fingers. 'You're Kentish Glory. You'll be the one doing the gallant rescuing, not the one standing in the flames and shrieking like a twit.'

Light Fingers had explained she couldn't read minds, but could look at something and ask herself 'what would Amy think?' and hit very near the mark. Like Amy with her mentacles, she got better when she practised.

'But it might be nice… once in a while…'

Amy looked at Light Fingers, at Frecks and Kali…

'No, Amy,' said Frecks. 'That's not the dream.'

Amy had a jumble of impressions from her dip into the Purple and sometimes thought she knew what was going to happen next… in a week or in twenty years. If she tried to focus, it all went away. Like Knowles when her cramming faded, she knew she'd known something – *for certain* – but was now vague about it. Some of her intimations, her feelings, had already been *wrong*.

'The wolves are gone from the woods,' said Smudge.

That was strange – Smudge rarely had good news to impart.

'Chased off by the Yettymen,' she continued. 'There've been footprints, scratches high up on trees, strange signs – not like last term's strange signs, *new ones*! There are no birds or bugs either. It's deadly quiet, except you know you're not alone so you listen out for the tiniest sounds. When there's nothing, not even a twig creaking or water dripping, you know the Yettymen are near.'

'You've been in the woods alone?' Amy asked.

'No, but I've heard from those who have.'

Amy paid attention. Frecks, Light Fingers and Kali gathered round.

They all had masks inside their blazer linings. They were all ready for adventure.

This was interesting. Amy's mental antennae pricked.

The Yettymen?

Another case for the Moth Club.

Drearcliff Grange School Register

Ariel

First Form

Susan Ah
Hilda Courtney
Jane Dogge
Phaedra Hunt
Demeter London
    (Captain)
Lydia Marlowe
Jean Orfe
Ivy Prosser
Anne Sercombe
Janet Thaw

Second Form

Maria Biddlecombe
Martina Bone
Emily Dace
Anne D'Arbanvilliers-
    Cleaver (Captain)
Georgaina Fell
May Forrest
Monica Frensham

Venetia Laurence
Lucia Maunder
Valeria Mrozková

Third Form

Hannah Absalom
Chastity Banks
Octavia Benjamin
Catherine Bourbon
Chloe Catchpole
Bizou De'Ath
Natalie Laverick
Evelyn Lowen
Catherine Trechman
    (Captain)
Sybil Vigo

Fourth Form

Christina DeManby
    (Captain)
Isabella Fortune
Arabella Hughes

Idominea Lescaulles
Titania Mondrago
Sally Nikola
Fleur Paquignet
Cassandra Wilding
Heather Wilding
Priscilla Wilding

Fifth Form

Susan Byrne (Captain)
Thomasina Campbell
Alexa di Fontane
Dorothy Dungate
Frances Farragh
Prima Haldane
Marion Keith
Sonali Shah
Charlotte Teller
Rosina Terrell

Sixth Form

Angela De'Ath
Jean DuGuid
Jane Ferrers
Enid ffolliott (absent)
Yeong-ae Kim
Brenda Manders
Patricia Peale
Doreen Stockwell
Alexandra Vansittart
    (House Captain)
Rebecca Youell

Desdemona

First Form
Elizabeth Chick
Jennifer Dawes
Pearl Dennison
(Captain)
Anne Gifford
Louise Hartley
Ruth Hipgrave
Taff Jones-Rhys
Helen Knight
Avril Parrish
Ellaline Terriss

Second Form
Janet Blake
Nancy Dyall
Philippa Farjeon
Dorothy Fulwood
Elisabeth Gaye
Kathryn Hall (Captain)
Lillian Hyson
Cynthia Moul
Violet O'Brien
Polly Palgraive

Third Form
Maude-Lynne Arbuthnot
Kali Chattopadhyay
Clodagh FitzPatrick
Moraticia Frump
Lydia Inchfawn
Thomasina Hoare-
Stevens
Emma Naisbitt (Captain)
Verity Oxenford
Amanda Thomsett
Serafine Walmergrave

Fourth Form
Janet Aden
Ella Bowman
Honor Devlin
Susan Foreman
Nicola Helfrich

Charlotte Knowles
Rosanna Kyd
Lucinda Leigh
Aurora Martine
   (Captain)
Clare Saxby

Fifth Form

Dorothy Abbott
Theresa Crockford
   (Captain)
Fiona Fergusson
Dilys Frost
Rosalind Kaveney
Saskia Kriegsherr
Amelia Lipman
Winifred Rose
Pamela Soon
Doreen Wychwood

Sixth Form

Gowan Caulder
Marigold de Vere
Constance Hern
Dolores Howe
Daisy Keele
Morrigan McHugh
Matilda Pelham (House
   Captain)
Adrienne Penny
Valmai Smith
Donna Wise

Goneril

First Form

Jane Addey
Selina Briss
Maureen East
Marina George
   (Captain)
Julie Godfrey
Julianna Keddle
Dianne Poynton
Sabine Saussure
Tzara Tetzlaff
Millicent Trundleclough

Second Form

Margaret Carmichael
Wilhelmina Fudge
Muyun Ker
Freya Outerbridge
Annie Pridhaux
Ruby Raven
Tabitha Spikins
   (Captain)

Lillie Stevenson
Jane Thicke
Emily Usborne

Third Form

Katherine Berthaiume
Rachel Cray
Miriam Ellacott
Joycelyn Hilliard
Hermione Jago (Captain)
Priyanki Khalsekar
Isabel Loss
Ekaterina Pendill
Jemima Sieveright
Linda Thiele

Fourth Form

Sophie Calder (Captain)
Helen Davisson
Cara Fielder
Aconita Gould
Mary Jones

Netta Kinross
June Mist
Dorothy Ooms
Ninja Sundquist
Phoebe Wellesley

Fifth Form

Hjordis Bok
Roberta Hale
Janice Marsh
Euterpe McClure
Helen O'Hara
Sarah Pinborough
Emilia Pitt-Patterson
Primrose Quell
Susan Su
Alicia Wybrew (Captain)

Sixth Form

Araminta Armadale
Eliza Beardsworth
Katherine Brown
Maisie Collins
Wendy Fernandes
Lucretia Lamarcroft
Gilbertine Myddleton
Florence Rhode-Eeling
  (House Captain)
Alraune Ten Brincken
Charmaine Yip

Tamora

First Form
Sarah Ackland
Mary Candlewick
Vera Claythorne
Olivia Duel
Damaris Gideon
 (Captain)
Louise Gilclyde
Laura Harvey
Iris Overton
Felicity Quilligan
Carlotta Smith

Second Form
Cleopatra Cotton
Elaine Finn
Cecily Garland
Miramara Ghastley
Siobhan Grimm
Clara Mill-Carston
Cunegonde Quive-Smith
 (Captain)

Victoria Silk
Tanya Six
Esther Stuckey

Third Form
Allegra Bidewell
Barbara Bryant
Selma Head
Mary Jarvis
Faith Merrilees
Bridget Mountmain
Silja Mueller (Captain)
Louise Sawley
Sarah Stallybrass
Francesca Stone

Fourth Form
Zenobia Aire (Captain)
Sarah Carnadyne
Ottilie Churchward
Miranda Crowninshield
Humphrina Jarrott

Gwendolyn Nobbs
Mara Rietty
Susannah Thorn
Phyllis Thorpe
Ruby Wool

Fifth Form

Erica Boscastle
Lucia Bewe-Bude
Caroline Cowper-Kent
Flora Griffin (absent)
Jacqueline Harper
Margaret Hume
Sylvestra Phillips
Sylvia Starr
Clementine Talbot
    (Captain)
Heike Ziss

Sixth Form

Henrietta Buller
Bryony Burtoncrest
Zealia Clock
Beryl Crowninshield
Sidonie Gryce (Head
    Girl)
Moria Kratides
Elva Kyle
Pandora Paule
Stheno Stonecastle
Felecia Tingle

Viola

First Form

Carol Coker
Alison Hills
Hazel Hood
Yung Kha (Captain)
Margaret Ring
Monique Soutie
Harriet Speke
Marianne Toulmin
Cecily Wheele
Jemima Williams

Second Form

Marie Adkins
Annabelle St Anne
Karen Featherstowe
Emanuelle Gotobed
Joan Hone
Eve Lapham
Juliet Lass
   (Captain)
Muriel Lavish

Helen Oakes
Marian Phair

Third Form

Heather Beeke
Theosopha Busby
   (Captain)
Simret Cheema-Innis
Ann Dis
Sarah Ladymeade
Abigail Pulsipher
Antoinette Rowley
   Rayne
Priscilla Rintoul
Angela Stannard
Morgana Vail

Fourth Form

Kitten Carnes
Barbara Chess
Isola Doone
Daphne Gallaudet

Philippa Hailstone
Unorna Light
Harmony Meade
Sara Paço (Captain)
Laura Tallentyre
Susannah Thorne

Fifth Form

Ida Acreman
Doris de Marne
Ellen Eyre
Sally-Anne Flyte
Oona Kite
Holly Queenhough
   (Captain)
Gladys Sundle
Mary Thompson
Lavinia Trent
Kathleen Vaughn

Sixth Form

Edith Brydges
Catherine Bunn
Unity Crawford
Amora Dove
Patricia Kearney
Margaret Lapham
Helena Mansfield
   (House Captain)
Martha McAndrew
Joanne Storey
Jocasta Upton

Staff

Dr Myrna Swan

Dr Ailsa Auchmuty
The Reverend Mr
   Pericles Bainter
Miss Ethel Bedale
Miss Violet Borrodale
Miss Elizabeth Downs
Miss Jennifer Dryden

Miss Catriona Kaye
   (acting)
Mrs Rosemary Wyke

Hilda Percy
Louise Humphreys
   R.R.C.
Nellie Pugh
Joxer Chidgey

Acknowledgements

THIS NOVEL GREW out of some research I did for *An English Ghost Story*, in which an author named Louise Magellan Teazle is supposed to have written a series of Drearcliff Grange School books. Mostly, that research consisted of reading Mary Cadogan and Patricia Craig's *You're A Brick, Angela!: The Girls' Story 1839–1985* – which remains one of the best books about popular fiction ever written, up there with Colin Watson's *Snobbery With Violence: English Crime Stories and Their Audience*, another influence on what I've been trying to do with a loosely interconnected series of stories and novels inhabiting a world of British pulp adventure.

Among my other research sources: Angela Brazil's *The Manor House School* and *The Third Class at Miss Kaye's*, Evelyn Smith's *Val Forrest in the Fifth*, Thomas Hughes's *Tom Brown's Schooldays*, a lot of dimly remembered books by Frank Richards and Anthony Buckeridge, and, of course, Ronald Searle's *St Trinian's: The Entire Appaling Business*. I should also thank Dr Morgan's Grammar School for Boys (which did have an utterly useless fives court), Haygrove Comprehensive and Bridgwater College.

A draft of the first section of this novel was published as 'Kentish Glory: The Secrets of Drearcliff Grange School' in my collection *Mysteries of the Diogenes Club* (MonkeyBrain Books). Thanks are due to Chris Roberson and Allison Baker for publishing that. At Titan, I am grateful to Nick Landau and Vivian Cheung, Cath Trechman (ace editor), Natalie Laverick, Jill Sawyer Phypers, Lydia Gittins, Cara Fielder, Chris Young, Katharine Carroll, Jenny Boyce and Martin Stiff (for another amazing cover). Thanks also to my agents Antony Harwood, James Macdonald Lockhart and Fay Davies. And to David Barraclough, Steven Baxter, Eugene Byrne, Alex Dunn, Barry Forshaw, Christopher Fowler, Sean Hogan, Stephen Jones, Paul McAuley and Brian Smedley.

I consulted various friends about their own school experiences – they're mostly acknowledged by being on the Drearclff Grange register. Kat Brown, Simret Cheema-Innis, Meg Davis, Grace Ker, Yung Kha, Maura McHugh, Helen Mullane and Sarah Pinborough all get Gold Stars as credits to School.

About the Author

KIM NEWMAN IS a novelist, critic and broadcaster. His fiction includes *The Night Mayor*, *Bad Dreams*, *Jago*, the Anno Dracula novels and stories, *The Quorum* and *Life's Lottery*, all currently being reissued by Titan Books, *Professor Moriarty: The Hound of the D'Urbervilles* published by Titan Books and *The Vampire Genevieve* and *Orgy of the Blood Parasites* as Jack Yeovil, and most recently the critically acclaimed *An English Ghost Story*, which was nominated for the inaugural James Herbert Award. His non-fiction books include the seminal *Nightmare Movies* (recently reissued by Bloomsbury in an updated edition), *Ghastly Beyond Belief* (with Neil Gaiman), *Horror: 100 Best Books* (with Stephen Jones), *Wild West Movies*, *The BFI Companion to Horror*, *Millennium Movies* and *BFI Classics* studies of *Cat People* and *Doctor Who*.

He is a contributing editor to *Sight & Sound* and *Empire* magazines (writing *Empire*'s popular Video Dungeon column), has written and broadcast widely on a range of topics, and scripted radio and television documentaries. His stories 'Week Woman' and 'Ubermensch' have been adapted into an episode of the TV series *The Hunger* and an Australian short film; he has directed and written a tiny film *Missing Girl*. Following his Radio 4 play 'Cry Babies', he wrote an episode ('Phish Phood') for Radio 7's series *The Man in Black*.

Follow him on twitter @annodracula. His official website can be found at www.johnnyalucard.com

Anno Dracula: Johnny Alucard

By Kim Newman

On the set of Francis Ford Coppola's troubled movie production of *Dracula*, Kate Reed meets young vampire Ion Popescu. She is compelled to help him escape and begin a new life in America, where he reinvents himself as Johnny Pop. He makes his name – and his fortune – selling a new, dangerously addictive drug that confers vampire powers on its users, and becomes a hit on the decadent New York art scene.

As he stalks the steeets of Manhattan and Hollywood, haunting the lives of the rich and famous, from Sid and Nancy to Andy Warhol, Orson Welles to Francis Ford Coppola, sinking his fangs ever deeper into the zeitgeist of 1980s America, it seems the past might not be dead after all…

Kim Newman returns to one of the bestelling vampire tales of the modern era in this brand-new novel in his acclaimed *Anno Dracula* series.

For more fantastic fiction, author events, exclusive
excerpts, competitions, limited editions and more

Visit our website
titanbooks.com

Like us on Facebook
facebook.com/titanbooks

Follow us on Twitter
@TitanBooks

Email us
readerfeedback@titanemail.com